WHEN THE LIGHTS GO ON AGAIN

ANNIE GROVES

When the Lights go on Again

HarperCollins*Publishers*

Published by HarperCollins*Publishers* 2010

1

A catalogue record for this book
is available from the British Library

ISBN: 978-0-00-726595-4

Set in Sabon by Palimpsest Book Production Limited,
Grangemouth, Stirlingshire

Printed and bound in Great Britain by
Clays Ltd, St Ives plc

Mixed Sources
Product group from well-managed
forests and other controlled sources
www.fsc.org Cert no. SW-COC-001806
© 1996 Forest Stewardship Council

FSC is a non-profit international organisation established
to promote the responsible management of the world's forests.
Products carrying the FSC label are independently certified
to assure consumers that they come from forests that are managed
to meet the social, economic and ecological needs
of present and future generations.

Find out more about HarperCollins and the environment at
www.harpercollins.co.uk/green

*As this is the final book in the Campion series
I would like to dedicate it to all the 'real life' families
and their descendants, who lived through WWII*

Acknowledgements

Susan Opie, and Victoria Hughes-Williams, my editors at HarperCollins. Yvonne Holland, copy editor extraordinaire, who, as always, has done a magnificent job.
All those at HarperCollins whose hard work enabled this book to reach publication.
Tony, who contributes so much to my books via the research he does for me.

ONE

Late August 1943

Jean Campion was standing in her kitchen waiting for the kettle to boil. Today was her birthday. Her soft brown wavy hair had been freshly cut and set the previous day especially for the occasion, the last drops of the precious Chanel scent that her son, Luke, had brought her back from Paris the first Christmas of the war, dabbed behind her ears. Jean smoothed down the cotton fabric of her blue floral print summer dress, loose on her now after nearly four years of wartime rationing. She had bought the dress from Lewis's in Liverpool, when her eldest daughter, Grace, had been working there, before the store had been bombed in the dreadful blitz of May 1940.

The kettle was coming up to the boil. From the front room, with the doors open into the hallway, Jean could hear the voices of her family, come to celebrate with her the birthday she shared with her twin sister, Vi. The voices of her daughters Grace and Sasha, her niece, Bella, her sisters, Vi

1

and Francine. Female voices. Female voices because they were at war and so many men were fighting for their country – and their lives. A heartfelt sigh escaped Jean's lips.

She was lucky, she reminded herself; many women she knew had lost sons and husbands. Luke might have been injured fighting in the desert, but at least he had recovered now, even if he had made that recovery far from home and, according to his most recent letter – which had miraculously arrived today – was about to rejoin his army unit.

She was lucky too in having the rest of her family close at hand. Grace, who was a nurse, might have moved to Whitchurch because her RAF husband, who was part of the very important and secret Y Section, had been posted there, but she too had her husband living at home with her.

Seb and Grace had come up from Whitchurch today on the train, and right now Seb and Jean's husband, Sam, were down at Sam's allotment, no doubt talking about the progress of the war and the recent invasion of Sicily by the Allied Forces, as well as Seb's desire to turn part of the rambling garden attached to the cottage they were renting into a vegetable plot.

Thinking of that invasion made Jean's heart thud with anxiety, for Luke, who was with the Eighth Army, and bound to be involved at some stage in the Allies' push into the Italian mainland to force back the Germans and Italians.

And Luke wasn't the only one of her children she had to worry about, Jean admitted, lifting her hand to smooth back a wayward strand of hair.

There was Lou, who of all things was now learning to fly aeroplanes, if you please, having been transferred by the WAAF into something called the Air Transport Auxiliary service. And Lou's twin, Sasha, despite having a nice steady job at the local telephone exchange and an equally nice steady fiancé working in bomb disposal, never seemed to be happy.

As she poured the boiling water onto the precious tea leaves, Jean thought how typically generous it was of her younger sister, Francine – a singer with ENSA, and recently married to a major in the army – to have brought her own rations with her for the birthday get-together.

On cue, the kitchen door opened wider to admit Francine, a rueful look of mischief sparkling in her eyes.

'I thought I'd escape from Vi by coming to see if you needed a hand.'

Francine was by far the prettiest one of the three sisters, with her strawberry-blonde curls and her heart-shaped face. Grace had the same pretty features.

As always, Francine was beautifully dressed, in a floral silk frock. She'd had the foresight to have some new clothes made whilst she'd been posted to Egypt with ENSA. You simply couldn't get clothes of the quality and style Fran had brought back with her in England now, not with rationing and the rules the Government had laid down for austerity clothing. Not that Jean minded having to stick by those rules, not when she knew the danger the country's poor merchant seamen had to endure bringing raw materials into the country for the war effort.

No, she didn't feel the lack of pretty things for herself, but she did feel it for her girls sometimes, Jean admitted, although Fran had been wonderfully generous, not just bringing a whole trousseau of clothes, including her wedding dress, back from Egypt for Grace, but also bringing lovely fabrics that she had shared with them all.

Fran pulled a face. 'I know that it can't be easy for Vi with Edwin having left her for someone else, but she doesn't exactly make it easy for others to sympathise with her, does she? I've never heard anyone complain so much, and over next to nothing.'

'That's just Vi's way,' Jean tried to defend her twin. 'She's always been like that, boasting when things are going well for her and complaining about life not being fair and her being hard done to when they aren't, but Edwin wanting a divorce, and the war, have made her worse. You can carry that tray through for me, if you will.' Jean nodded at the tray with the pretty china tea set that Grace had given her the first Christmas of the war. 'And I'll bring the teapot.'

Over a decade younger than Jean and Vi, Francine had been through such a lot. Pregnant at sixteen by a married man she naïvely believed loved her, Francine had given in to pressure from Vi and her husband to allow them to bring up her baby as their own before she left for America to make a new life for herself there as a singer.

But then the war had brought her back to do

4

her bit for the country, and Francine had found out that Vi and Edwin had not been the loving parents to little Jack that she'd expected. That had been ever such a bad time. Poor Jack had run away from the people Vi had sent him to, supposedly to keep him safe from the war, and Jean had seen what Francine had gone through, wanting to claim her little boy and mother him, whilst Vi and Edwin did their utmost to stop her. And then had come the terrible tragedy of Jack being killed when a bomb had dropped on the farm to which he'd been evacuated. Such a terrible thing to happen. Of course, things had never been the same between Francine and Vi after that.

'I don't know how Bella puts up with Vi,' Francine told Jean. 'Vi's done nothing but complain about how hard done by she is since she got here, when it's perfectly plain that she has poor Bella running round after her, as well as working full time managing that nursery.'

Bella, the elder of Vi's two children, was in charge of a government nursery in Wallasey where she and her new husband, a Polish fighter pilot, lived.

'Vi's worried that, now that Bella's married, once the war's over she's going to be left on her own. She might complain about having Bella living with her when Bella has got a perfectly good house of her own, but she'd be lost without her,' Jean told Fran.

Fran had picked up the tea tray but now she put it down again, the tone of her voice softening, as she told her sister, 'I had a letter from Marcus this morning. His regiment is still on home duties but he thinks now that we've got Sicily, if we can win Italy, it won't be long before we invade Western Europe, and that his regiment is bound to be part of that. I feel so guilty at times, Jean. One half of me is jubilant because we're beginning to win the war at last, even though I know that there is still more fighting to be done, but the other half of me is so terribly afraid for my own happiness and for Marcus. Life is so precious and so very fragile, and loving Marcus makes me feel so vulnerable. If I should lose him . . .' She gave a deep shudder. 'I'm being selfish, I know. After all, there isn't a woman in the land who doesn't feel as I do for someone.'

The two sisters exchanged understanding looks.

'You have Luke with the Eighth Army,' Francine continued, 'Bella has Jan with the RAF, and even Vi has Charlie in the army, although to listen to her she seems more concerned about him losing out if Edwin's mistress has a son than she is about Charlie losing his life.'

Jean knew what Francine meant. With a victory predicted for the Allies and an end to the war, peace seemed so tantalisingly close that it was harder than ever for those at home to hold back their fears that their loved ones fighting for that peace might not survive to share it with them.

'Mum, Auntie Vi's complaining that she's parched,' Grace announced, coming into the kitchen. Pulling a face, she added, 'She's done nothing but complain since she and Bella got here.'

'We're on our way,' Jean answered, laughing.

*　　*　　*

6

As Francine followed Jean through the door with the tea things, her mind was still on Marcus. Neither of them had said so in as many words, but Francine knew how much it would mean to him were she to start a baby before he was sent overseas, and not just because they loved one another, or even because his child would be a living reminder of their love, should he fall in combat. Each of them had already lost a child to the war: Marcus when his first wife, who had been pregnant with their first child, had been killed in an air raid, and Francine herself when the same thing had happened to Jack, the child who had never even known she was his mother and with whom she had shared such a short and poignant handful of days on her return to Liverpool from America. Superstitiously, Francine felt that if she did conceive then Marcus would survive the war because, after all they'd been through, God simply wouldn't let them have a child if both of them weren't going to be there to love and protect it.

For that reason she had waited with eager anticipation each month, only to be disappointed when her period arrived with relentless regularity. And now Marcus was warning her that he was expecting to be sent into action.

As she pushed open the door to Jean's small front room the sight of its exclusively female occupants reinforced everything that she had been thinking about the reality of the war and what lay ahead.

'I wish you could stay up here long enough to spend a couple of days in Whitchurch with us,'

7

Grace told Francine later on when they were washing up, whilst Jean took some sandwiches and a flask of tea down to the allotment for Sam and Seb.

The kitchen should have been cold and unwelcoming, facing north as it did, but Sam had painted it a bright yellow before the war, and Francine always thought that in addition to the warming colour the homely room held something of Jean's own comforting warmth about it.

'Next time I come up I'll have to do that,' Francine agreed,

'Will you be coming back up soon? Only it's so hard to get Mum to come out to see me, she's always so busy here, and I know she'd come if you were coming,' Grace pressed her, adding coaxingly, 'Seb's going to be away in a month's time on a course at Bletchley Park and it would be lovely if you could both come then.' She gave a small sigh. 'I know I'm lucky to have Seb stationed here in England, and even luckier for him to be living out so that we can be together, but I do miss Liverpool and home.'

Poor Grace, Francine thought. It was obvious to Fran that what her niece didn't want to say was that she missed her mother.

'Of course I'll come,' Francine agreed on a rush of sympathy, 'and I'll make sure that your mum comes with me.'

Grace's face lit up. Putting down the cloth with which she was carefully drying the tea set, she gave Francine a fierce hug.

'Thanks ever so, Auntie Fran.'

'You are happy in Whitchurch, aren't you?' Francine asked. What she really meant was, was Grace happy in her marriage, but that was something she was reluctant to ask straight out.

'Oh, yes,' Grace answered immediately and, very obviously, truthfully, to Francine's relief. 'It's just that Whitchurch is only a small place and all the girls I work with are local and have their families there, and somehow that makes me miss my family even more. Then when I do come home I hardly get to speak properly to Mum, she's so busy. You *will* come and stay with me and bring Mum, won't you?'

'I promise,' Fran confirmed.

TWO

'Lou, you are soooo lucky. You brought that Harvard down daisy-cutter perfect first time, but when I had to do it I came in too high and had to go round again.'

'It didn't feel like a perfect landing,' Lou assured her friend and fellow ATA pilot June Merryvale as they walked away from the airfield and its hangars, carrying their parachutes with them.

The breeze filled out the loose fabric of their Sidcot flying suits, worn not, as it was rumoured so many of the ferry pool pilots did, over merely their underwear, but over their smart navy-blue uniform trousers and pale blue shirts. The same breeze was lifting the wind sock on the airfield and also tugging at Lou's curls, the tips of her hair sun-bleached now by the summer sunshine.

The two girls had been posted to the ATA training airbase at Thame at the same time for their ongoing training from flying Grade 1 only planes to flying Grade 2 planes – advanced single-engined aircraft, primarily fighter aircraft, such as Hurricanes, Spitfires, Typhoons, Mustangs, Airacobras, and even

10

'tricky' aircraft like the Walruses. The aircraft, though, that Lou most longed to fly was the Spitfire, the small fighter plane that those women pilots who had flown them declared were perfect for female flyers.

Spits – Lou's heart lifted with excitement every time she thought of flying one. She knew that some of the RAF men disapproved of girls flying at all, but especially disliked and resented the idea of girls flying Spitfires, feeling that only the male ATA pilots – those pilots who for one reason or another could not fly in combat, but who were still good airmen – should be allowed to do so.

So much had happened since she had undergone her ab initio training at Barton-in-the-Clay, the small grass airfield where she had spent the regulation two weeks having lessons in 'ground school', followed by bumps and circuits in the school's Gypsy Moth training plane. From there she had gone on to solo flight, before being assigned the thirty cross-country flights every would-be ATA pilot had to complete successfully before getting her 'wings'. These flights, designed to hone the skills the trainees had been taught in ground school, had involved putting into practice their navigation ability. The rule was that all ATA pilots, no matter how skilled, had to stick to 'contact' flying, which meant that they had to fly beneath any cloud cover so that they could navigate using their maps and what was visible on the ground below them. One of the worst test flights, so far as Lou was concerned, had been when she'd had to navigate round the Spitfire factory at Castle Bromwich avoiding the barrage balloons that protected the site.

Every ATA pilot was expected to progress to more complicated planes as speedily as she could – it was her role, after all, to move as many planes as possible around the country – but in accordance with her own confidence and the wisdom of those teaching her.

Once an ATA pilot was qualified and had her wings, she was then sent to one of the ATA ferry pools where she would be given 'chits' to collect and deliver planes.

The ferry pools used Avro Ansons in a taxi service to get the pilots to the planes they had to deliver. The pilots then had to collect the planes, and deliver them to MUs, as the maintenance units were called. Only then would the planes be fitted with their onboard navigation systems and other equipment. This was why the ATA pilots had to learn to fly without anything other than basic instruments, and were forbidden to go above the clouds, or from an MU to an RAF station.

Every new recruit was told hideously graphic tales of pilots who had ignored this rule and ended up losing their planes and their lives.

Here at Thame, though, which was close to ATA's Ferry Pool Number 5 at Luton, Lou had also heard tales of certain daredevil ATA female pilots who not only ignored the rules to fly above the cloud but who also performed acrobatic manoeuvres with the fighter planes they were delivering, something that was strictly forbidden and for which they were not trained.

Lou couldn't imagine herself ever being skilled enough to do that, even though she had made such good progress in Grade 1 that she had been sent back to Thame to undergo her conversion course to Grade 2 in record time.

'We've both got an off-duty weekend coming up – why don't the two of us spend it in London?' June suggested.

'I'd love to,' Lou told her truthfully, hitching her parachute higher onto her shoulder, 'but I can't. I haven't been home in an age. My twin has been engaged for over two months and I haven't congratulated her properly yet.'

Good pals though they had become, Lou didn't feel she could confide in June how guilty she felt that she and Sasha had drifted so far apart that sometimes, reading Sasha's short, stilted letters to her, Lou felt as though they had become strangers, and that they had nothing in common any more.

'Oh, well, never mind,' June accepted philosophically. 'But promise that you'll come with me the next time we get a weekend pass.'

'Of course I will,' Lou agreed, wincing as the Tannoy broke into life, announcing that the two pilots whose names had been broadcast were required to present themselves at the admin block for ferry duties.

Lou couldn't wait until she was properly qualified. What a thrill it would be to hear her own name being broadcast. Inside her head Lou replayed the message delivered in the stentorian accents of the base's admin controller, but substituting her own name for those of the girls called.

Their admin controller was, like the original instructors for ATA, a BOAC employee. Now, though, the Government, in the belief that the Allies would win the war, had allowed BOAC to recall all its own instructors to start preparing post-war training for the corporation. The job of training ATA pilots had been handed over to instructors who had themselves been ATA pilots, many of them women who had the advantage of knowing exactly what the work of an ATA pilot entailed.

Lou's instructor this morning, Margery Smythe, who had sent her out on her first solo Grade 2 flight, was a firm disciplinarian but very fair and encouraging.

She had been so lucky to have been upgraded on to a Grade 2 course so speedily after having first qualified, Lou reflected as she tucked into her salad lunch in the canteen. She'd be flying again this afternoon and she didn't want a heavy meal lying on the butterflies she knew would invade her tummy. June had qualified two months ahead of her and insisted that Lou had to be 'super good' to have been pushed up a grade so quickly.

Lou suspected, more modestly, that it was more a case of her being in the right place at the right time. Not that she hadn't been thrilled and excited. She had, the words almost falling over themselves as she wrote them when she sent Sasha a letter telling her about her potential up-grade to fly advanced single-engined planes, but in her response her twin hadn't even mentioned Lou's triumph. What made Lou feel even more guilty now was that secretly she would much rather have spent her precious leave weekend in London with June than in Liverpool with her twin sister.

'I just hope that when we finish this conversion course we're both posted together, that neither of us gets posted to Ratcliffe,' June announced, breaking into Lou's thoughts.

Lou finished chewing a rubbery piece of Spam, and demanded, 'Why, what's wrong with Ratcliffe?'

June raised her eyebrows and shook her head so vigorously that the bun into which her auburn hair was knotted threatened to unravel.

'Haven't you heard about those Americans who joined ATA who are based there?'

'No, what about them?' Lou demanded.

'They've put it about that they can outfly and outplay any other ATA female pilot, and they've got the reputation to prove that they mean it. There was a pilot at my last ferry pool who swore blind that she'd seen two of them deliberately racing one another to see who could put down first. They don't like us and they're quite happy to show it, or so I've heard.'

'There were a couple of American pilots at my last posting and they were nothing like that.' Lou felt obliged to defend the two senior and very dedicated American women she'd seen flying in and out of Barton-in-the-Clay.

'Well, I'm only telling you what I've heard, and I certainly wouldn't want to be posted to Ratcliffe. I like a good time but when it comes to some of the things I've heard that they get up to, I'm afraid I draw the line.'

'What kind of things?' Lou pressed her.

'Like I just said – wild parties. Very wild parties. The kind where you end up in some man's bed,' June emphasised darkly. 'I mean, I'm no prude, *but.*'

If what June had said was true then she had to agree with her, Lou reflected as they cleared what was left on their plates into the slop bin and then placed them on the trolley for washing.

'I've got my first solo this afternoon.' June rolled her eyes. 'I'm dreading it. What about you – what are you doing?'

'Margery is going to go through the details of my three cross-country solo flights with me, ready for the first one tomorrow. She's not told me yet which plane I'll be flying, though.'

'See you tonight then.'

Lou nodded.

Although most of the ferry pools didn't have accommodation blocks, and ATA pilots were normally billeted with local people or clubbed together to rent somewhere between them if they could, at Thame Sir William Currie had put one wing of his Tudor mansion at the disposal of ATA to provide a 'live-in mess'.

After living in basic WAAF accommodation at an RAF base before transferring to ATA, Lou had been round-eyed with disbelief when she had first been shown her new quarters – a wood-panelled room with its mullioned windows overlooking the knot garden.

She even had a four-poster bed, with the same heavy ruby-red velvet curtains as were hanging at the windows. Her room had its own fireplace, and a large polished wardrobe and a chest of drawers, both of which smelled of lavender.

On the wall next to Lou's bed hung a sampler, requesting 'Bless this House', stitched, so she had been told by the housekeeper, by Sir William's great-aunt as a young girl.

'Their' wing of the large house was accessed via the main hall with its magnificent polished wood staircase, the banister carved with symbols from Sir William's family crest. Since ATA did not have an officer structure – pilot seniority being denoted by length of service and ability to fly a variety of planes – there was no official 'mess'. Instead the girls ate their meals in the base's canteen or occasionally by invitation in the house's elegant dining room, furnished with an antique Hepplewhite dining-room table and chairs, eating off delicate china and using silver cutlery, with Sir William as their genial host. One of the drawbacks, though, as far as Lou was concerned, were the bathrooms, with their huge baths, which they were allowed to fill with only two inches of hot water.

'Yes, see you tonight,' Lou confirmed as she set off in the direction of the hangars.

THREE

'Yes, Charlie, of course I understand why Daphne won't be coming with you, with her own mother not being very well, but I must warn you that Mummy is bound to be disappointed. You know how much she thinks of Daphne.' Bella Polanski pushed the thick waves of her golden-blonde hair back from her face as she spoke patiently but firmly into the telephone receiver. Her blue eyes were shadowed with disappointment as she assured her younger brother that she had got the message that his visit to Wallasey would be a solo affair.

Privately, Bella acknowledged later, she wished that Charlie was going to be accompanied by his wife, even though that would have meant Bella giving up the comfort of her double bed to Charlie and his wife, leaving her to sleep in the boxroom's single bed, and even though she and Daphne had never been close. And it wasn't for her mother's sake either that she would have preferred Charlie not to have returned home alone. Vi had been puffed up with pride when Charlie had announced that he was to marry Daphne Wrighton-Bude, the

18

girl whose brother Charlie had rescued at Dunkirk but who had sadly not survived his injuries, and their father had rewarded Charlie very handsomely financially for his good sense in marrying a girl from such a good family. Not that Charlie was likely to get any money out of their father now that he had left their mother for his assistant, Pauline. Vi had been over the moon when Charlie had told her that he and Daphne were expecting their first child, but then just after Bella and Jan had married had come the sad news that there was not to be a baby after all. Bella, having suffered a miscarriage herself during her own first marriage, had written immediately to Daphne but the only reply she had received had been a frosty little note from Daphne's mother acknowledging her own letter.

From her small office at the nursery, it was impossible for her to see out into the nursery itself but she didn't have to do that to be able to visualise the look of tenderness on Lena's face as she worked with their small charges.

The best thing she had ever done, aside from marrying Jan, had been to listen to her conscience the day she had seen Lena in the street in Liverpool, distraught and heavily pregnant with her brother, Charlie's illegitimate baby. Moved by the young girl's plight, Bella had taken her home with her. Out of that one act of compassion had grown a friendship that had turned Bella's own life around. Lena was happy now, a proud mother of Bella's adored niece, a happy wife to Gavin, a mother-to-be to his own baby, and Bella's right hand and a highly valued member of Bella's loyal team of nursery nurses. After their marriage Bella had offered her own house to Lena and Gavin and had moved back to live with her mother. She'd been delighted when Lena and Gavin had married and Bella felt that the last thing they needed now was for Charlie to reappear on the scene to start making trouble in that way that he had.

On the other hand, Bella also knew how much it would mean to her mother to see Charlie, especially when Charlie himself had hinted to Bella during his telephone call that he expected to be sent into action soon.

She would have to tell Lena about his proposed visit, of course.

She found Lena in the day room of the nursery, soothing one of their new intake of little ones, who had woken up from her afternoon nap confused by her surroundings. Small and curvaceous, with olive-toned skin and thick dark hair, Lena was strikingly attractive, her looks and colouring a perfect foil for Bella's peaches-and-cream beauty.

The nursery was a light airy place, with two large main rooms, a day room, and a sleeping room where the children could have their afternoon naps. The walls of the day room were painted bright yellow and decorated with the children's drawings. High chairs for the babies were pushed back against one of the walls, ready to be pulled up to the scrubbed wooden table where the children ate their meals, whilst there were proper chairs for the older children, and four deep comfy armchairs for the staff to sit in when they settled down to read the children their afternoon story, or give some upset child a special reassuring cuddle.

Lena, who was sitting in one of these, had settled the toddler on her lap to dry her tears. She looked up at Bella with a warm smile.

'You aren't going to be able to do that for much longer,' Bella warned her. 'You won't have enough room.'

Lena laughed and looked down at the swelling beneath her navy-blue cotton maternity smock, with its white Peter Pan collar and pretty bow.

'He doesn't like it at all when I put one of the babies on my knee. He kicks away at them like billy-o.'

'He?' Bella teased her, her own pre-war floral cotton dress slightly loose on her slender frame, thanks to the rigours of rationing. Bending down to lift the now smiling toddler from Lena's lap and watching her whilst she toddled off happily to join a group of children who were playing with some wooden building blocks, she reminded Lena, 'You were sure that Janette was going to be a boy but you were wrong.'

'Yes, I know, but I'm really sure this time that it's going to be a boy.'

It would certainly probably be a good thing if Lena and Gavin's baby were a boy, Bella reflected. Gavin was a wonderful father to Lena's little girl and adored her, but Bella felt privately that there would be less chance of comparisons being made between the child that Charlie had fathered, and the one that was Gavin's own, if this next baby was a boy.

Thinking of Charlie reminded her of why she had come to find Lena.

'I'll go and make us both a cup of tea, shall I?' Lena suggested, starting to get to her feet, but Bella stopped her, shaking her head.

'There's something I want to tell you.'

Immediately Lena's face lit up. 'You've started a baby,' she challenged Bella excitedly. 'You and Jan. Oh, Bella, I'm so pleased.'

'No, it isn't that. It's Charlie. He's coming home this weekend. He told me that he's expecting to be sent into action soon and that he wanted to come up and see Mummy.'

They exchanged understanding looks.

'You'll want to tell Gavin, of course,' Bella went on, 'although I don't think you're likely to run into Charlie. He's bound to want to give you a wide berth after the way he's behaved.'

'It wasn't his fault that I was daft enough to think he wanted to marry me when all he wanted was a good time.'

'It was his fault that he didn't tell you that he was already engaged to be married, Lena.'

'It doesn't matter now,' Lena assured her. 'In many ways I reckon he did me a favour.'

'A favour? When he left you carrying his child?' Bella protested.

'Well, if it hadn't been for me being pregnant I'd never have got to meet you, and look at all the things you've done for me, Bella – giving me a home and a job, and being such a good friend to me. If it wasn't for you I'd never have met Gavin, and I'd probably have come to a bad end

22

instead of being married to the best husband a girl could have, and having the best friend in the world. Don't you worry about me accidentally bumping into your Charlie. If I did, I'd tell him how lucky I reckon I am.'

'Oh, Lena, you're a real tonic and no mistake,' Bella laughed.

'Hug, Auntie Bella, hug.'

The sound of her niece's voice had Bella going immediately towards the little girl to pick her up and cuddle her close. She smelled of that lovely vanilla and baby powder scent, and Bella's hold on her tightened as she breathed it in.

Lena's innocent comment about Bella being pregnant herself had caused a little ache deep inside her body. Once she had been going to have a child, but because of her first husband's physical assault on her she had lost that baby. Jan had been there then to help her, although then she had believed she hated him.

They had talked during the brief time they had shared together before Jan had had to rejoin his Polish RAF Squadron down on the South Coast, and Bella had told Jan then that she didn't want to have a baby until the war was over, and until he could be with her.

'I'm so afraid, Jan,' she had confessed to him. 'After what happened before. I couldn't bear that to happen again.'

'It won't. It was Alan who caused your mis-carriage,' he had tried to reassure her.

'I know that, but I'm still afraid. I need you to be there with me – I need your strength. Somehow

I feel that if you are there then everything will be all right . . . our baby will be all right,' Bella had told him.

Jan had kissed her then and she had kissed him back, and he had told her that everything would be as she wished. She knew she had made the right decision, but that couldn't stop her aching with longing to feel Jan's child growing inside her. It wouldn't be long now until the war ended. Everyone said so. All she had to do was wait.

Wait and pray that Jan would come safely through it. Bella hugged her niece even more tightly. The Polish Squadron within the RAF had a reputation for bravery and daring. Jan had already been shot down once whilst in action. If she should lose him . . . but she mustn't think of that. She must think instead of doing her own bit for the war effort, of playing her part and, of course, of dealing with the fuss her mother would make once she learned that Charlie was going to pay them a visit but that Daphne would not be with them.

So Charlie was coming home. Lena put a calming hand on her stomach as the baby within it kicked hard as though in protest against the intrusion into her thoughts of someone else. Lena looked down at her daughter. She was a beautiful little girl with the same dark curls that Lena herself had inherited from her Italian father, but where Lena's skin had a faintly olive tone to it, Janette was fair-skinned and blue-eyed. Everyone who saw the three of them together remarked on the fact that whilst her daughter's hair was the same colour as Lena's own, her eyes were the same colour as her father, Gavin's. Only of course Gavin had not fathered her at all, even if she called him Daddy and the two of them adored one another. Charlie had fathered her. Charlie, whom Lena had so naïvely and foolishly believed loved her and had meant what he had said when he had promised to marry her.

How silly she had been giving her heart and her body so immediately to Charlie. She was much wiser now, and with this new baby on the way she had everything she could possibly want.

So why did the fact that Charlie was coming home make her feel so restless and . . . on edge? A sudden flurry of kicks from the baby punished her for her thoughts and reminded her of where her duty lay. She was so lucky to have what she did, Lena told herself. So very lucky.

Katie enjoyed her voluntary work at the American Red Cross's home from home for the American military at Rainbow Corner in Leicester Square, although she had to admit that it could be very demanding, especially on evenings like this one, when she was running late. She'd earned herself a disapproving look from the senior voluntary worker in charge on the reception area as she'd hurried in and made a dash for the cloakroom, where she'd removed her blue blazer and her neat white hat with its navy-blue bow trimming.

There'd be no chance of begging five minutes to snatch a hot drink and something to eat, Katie thought ruefully, quickly dabbing Max Factor powder onto her nose and then applying a fresh coat of pink lipstick, before combing her soft dark gold curls. Working at the Postal Censorship Office did not require her to wear a uniform, and the warmth of the September sunshine had meant that she had gone to work this morning wearing a neat white blouse under her precious 'good' blazer, and a red skirt with a pattern of white daisies on it, not really thinking about the significance of the colours until a small group of British Army high-ups had passed her when she left work, one of them commenting approvingly, 'Red, white and blue, eh? Jolly good show, young lady. That's the spirit.'

It was almost miraculous how things had changed since El Alamein and the Allies' success. The air of tension and anxiety that had filled London's streets like the dust from its bombed-out buildings had begun to lift, to be replaced by a sense of energy and optimism. The years of sacrifice, both in terms of human life and going without, of having faith and holding strong, were finally beginning to pay off. You could see it in the pride with which everyone was beginning to hold themselves, especially those in uniform, even if the shadow of Dunkirk and all the losses that had followed it were still there.

Victory – it was so close that you could almost taste it, almost . . . inside your thoughts, in your conversations with others, but it wasn't real yet, and there were still hundreds, thousands, perhaps, of young men who would have to sacrifice their lives before it could be achieved.

26

Some of those young men would be those who were here tonight in the Rainbow Club, Katie knew: eager, enthusiastic, brash young Americans, come to show the Brits how to win a war and not in the least abashed about saying so either.

They didn't mean any harm, not really. They just didn't realise the effect their well-fed, smartly turned-out appearance had on a nation that had undergone four years of warfare and rationing. And it wasn't just Britain's armed forces that some Americans seemed to look down on. There had been more than one occasion on which Katie's face had burned with indignation and anger over the way she had heard American servicemen describing British girls, although to be fair she had to admit that the behaviour of some girls did leave a lot to be desired.

At night the streets round Piccadilly were filled with girls offering GIs 'a good time'; couples openly having sex in doorways and whatever dark corner they could find, with the result that used condoms littered the streets, whilst, according to the authorities, venereal diseases were on the rise.

All this was to be deplored, and it was strictly forbidden for the young women who were judged suitable to work at Rainbow Corner to get involved in relationships with the Americans they met there.

Of course, there were girls who broke that rule, although Katie wasn't one of them. Not that the young GIs hadn't tried to date her – they had. Katie, though, always refused. She didn't want to get involved – with anyone.

A sudden influx of young airmen brought an end to her introspection.

'Boy, oh boy, it smells good in here,' one of them remarked enthusiastically, breathing in appreciatively. 'Coffee, doughnuts and hamburgers, Home sweet American Home.'

They'd arrived on one of the special trains put on to ferry American servicemen from their bases into London for their weekends off, and they were keen to let Katie know how they planned to spend their weekend.

'Girls, girls and more girls – that's what we want, isn't it, guys?' the one who was obviously the leader informed Katie, looking round at the others.

'Sure is,' they agreed in unison.

'I'm afraid we can't help you there,' Katie responded lightly, 'but if you'd like a map of London, or directions to anywhere . . .'

'Yeah, we'll have some directions to the nearest cat house,' one of the men grinned.

Katie suspected that they'd already been drinking, but she didn't really want to get them into trouble by calling for assistance. American GIs were meant to respect Rainbow Corner as though it were their home and occupied by their mother.

'Why don't you boys go and get yourselves a Coke and make yourselves at home?' Katie suggested.

'That ain't what we've got in mind,' drawled the one who had first spoken, leaning on the counter, breathing alcohol fumes in Katie's direction, while the others gathered round him. 'How about obliging us yourself? We don't mind taking it in turns, do we, guys?'

28

Some more men had walked in and had obviously overheard the comment. One of them – an officer, Katie guessed from the insignia on his uniform – walked over to the desk with a grim expression and announced curtly, 'We don't treat the kind folks, who are good enough to give up their free time to make us welcome, like that, Soldier, and I suggest you apologise to the lady right now, otherwise I'm gonna be calling the MPs.'

One look at the officer had an immediate sobering effect on the small group.

'Yessss, sir,' the culprit stammered as he stood up straight and saluted, a shamed-faced, 'Sorry, ma'am,' crossing the desk, before, to Katie's relief, the young men disappeared at some speed, into the club.

'Thank you for that,' she told her rescuer.

He shook his head, his mouth tightening into a grim line.

'You shouldn't have had to thank me,' he told her bluntly. 'Do you get much of that kind of behaviour?'

'No,' Katie told him truthfully.

'I'm afraid that some of these young idiots try to treat this country as though they're an invading force, not its ally,' the officer commented.

Katie smiled but didn't say anything. What he had said was, after all, true.

A younger officer came hurrying in saluting her rescuer.

'The general's car has arrived, sir.'

'I'll be right with you,' Katie's rescuer answered him, looking back at her. 'I'm sorry you had to put up with those young fools,' he told her before turning on his heel to leave the building.

'Wow, who was he?' the other girl on the reception desk, who had been taking her break, demanded as she reappeared just in time to see Katie's rescuer disappearing.

'I don't know,' Katie answered.

'Looked more like he should be mixing with the top brass at the American Embassy than coming here. That was a major's insignia he was wearing.'

It was obviously one of those nights, Katie reflected later when she arrived back at the billet she shared with four ATS girls in Cadogan Square, to find Peggy Groves, the most sensible and senior of the young women, waiting anxiously in the kitchen, twisting her engagement ring round on her finger. Katie noticed her khaki uniform skirt was looser on the waist than it had been. Thanks to rationing, they were all quite literally having to 'pull their belts' in.

'I'm waiting for Gerry to come in. I've decided that it's time I had a word with her about the way she's behaving. For her own sake, not just because it reflects on all of us.' An anxious frown was creasing Peggy's forehead. 'I was working late at the War Office this evening and when I got back the retired colonel from three doors down collared me to complain about what he referred to as "our goings-on".'

Peggy lit up a cigarette and drew deeply on it, the light from the kitchen's ugly single bulb shining on her dark auburn hair. 'If word of

Gerry's behaviour gets to Lord Cadogan's ears, we could all end up looking for a new billet, and I can't say that I would blame him. I know that Gerry's always been a bit on the wild side and that she's been through a hell of a lot, losing both her brothers this summer.' Peggy gave a shudder and stubbed out her cigarette. 'It's the kind of news we all dread getting.'

Katie nodded. Gerry's brothers had both been pilots with Bomber Command and everyone knew that the death rate amongst those who flew bombing missions to Germany was very high – higher than that amongst fighter pilots.

'We've all tried to give her a bit of leeway and cut her some slack,' Peggy continued. 'If there's one thing this war has taught me it's not to judge others. Gerry isn't the first girl to throw herself into living life to the full, with all that that means, following the death of someone close, and it's not for me to stand in moral judgement on her. She's a decent sort at heart, but she can't keep carrying on the way she is doing, drinking too much and sleeping around with as many men as possible, coming in at all hours, and in the state she does, with torn stockings and her clothes not fastened properly.'

Katie knew what Peggy meant. They were all aware of the change the deaths of her brothers had caused in Gerry. Before, she had spoken openly about the fact that she liked a bit of fun, but now there was a desperation about her behaviour that worried them all.

'Do you want some cocoa?' Katie asked, going to fill the kettle.

Peggy nodded, and then frowned again as they heard someone knocking on the front door.

Without saying anything they hurried into the hallway, automatically switching off the lights as they did so, so as not to break the blackout laws.

When Peggy opened the door, Katie could see a couple of GIs supporting Gerry between them, a taxi with another GI standing beside it waiting at the kerb with its meter ticking.

'Get a move on, you guys,' the GI standing beside the taxi urged them. 'We don't want the MPs catching up with us again.'

His warning of the possible arrival of the Military Police was enough to have the two GIs let go of Gerry, who would have fallen headlong into the hallway if Katie and Peggy hadn't caught her. She smelled of whisky, and something else – a rank sexual male odour that made Katie gag.

'We'd better get her upstairs to her room,' Peggy told Katie as they exchanged despairing looks.

It wasn't easy. Gerry was so drunk that her limbs were like those of a rag doll, her speech confused, but eventually Katie and Peggy managed to get her into her room and onto her bed.

'We'll have to turn her onto her side, in case she's sick in the night, otherwise she could choke,' Peggy told Katie practically. 'Come on, Gerry,' Peggy instructed her firmly. 'You're going to have to sit up.'

'Don't want to sit up.' Gerry told them. 'Don't want to do anything,' but determinedly, and with Katie's help, Peggy managed to get Gerry into a semi-sitting and much safer position.

'I don't really like leaving her on her own in this state, but I've got to be at the War Office earlier than usual tomorrow. There's an important meeting taking place,' Peggy confided to Katie, when Gerry fell asleep minutes after they had got her sitting up.

'I'll stay with her, if you like,' Katie offered.

'Would you?' Peggy gave her a grateful look. 'I know that strictly speaking it isn't up to us to look out for her, but—'

'We're all in this war together,' Katie stopped her. 'I like Gerry and I feel sorry for her. She doesn't really mean any harm.'

'No, she doesn't,' Peggy agreed.

It was over two hours later when Gerry woke up, her attempt to stand waking Katie, who had been dozing in the chair beside her bed. Throwing off the thin grey blanket she had wrapped round herself, Katie got to her feet just in time to prevent Gerry from losing her balance.

'Oh, Katie, it's you. That's funny,' Gerry announced. 'The last thing I remember is being with some GIs.'

'Yes, they brought you back here,' Katie agreed.

'And you don't approve. Oh, it's all right, I can tell by the sound of your voice what you're thinking.' Gerry shivered. 'I thought that by living I'd be able to make up for the fact that my brothers are dead; that if I had fun then I'd be having fun for all three of us. I wanted to live for all three of us, Katie, but I can't. I can't . . .' Her voice broke and her body heaved with the intensity of the ragged sobs shaking her.

'The more I try, the worse it gets, and the worse I feel. Sometimes I wish that I was dead as well. At least that way we'd all be together and my parents wouldn't have to worry any more; they wouldn't look at me and think that there should be three of us. It's so hard there, just being me.'

Katie ached with sympathy and sadness for her.

'Sometimes I just want to go to sleep and never wake up again. Have you ever felt like that, Katie?'

All Katie could do was hug her tightly, but Gerry's anguished outburst had filled her with concern, and she knew she had to say something.

Taking a deep breath she told Gerry quietly, as she released her, 'I do understand how you feel and, well, I think I'd feel the same, but we can't always just think of ourselves, Gerry.'

The other girl was looking at her now.

'You are all your parents have left, Gerry. You are the future of your family. You and the children you will have, not just for yourself but for your brothers as well. Sometimes it takes more courage to live than it does to die. Your brothers were incredibly brave and I know that you can be just as brave.'

For a moment Katie thought she had done the wrong thing. Tears were pouring silently down Gerry's face, but then Gerry flung herself into Katie's arms.

'I just don't deserve a friend as good as you, Katie,' she wept. 'You're right. The boys would be furious with me for being such a coward. From now on things are going to change. I am going to change.'

They hugged again, Katie close to tears herself.

Later on, as she stood in her own room, her hands wrapped round the comforting warmth of her mug of cocoa, Kate reflected sadly on the effect that the war was having on the emotions of young women, herself included. Some, like Gerry, sought escape from its harsh realities in drink and 'having fun'; others, like Katie herself, avoided anything other than friendship with young men, for fear of the emotional pain of losing them, whilst women like Peggy Groves, engaged or married, prayed every night that their men would return home safely. If she and Luke Campion had still been engaged, she too would have been one of those waiting and praying and hoping against hope.

But she was not still engaged to Luke, Katie reminded herself. That was over and in the past, just like the despair she had suffered when Luke had first broken off their engagement. But ending it had been the right thing for both of them. As much as she had loved Luke – and she had – she had found his dark moods and jealousy difficult to cope with. The turbulence of her parents' marriage had left her yearning for the calm of a love based more on the comfort provided by friendship than passion, Katie admitted, but she had not known herself well enough then to be able to see that. She had not known herself and she had not really known Luke either; they had never properly discussed themselves with one another. No, she no longer wept for their broken engagement or her own broken heart.

* * *

'What do you reckon, Corp? Think we're going to make it?' Andy asked Luke as they kept their heads down, waiting for the landing craft they were on to get close enough to Salerno's beachhead for them to disembark.

Luke and Andy had joined up virtually together, trained together, and fought together in the desert, and now here they were about to disembark onto Italian soil.

Their unit, along with the remnants of other British units, were now being deployed in Italy under the command of General Mark Clark, of the American Fifth Army, the aim, to break through the German defences and push all the way to Rome.

Right now, though, Luke reflected, as he tried not to let the screams and moans from a landing craft that had just been hit by a German shell, get through the protective wall that every soldier learned to draw around himself, for some odd reason it was Katie who was at the forefront of his mind. Determinedly he pushed her image away to focus on his men and his responsibility to them.

On the beach ahead of them men from the advanced landing craft had started up a smoke screen to protect the landing of the infantry and the equipment.

The sergeant in charge of their troop was giving the command for the men to make for the beach. Wading through churning water, Luke chivvied his own men on, ignoring the sight of a corpse floating in the sea next to them.

All along the landing area men were coming ashore, amid the cacophony of noise and the acrid smell and taste of smoke, and the enemy shells falling around them, to get their equipment safely beached, before starting to push inland, alongside 146th Field Regiment RA, which was now attached to the 7th Armoured Division.

'Fighting this ruddy war certainly doesn't get any easier,' Andy found time to mutter, in an aside to Luke, as the men fell in and started to push forward. The first rule of any beach landing was that you got off the beach as fast as you could, and as far as the enemy would let you.

This time that distance wasn't very far, a mile or so Luke reckoned, before all hell broke loose and they were under attack from the Germans.

She had done it. Lou felt like whooping with joy as she taxied her plane neatly to a standstill, after her tenth cross-country flight. This one had been the hardest of all: from Thame to the Castle Bromwich aircraft factory – the largest Spitfire factory in the country – surrounded on three sides by barrage balloons to protect it. Lou had not had to land on the airstrip there this time to avoid clogging it up when it was needed for the removal of Spits to the maintenance units. Instead she had been instructed to drop down almost to a landing height and then lift off again. As the barrage balloons stretched to the western side of the airstrip, all landings had to be made to the west and all take-offs had to be made to the east. Today, even with good visibility and a lightly buffeting wind, Lou had been aware of what a challenge it must be to perform those manoeuvres when weather conditions were unfavourable.

Lou had been glad she had listened to the advice of her instructor, Margery, who had told her to return via the maintenance units of Little Rissington, Kemble and Aston Down, where ultimately she would be expected to deliver the new Spitfires for their mechanical fitting out, and then Number 6 Ferry Pool at Ratcliffe before returning to Thame. Since the Fosse Way passed the boundary to Ratcliffe's airstrip, once she had the road in her view, Lou had stuck with it, holding her breath when they had run into some unexpectedly low cloud.

Technically she was not allowed to fly above it but if she dropped down too low to get under it she could end up dangerously close to the ground. In the end she decided to keep to a steady course and fly through it in the hope that it was only an odd patch. To her relief her guess had been right, and they were soon out of the cloud. Even better, she had been able to maintain a steady course.

It was her longest and most complex cross-country so far, and she was thrilled when, once they were both outside the aircraft, Margery told her approvingly, 'Very nice, Campion. Well done.'

Just seeing those gleaming Spitfires all lined up awaiting transportation had filled Lou with excitement. It had been a wonderful day, she acknowledged happily to herself, removing her flying helmet and shaking her head to free her tangled curls.

She had allowed June to persuade her into going to a dance this evening at a nearby American bomber base. A whole crowd of them were going, thanks to an invitation passed on to them via a male American ATA pilot. Several American male pilots had joined ATA in its early days, before America had joined the war.

Although ATA had now opened its doors to girls from ordinary backgrounds, the ethos put in place by the original eight pilots, all young women from privileged and well-to-do backgrounds, still prevailed. ATA pilots were not subject to any of the rules and regulations imposed by the Armed Forces: there was no parading, no drill, no hier-archy, no jankers, no rules about wearing uniform instead of civvies. Instead what there was were a set of unspoken 'rules' accepted and adhered to as a matter of principle and honour.

These included such practical aspects of their work as upholding the reputation of ATA for delivering planes to their destinations safely and efficiently; but, equally importantly, unwritten rules such as always presenting a feminine appearance, wearing lipstick, and nail polish, not getting out of one's plane at an RAF base until one had removed the ugly flying helmet and replaced it with a pretty silk scarf.

The newer intake of ATA pilots might not be in a position to take off in their cars for London to have dinner at places like the Savoy and the Ritz, and go to exclusive clubs like the 400, but when the opportunity came to attend social events ATA girls were on their honour to look good, which was why Lou blessed the insight and the generosity of her aunt Fran as she changed into her outfit for the evening.

The arrival, for her birthday earlier in the year, of a large parcel that had contained several stunningly pretty dresses from her aunt had truly delighted Lou.

In the note that had accompanied them, Francine had written that she hoped that Lou might be able to make use of the dresses, which she no longer needed.

Luckily, all the females of their family seemed to share the same neat waist and slender figure, and the dresses were a perfect fit. Lou had later learned that their aunt's birthday gift to her twin had been some beautiful Egyptian cotton bed linen for the bottom drawer Sasha had started now that she was engaged.

Tonight Lou had decided to wear the dress that was her favourite. In a shade of soft green silk printed with large white polkadots, which somehow deepened her summer tan whilst emphasising the way the sun had bleached the ends of her hair, the dress was halter-necked, with a neat-fitting bodice, which fastened with pretty white buttons and a white belt that fitted round Lou's small waist, whilst the semi-circular skirt floated prettily against her legs. To complete the outfit there was a little short white jacket lined in the same fabric as the dress.

Lou and June were being given a lift in her car by Hilary Stanton, one of the more senior girls, who was standing beside her car smoking a cigarette as they went to join her.

'Good choice of frock, Campion,' she praised Lou. 'I've heard that several of the American pilots based at Ratcliffe, who've joined ATA, will be there tonight, so we'll definitely want to put on a good show.'

'Of course, we all know why Hilary disapproves of the Ratcliffe pilots,' June had commented to Lou earlier. 'It's because of all the talk going round about the American pilots being real dare devils. Like I said before, there are all sorts of stories going round about them buzz-diving the general public for fun, flying under low bridges, flying above the cloud cover, and showing off.' June had pulled a face and added, 'They like to think of themselves as dead-end kids who are up for anything and everything, and who can fly planes when the weather is so bad that even the birds are walking.'

'That's all very well for them,' Lou had answered, 'but we've got a job to do that matters more than showing off and partying.'

Now, as she and June piled into Hilary's car along with two other girls, Lou acknowledged that she wasn't all that keen to go to the dance. However, she had promised June that she would, having had to refuse to go to London with her at the weekend, and then of course there was the added lure of the fact that the music would be provided by none other than Glenn Miller's band.

It didn't take them long to reach the American airbase, driving down narrow winding country lanes that lay almost hidden between high hedgerows, heavy now with blackberries and wild rosehips, and through picture-perfect villages, drowsing in the fading September sunlight.

As soon as they got close to the base, though, the scenery changed. Barbed wire replaced the hedgerows, and the gently undulating landscape was ironed flat, and pinned down with all the para-phernalia of an air force base: hangars, searchlights, wind socks, landing strips and the obligatory guard house by the entrance, through which they were allowed to pass once they had given the American ATA pilot's name.

As they drove past the airfield they could see the long line of bombers outside the hangars.

The base was a large one and, of course, rela-tively new, the area outside the mess where the dance was being held busy with American airmen in immaculately smart uniforms.

Not that the girls needed to be in the least bit ashamed of their appearance, Lou decided, proud to champion her own colleagues as, once the car was parked and they had all climbed out, she and June went to join the small crowd of ATA pilots who had already arrived.

'It's not going to be Glenn Miller after all,' one of the girls warned Lou, obviously disappointed herself. 'They've got another band playing instead.'

They all went into the mess together, exchanging greetings with the Americans who came forward to welcome them.

The American airmen's mess was far smarter than any mess she had ever been in before, Lou felt obliged to admit, trying not to look too impressed as she strained to listen to what the young American airman standing next to her was saying to her above the noise of other conversations around them. He was pleasant enough, with good teeth and a nice smile.

'Look over there,' June suddenly hissed directing Lou's attention to where a diminutive blonde with a mass of curls was sitting on a table, holding court to the group of men pressing round her. Unlike the other women in the room, who were all wearing frocks, she was wearing a pair of American jeans rolled up to reveal her enviably tanned and slender ankles and calves, a leather belt drawing the fabric in at her waist to show off its narrowness. She was chewing gum, and drinking beer from a bottle, and generally acting as though it was her right to be the centre of attention. For no reason that Lou could rationalise she felt a sharp stab of hostility towards her.

'Joyce Botham has just told me that she's one of the American ATA pilots. Her name's Frankie Truebrooke.'

Lou nodded and was about to turn away when the sight of an RAF uniform amongst the American pinks and greens caught her eye.

Perhaps she had stared too hard and for too long, Lou didn't know, but Frankie Truebrooke suddenly gave her a hard look and then turned to say something to the RAF pilot, whose face was hidden from Lou's view by the other men crowding around her. The RAF pilot moved, obviously directed to look at her by Frankie Truebrooke, and Lou's heart did a steep dive at such speed that she could hardly breathe.

Kieran Mallory! Tall and broad-shouldered with coal-black hair, grey eyes and a knowing smile, Kieran Mallory was strikingly handsome. And of course he knew it, Lou thought bitterly. Kieran Mallory was the very last person she ever wanted to see again. Quickly Lou looked away, not wanting to make eye contact with him, because she didn't want any kind of contact with him at all. What had Frankie Truebrooke said to him about her? And, more important, what would he say to the American about Lou? Would he tell her that both Lou and her twin sister had once had huge crushes on him; that he had deceived them both into believing that they were special to him? Lou could feel her face beginning to burn with angry humiliation. She was a different person from the silly girl she had been then. He and Frankie Truebrooke were well suited, Lou decided, with a toss of her head.

The band had started to play – indeed not Glenn Miller's band, sadly, but they sounded pretty good anyway, Lou acknowledged. The young airman, Cliff, with the good teeth and the nice smile, to whom she had been introduced, politely asked her to dance and, just as politely, Lou accepted.

Dancing sedately with Cliff to the tender strains of 'Moonlight Becomes You', Lou noticed that towards the end of the number Frankie Truebrooke, who was dancing with a fellow American, pulled away from her partner and ran over to say something to the band leader.

Then as the notes of 'Moonlight Becomes You' faded away Frankie Truebrooke, who was still standing in front of the band, clapped her hands together and announced, 'This is an American airbase, filled with fine American airmen, and we're gonna show you Brits that we can outdance you as well as outfly you.'

There was a moment of uncomfortable silence and exchanged uncertain looks, and then one of the airmen whooped in approval of Frankie's challenge and grabbed hold of her hand just as the band swung into a hot-paced jitterbug number that quickly turned into a floorshow given by Frankie and her partner whilst other dancers stood back.

She was good, Lou acknowledged, but not as good as Lou and Sasha themselves had been. There were many many times when Lou missed her twin and their old relationship, with its closeness and its shared ambitions, but right now she really wished that Sash was here so that they could do their bit for British morale and show Frankie a thing or two about really good jitterbugging.

Impulsively she turned to Cliff and demanded, 'Can you jitterbug?'

When he nodded, Lou didn't waste any more time. Grabbing hold of his hand she hurried him onto the floor, immediately picking up the beat of the music. She and Sash had loved dancing so much, and the magic it had always held for her was still there; there were some things, some skills, that were never forgotten.

As she let the music seize her and take her, Lou could hear the astonished and admiring gasps from the ATA girls now crowding round the edge of the dance floor to watch them, and cheer her on, their

45

support reinforcing her determination to make Frankie Truebrooke regret her arrogant claim.

Cliff, who had initially looked apprehensive, was now throwing himself into the spirit of things. Luckily he was a good dancer himself, but it was Lou who held everyone spellbound and who the band played for as they recognised her skill, whilst her comrades clapped and cheered her on.

Thank goodness she'd decided not to bother wearing stockings because her legs were tanned, Lou thought, as Cliff swung her round, then up and then down again.

Laughing up at Cliff, she wouldn't have seen the bottle that Frankie had thrown down deliberately to trip her up if it hadn't been for the fact that Kieran Mallory had moved, no doubt wanting to get closer to the American, and his movement had caught her attention, showing her the bottle rolling towards her. She heard her friends gasp; she could see the look of malicious triumph on Frankie Truebrooke's face, but Lou knew what to do. In a manoeuvre that had been part of one of the routines she and Sasha had taught themselves, Lou changed feet, and hands, and spun round anticlockwise, turning under Cliff's arm, in a movement that pushed him to the side, and took them both safely away from the bottle.

The roar of approval and the hand clapping that resulted from the British ATA contingent said everything that needed to be said, Lou recognised, both about Frankie's spitefulness and her own quick reaction to it.

Of course, when she came off the dance floor all the Brits gathered round her, wanting to praise her.

'Well, you're a dark horse,' said June, tugging on Lou's arm. 'You never said a word about being able to dance like that.'

'It's just something Sash and I taught ourselves,' Lou insisted, feeling uncomfortable about all the attention she was getting now that she had stopped dancing.

'You were a wow,' another of the girls approved. 'You knocked that show-off American sideways, you were so good.'

Everyone was making such a fuss that Lou began to wish that she hadn't given in to the impulse to show Frankie that she wasn't the only one who could jitterbug.

'You didn't just outdance Frankie Truebrooke, you've outclassed her as well,' Hilary told Lou, later on in the evening when they were on their way back to their own base. 'She needed teaching that kind of lesson, and I for one am glad that one of us was the one to do it. She's got a reputation for being spoiled and wild,' Hilary continued, 'and she likes stirring up trouble. One of my pals was posted to Ratcliffe and she said that Frankie was always trying to prove how much better she is than everyone else, but especially the British ATA pilots. Apparently she likes to boast that the ranch her father owns in Texas is bigger than the whole of England and that she's been taught everything she needs to know.'

'Except good manners,' June pointed out trenchantly.

'Absolutely,' Hilary agreed. 'You really put her nose out of joint tonight, Campion. It was about time someone showed her what it means to be British and I am so glad that it was one of us. I felt dreadfully sorry for that nice RAF flight lieutenant she was trying to lead on, though.'

Lou had to bite on her tongue not to retort that Kieran Mallory was far from nice and would certainly not need any leading on.

FOUR

The first thing Lou noticed after she had stepped out of Liverpool's Lime Street Station, packed with travellers, most of them in uniform, was how grey and grimy Liverpool looked after the pretty English countryside she had been living in. Quickly she pushed away her disloyal judgement on the city. Liverpool was her home, it was the place where she had grown, and most of all it held the people she loved.

She was wearing her uniform, more for her parents' benefit than her own. Her father was a traditionalist and a bit old-fashioned, and Lou suspected that he wouldn't understand or indeed approve of the way things worked in ATA. Not that she minded wearing her smart tailored navy-blue skirt with its matching jacket worn over a lighter blue blouse. Unlike the well-to-do pilots, who all had their uniforms tailored for them at a store in London called Austin Reed, Lou had been perfectly happy with the neat fit of her regulation-sized clothes. Rammed down onto her curls was the peaked forage cap that none of the girls really ever wore, her golden wings stitched proudly to her jacket denoting that she was now a Third Class ATA pilot.

After the sleepy green peacefulness of the narrow country lanes around their base, connecting small rural villages and towns, the busyness of Liverpool's streets, teeming with traffic and people, came as something of a shock. Her strongest memories of her home city were those of the dreadful days of Hitler's blitz at the start of May 1941 and the terrible time after that when her sister had nearly lost her life in the bomb-damaged streets. Then the city had been silent, mourning its dead, and filled with grief, its people weighed down with the enormity of the task that lay in front of them.

Now all that had gone and in its place was a sense of expectation and energy, brought about, Lou suspected, by the country's growing hope that Hitler was going to be defeated.

The city centre was busy and bustling with men and women in every kind of uniform: British Army, Royal Navy, and the RAF; American infantry and airmen, Poles, Canadians New Zealanders and Aussies.

As she passed the street that led to the Royal Court Theatre, Lou felt her heart give a flurry of angry thuds. It was there that she and Sasha had first met Kieran Mallory, the nephew of its manager, Con Bryant. They had gone there naïvely hoping to be taken on as dancers. Instead of sending them on their way, Kieran and his uncle Con had deliberately encouraged them to believe that they had a stage future ahead of them. And by playing each of them off against the other, pretending to each behind the other's back that he liked her the best, Kieran had cleverly come between them, fostering a mistrust and jealousy that had ultimately almost led to a terrible tragedy.

That was all in the past now, Lou reminded herself. Sasha was happily engaged to the young bomb disposal sapper who had saved her life, and Lou herself had achieved her ambition of becoming a pilot.

But the division between them was still there.

Not because of Kieran Mallory, Lou assured herself. He meant nothing to either of them now and she certainly wasn't going to give him an importance in her life that he didn't deserve.

Her nose, accustomed now to the smell of aviation fuel, hot engines, and Naafi food, set against a countryside background, was now beginning to recognise the smells of home: sea salt-sprayed air mixed with smoke and dust; the smell of vinegar, fish and chips wafting out of a chippy as she made her way up through the city streets toward Edge Hill; the scent of steam and coal from the trains in the Edge Hill freight yard, those smells gradually fading as she walked further up Edge Hill Road, leaving the city centre behind her, so that by the time she was turning into Ash Grove, Lou could have sworn she could smell the newly turned earth from the row of neat allotments that ran behind the houses and down to the railway embankment, one of which belonged to her own father. Her heart lifted, and just as though she were still a little girl, she suddenly wanted to run the last few yards, just as she and Sasha had done as children, racing one another to see who could reach the back door first, and somehow always getting there together, falling into the kitchen in gales of giggles. It had always been Sasha, though, who had still looked neat and tidy, whilst Lou had always been the one with a ribbon missing from one of her plaits and her ankle socks falling down.

In those days, when they had got home from school they had measured the days from the way the kitchen smelled. Mondays, the smell would be of lye soap and laundry, because Monday was wash day, just as on Fridays the smell would be of fish. They were not a Catholic family but their mother had still followed the traditional habit of serving fish on Fridays. Thursday's smell had always been Lou's favourite because Thursday was baking day, and they would return home from school to find the kitchen wonderfully scented with the aroma of cakes or scones, or whatever it was their mother had been baking.

Those had been such happy days. She had never dreamed then of what might lie ahead of them, never imagined that there would ever be a time when she and Sasha would not do everything together. Then such a thing had been unthinkable. Then . . .

The back door was half open. A pang of unexpected happiness, tinged with uncertainty, made Lou hesitate, suddenly conscious, now that she was here, how very much she wanted to make things right with her twin and for them to be close again.

She pushed open the door.

'Lou!'

Jean stared in delight at her daughter, taking in her air of calm confidence and the smartness of her appearance.

'Mum.' Lou's voice thickened with emotion as she was enveloped in her mother's loving embrace.

'You've grown,' Jean told her. 'A least an inch.'

'It's this cap,' Lou laughed. 'It makes me look taller. Oh, Mum, it's lovely to be home. I do miss you all, especially Sash.'

The once bright yellow paint on the kitchen walls might look a little faded and war-weary now, but the love that filled the small room hadn't changed, and nor had her mother.

'Tell me all about everyone,' Lou begged her mother. 'I get letters, but it isn't the same as seeing people. How's Grace liking Whitchurch? And what about Auntie Fran? And Sasha, Mum, how is she?'

Jean sighed and shook her head slightly.

'I'm worried about her,' she admitted. Normally she would not have dreamed of discussing one of the twins with the other, but Lou had such an air of quiet competence about her now that unexpectedly Jean discovered that it was actually a relief to be able to voice her concerns about Sasha to someone who knew and understood her so well.

'There's nothing wrong between her and Bobby, is there?' Lou asked anxiously.

'I don't think so, Lou. I just don't know what's wrong with her, except that nothing seems to please her these days.'

Outside the back door Sasha stiffened, anger

and resentment filling her. So that's what she got for using some of her precious time off to come home early to welcome her twin – overhearing Lou and their mother talking about her behind her back.

Sasha pushed open the door and marched into the kitchen, her unexpected appearance forcing an uncomfortable silence on the room.

'Don't worry about me,' she told her mother and sister. 'I'll go up to my room so that you can go on talking about me behind my back.'

'Oh, Sasha, love, don't be like that,' Jean pleaded.

She was upsetting her mother, Sasha could see, and immediately her anger turned to guilt and misery. She knew that her mother was anxious about her, but how could she tell her about the shameful secret that was eating into her? How could she tell her what a coward she was, especially now with Lou standing there in her smart uniform. Lou, her twin, whose letters home were full of the exciting and dangerous things she was doing.

Wanting to change the subject and lighten the mood in the kitchen, Lou announced, 'I wish so much you'd been with me last night, Sash. A group of us went to this dance and there was this dreadful show-off American girl pilot who was trying to prove that us British girls couldn't jitterbug, so I had to show her that she was wrong. I did pretty well but it would have been so much better if you'd been there.'

Was that a hint of a smile relaxing Sasha's frown?

'Oh, and I've got to tell you this. You'll never guess who was there,' Lou continued. 'Kieran Mallory, and—'

Immediately Sasha's smile disappeared. 'Kieran Mallory? Why have you got to tell me about him? Do you think I actually need reminding about what he did, or how keen you were to get in his good books? I thought we'd agreed that we'd never talk about him again.'

Lou didn't know what to say.

'It was thanks to you and him that I nearly got myself killed,' Sasha threw at her, red flags of emotion burning in her cheeks. 'I would have been killed an' all if it hadn't been for my Bobby, saving me like he did by taking my place in that bomb shaft.'

Guilt filled Lou. 'Sash, you know how dreadful I feel about that.' Remorsefully she reached out her hand to her twin, but Sasha stepped back from her.

'It's easy enough for you to say that, but it doesn't seem to have stopped you taking up with Kieran again.'

'I haven't taken up with him,' Lou protested. 'I only mentioned him because I wanted to tell you that he was with this dreadful American girl!'

'And that's why you wanted to outdance her, isn't it? So that you could show off to him.'

'No,' Lou protested. 'It wasn't like that at all.'

'Then why are you so keen to tell me that you've met up with him again? If you're trying to make me jealous of you, Lou, you needn't bother. My Bobby is worth a hundred of Kieran Mallory.

You're welcome to him. Don't bother making me any tea, Mum. I'm meeting Bobby at tea time and we'll have something at Joe Lyons.'

Lou was too astonished and, yes, hurt as well, by Sasha's unexpected and unjustified attack on her to say anything to defend herself. She'd only mentioned the incident because she'd wanted to take Sasha back to a time when they'd been close to one another. It had never occurred to her that Sasha would place the interpretation on her little story that she had.

Without waiting for any response Sasha pulled open the door into the hall and walked out.

Jean and Lou looked at one another in silence as they heard her feet going up the stairs.

'It isn't like Sasha thinks, Mum. I wasn't telling her about Kieran for any reason. Sasha's right, though,' Lou continued soberly. 'What happened to her was my fault. If we hadn't quarrelled and she'd decided to go home without me, she'd never have gone across that bombed-out building and fallen into that bomb crater. I should have gone back with her the moment she said she didn't want to go any further, instead of waiting like I did, thinking she'd change her mind and come running after me and Kieran.'

Lou looked so guilty and upset that Jean's heart ached for her.

'It was an accident, with no one to blame, Lou love, and thankfully in the end neither of you came to any harm. I can't tell you how many years it aged me and your dad when we saw the two of you in that bomb crater, you holding on to Sasha for dear life and her half under that bomb.'

56

Jean exhaled and then said firmly, 'I'm going to put the kettle on and make us all a nice cup of tea.'

She turned away from Lou to fill the kettle. 'And as for this Kieran Mallory . . .' she continued, her back to Lou as she turned on the gas and then struck a match to light the burners.

'He doesn't mean anything to me now, Mum,' Lou assured her. 'Me and Sasha were well and truly taken in by him and that uncle of his who managed the Royal Court Theatre.'

Jean was glad that she had her back to her daughter. Somehow, perhaps because at the time she had been so dreadfully anxious for Sasha and then so relieved when she was finally safe, she'd never made the connection between Kieran Mallory and Con Bryant, although Jean recognised that it must have been there for her to make. Now that she had, though, a fresh apprehension filled her. Con might be dead and buried – Jean had seen the announcement of his death in the local paper – but that did not alter the fact that he had been the cause of such dreadful misery and potential shame to the family when he seduced Francine, and left her pregnant, something which Lou and Sasha knew nothing about. And now here was his nephew, coming between her daughters, a nephew who sounded very much as though he was made in the same mould as his uncle; the kind of man no mother wanted going anywhere near her daughters.

Lou had said that he didn't mean anything to her, and Sasha was safely engaged to Bobby so there was no real reason for her to worry, Jean tried to comfort herself.

Irritably Charlie Firth gunned the engine of the Racing Green MG and dropped it down a gear so that he could overtake the lumbering army lorries travelling in convoy ahead of him. He hadn't been in the best of moods when he'd left his base in the South of England for the long drive home to Liverpool, and the slow crawl along roads filled with military traffic hadn't done anything to improve that mood. Spending, or rather wasting, what could well be his last bit of decent leave before his battalion was posted overseas and into action on a visit to his mother was the last thing Charlie would have chosen to do – not when London and all it had to offer in terms of a good night out with a pretty and willing girl was so conveniently close to the base. Unfortunately, though, he'd had no choice. Thanks to his ruddy wife and her equally ruddy parents, and their insistence on Charlie doing the gentlemanly thing and giving his wife a divorce.

Charlie swore viciously as he took a sharp corner at speed and almost knocked a pair of cyclists off their bikes. He could just imagine how his mother was going to react to the news that Daphne wanted a divorce. Not that Charlie really cared how his mother felt; it was the effect the news of his divorce was likely to have on her willingness to 'help him out' with those useful 'loans' he kept tapping her up for that worried him. His mother was a snob. She had boasted to anyone who would listen that he, Charlie, was marrying a girl with a double-barrelled surname and she wasn't going to like what Charlie had to tell her. And he did have to tell her because if he didn't there was no guarantee that if he didn't get his side of the story in first, his in-laws, the Wrighton-Budes, just might give her theirs.

They'd never considered him good enough for their daughter, although Charlie had only discovered that on his wedding day, when Daphne's cousin had let slip that Daphne's parents and, indeed, Daphne herself had been expecting a local land-owning neighbour's son to propose to her, and when he had married someone else instead marriage to Charlie had been seen by them as a face-saving exercise.

Now, though, this neighbour's son was a widower, thanks to the war, and free to remarry, and it seemed that the woman he wanted to marry was Charlie's wife.

Naturally Charlie had expressed shock and anger when this news had been relayed to him by his father-in-law, but the old fart had out-manoeuvred him by announcing that he knew all about the girls Charlie saw when he was on leave in London, because he had apparently been having Charlie followed, so that evidence could be gathered to back up Daphne's claim for a divorce. Charlie's father-in-law had actually had the gall to add that in view of his taste for variety, Charlie might actually welcome the freedom of a divorce.

Charlie, however, wanted no such thing. Announcing that he was married, as he had discovered, was a very effective way of sorting out the girls who wanted to play the game his way and have a good time, from those who were after something more permanent. Now his father-in-law was demanding that Charlie did the decent thing, so that Daphne, her name clear of any wrongdoing, could get her divorce and be free to remarry.

No, he wasn't looking forward to the coming weekend at all, Charlie admitted.

There'd be no point in trying to tap up Bella, his sister, for a few quid; they'd never been what one might call close, but their relationship had really deteriorated after Bella had taken in that girl who reckoned that he'd fathered her brat.

He had reached the outskirts of Liverpool now, the Mersey a grey gleam to his left, made even greyer by the hulls of the naval vessels and merchant convoys filling the docks.

Liverpool was the port used by most of the convoys crossing the Atlantic, bringing in much-needed supplies of raw materials and food. Not that the vitally important role his home city was playing in the war effort interested Charlie.

Wallasey was considered far more exclusive than Liverpool, the town holding itself apart from the city in the manner of a 'lady' keeping her distance from her servants, whilst being dependent on them.

The last few miles of the drive increased Charlie's ill humour. He'd have given anything to turn the car round and drive back to London, he acknowledged as he pulled up outside his mother's house.

In the front window a lace curtain twitched ever so slightly, but Charlie was too preoccupied with his own sense of injustice and ill-usage to notice.

'Bella, it's Charlie. He's here,' Vi Firth announced, letting the lace curtain drop and then hurrying into the hallway, patting the rigid waves of her new hairdo, before going to open the door.

Lord, but his mother looked drab and dull; no wonder his father had left her for someone younger and livelier, Charlie thought unkindly as he submitted himself to Vi's tearful embrace.

'Such a shame that dearest Daphne couldn't come with you. I can see that I'm going to have to travel down to see her,' Vi informed Charlie, before turning towards the kitchen and calling out in a far sharper voice, 'Bella, do hurry up with that tea. Your poor brother has been driving for hours.

'Having Bella living here with me is so difficult at times, Charles. You wouldn't believe how selfish she can be,' Vi confided to her son in a lower tone. 'I blame that nursery. I never wanted her to go and work there, or marry that Pole. Of course, if your father had been here to put his foot down . . .' Fresh tears welled in Vi's eyes.

'No one would have stopped me from marrying Jan, Mummy,' Bella announced, appearing in the open doorway from the hall to the kitchen, obviously having overheard their mother's comment.

'Where is that tea, Bella?' Vi interrupted her.

'In the kitchen,' Bella answered her.

'Oh, really, Bella, I thought you'd have made more of an effort for your brother, and prepared a tea tray for the lounge. This dreadful war is

61

causing standards to slip dreadfully,' Vi complained to Charlie.

Charlie fought to conceal his growing irritation. A good stiff drink was what he wanted, not a cup of tea, but he judged it wiser not to say so, not with the old girl almost having turned into a bit of a lush herself after his father had left. It wouldn't do to fall out with his mother before he'd won her round, gained her sympathy and got some money out of her, and there was no point in falling foul of Bella otherwise she'd set off giving him an ear-bashing.

An hour later, having spent most of that time forced to listen to his mother cataloguing her various grievances, Charlie was beginning to wish that he *had* thought to bring a bottle of army rations gin with him to calm his mother down and put her in the right mood for what he had to tell her.

'. . . and I still don't see why you couldn't have let Charlie sleep in your bed tonight, Bella, whilst you used the spare room,' his mother was now berating his sister. 'He needs a decent night's sleep after driving up here.'

Scenting an opportunity to deliver his bad news, Charlie assumed a morose, mournful expression and heaved a heavy sigh.

'Don't worry about me, Ma. I've hardly slept a wink this last week since . . .'

'Since what?' Vi demanded anxiously when Charlie deliberately did not continue.

Charlie shook his head. 'I don't want to burden you with my problems, Ma, especially after what you've been through with Dad.' He paused and waited, and, true to form, just as he had expected she would, his mother immediately pressed him.

'Charlie, I'm your mother; you must tell me what's wrong.'

Charlie shook his head and then cleared his throat as though struggling with his emotions.

'I'm not going to blame Daphne. It isn't her fault. It's mine. I should have realised when her cousin let the cat out of the bag about how Daphne had been involved with someone else before she met me, that she might not love me as much as I love her.'

'So much that you got another girl pregnant whilst you were engaged to her,' Bella cut in in a sharp voice, earning herself a look of censure from their mother and a rebuking.

'I won't have you bringing that up, Bella. If anyone was to blame, it was that dreadful girl.' Turning back to Charlie, Vi told him firmly, 'I shouldn't let it worry you if you and dearest Daphne have had a bit of a tiff, Charlie.'

Trust his mother to be obtuse, Charlie thought impatiently. She'd always been good at not seeing what she didn't want to see, and making a fuss over bits of something and nothing because it suited her to do so.

'A bit of a tiff? I wish that it was just that, Ma.' Charlie stood up and paced the kitchen floor as though in the grip of an intense emotion that was almost too much for him. 'Like I said, though, I'm not blaming Daphne.' He gave a bitter laugh. 'No, if anyone's to blame for her turning against me then

63

it's her mother. She never really liked me.' There, that should do it, Charlie reckoned. His mother had never forgiven Daphne's mother for the way she had behaved over the wedding, treating Vi as though she was a poor relation she'd rather not have known the mother of her daughter's husband-to-be.

Vi's reaction was as gratifying as it had been predictable. Her mouth pursed, her bosom swelling with righteous indignation.

'And who is she when she's at home, not to like you? You saved her son's life – well, as good as. It wasn't your fault that he went overboard again and drowned after you'd rescued him at Dunkirk. Mind you, I have to say that I never really took to her. Well, look at the way she was always interfering and stopping poor Daphne from coming up here. Selfish, that's what I call it.

'You must speak to Daphne, though, Charlie, and be firm with her. She's your wife now, after all.'

Charlie shook his head. 'It's too late for that now.'

'Too late? What do you mean?' Now Vi was seriously alarmed.

'Daphne wants a divorce. And the truth is, well, I feel honour bound to agree, especially knowing that—'

'Knowing what?' Bella challenged her brother. She knew Charlie far too well to be taken in by the little side show he was putting on for their mother. And besides, being honour bound to do anything simply wasn't Charlie. If Bella had needed any confirmation of that she only had to think of the way in which Charlie had stolen her jewellery and then tried to blame the theft on Jan. And, even worse, how he had seduced poor Lena and then deserted her, leaving her pregnant.

Charlie exhaled unevenly.

'This chap – the chap who Daffers was involved with before me – is a widower now, and it seems that he . . . that they – well, I'm pretty sure that all Daffers intended to do was to offer him her condolences, since he's a close neighbour, and that he's the one to blame for things getting out of hand. She's not the sort to deliberately . . . Well, like I said, I can't and won't blame her, but the truth is that things have gone further than they should and poor Daffers . . .' Charlie paused for effect, and heaved a deep sigh.

Her brother really ought to have gone on the stage, Bella thought grimly.

'Charles?' Vi begged.

Charlie took another deep breath. 'I hate to have to say this but the fact is that they were caught out in a compromising situation and now, for her sake, the sooner this chap is able to make a decent woman of Daffers, the better. Of course I could refuse to co-operate, but – well, when you love someone you want them to be happy, and if the only thing I can give her to show her how much I love her is my agreement to being named as the guilty party in our divorce, to protect her, then that is what I will do.'

There were a dozen probing questions at least that Bella wanted to ask but now wasn't the time.

Vi, who had half made to stand up, was now sitting back in her chair, one hand placed over her heart, the other clutching the edge of the table for support.

Bella knew how much Charlie's news would upset her mother, and what a blow it would be to her. Pity for her softened Bella's awareness of how difficult their mother could be. Charlie's divorce would be very hard for her to bear, and she would see it as another humiliation on top of the humiliation she had already suffered over their father leaving home to live with his assistant.

Everything that Bella was thinking was confirmed when her mother turned to Charlie and told him, 'Daphne may have behaved very badly, Charlie, but she is your wife. I shall write to her for you and tell her that, and I shall write to her mother as well . . .'

The last thing Charlie wanted was his mother getting in touch with Daphne or her family and discovering the truth. Furious with his mother for making things difficult for him, he longed to be able to escape – from her and from the problems she was causing him. As always when he was confronted with an obstacle to his plans, he blamed everyone apart from himself.

'No! You mustn't write to Daphne or her parents,' he began furiously.

'Why not?' Vi demanded.

Bella had seen and heard enough. She could tell from Charlie's expression that things weren't going the way he had planned and that the situation was going to get very unpleasant unless she did something to avoid that.

'Mummy, you can't interfere. It wouldn't be right. It wouldn't be dignified, or worthy of you. Charlie has just told us that he feels honour bound to let Daphne have her divorce and it is only right that you respect his decision, and be proud of his . . . his generous and honourable treatment of her.'

Charlie listened to Bella with relief. She certainly knew how to handle their mother.

'That's right, Ma,' Charlie agreed. 'A man's honour is very important to him. Especially when he's in uniform and he's about to go into action. I'm not saying that I wasn't tempted to plead with Daffers to change her mind, but a man's got to be a man – and honourable, of course.'

Charlie was right, Vi acknowledged reluctantly. It was important that he did the right thing, and that he put being honourable above his own feelings. And that would certainly show that stuck-up Mrs Wrighton-Bude, Daphne's mother, which of their two children knew the right way to behave. How ashamed she must feel having to explain to all her friends – her 'bridge club set' – that her daughter had behaved in such a shameful way and her with a husband who loved her, who had saved her brother's life and who was about to be sent overseas to fight for his country. In her shoes Vi didn't think she'd have been able to show her face anywhere. She, on the other hand, would be able to tell everyone just how well Charlie had behaved. Poor Charlie, whose heart had been broken.

'Well, I suppose I shall have to feel sorry for Mrs Wrighton-Bude,' Vi announced, 'for having been so shown up by her daughter in such a dreadful way. She must feel so ashamed, because of course it will reflect on her and the way she has been brought up.'

'I wanted to come up and tell you rather than send a letter.' Charlie quickly picked up the ball Bella had set rolling for him, keen to get the most benefit he could from his mother's sympathy for him. 'Not that it was easy. All the way up here I kept on thinking that Daphne should be with me . . .'

'You're over-egging the bread,' Bella warned him in a quiet murmur, but Charlie ignored her, going over to Vi's chair.

'These last few weeks have been pure hell, and to make the whole thing even worse, I've practically bankrupted myself driving over to see Daphne and her parents and then sorting out . . . well, everything that needs to be done, so that I can provide the necessary evidence that will enable Daphne to sue me for adultery.'

When Vi shuddered, Charlie assured her untruthfully, 'It's all right, Ma. It's all done very neatly; the solicitor arranges it all. I just have to say that I was at such and such an hotel on such and such a night with a Miss A – even though neither of us was anywhere near the place. Our names will appear in the hotel register and that will be enough. Of course, the whole thing is damnably expensive. More so than if I had actually been guilty of adultery. My solicitor was rather shocked that Daphne's father hadn't offered to cover all my expenses, but, well, call it foolish pride, but I couldn't bring myself to go cap in hand to him, to ask him to help me out, even though three hundred pounds is nothing to him.'

'Three hundred pounds?' Vi gasped.

'Yes. Luckily I'd got a bit put by. I'd been saving for after the war, thinking that me and Daphne would be wanting to buy our own home then.'

Vi's emotions overwhelmed her. 'Oh, my poor boy, I'll do what I can to help you, but the most I can manage is a hundred.'

He'd done it. Charlie crowed inwardly in triumph.

'I hate taking money from you, Ma, especially after what Dad's done. I'll pay you back, I promise. At least now all I've got to worry about is doing my bit for the country, and making sure we get this war won.'

'It's definite that you're going into action, then?' Bella asked.

'Looks like it,' Charlie confirmed. 'All leave's cancelled after this weekend, and we've been told we've already got orders to ship out. No one's saying for definite, but it's got to be Italy, with Sicily already invaded and won, and some of our men already with the American Fifth Army at Salerno.'

Bella nodded. What Charlie was saying confirmed what everyone seemed to be expecting. She had no idea what part her own Jan would be playing in any invasion of Italy. Jan's fighter pilot squadron based in the South of England covered the South Coast and the Channel, and as far as Bella was aware, it was the heavy bombers, both American and British, that were being used to make raids on Germany's defences in Italy and Germany itself.

If Italy could be captured then the way would be open for the Allies to really drive back the Germans.

Italy – that willing little bed partner Bella had made all the fuss about had had an Italian look about her, Charlie reflected, well pleased now with the result of his hard work, and typically and conveniently forgetting that it had been Bella who had saved the day for him.

Life just didn't seem fair, Vi thought bitterly.

She had been so proud when Charlie had married 'up' to a girl with a double-barrelled surname, and so had Edwin. But then Edwin had been tempted away from her by that dreadful scheming creature who had worked for him and with whom he was now living openly in sin, despite the fact that, technically at least, he and Vi were still man and wife. And now here was Charlie, her son, saying that his wife wanted a divorce. How could life be so cruel and unfair, especially to her? She had always lived a blameless life, selflessly devoting herself to the good of others, looking around for the right kind of husband; marrying Edwin for practical, sensible reasons, unlike her twin, Jean, who had fallen in love with the first man who had asked her out, and then marrying him without even considering what his future prospects might be.

Then she'd taken in their younger sister's illegitimate child, who had caused her nothing but trouble, only to have Fran carry on as though she and Edwin had been cruel to the boy instead of giving him the best of everything.

She'd even insisted that Edwin buy this house here in Wallasey, for Edwin and her children's sake rather than her own, so that Bella and Charlie could mix with a better class of people. It was because of the sacrifices she had made that Edwin had done as well as he had, and the family had risen to the position where others looked up to them and envied them.

Then the country had gone to war and everything had changed, and Vi didn't like those changes.

But it was poor Charlie she must think of, not herself. She must make sure too that people knew how badly Charlie had been treated, and how honourably he had behaved in return. Just mentally thinking the word 'honourably' made Vi feel better. No one could argue against or criticise a young man who behaved honourably.

FIVE

'Oh, you're still awake.'

The tone of Sasha's voice made it very clear to Lou that Sasha didn't welcome the fact that Lou was sitting up in bed in their shared bedroom, instead of being asleep.

Lou had been giving a great deal of thought to Sasha over the course of the evening, her concern for her twin growing with everything that her mother had said about Sasha – and, more importantly, everything she had not said.

Lou had learned that 'Sasha isn't doing Bobby any favours by trying to force him to turn his back on his comrades in the bomb disposal service by asking for a transfer into other military duties' – her father's comment.

And, 'I can understand that poor Sasha worries about Bobby doing such a dangerous job, but having a go at your dad because he won't help her to persuade Bobby to ask for a transfer isn't the right way to go about things. Your dad's a man of principle and he respects Bobby for insisting that he intends to stick with his comrades' – their mother's statement. And all the things in between that hadn't been said but which Lou had been able to sense with the maturity that being in uniform and having to work as part of a team with others had brought her.

'I could tell this afternoon that she wasn't herself,' Lou had admitted to her mother when they had been in the kitchen together after tea, washing up the tea things, a family ritual that Lou had once done everything she could to escape, but that today she had loved because of the opportunity it gave her to share a special closeness with her mother, as two adult women.

'I thought that it must be because of me and because she thought I'd been talking about her behind her back.'

Jean had sighed and shaken her head. 'There's no reasoning with her these days. I wouldn't mind so much if I thought that she was happy, but when I can see that she isn't . . .' She'd turned to Lou, her hands still in the washing-up water, red and slightly chapped from all the hard work they did. Looking at them, Lou had felt a surge of fierce love for her mother, and an equally intense wish that she could do something not just to put things right between her and Sasha, but to help her mother as well.

'I'll try and talk to her, if you like,' she had offered. 'I'd planned to tell her anyway how sorry I am that I was so mean to her when she and Bobby first started going out, because I didn't want things to change and I just wanted it to be me and her, like it had always been.'

Lou had guessed that their mother had expected Sasha to return home early from her tea out with Bobby because Lou was home, and that she was upset because Sasha had not done so. Because of that Lou had set herself the task of showing her parents, and especially her mother, that she was not upset or offended and that she was happy in their company, telling them about her own life in ATA, or at least giving them a carefully edited version of it so as not to alarm her mother, listening to the news with them, laughing when her father reminded her of the racket she and Sasha used to make with their music and their dancing, and listening with genuine interest whilst Jean brought her up to date on things that were happening within the family.

But all the time Lou had been trying to think of the best way to break down the barriers between her and Sasha.

'No,' she answered her twin now with a warm smile, 'I wanted to wait up for you so that we could have a proper chat. Do you remember how we used to talk so late into the night that Mum threatened to make us sleep in separate rooms?'

When Sasha didn't respond but turned away from her instead, and started getting ready for bed, Lou tried again.

'Mum and Dad were both saying how much they like Bobby.'

Sasha, who had put one foot on their shared bentwood chair whilst she removed her stockings, stiffened but didn't say anything.

'I'm really sorry that I was such an idiot and

behaved so badly when you and Bobby were first seeing one another, Sash,' Lou apologised generously. 'I was so immature and selfish, wanting to keep things between us the way they had always been.'

Sash had returned to removing her stockings. Her twin had lost weight, Lou recognised. Even the dim light of the bedside lamp couldn't conceal how pinched her face looked. Lou looked towards the window with its heavy blackout covering. If only Sasha would just make some response, but her twin was behaving as though Lou simply wasn't there.

Lou wasn't going to give up, though. Not for one minute.

'I was so jealous of Bobby,' she continued, laughing at herself, 'him being with bomb disposal and being a real hero. You must be so proud of him, Sasha.'

Now at last her twin reacted, turning to face Lou, her eyes blazing with emotion in her pale face.

'Proud of him for risking getting himself killed when he knows what that would do to me? When he could ask for a transfer out?'

Sasha's voice held so much anger and so much pain that Lou could feel that pain in her own heart.

'I hate this war. I hate it and I just want it to be over, before it can take Bobby from me,' Sasha burst out.

In a flash Lou was pushing back the bedclothes and getting out of bed, her one thought to comfort her twin, as she ran across the space that divided their single beds.

'Oh, Sash, I'm so sorry.' Lou reached out to put her arms around her twin.

'No you're not. You're enjoying this war, like everyone else: Mum and Dad, and Grace and Seb, and . . . and everyone. Well, I'm not enjoying it. I hate it. I hate everything about it, everything.'

Sasha had torn herself free from Lou's embrace before Lou could stop her, snatching up her toilet bag, obviously intending to go to the bathroom.

Lou watched her go, her heart aching for her twin, knowing instinctively, because they were twins, that what Sasha had really wanted to say was that she hated everyone involved in the war rather than merely everything.

Poor Sasha. Of course her twin must be worried about Bobby, especially with him having such a very dangerous job. Lou wasn't in love herself so she felt that she couldn't truly appreciate how it must feel to know that the person you loved and wanted to spend the rest of your life with might be taken from you. On the other hand, she did know girls who were engaged and married, and whilst they were naturally anxious for their loved ones their feelings about the war did not match Sasha's. Feeling very troubled and concerned for her twin, Lou went back to bed.

Sasha was an awfully long time in the bathroom. Because she was upset or because she was hoping that Lou herself would be asleep by the time she returned, Lou wondered. If that was the case, perhaps right now the best thing she could do for her twin was grant her that privacy, Lou accepted tiredly as she stifled a yawn. It had been a very long day and hopefully there would be time for them to talk properly to one another tomorrow, when Sasha was feeling calmer.

When she opened the bedroom door and saw that the room was in darkness, Sasha let out her pent-up breath in shaky relief. There was no point in her trying to explain to her twin how she felt. Lou simply wouldn't understand.

Putting her wash bag on the dressing table, Sasha felt in the pocket of her dressing gown for the familiar reassuring security of her small torch. She had bought it and its batteries on the black market, and it and Bobby's engagement ring were her most precious possessions. Both of them gave her comfort and helped her to feel safe.

Very carefully she put the torch under her pillow and then quickly removed her dressing gown. If she concentrated and didn't think about the dark and the ice-cold shudders of fear it sent crawling down her spine, she could be in bed and reaching for her torch before it had the chance to take hold of her. What she must not do once she was in bed was think about how the weight of the bedclothes reminded her of being trapped in the bomb shaft, knowing that if Lou let go of her she would slip completely beneath it, swallowed up by the darkness, and the weight of the bomb and the earth around it pressing down on her smothering her.

She was in bed now but she was trembling so much she couldn't get hold of the torch. A cold sweat was filming her forehead, panicky nausea gripping her stomach, her heart pounding and her lungs refusing to expand to take in air. A horrible choking sensation tightened her chest, as the seconds ticked by, her panic only releasing her when she finally held the torch and switched it on. Light. It made her feel so much safer and calmer. With the little torch on she knew she wouldn't wake up in the middle of the night fearing that she was still trapped beneath the bomb and that she was going to die.

It had all been so different when she had first been rescued. She had been so happy then, so grateful to Lou for staying with her, and even more grateful to Bobby for taking her twin's place and then her own so that she could be rescued. It had been only after Lou had joined the WAAF that she had started having these awful feelings of panic and fear, flashbacks to how it had felt to be trapped under the bomb. At first she had tried to ignore those feelings, hoping that if she did they would simply go away, but they hadn't. Instead they'd grown worse, tormenting her at every turn, making her afraid to go to sleep in case she woke up in the darkness thinking she was still trapped. The torch protected her, keeping the darkness at bay, but nothing could protect her from her fears. Fears that were all the worse for her knowing that every day Bobby risked losing his own life because he worked in bomb disposal. The thought of him being trapped as she had been terrified her. She had forbidden him to talk to her about his work because she simply couldn't bear hearing about the shafts they had to dig to get down to some of the bombs. She had nightmares about those shafts;

about being trapped in one of them with the earth burying her, slowly choking her to death.

There was no point in her trying to explain to anyone how she felt. Who would understand? Not Bobby, who laughed at her when she said that his work was too dangerous, not Lou, who loved nothing more than risking her own life flying in a plane, not the girls she worked with at the telephone exchange, who all had boyfriends or husbands, doing their bit for the country, not her elder sister, Grace, either, who talked about the bravery of the wounded soldiers she nursed, and certainly not her parents, who were so proud of Luke. They would all think she was a coward and be ashamed of her. She felt ashamed of herself. Ashamed and afraid and so very alone.

Tears trickled down Sasha's face, her hold on the little torch tightening, her last thought before she fell asleep that she must wake up before Lou so that she could switch off the torch so Lou wouldn't know about it.

SIX

'That's nearly a full week's ration of butter you've just spread on your toast,' Bella pointed out crossly to her brother, as she poured herself a cup of tea. Her mother's kitchen was nothing like as pretty as her own, or as homely and comfortable as her aunt Jean's, even though Vi had had the kitchen newly fitted out with the very latest gas oven, and a smart metal unit painted cream and green, as well as a brand-new table and four chairs, when the family had moved into the house just a couple of years before the start of the war.

'Well, you can get some more easily enough from that nursery of yours, without anyone being the wiser, since you run it, can't you?' Charlie demanded, without lifting his gaze from the paper he was reading.

'You may think it acceptable to steal from others, Charlie, but I certainly don't,' Bella told him pointedly.

Charlie heaved an irritable sigh. 'Oh, for God's sake stop moralising, Bella, just because you've become a Goody Two-Shoes. I remember how you persuaded Alan to marry you, even if you'd rather forget.'

Bella wasn't going to deny that she had tricked her first husband into marrying her. She had been a different person then, a stupid shallow selfish person who had learned the hard way that what she had done was wrong. Alan was dead now and she had been given the chance to make a new life for herself with the man she loved.

'What I did was wrong, but I've paid for my wrongdoing. Unlike you, Charlie.'

Charlie threw down the paper. 'If you're referring to that brat you keep insisting is mine, I've a good mind to go round and see—'

'Don't you dare go anywhere near Lena. She's happy now, with Gavin, and she doesn't need you upsetting her,' Bella interrupted him, realising too late when she saw the look in his eyes that she had said too much and by doing so had created exactly the situation she had wanted to avoid, sparking Charlie's interest in Lena, instead of protecting her.

'Who says I'd be upsetting her? She might be glad to see me. She certainly was the last time I saw her.'

Charlie goaded Bella with a leering smile that made Bella fear even more for Lena. Lena had loved Charlie so much. He had broken her heart, and even now she was still so young.

She was worrying over nothing, Bella told herself. Lena had no interest whatsoever in Charlie. She wasn't in love with him and she didn't secretly yearn for him. She had told Bella that herself when she had told her how much she loved Gavin. But even so, Bella felt anxious on Lena's behalf.

'Do you see much of the old man?' Charlie asked, judging it wise to change the subject.

'Nothing at all,' Bella answered. 'Nor do I want to. He's treated Mummy dreadfully. And if you're thinking of taking your sob story about Daphne to him, Charlie, in the hope that he'll be as easily taken in and as generous as Mummy has been, I really would advise you not to. Pauline will soon see through you and she certainly won't let Daddy give you any money.'

Bella was too shrewd by half, Charlie acknowledged.

'She never had that kid she was supposed to be expecting, did she?' he asked.

'No. I think she must have been pretending to be pregnant as a way of making sure that Daddy left Mummy, but once she realised that Mummy wasn't going to divorce him and that the best she could hope for was to be his mistress, a pregnancy was probably the last thing she wanted.'

'Hmm, well, I still might as well go and visit the old man, seeing as I'm up here,' Charlie told Bella, ignoring the look she was giving him. 'He's still living out at Neston, I take it?'

'As far as I know, yes,' Bella confirmed. She didn't think for one minute that their father would be as generous towards Charlie as their mother had been, but at least while he drove out to the Wirral she wouldn't need to worry about him deliberately trying to cause trouble and upset Lena.

*   *   *

'Thanks for agreeing to come with me to this official do at the American Embassy tonight, Katie, especially at such short notice,' Gina told Katie gratefully as they sat in the café in Peter Jones in Sloane Square, drinking tea.

Katie smiled at her friend. They had originally met at work and had got on well from the moment Gina had introduced herself. Although she came from a well-to-do county family, there was no edge to Gina.

Gina told Katie ruefully, 'I dare say I only got the invitation myself because they're a bit short of females and my name happened to be on one of those dreadful lists of "respectable and acceptable" young women the American top brass seem to insist on.'

They smiled at one another in mutual amusement, two stylish young women anyone observing them would think acceptable anywhere. The camel-coloured coat Gina had on toned perfectly with the fallen leaves outside, her brown beret toning with her hair and matching her well-polished dark brown shoes. She was taller than Katie and her good complexion was her best feature.

Katie was wearing a cherry-red hat trimmed with some feathers from one of her mother's old stage outfits, with her own grey winter coat, the little hat tilted at a slight angle like the hats on the models in Peter Jones.

'I wouldn't go, but one feels it's one's duty to represent our own Armed Forces and remind the Americans how proud we are of them. Of course, I wouldn't be going if Leonard wasn't at sea,' Gina continued.

Katie eyed Gina affectionately. Leonard, Gina's husband, was a captain in the Royal Navy, and they hadn't been married very long.

'I was only thinking this morning of the way things work out.' Gina shook her head. 'If you and I hadn't gone to Bath when we did, then we would never have met Leonard and Eddie.'

'You and Leonard were obviously meant to be,' Katie responded gently. She knew from what Gina had told her when they had first become friends, just after Katie had transferred to the Holborn Office of the Postal Censorship Department, that Gina had expected to marry another young man before she had met Leonard. That young man had been killed in action and it had taken courage on Gina's part to risk loving another man in uniform.

'What about you and Eddie?' Gina challenged her. 'After all, one day he will inherit his father's title.'

Katie laughed and shook her head. Eddie was Leonard's younger cousin, Leonard's mother and Eddie's father being sister and brother. Like Leonard, Eddie was also in the navy. Terrific fun and an equally terrific flirt, Eddie made Katie laugh and she liked him as a friend, but that was all.

'Eddie and I are just friends. I'm glad that you've asked me to go with you,' Katie responded to Gina's initial comment. 'I know this sounds selfish of me but it will be a pleasant change to go out and be a guest instead of being the one running around after others.'

'You, selfish?' Gina scoffed. 'You are the least selfish person I know, Katie. You're working far too hard, you know, all day at the Censorship Office and then nearly every single evening at Rainbow Corner. I thought you were only going to be there three nights a week?'

'I was, but they've got so busy with all the Americans being brought over that they're desperately short of volunteers.'

'Do you think it's true, Katie, what everyone's saying about the Forces getting ready to invade France?' Gina asked.

'Well, we shall have to if they're going to defeat Hitler,' Katie answered.

'I know,' Gina acknowledged, 'but after what happened to the poor men in August last year when the invasion of Dieppe failed and so many men were killed and wounded . . .'

The two girls exchanged sad looks. The young men who had gone so bravely to their deaths had all been Canadian volunteers from overseas, who had wanted to do their bit for the country with which so many of them had family ties.

'I'll come to you for six o'clock, shall I? Then we can walk round to the American Embassy from your billet?'

Katie agreed.

'I'm hoping to visit Leonard's parents next weekend,' Gina told her as they both stood up. 'I promised Leonard that I'd try to go and see them and the children as often as I can whilst he's away.'

Leonard had two children from his first marriage to a Frenchwoman, a son and a daughter of four and three. Odile, their mother, had been killed in a car accident with her lover, and the two children lived in the country with Leonard's parents.

'The children are so sweet,' Gina confessed. 'Little Adam asked me ever so seriously the last time I saw them if he and Amy could call me Mummy. Poor little things. Leonard told me that Odile didn't have much time for them. I've never thought of myself as maternal, but now . . . I'm really beginning to miss them when I'm in London.'

'I think that they are very lucky to have you as their stepmother, Gina.'

'Well, I don't know about that,' Gina protested, but Katie could see that she was pleased.

'And Tommy's housemaster at the Grammar School has said as how he thinks that Tommy is a very bright boy and that I should be thinking about him perhaps going on up to Oxford if he works hard. He says that Tommy's got a really good ear for languages.' Emily couldn't help boasting a little as she worked alongside the other women on that week's rota for doing the church flowers, at Whitchurch's historic Queen Anne church, St Alkmund's.

'He's a lovely lad and no mistake, Emily,' her friend and neighbour Ivy Wilson agreed loyally. 'Looks ever so smart too in his uniform.'

The Grammar School divided its pupils into four houses, each house represented by its own uniform colour. Emily had been lucky enough to have been told by the dressmaker, who altered her own clothes, that she had another customer whose son had just finished school and who no longer needed his uniform. Acting as a go-between, the dressmaker had negotiated a price for the uniform that was acceptable to both parties, and so Tommy had been able to start Grammar School in a proper uniform.

'Don't worry about the blazer being a bit big for him,' the dressmaker had reassured Emily 'He'll grow into it soon enough. Grow like weeds, young ones do.'

'Well I never, Emily, that was ever such a good idea of yours to add a bit of greenery to the flowers to make them go a bit further. A real asset to the flower rota, you are, and no mistake,' Ivy continued warmly.

Listening happily to her neighbour's praise, Emily congratulated herself, not for the first time, that moving here to Whitchurch was definitely the best thing she had ever done.

The church, with its square tower, had been rebuilt from sandstone in the early 1700s, and blended perfectly into its surroundings, the grave-yard with its time-worn gravestones testament to the many generations of local families who had worshipped there. Its main claim to fame was that beneath its porch the heart of Sir John Talbot, Earl of Shrewsbury, made famous by Shakespeare, was buried.

The vicar and his wife were a kind, well-thought-of couple, and the female members of the congregation were enthusiastic about doing their bit for the war. In general Emily had found them a friendly group, who had welcomed her warmly amongst them. Apart from Ina Davies, who was eyeing her disparagingly now as she sniffed,

'Personally I wouldn't have said that all them leaves are right for church flowers. Not that my opinion matters, of course, but to my mind there's something a bit common about them.'

Emily and Ivy exchanged looks. For some reason Ina Davies had taken against Emily right from the start when she had first moved to Whitchurch, often making critical and sometimes hurtful comments about Emily in Emily's own hearing. According to her neighbour, Ina wasn't well liked in the community but people put up with her out of their good nature.

'Give over, Ina,' Ivy protested. 'They set off them dahlias a treat.'

'And as for that son of yours being good at languages,' Ina continued, ignoring Ivy's comment, 'I should think he would be, given the amount of time that German POW spends at your house. I don't think I'd want any lad of mine spending so much time with someone like that, a Nazi! 'Oo knows what he might be telling him.'

'Wilhelm is not a Nazi. He was forced to join up and fight,' Emily protested.

'That's easy enough for him to say now. Stands to reason he's going to want to protect himself by pretending he was forced to support Hitler. Mind you, I've got to say that it seems to me that there's something funny going on when someone who reckons to be British starts defending a German. My Harry says he's never seen the like of it,' Ina continued. 'A German POW coming and going like he does, making himself at home, brazen as anything and acting like he isn't a POW at all . . .' She pursed her lips in disapproval. 'My Harry says he's surprised that someone hasn't said something to the authorities and got something done about it.'

The atmosphere in the church had changed, the other women looking meaningfully at one another and, Emily thought, questioningly at her, the happy mood in which they had all been working together changing to one of discomfort.

It was a relief to Emily when the flowers were finished and she was free to leave.

'Don't worry about what Ina had to say,' Ivy tried to comfort her as they walked home together. 'She's always had a nasty side to her and been a bit of a troublemaker. I reckon she's jealous that you've got Wilhelm looking after your garden for you, and doing a good job on it too, whilst she's got to rely on her Harry who wouldn't know one end of a carrot from another. Course it doesn't help that their Christopher was taken prisoner at Dunkirk. She reckons the POWs we've got here have it easy compared with her Christopher, but that's not your fault and she's got no right picking on you like she did. Not that anyone will pay any attention to her, not knowing what she's like.'

Emily was grateful for her neighbour's kindness, but Ina's comments had left her feeling upset and uncomfortable.

SEVEN

Things hadn't gone as well in Neston as he had
hoped, Charlie admitted as he drove through
Wallasey, heading for his mother's. His father had
flatly refused to give him any money, demanding
to know how Charlie expected him to be able to
afford to give him money when he was having
to support two households. And that despite the
fact there had been two cars parked on the drive
of the fancy house his father was renting, and
Pauline had been tricked out in what looked like
three strands of real pearls and a ruddy great solitaire diamond 'engagement' ring. Charlie had tried
flattering her, hoping that by buttering her up a
bit she'd weigh in on his behalf with his father,
but he hadn't reckoned on how hard-faced she
was, Charlie admitted, scowling as he remembered
how his father's mistress had waited until his father
wasn't there before telling him that any spare cash
his father had would be going into her bank
account and not Charlie's.

Hard as nails, that's what she was, and now
he'd wasted almost the whole of Saturday and his

precious petrol driving out to Neston to no purpose. He couldn't wait to get back to his base and then into London for some decent fun.

Charlie started to turn into the road where his sister's house was, intending to take a short cut down it to his mother's. A young woman wearing a swing-back brown coat, a neat-fitting hat perched on her dark hair, was walking along the pavement, her child in a pushchair. Charlie recognised Lena immediately, with a feeling like a violent punch in the chest.

God, but she was pretty. Pretty, willing, married to another man, and Bella had warned him off her. Any combination of two of those facts would have been enough to have Charlie itching to break the rules and have some fun. Throw in his bad temper and his boredom, and seeing Lena was exactly the antidote he needed to cheer himself up.

Lena was aware of the car on the road behind her slowing down. Automatically she turned round, assuming it must be one of their neighbours, the colour coming and going in her face as Charlie brought the low-slung MG alongside her, slowing it down to match her walking pace as he leaned towards her and gave her his best smile, stopping the car and telling her cockily, 'Hello there, gorgeous. Remember me?'

She should have ignored him, Lena knew that. He was nothing to her after the way he'd treated her. She had a good husband now in Gavin, and in another few months she and Gavin would be giving Janette a little baby brother or sister – a baby that would have a father who had wanted it right from the word go. Not like Charlie.

Her legs had turned to jelly and she was glad to have Janette's pushchair to hold on to. She'd forgotten how confident Charlie was, and how good-looking. She waited for her heart to react to him with the excitement it had done when she had first known him but instead of thudding with excitement it was thumping with dismay and anxiety. She wished he wasn't here, she wished he hadn't seen them; she wished he hadn't stopped and most of all she wished that Gavin was with them, Lena acknowledged.

It was a funny feeling knowing at last, after all the times she'd secretly worried about how she might feel if she ever saw him again, that she was truly safe, and that she felt nothing at all other than deep gratitude for the fact that Gavin loved her and she was safely and happily married to him. In fact, it was a marvel to her now that she had ever found Charlie attractive at all, despite his good looks. Good looks were nothing when compared to a kind and loving heart.

'Pleased to see me, are you?' Charlie grinned at Lena. 'I'm here all weekend; I could come round and we could have a bit of fun together, just you and me.'

'We're both married now,' Lena pointed out firmly.

'So what? Come on, Lena, you remember how good it was with you and me, don't you?' Charlie coaxed, moving close to her, putting his hand on

92

her arm and looking down at her breasts, feeling his body harden in anticipatory eagerness.

High up in the old oak tree at the bottom of the garden, sawing off one of the branches, Gavin had a clear view of the bottom of the street and what was happening there. He'd been on the point of climbing down when Charlie had first stopped his car, but now, with Charlie holding Lena's arm and his wife showing no signs of moving away, Gavin felt too heartsick to do anything. Lena had really fallen for Charlie – Gavin knew that – and although she'd told him that she hated Bella's brother now for the way he'd treated her, in his own heart Gavin had secretly worried that Lena didn't love him as much as she had done Janette's father. Now it looked as though he'd got proof that he had been right.

'I've got to get home. My Gavin will be waiting for his tea,' Lena told Charlie, pulling away from him. 'And little Janette will be wanting to see her daddy as well,' she added pointedly.

Charlie frowned. 'Her daddy? The kid's mine, not his,' he told Lena, her refusal to play along with him making him belligerent. Charlie hadn't given a moment's thought to the child he had fathered, apart from being relieved that his parents had flatly denied that it could be his, and yet now hearing Lena refer to someone else as its father, a dog-in-the-manger possessiveness took hold of him.

'Gavin is Janette's father,' Lena contradicted him. 'He's the one who's provided for her and he's the one she loves.'

Before Charlie could stop her she had wheeled the pushchair past him and was walking away from him as fast as she could.

Ruddy women, Charlie cursed her under his breath. Well, there were plenty more where she'd come from. And as for the kid, why should he care about someone else being her father? He didn't want to be saddled with her or any other kid. The man who'd married Lena was a proper fool. You'd never catch him taking on another man's kid.

Getting back into his MG, Charlie slammed the door and roared off at speed. He'd had enough of Wallasey, and he couldn't wait to leave the place and the people in it behind him, he decided as he drove past Lena.

'See anyone whilst you were out?' Gavin asked Lena as casually as he could. Lena had called him into the kitchen for the cup of tea she'd made for him.

Lena hesitated. She desperately wanted to tell Gavin what had happened but she knew him and she knew how protective of her he was. If she told him there was no saying that he might not go straight round to Bella's mother's and call Charlie to account for the way he had behaved towards her. Lena didn't care what her Gavin might do to Charlie, but she did care about Bella, and she knew it would cause trouble between Bella and her mother if Gavin went rampaging round there, demanding that Charlie gave an account of himself. Mrs Firth doted on Charlie. He could do no wrong in her eyes, as Lena herself had good reason to know.

No, it was best that she didn't say anything to Gavin, she decided, as she shook her head and fibbed, 'No.'

Lena had lied to him. Gavin felt the pain explode inside his chest. His Lena, whom he loved so much, had lied to him and all because of that no-good rotter who had already hurt her so much. Gavin looked away from Lena. Janette was smiling up at him from her high chair. The minute he'd stepped inside she'd held up her arms to him to be lifted out, and Gavin had felt that same spike of emotion now that he'd felt the very first time he'd held her, minutes after her birth. She was his girl, his child, the child of his heart, and he loved her every bit as much as he would do the new baby Lena was carrying.

The new baby. A knife twisted in his heart. Was Lena wishing that she hadn't married him and that she wasn't having his child now that she'd seen Charlie again?

They were almost midway through September, but although the days might be growing shorter, double summertime meant that thankfully it was still possible to go out in the evening in daylight, even if blackout curtains had to be put in place ready for one's return in darkness, Katie reflected, carefully applying a thin coat of precious lipstick, using a small brush so as to use as little as possible of what was left of her favourite Max Factor pink, bought just before the war. Once that was done she ran her comb through her thick naturally curly dark gold hair and then studied her reflection

95

critically in her bedroom's full-length mirror. The outfit she was wearing had been a second-hand find, bought when she and Gina had spent a couple of days together in Bath, just before it had been badly bombed, and the silk of her dress floated delicately round Katie's slim legs. She did feel rather guilty about the fact that she was wearing a pair of silk stockings that had been given to her by a grateful young American GI who had enjoyed the tour of London's historical sites she had planned for him so much that he had insisted on giving them to her as a 'thank you'. The ATS girls with whom she shared the house in Cadogan Place had teased her unmercifully about both the stockings and the young GI, but Katie knew that his desire to thank her had been genuine and not a prelude to some sort of 'come on'.

She had been extremely lucky in her billet, she knew; the house, right in the centre of the city, was in a terrace of elegant late Georgian buildings. Her bedroom was enormous, with a high ceiling and its own bathroom. Luxury indeed, as Katie's parents were fond of reminding her when she made her fortnightly visits to Hampstead, where her mother and father were now living with friends in a rather run-down Victorian house, both of them missing living in the city, having moved further out during the blitz.

From her bedroom window Katie could see Gina walking towards the house, which fortunately was only a short walk from the tube station close to Harrods. Gathering up her handbag and the warm woollen silk-lined stole on permanent loan to her from her mother, Katie made her way downstairs to join her friend.

The American Embassy was situated in Grosvenor Square and within easy walking distance of Cadogan Place, as Gina had already said.

'I had a wonderful surprise when I got back to my aunt's this afternoon,' Gina told Katie as they set out. 'Leonard telephoned from Devonport. They're under sailing orders, and of course he couldn't say where they were going, although my guess is that it has to be Italy, now that we've got a toehold in Sicily. It was lovely to hear his voice. Hearing that he'd got some leave coming up would have been even better, of course. I mustn't be greedy, though. Not after him getting two weeks' leave when we got married, and a forty-eight-hour pass the other weekend. He couldn't say outright, but he did hint that he might be home for Christmas. I do hope so. Leonard's parents living so close to my own means that we could see both families, and, of course, the children. Once the war is over we want them to come and live with us full time, but of course it's best that they stay where they are for now.'

A pair of smartly dressed American marines were on duty outside the American Embassy, faces fixed in stern expressions, eyes forward. An equally smartly uniformed young woman checked their names off her guest list, in the imposing hallway with its marble busts and highly polished floor, the American flag very much on display.

'I rang and told them I'd be bringing you with me,' Gina murmured to Katie, who nodded in response. It was well known that with so many good-time girls on the fringe of London society eager to strike up friendships with the Americans, especially those who were officers, only unattached women who had been vetted were on the official invitation lists.

The American Embassy was very much the hub of the American Military Command in London. Military uniforms outnumbered the diplomatic uniform of city suit and Brooks Brothers shirt almost ten to one, from what Katie could see, as she and Gina stood together just outside the double doors leading into a large reception room, its crimson-papered walls hung with portraits of past presidents, the elegant plastered ceiling and cornices painted white with the detail picked out in gold. Beyond this room a further set of double doors on the opposite wall were open to reveal another room, this one painted a rich royal blue, its windows framed by royal-blue velvet curtains trimmed with gold braid. All very rich and expensive-looking, Katie thought, and not a bit shabby as so many British buildings had become.

A group of what looked like newspapermen were all clustered together on one side of the room, drinks in hand, cameras slung from their shoulders, as they studied the other occupants of the room, a group of military men standing in front of the imposing marble fireplace.

It was easy to see which women were Americans, Katie reflected. All the British women there might have done their best, but their clothes, no matter how smart, did not have the up-to-the-minute freshness and fashion of those sported by the Americans.

'Ah, Gina, there you are. Dreadful crush, what?'

'Uncle Rupert, I'm surprised you managed to spot me in this crush,' Gina laughed as she was enveloped in a bear hug by her relative. 'Uncle Rupert, I've brought Katie with me. She was my bridesmaid.'

'Of course, remember her well. Delighted to meet you again, m'dear. Dashed pretty girls, both of you. We'll show these Americans a thing or two, what? What are you drinking? Champagne, I expect. Best drink for pretty girls.'

With that skill possessed by upper-class men of a certain age and confidence, out of nowhere, or so it seemed to Katie, a waiter was summoned to produce two glasses of freshly poured champagne.

'And where's that husband of yours, Gina?'

'I really couldn't say,' Gina informed him.

'That's right, good girl. Careless talk costs lives and all that. Still enjoying your job? Not getting too many saucy letters to read, I hope?'

Behind her uncle's back Gina gave Katie a rueful look, which made Katie both want to laugh and at the same time made her feel sad. So many of the letters they had to check did contain the most intimate of messages, sent, though, from the heart, in most cases, from men desperately missing the one they loved and equally desperate to assure them of their love and be reassured in turn that they were loved.

It wasn't long before Gina's uncle Rupert had introduced them both to an American colonel of his own generation, who announced immediately that he must introduce two such charming girls to his junior officers, adding with a smile, 'Because if I don't, they will think that I'm keeping you to myself, and then I reckon I could be in danger of having to subdue a mutiny.'

Two minutes later Gina and Katie were almost surrounded by half a dozen young Americans in army uniform,

'Definitely Ivy League,' Gina murmured in a swift aside to Katie. 'That's the equivalent of our Eton and Sandhurst cadets.'

Katie nodded. Her father's pre-war career as the conductor of some of London's most famous bands, and the fact that she had always accompanied him when he played, to help him with all the practical aspects of his work, meant that she had had enough contact with the upper classes and the well-to-do not to feel awkward or intimidated in the company of people from a social class above her own.

The young Americans might be inclined to be a little boastful and a little thoughtless about how a British girl might feel hearing them talking about how they were going to win the war, but Katie was wise enough to put their comments down to excitement and inexperience, although she noticed that Gina looked rather nettled, and so wasn't surprised when her friend excused them both with the fib that they had to 'catch up with some friends'.

'I know they are our allies, but I hate it when they are so beastly about our boys,' she told Katie crossly once they had escaped. 'Talking like that about showing Hitler what real fighting men are and showing us a good time.'

'I don't think they meant any real harm,' Katie tried to pacify her. 'They're only young and, unlike our boys, they don't really know what war is all about yet.' Unlike Luke. He knew what war was all about. Luke! Hadn't she made herself a promise that she would not allow him into her thoughts?

'I do wish you could fall in love with Eddie, Katie.'

Gina's plaintive words made Katie smile.

'Eddie doesn't really want any girl to fall in love with him. He just wants to have a good time with lots of different girls.'

'That's where you're wrong,' Gina told her. 'Eddie is a flirt, but he's really keen on you, and I mean *really* keen. If you were to give him the least bit of encouragement, I suspect he'd have an engagement ring on your finger as fast as anything. He might be a flirt but you can be sure that he knows that he has a duty to provide an heir for the title.'

'That's nonsense and you know it. Eddie's parents will expect him to marry a very different sort of girl from me, and someone from a similar background to his own.'

Katie said this without any feeling of resentment. In her opinion it was only natural, with Eddie's father having a title, Eddie's family should want him to marry someone who understood that sort of thing.

'Once I dare say they would have done,' Gina

agreed, 'but right now I think they'd just be glad to see him married. As I've just said, if anything were to happen to him, there's no one to succeed him to the title, and there won't be until he marries and has a son. Not that anyone can get Eddie to talk seriously about that. He maintains that nothing's going to happen to him because he's got Leonard to keep an eye on him.'

'I like Eddie, Gina,' Katie answered, 'but that's all. However, even if I loved him I don't think we'd be right for one another. Our backgrounds are so very different. Now, whilst the war's on, that kind of thing might not matter but once the war is over it will be different.'

She was an ordinary girl and whilst she had liked Eddie's parents when she had met them at Gina's wedding, and they had been kind to her, Katie knew that a life like Eddie's mother's, as the lady of the manor, was not one that she would ever want.

'I hope them ruddy naval gunners know the difference between our own lines and them panzers,' Andy told Luke breathlessly, both of them dropping flat to the ground as they heard a fresh burst of exploding tank shells.

It was two days since they'd come ashore at Salerno, followed by intense fighting with the Germans as they'd tried to push them back from their entrenched position. But now, with the panzers having moved down from the hills beyond Salerno to surround the bay, it was looking dangerously as though they were the ones who were going to be pushed back into the sea, not the Germans forced to give way so that the Allies could advance.

The naval guns to which Andy was referring, as the men dug in, belonged to the battle cruiser *Warspite* and three destroyers out in the bay, all of which were pounding the panzer-infested hills, whilst the panzers returned fire into the Allies' lines.

'Hellfire, that was close,' Andy protested, cramming his helmet down onto his head and wriggling deeper into his foxhole as a shell exploded within yards of their position, sending up a spray of earth and stone to mingle with the blood of the men it had hit, whilst the field guns of the 146th Field Regiment of the Royal Artillery, positioned behind the infantry, tried their best to give the Germans a pounding. The smell of war was everywhere: blood, smoke, cordite, unwashed male flesh and khaki.

'You know what I think of at times like this, what keeps me going?' Andy confided to Luke.

Luke shook his head. He knew what, or rather who, he thought of. Katie. He thought of his mum and dad and his family, of course, but first and foremost he thought of Katie and how badly he had treated her. If he didn't fight to live he would never get the chance to apologise to her. And he wanted to do that. He wanted to set the record straight and square things with her. There was no going back to what they had once shared, but he owed her that apology. It and Katie were on his conscience.

But what if he didn't survive? What if he never did get the chance to tell her? Did he really want her to go through the rest of her life thinking badly of him, telling the chap she eventually married how badly he, Luke, had treated her?

'What I think of is me mum's Sunday roast dinners,' he could hear Andy telling him wistfully. 'Aye, and there's no way I'm ever going to let any ruddy German stop me from tasting one of them again.'

Luke nodded. It was his duty, after all, as corporal to listen to his men and to put heart into them when they needed it, but his most private thoughts were still on Katie.

Katie. How was she going to know everything he wanted to tell her if he never made it home? Another burst of shells exploded around them.

He'd write to her, Luke decided. He'd write to her just as soon as he got the chance – if he got that chance.

EIGHT

'Good weekend at home?'

'Yes thanks, June,' Lou fibbed.

'I love being in ATA and I always think that I don't miss my family until I get some leave and I go home,' June told her. 'It's funny, isn't it, how we sort of have two separate lives – the one we have here and the one we have with our families? My ma would go spare if she knew a quarter of the things we get up to. I don't even smoke at home, never mind tell her about the near misses I've had flying.'

Lou smiled. In truth she was glad to be back at the base. Because she didn't want to have to think about Sasha and how much her twin had changed? Lou's forehead crinkled into a worried frown. She had tried to talk to Sash, hadn't she, and more than once, but her twin had rejected every attempt Lou had made to bridge the gap between them.

In desperation, before she had left, when they'd been alone in their shared bedroom, Lou had grabbed hold of her sister to stop her leaving and had told her firmly, 'Look, I know that something's wrong. We're twins, remember. Twins, Sash. All I want is for you to be happy.'

'I am happy,' Sasha had insisted angrily. 'Just because I don't want to learn to fly aeroplanes and go round showing off my uniform and have everyone thinking I'm wonderful, that doesn't mean that I'm not happy.'

'Oh, Sash, don't be like that, please,' Lou had begged. 'I wasn't trying to suggest that what you are doing is any less worthwhile than what I'm doing. When I said you aren't happy, I meant you, here, inside yourself.' Lou had touched the spot over her twin's heart to emphasise what she meant, but once again Sasha had chosen to misunderstand her.

'Do you really think I don't know what you really mean?' she'd demanded. 'You think that just because you've met up with Kieran Mallory again that I'm jealous, don't you? Well, I'm not. I couldn't care less about him.'

'Neither could I,' Lou had tried to reassure her twin. 'And I wasn't talking about Kieran Mallory anyway.' She'd paused, not sure how much to say, but then deciding that she had to say something. 'Sash, both nights whilst I've been home you've fallen asleep with your torch on . . .'

'So what if I have? Can't a person read in bed if she wants to without someone else making a fuss about it?'

Sasha had pulled away from her then, hurrying out of the bedroom before Lou could stop her.

Something *was* wrong with Sasha. Lou knew

that instinctively, even if she couldn't come up with a logical explanation of why she felt the way she did. On the face of it Sasha should be happy. She was engaged to Bobby, who loved her and who she said she loved in return. She was doing her bit for the war, working at the telephone exchange, and at the same time living at home with their parents just as she had wanted to do.

Was it because of Kieran Mallory that Sasha had been so upset and angry, refusing to make up the distance that now existed between them? Did her twin secretly have feelings for him, even though she insisted that she didn't?

He had come between them once already and Lou did not want him to come between them again. If Sasha didn't want to confide in her then perhaps she ought simply to respect her twin's decision.

'How was London?' she asked June now, reluctantly putting her concern about Sasha to one side.

'Crazy. For a start, it's full of Americans. You can't walk down any of the main streets without getting blocked in by Americans passing one another and having to salute. Mind you, I have to admit that they know how to have fun. There was a dance on at our hotel on Saturday night, and before we knew it the place was swarming with GIs. They certainly know how to treat a girl,' June giggled. 'We met up with them on Sunday. They picked us up in these Jeeps and then roared round London in them. We ended up at this club – the 400 Club. Members only, supposedly, but after they'd waved some five-pound notes under the doorman's nose he let us in. There was a terrific band playing. The place was full. I saw one of the upper-crust ATA girls there, Diana Barnato, with a crowd that included several RAF high-ups. You should have been with us, though, Lou.'

'Next time I will be,' Lou promised.

'I'm going to keep you to that promise,' June warned her. 'Let's make a definite date for going down in November then, shall we?'

Lou agreed. They normally worked ten days on and then had two days' leave with a fortnight's holiday a year, so Lou knew that there wouldn't be too much of a problem in planning their London trip for November.

She'd been lucky, she reflected. Much as she'd loved being in the WAAF, the freedom from military rules and regulations that being in ATA gave her was a definite bonus. The fact that ATA had needed more pilots had made it easy for her to be transferred out of the WAAF and into ATA. However, whilst she enjoyed her new freedom, Lou firmly believed that she had benefited from the discipline of the WAAF, and all that that had taught her about herself and her own capabilities.

She'd got another of her cross-country flights in the morning – solo this time. She just hoped she was up to it, Lou reflected as she prepared for bed. That was the trouble about having a weekend off: you lost that surge of excited energy that pushed you to prove that you could do everything and more that your superior demanded of you.

*　　*　　*

They'd taken on some new girls at the telephone exchange, and Sasha had been asked to keep a helping eye on one of them, Alice White, a confident, pretty blonde, through her first few weeks as an operator.

They were having their lunch in the canteen, sitting with several other senior girls like Sasha, who were watching over the new recruits, everyone exchanging tales of how they had spent the weekend, when Alice gave a theatrical shudder and announced, 'Well, I saw the most awful thing on Saturday. I'd been round to my nan's with Mum, and we were on the way back when we heard this explosion. Near deafened us, it did, and it was like all you-know-what had broken loose. A fire engine came racing past, and an ambulance, and we could see all this smoke, and then when we got round the corner we had to turn back 'cos the army had got the whole road cordoned off because there'd been a bomb found and it went off whilst they were trying to defuse it. Blown to bits, them that was defusing it were, so I heard,' Alice finished.

Somehow Sasha had managed to sit through Alice's excited description of what had taken place, but now she was shaking from head to foot.

'Sash, are you all right?'

The anxious words came from Sasha's closest friend at the exchange, Mary Talbot, an older quiet girl, who was married to a submariner.

'Yes . . . yes . . . I'm fine,' Sasha lied.

'Sasha's fiancé is with the bomb disposal lot, Alice,' she heard Mary explaining.

Immediately Alice was contrite. 'Oooh, Sasha, I'm ever so sorry,' and then she tactlessly went on,

'You don't think that your fiancé was one of them that was there, do you? I could never be engaged to a lad doing something so dangerous. I'd be on pins all the time, worrying about him. Give me a lad that works in a reserved occupation any day of the week over one that's in uniform.'

Sasha had stopped listening. Hearing Alice tell her story hadn't just filled her with sick fear for Bobby, it had also brought back her own experience of being trapped: pinned down virtually by an unexploded bomb. It was two years now since that dreadful night, and she had been saved, rescued by Bobby, but she couldn't stop thinking about it. In fact she thought about it more now than she had done after it had first happened. When was it going to end? When was the memory of that night going to stop tormenting her? What if it never did? A horrible cold and then hot panicky feeling filled her. Her chest was tightening up and her throat closing as though she wasn't going to be able to breathe.

'Sash, what is it? What's wrong?' Mary's anxious demand snapped her back to normal. Her hair felt damp with sweat, and her heart was pounding as though she had been running. She was a coward; a silly scared coward who didn't deserve to have someone like Bobby to love her.

Thank goodness she didn't need to worry that Bobby was one of those who had died in the explosion Alice had described. Sasha knew that he was safe because he'd gone to church with her family on Sunday and come back with them for Sunday lunch.

* * *

It was Monday afternoon when it happened: the sound of glass breaking and splintering filling the whole house, and reminding Emily of Liverpool and the blitz. Emily had been holding the washing basket she'd just brought in with the dry washing off the line, but she abandoned it on the kitchen floor as she rushed through the hall and into the front room to find glass everywhere, from the broken panes in the pretty Georgian window, and right in the middle of the floor the cause of their destruction in the form of a large brick.

Emily had felt so sick and shocked that all she'd wanted to do was sit down and have a good cry, and that's what she would have done too, she suspected, if her neighbour, Ivy, hadn't come hurrying round, having heard the noise herself.

'Well, what a thing to happen. Someone's done this on purpose, if you ask me,' she pronounced, having been shown the front room by Emily. 'After all, bricks don't throw themselves through windows, do they?'

Taking charge, she shepherded a still-shocked Emily back into the kitchen, filled the kettle and then put it on the Aga.

'Alf Simms will have to be told.'

Alf was their local police sergeant.

'I'll give the police station a ring now. Mark my words, it will be evacuees that have done it. There's a few of them caused nothing but trouble since they arrived here. Now you just sit here, whilst I telephone. It's lucky that no one was in the room when it happened.'

Emily listened gratefully to her neighbour. She

was shocked, she admitted. Whitchurch was such a quiet place, not the kind of place at all where people threw bricks through windows.

Within half an hour of her neighbour telephoning the police station, Alf Simms was propping his bicycle up on the back wall of Emily's cottage and accepting a cup of tea from Ivy, having removed his helmet and placed it down on Emily's well-scrubbed kitchen table.

'I've told Emily that it's bound to be evacuees that have done it,' Ivy told him. 'Given her ever such a shock, it has, though, hasn't it, Emily? I could hear the noise from my own kitchen. Terrible, it was. Made me think at first that a bomb had dropped. It oughtn't to be allowed, evacuees going round scaring the living daylights out of decent people.'

Alf drank his tea, sucking on his teeth as he put down his empty cup next to his helmet.

'I'll go and take a look at the scene of the offence, if you don't mind.'

'Yes, of course,' Emily agreed.

'Best that you ladies stay in here. We don't want any accidents with that broken glass. You'll have to get Bob Walker in to fix it for you. I'll call in and tell him for you, if you like. I've got to cycle past his place on my way back to the station.'

'Oh, yes, thank you. I hadn't got as far as thinking about repairing it,' Emily admitted.

'You'll still have to put up your blackout curtains, of course,' Alf warned.

It seemed an age before he returned to the kitchen, carrying the brick.

'Looks to me like this is a Manchester brick,' Alf informed Emily and Ivy. 'Hard and heavy, they are, so I reckon that whoever threw it knew what he was doing.'

'Well, some of those evacuees—' Ivy began.

But Alf cut her short, explaining portentously, 'When I examined the scene I found this piece of paper underneath the brick.' From his pocket he removed a small folded piece of lined paper. 'Upon further examination of it, I discovered that it contained a message.' Unfolding the paper, he continued, 'That message reads: "Traitor. German Lover."'

Emily covered her mouth with her hand, too shocked and upset to say anything.

She was still feeling shocked and upset when Tommy came home from school. Of course he wanted to know why the window was being repaired and what had happened. Emily would have preferred to let him think that the panes had fallen out by themselves but she knew that in such a small town details of the incident would have spread and that Tommy was bound to hear about it from his school friends.

Naturally she played things down when she told him, omitting to say anything about the note, as Alf had already charged both her and her neighbour not to discuss it with anyone 'whilst investigations are in progress'.

Ivy, though, didn't include Emily in that ban and was very vocal in her views on the situation.

'It's like I said,' she repeated to Emily later in the evening, her desire to discuss the situation making Emily glad that she had just sent Tommy upstairs to get ready for bed. 'It stands to reason that it's them evacuees. After all, no decent right-thinking person would do something like that. I mean, look at all the good work the German POWs have done round here, working on the land. They might be on the other side, but like the vicar said when they first came here, the war's over for them now and we've got a duty to treat them in a Christian way. Besides,' she added practically, 'there's many a local farmer would be hard put to do his bit for the country without having POWs to lend a hand. Look at all the hard work Wilhelm has put in your garden. Growing nearly everything of your own now, you are. That fruit you and me have just bottled and the chutney we made will see us both very nicely through the winter and into next summer.'

Her neighbour's comments were meant to comfort and reassure her, Emily knew, but it wasn't just herself she was concerned for. She was concerned for Tommy as well, and for Wilhelm himself. A lovely man, he was; she'd thought that right from the start, and there wasn't a day went by when she didn't find something more to like about him.

There'd been articles in the papers recently about an exchange of POWs between Britain and Germany, and Emily just hoped that it was this that had fomented the attack on her windows and not Wilhelm himself.

'You should perhaps think of getting a dog,' her neighbour continued. 'I'm not keen on them meself, what with them muddy paws and that, but like as not if you had one its barking would give you a bit of warning if those evacuees were to try any more funny business.'

Emily pondered what Ivy was saying. She'd never had a dog herself, and if the truth were known she was a bit nervous around them. She knew, though, that Tommy would be thrilled at the prospect, and anything that staved off another event like this afternoon's was something she could only welcome right now.

True to her nature, though, Emily said cautiously to her neighbour, 'I'll have a word with Alf and see what he thinks about me getting a dog. I wouldn't want to have people complaining about a barking dog keeping them awake at night.'

'Well, of course not, but it could be trained just to bark at strangers. Your Tommy could do that. Boys and dogs – well, they go together like apple pie and custard,' Ivy assured her, taking pity on Emily's townee ignorance.

'I'll speak to Alf tomorrow,' Emily told her.

'Katie, can I have a word?'

Katie looked up in some surprise when she saw Gerry standing hesitantly at the half-open door to her room. She was meeting Gina for lunch, seeing as they both had a day off, and she'd come upstairs to get her coat.

'Of course you can,' she assured Gerry. 'Come in.'

'Thanks. Only I didn't want to say anything downstairs in front of the others.' Gerry pulled a small face, as she took a packet of cigarettes – service issue, Katie noticed – out of the pocket of her slacks and offered Katie one.

Katie shook her head and waited whilst Gerry lit her own cigarette and inhaled deeply before expelling the smoke. Gerry certainly looked much better than she had done the night she had come back in such a state and broken down, Katie acknowledged, although she was still burning the candle at both ends, as the saying went.

'I just wanted to thank you for what you did . . . you know, that night.' Gerry's voice was slightly stilted and quiet.

'You don't have anything to thank me for, Gerry,' Katie responded gently. 'I didn't do anything special, or that anyone else wouldn't have done.'

Gerry stubbed out her unfinished cigarette with an awkward movement.

'Yes, you did. You listened to me and you understood. You didn't tell me to . . . to pull myself together, or say that I was in danger of disgracing everyone else.' Gerry sighed. 'Oh, I know that Peggy means well and that she's probably right.'

'She was concerned about you, Gerry; we all were.'

Gerry nodded. 'I've been thinking about what you said, about my parents and everything. You were right, Katie. I really wish that I could be like Peggy and, well, find the right one, but . . . Have you ever been in love, Katie?'

'Yes,' Katie admitted. She desperately wished that Gerry hadn't asked her that particular question.

'What happened?'

'Nothing really. We just decided that we weren't suited.' Katie forced herself to sound natural. It wouldn't help Gerry, after all, to learn the truth and might even put her off trying to settle down.

Gerry stood there uncertainly for a moment longer.

'Well, I just wanted to say thanks for everything.'

She had gone before Katie could say anything, leaving Katie feeling relieved that she hadn't asked her any more about Luke.

Poor Gerry. She was just as much a casualty of the war as her brothers had been, although in a different way.

A knock on the front door right when she was in the middle of her weekly bake wasn't something that Emily really welcomed. Wiping her floury hands, then dragging off her pinafore, she hurried to answer the impatient knock, surprised to discover Alf Simms, the police sergeant, standing on her front door step, his bicycle propped up against the wall below her repaired front window.

'Sorry to disturb you,' he began, 'but since you was saying that you thought you might get a dog, I was wondering, if you'd like this little 'un.' As he spoke he was walking back to his cycle and opening the saddlebag on the back. 'Found her this morning, the only one left alive in a litter, left behind by some folks who'd been living illegal, like, camping in Taylor's Wood, up by Hugh

Williams' Farm. Caused a real nuisance, they did, stealing chickens and that.'

Although she was listening to the sergeant Emily was focusing on the small bundle of black, tan and white fur he had lifted from the saddlebag.

'Too young to be without its ma, it is,' Alf told Emily knowledgeably. 'It's no more than four weeks old, I reckon, and chances are it wouldn't have survived another night. It will need feeding every few hours. I called at Williams' farm and Mrs Williams has sent down a bottle and some milk. Mind you, she reckons the poor little thing won't survive. Too young, she says.'

Emily, who until that moment had been on the point of thanking the sergeant but refusing his gift by pointing out that what she needed was a fully grown well-trained dog to protect the house, not a weak four-week-old puppy, somehow found that the pathetically fragile bundle of fur had been passed into her hold, and that she was stroking the shivering little creature, appalled to find that she could feel its bones beneath its fur.

Ten minutes later, her baking put on hold, she was sitting beside the Aga, trying to coax the puppy to take some of the milk she had warmed for it. The puppy, though, wrapped up now in Emily's oldest winter jumper, wouldn't have anything to do with the carefully prepared baby's bottle, and it seemed to Emily that she could almost see the poor little creature slipping away before her eyes, giving up on life before it had really had a chance to experience it. Poor, poor little thing. A determination filled Emily. She was not going to let it die. Patiently she poured some of the milk into a dish, and then dipped a corner of a piece of cloth into it, squeezing the milk from it into the puppy's mouth. The first few times she tried the puppy didn't respond, but then just when she thought it was too late and the limpness of its little body meant that she had failed, suddenly the puppy started to suck on the cloth.

A little at a time, that was all she would give it, Emily told herself, remembering what the doctor had told her when she had first taken Tommy in, half starving and so thin you could see his ribs sticking out.

Of course when Tommy came home from school and found the puppy curled up in a basket in front of the Aga he was ecstatic, and nothing would do but that Emily showed him how to feed 'Beauty', as he had – in Emily's view at least – somewhat inappropriately named the puppy.

'Look how big her feet are,' Tommy told Emily.

'Paws – dogs have paws, not feet,' Emily corrected him. The puppy's 'feet' were indeed large in comparison to the rest of her.

'I can't wait to show her to Wilhelm,' Tommy told Emily. 'He'll be able to help me train her.'

Delightful images of Tommy, the puppy, Wilhelm and herself enjoying an idyllically happy life together filled Emily's imagination. In those images she automatically visualised herself wearing a simple plain wedding ring. A wedding ring. They had talked about it, but both of them knew that, whilst the war was on, a dream was all that their getting married to one another was.

NINE

She'd done it. She was now authorised to fly Class 2 planes – advanced single-engine aircraft, which included Hurricanes and Spitfires. Lou had felt a bit selfconscious but very proud accepting the congratulations of the other ATA pilots over breakfast this morning.

'I'm really pleased that you're going to be staying here,' had been June's comment when Lou had told her that she'd been informed that she would be remaining at Thame, attached to Number 5 Ferry Pool.

Lou glanced at her watch, her tummy muscles tightening with a mixture of excitement and nervousness. Five to nine. At nine o'clock on the dot all the pilots had to report to their respective ferry pools, no matter what the weather, to collect their delivery chits for the day from the pool operations officer.

The ops room was filling up with other ATA pilots when Lou went in, hanging back a little shyly, and feeling very 'new', even though she was familiar with the procedure from her previous ferry pool posting.

'Castle Bromwich for you this morning, Campion,' the pool ops officer informed Lou breezily as she passed Lou her chit.

Castle Bromwich? The Spitfire factory? Lou almost dropped her chit. Her heart was thumping with pride and delight, her hands trembling slightly as she read her chit. She was to be dropped off at Castle Bromwich, where she would pick up a new Spitfire and fly it to a maintenance unit base, to be fitted out for action. At the MU she'd then pick up another Spitfire, which she would then fly to an RAF base before returning to Castle Bromwich and going through the entire process again with a second Spitfire, with the taxi Anson picking her up at the RAF base later in the day to bring her back to Thame.

Somehow managing to put to one side her sense of awe and excitement, Lou followed the procedure all the pilots had been taught, which involved checking the weather report with the pool Meteorological Office, then checking with Maps and Signals to see if any changes had been made with respect to flying hazards such as barrage balloons, and restricted areas. Having done that, Lou then quickly read through the handling and pilot's notes, which all ATA pilots were given – put together by ATA pilots themselves – and which contained detailed information on the workings and flying of every aircraft the pilots were likely to handle. As well as all the technical information a pilot might need the notes contained little warnings from other pilots of the foibles an aircraft might possess, and Lou quickly saw that it was apparently a mistake to leave a

122

Spitfire standing on the airstrip instead of taxiing it to where it needed to be immediately on landing, because the engine had a tendency to overheat. If that happened it would cut out, which meant that the plane could not be moved until the engine had cooled down. Lou certainly didn't want to embarrass herself on her first Spitfire flight by leaving her aircraft stuck on the landing strip, preventing any other aircraft from landing until hers could be moved.

By half-past nine the taxi Anson was full of ATA pilots, eager to get on with their day's work. Lou looked down at her small overnight bag – an essential just in case for some reason she couldn't get back to Thame and had to find a billet for the night. Her nails and lips were painted the obligatory ATA red, and she'd tucked into her pocket a pretty red, white and blue patterned scarf, which had been a Christmas present from her aunt Francine, remembering the unwritten rule that she must step out of the plane looking glamorous and serene.

Some of the pilots, like Lou, were already wearing their Sidcot flying suits, with their warm detachable linings and boots. Others, the more experienced pilots, Lou suspected, would be wearing one of the much-coveted Irvin flight jackets, and their uniform slacks. The flying jackets had originally only been issued to 'fighting forces' although the Government had relented and now allowed ATA pilots to purchase one at their own expense if they wished to do so. Lou was determined to save up for one.

Three other girls were dropped off along with Lou at Castle Bromwich, the four of them making their way to the operations room where they had to queue to present their chits to the ops officer.

Half an hour later, Lou was strapped into 'her' plane. All she could see in front of her was a big black semicircular instrument panel, a dome of sky around it and her rear-view mirror. Nervously she focused on the six central instruments: airspeed indicator, artificial horizon, rate of climb indicator, altimeter, turn indicator and gyroscopic compass. The plane fitted round her as snugly as though it had been made for her. Now she knew what the other pilots meant when they said that the Spit was a woman's plane.

She was third in the queue to take off. Her stomach muscles cramped and then there was no time to worry, no time to do anything but release the brakes and feel the power kicking her in the back, then surging through the plane, almost as though the plane itself was desperately eager to be airborne, Lou thought, as a thrill of excitement pounded in her body in much the same manner as the Spit's Merlin engine was pounding in its. Cautiously Lou taxied down the runway, picking up speed as she did so, holding her breath when the plane started to lift and then exhaling on a breath of pure joy as the Spit almost soared through the air. This was a plane designed to fly at speed, Lou recognised immediately, well able to understand now why so many of the ATA pilots spoke yearningly of longing to break the rules in it, and soar high and fast above the clouds.

Even at a steady safe pace, Lou felt the sheer exhilaration of flying such a delightfully responsive plane. It would be dangerously easy to be reckless, she acknowledged. But her job was to get the Spitfire safely to its maintenance unit to be fitted out for combat, not to enjoy herself. She knew the route off by heart but she still looked at her map and then down at the ground, heading for the familiar landmark of the A1 as she flew south, checking the map for any possible barrage balloon sites she might have forgotten, before turning east towards her destination.

It was a perfect day for flying, with good visibility, high cloud and a light southwesterly wind. The site of the maintenance unit, like most, was hidden from enemy aerial view by trees, and Lou held her breath a little as she brought the Spitfire down, warning herself not to brake too hard because on the ground the plane was nose heavy and would tilt forward if one applied too much brake.

If her landing was textbook perfect, right up to her neat taxi off the runway to where several other planes were already lined up, that was down to the plane itself and not her, Lou told herself. She brought the Spit to a standstill and then quickly removed her helmet and her goggles, shook her curls free, tied her dashing scarf round her neck, before wriggling out of her seat and climbing out onto the wing, accepting the helping hand extended to her by a burly mechanic.

There was just enough time to gulp down a drink of tea, and take a bite of the chocolate bar the girls were issued with, just like their male RAF counterparts, before their transport back to Castle Bromwich was ready for them – a transport plane on its way north, which would stop off at Castle Bromwich so that they could pick up their next planes to ferry back to the maintenance unit.

By the time she was strapped into her third and final ferry for the day, Lou's confidence had grown, but she still remembered to follow the instructions she had been given whilst training, feeling the now familiar kick of the Spit's engine and the surge of power that followed it as it lifted into the sky apparently effortlessly.

Along with the other girls, Lou had checked on the weather before taking off and been told that nothing had changed. ATA pilots flew only in daylight as they used ground landmarks to guide them and not instruments.

Lou headed for the A1, following it until she reached the point where she had to turn east, humming to herself under her breath, only to stop abruptly when suddenly out of nowhere she was in cloud. What had happened? Had she somehow or other accidentally let the plane go higher than she should have done? Lou studied the instrument panel, not sure whether to be relieved or not when she saw that she hadn't. Her met report hadn't given any warning about low cloud, which must mean surely that it was just an unexpected patch she had flown into. She was on course, all she had to do was keep flying and the cloud was bound to disperse.

Only it didn't. If anything it was getting thicker. Lou tried dropping closer to the ground, hoping that she would be able to get beneath the cloud, and then when she didn't real anxiety gripped her. She couldn't continue to fly through the cloud; it simply wasn't safe and they were always being told not to take risks with themselves or their planes. Frantically Lou tried to calculate how far she had come before looking at her map for the nearest airfield, knowing that the safest thing she could do was to land the plane, and wait for the cloud to lift.

The nearest airfield was a bomber base, where Lou hoped that the landing strip would be clear since Bomber Command flew night raids over the Channel and into Germany.

Very carefully she started to take the plane down, her heart in her mouth as she prayed for the mist to lift, The base was 650 feet above sea level, which meant that she could drop down to 750 feet, giving herself a clearance of 100 feet, at which level surely she would be under the cloud and able to see the airfield? But at 750 feet Lou couldn't see a thing apart from cloud.

At 700 feet her heart was thudding far too fast, apprehension crawling along her spine; 680, and she dared not go any lower. And then, to her relief, just when she was beginning to think that both she and the Spitfire were destined for destruction, she could see the grey shapes of hangars looming towards her out of the mist, followed by the wonderful site of the runway.

This time she didn't care one bit about a perfect

127

landing. All she wanted was to get the plane down safely, and she had to fight not to reach for the brake when she finally hit the tarmac, cutting her speed until she was able to bring the Spit to a halt alongside a Lancaster bomber.

She must be better trained than she had known, Lou decided shakily as she realised when she stepped out onto the Spit's wing that she had actually remembered to remove her helmet and goggles.

'What the hell do you think you're playing at landing here? Where do you ruddy well think this is? We fly bombers here, not ruddy Spitfires?' an angry male voice demanded, an RAF mechanic standing with his hands on his hips glowering up at her whilst what she assumed were the crew of the bomber she had stopped next to looked on in interest.

'I got into thick cloud, and couldn't risk flying on—' Lou began, only to have the mechanic continue, 'Ruddy women pilots, ruddy useless, they are, the whole lot of them. They shouldn't be allowed, if you ask me.'

Lou was beginning to feel slightly sick and very shaky.

'I need to speak to your ops officer. If you could help me down and direct me to the ops office . . .'

'What use would that be? You'd never be able to find it in this mist, would you?'

The crew began to laugh. Lou was perilously close to tears. But she wasn't going to humiliate herself or ATA by letting the men see how upset she was.

She was just about to try to scramble down off the wing by herself when one of the men detached himself from the group, telling the mechanic in a familiar voice, 'Leave it out, Len. It's not her fault she got caught out by the weather.'

Kieran Mallory, with his flight lieutenant's wings stitched to his uniform, Lou noted as she was forced to wait and watch as he strode towards her to help her down.

The grip of his hand on hers felt warm and unexpectedly comforting. Comforting? Kieran Mallory? After the harm he had done to her and Sasha's relationship? After the hurt he had caused them both?

Lou's 'thanks' was stilted, as she determinedly refused to look at him. But either he wasn't aware of her desire not to have anything to do with him or, more likely, Lou thought darkly, he was taking a delight in ignoring it and tormenting her.

'You did well to come down through this mist,' he told her. 'I watched you coming in. Just as well you came in from the west, otherwise you wouldn't have cleared the ops block.'

Privately Kieran had been astonished when he'd recognised the ATA pilot who had brought down the Spitfire with such skill was Lou. He'd got less than fond memories of the twins and all the problems they'd caused him . . . It had been a relief to join the RAF, where all he'd had to worry about were the practicalities of learning to fly, instead of having to worry about all the problems he'd had in Liverpool. Kieran might have grown up surrounded by females, and then, after his father's death, having to keep an elder brotherly eye on his younger brothers and sisters, but that didn't mean that he enjoyed that kind of responsibility.

He pulled a packet of cigarettes out of his pocket and offered Lou one. She didn't smoke very often but right now she needed a cigarette. Kieran's comment had left her feeling even more shaky at the thought of what it would have meant if she had hit the ops block, not just for her and the Spitfire, but for all those working in the block.

Kieran leaned forward to light Lou's cigarette for her.

To Lou's chagrin her hand was trembling so badly she couldn't even hold the cigarette steady.

Automatically Kieran reached out to steady her hand.

Kieran's hand was so much larger than her own that hers was practically engulfed by his. Lou could feel the warmth from his skin against the chill of her own.

'Your mechanic wasn't very impressed by my flying,' she pointed out, gamely trying to make conversation as Kieran leaned closer to light her cigarette. She could smell the Brylcreem in his hair and the maleness of his skin, those scents somehow too intimate for her own comfort, causing her to draw back from him in a jerky uncoordinated movement.

'He's a bit anti women at the moment. His girl has just dropped him.'

Lou nodded and drew on her cigarette, exhaling before she told him, 'I need to go and check in with Ops here. I'll have to ask them to get in touch with the maintenance unit I was heading for and my base, and ask them what they want me to do.'

'I'll walk you over. Been giving any more dance demonstrations lately?' Kieran asked her.

Lou shot him a mutinous look. 'No I haven't. Have you dated any more American ATA pilots?'

'Who said I have dated any of them?'

'You were with Frankie Truebrooke at the dance,' Lou pointed out and then, worried that she'd said too much and that he'd think she was actually silly enough to mind who he dated, she added hastily 'Not that it matters to me who you date.'

And nor did it matter to him what kind of danger she got herself into, Kieran told himself. Just because he'd known her as a naïve kid with stars in her eyes back home in Liverpool, ready to trust anyone, that didn't mean that he had to make himself responsible for her safety now.

A large building loomed out of the mist in front of them.

'Ops is over there,' Kieran told Lou, nodding in the direction of one of the doors.

'Thanks.' Lou turned away from him, refusing to give in to the temptation to turn round to see if he was still there. It was only when she got to the main door into the admin block that she allowed herself to turn and look back, only to find that Kieran had gone, swallowed up in the mist as he no doubt returned to his men and his plane.

Half an hour later, after Ops had spoken to the Maintenance Unit and Thame, Lou was told that she had done extremely well to put the plane down safely and that the girl who had taken off after her had not been so fortunate, miscalculating the situation and losing both her life and the plane.

That sobering news had Lou shivering inside her flight suit.

The weather she had run into had not been forecast, she was told, and had been caused not just by a new weather front rolling in but because the dew point had been unusually high for the area, meaning that with a very slight variation of temperature, the sky over the whole of the middle of England had suddenly condensed into cloud.

'Let's just hope it clears for tonight,' the ops officer told Lou, which she interpreted to mean that the base must have bombers going out on a night-time bombing mission.

Even if the sky should clear, though, Lou would not be flying anywhere until the morning.

A bed would be found for her in the Waafery, and in the morning she could resume her journey, provided the weather was suitable.

By now it was almost dusk, and Lou welcomed the thought of a hot meal and, even better a hot shower, as she accompanied the Waaf corporal summoned to escort her over to the Waafery.

'There's a letter for you, Katie,' Peggy Groves informed Katie.

Katie thanked her as she put down her bag and sank down into one of the kitchen chairs. She'd hung up her coat in the hall when she'd come in, but the kitchen was so cold she wished she'd kept it on. The kitchen faced north, a rectangular-shaped

132

room with a stone sink under its single small window, the porcelain chipped here and there. The walls were painted an unpleasant shade of pea green, but thankfully the gas cooker was relatively modern and the geyser by the sink worked efficiently to heat the water for washing up. When the house had been requisitioned Lord Cadogan must have instructed his staff to remove everything that was of value. The table and chairs looked cheap and had obviously seen better days, although the table was a decent size. The cupboards that ran the length of one of the long walls might once have held expensive china but now all that was in them was a collection of thick pottery. Dark brown linoleum covered the floor, adding to the room's drabness.

They were very busy at work. With so many men overseas, the numbers of letters they were having to check was growing by the day. Some of them were so poignant and others so heartbreaking that it was impossible to prevent their contents shadowing her own thoughts, Katie admitted. The letters that affected her most were those from fighting men saying how much the letters they were receiving from those they loved meant to them, how they cheered them on and supported them, and how even the most mundane details of everyday life were things they cherished in the midst of battle, reminding them as they did of all that they were fighting for.

Katie's supervisor had said much the same thing when she had thanked them all for working longer than normal hours, telling them, 'We all know from the correspondence we see how vitally important letters are to our boys in uniform; and how very grateful those unfortunate men who have no one of their own are to receive letters from volunteers who write to them.'

'I'm just making some tea, do you want a cup?' Peggy asked.

'I'd love one,' Katie responded gratefully, going over to the dresser on which the girls put all the mail neatly sorted for each girl.

Her letter was from her parents, the envelope written in her father's heavily slanted style. Katie frowned slightly. It was unusual for her parents to write to her – they had access to a telephone and so did she – and the letter felt fat and heavy.

Opening it, she discovered that there was another envelope inside and the shock of recognising Luke's handwriting sent Katie's heart into a flurry of accelerated beats. Once the sight of a letter from Luke would have filled her with delight and joy; now though, she was almost reluctant to pick this one up, never mind open it.

There was no reason for Luke to write to her, so why had he?

'Are you all right?'

Peggy's concerned question had Katie forcing herself to smile.

'It's a letter from my ex-fiancé,' she felt bound to explain. 'Seeing his handwriting was a bit of a shock. I can't think why he should write to me.'

'Maybe it's a letter that he wrote to you whilst you were still engaged, that's been held up somewhere?' Peggy suggested.

Peggy's suggestion made Katie even more reluctant to open the letter.

'The others will be coming in soon. Why don't you take your tea up to your room so that you can read your letter in peace?' Peggy suggested.

'In private' was what Peggy meant, and Katie was grateful to her for her tact.

'Yes, I'll do that.' Katie picked up the cup of tea Peggy had poured for her.

Never had the short walk up the stairs to her room seemed so filled with apprehension. Her heart was thudding as though she had climbed a mountain.

Once she was inside her room Katie removed her hat, carefully putting her hatpin back in it. Things like hatpins were virtually irreplaceable because they were metal and every scrap of metal in the country was needed for munitions. Having done that, Katie sat down on the edge of her bed, her cup of tea on the bedside table.

On the back of the envelope Luke had written his military BFPO address, which Katie, familiar with such addresses, swiftly recognised that it must mean he was in Italy. Also, that he must be in action. But where? The newspapers were full of reports of the Allied forces' struggle against the Germans as the Allies pushed towards Rome. She opened the envelope carefully – because she wanted to preserve the address? Of course not.

Inside were two thin sheets of paper.

Dear Katie,
    I hope you won't mind me calling you that, because my memories of you are very dear to me, Katie. Don't worry, though, I'm not writing

to you to ask you to take me back. You'll have moved on now and, for all I know, there may be another man in your life who has far more right than I do to call you his dearest.

I don't have your address so I have sent this letter to your parents asking them to kindly forward it to you for me.

The reason I'm writing to you, Katie, is to tell you how much I regret the way I treated you, how ashamed I am of my own behaviour, and how much I hope that you can find it in your heart to accept my apologies and forgive me.

The letter I wrote to you ending our engagement was written in the heat of the moment and in a mood of bitter jealousy, but that does not excuse or justify the fact that I made accusations against you, not only without giving you the chance to put your side of the story, but which I knew in my heart of hearts could not be true.

War teaches a person many things, Katie. When I was lying in hospital after I was wounded I had a lot of time on my hands to think about things. I'd already had an ear-bashing from one of the nurses, who said that she wouldn't put up with a fiancé who didn't trust her, and who was questioning her all the time.

I wouldn't let myself trust you because I was so afraid of losing you and so I drove you away. I loved you, Katie, but I didn't understand that loving a person means trusting them, not trying to control them because you're afraid of losing them. I was too much of a coward to let you see how afraid of losing you I was. I deserved to lose you, Katie. I know that now. But you didn't deserve to be treated the way I treated you. If I hurt you I'm sorry. That wasn't my intention. I was too selfish to think of your feelings. All I could think of was my own and how much I was hurting. I look back on the person I was then with both shame and guilt. No amount of regret, though, can change the past, nor should it.

I'm writing to you now, Katie, because I want to admit my faults to you; to accept all the blame for what happened between us and because I want to apologise to you whilst I can. If it should be that I don't come through this war I don't want to die with it on my conscience that I let the opportunity to do so go.

You're a wonderful girl, Katie, one of the best, and I wish you all the happiness in the world because you deserve it.

Luke

PS. There's no need to feel obliged to write back to me, but if you are generous enough to write telling me that you accept my apology, should you feel inclined to do so, I would welcome hearing from you.

Katie had no idea what she had expected to read, but it certainly hadn't been any of this. The writing might be Luke's but the sentiments, the openness, the sense she got from what he had written of how much he had changed, of how much he had grown, left her feeling almost as though the letter had come from a stranger.

Katie got up from the bed and paced the room. Her thoughts were confused. To have heard from Luke at all had been a shock, but to read his apology, to know that he had recognised and accepted not just that he had misjudged her but that he understood why he had done so, was even more of one.

Luke's letter had set her free from the emotions that had tied her to their shared past, Katie recognised. No longer would she find herself troubled by that sense of something not finished, which had haunted her and prevented her from getting on with her life, because of the way in which Luke had ended their engagement without giving her the opportunity to defend herself. That was now gone; that troubled place within her soothed. Katie could feel gratitude and relief welling up inside her. She was grateful to Luke for having the courage to write to her, and if he had been here she would have wanted to tell him so, she knew.

Since he had ended their engagement it was almost as though she had been treading water, unable to go back and unwilling to move forward, because of all the questions she had not been able to ask him. Now those questions were answered; now she could truly put the past behind her and start to live again, free from the torment of not knowing, which had held her back. Katie could

138

feel her spirits lifting, the burden of unhappiness she had been carrying slipping from her shoulders like a physical weight. The wound Luke had inflicted on her was finally, and almost miraculously it seemed to Katie, healed.

She stopped pacing and hurried over to the chest of drawers next to the wardrobe, removing from it her writing case.

Then, before she could have second thoughts, she sat down and began to write.

Dear Luke,

I am so glad that you wrote to me as you did. I won't say any more on that subject other than to thank you for your generosity.

I am still working with the same organisation, although I am in London now, so I can guess where you yourself are, and I can understand why you wrote as you did with regard to surviving the war. I very much hope that you will do so, Luke, for your own sake, for the sake of your family, and for the sake of the girl who will one day become your wife. I know that you will find that girl, Luke, and that you will make her very happy.

Do take care of yourself.

As she wrote those words Katie thought of all that she had read about the fighting in Italy, as the Allied forces pushed back the Germans and advanced towards Naples. The Allied losses had been heavy, especially at Salerno. Katie's heart turned over. If Luke was one of those lost he would never see her letter, never know that she understood and accepted his apology.

Her hand trembled as she signed her name at the bottom.

'You're in a hurry,' Peggy commented, standing in the hallway to let Katie go past her as she ran down the stairs.

'I've got a letter I want to get in the post,' Katie told her, grabbing her coat from the hall.

The evenings were still light but the air was beginning to smell of autumn now, the leaves on the tree showing their tiredness – rather like the people of London and the rest of the country, Katie thought as she walked quickly to the nearest post office.

It was no secret that the Allies were now planning a second front against the German occupation of France. If that were to go ahead, if it were successful, then the end of the war would be in sight. So many ifs – too many, it sometimes seemed, for a war-weary nation, its people exhausted by the demands that the war had made on it.

A man in RAF uniform, seeing Katie walking towards him as she made her way back to her lodgings, gave her an admiring look.

Katie, seeing it, found that instead of shutting herself away from the young officer's admiration and ignoring it, right now she felt more inclined to smile. Every minute, every second of life was precious and should be enjoyed, relished, savoured for the wonderful gift that it was. Why deny the young officer her smile as a reward for his admiration when it cost her nothing to give it and committed her to nothing other than a brief exchange between strangers that left both of them lifted by that exchange?

She was free now, Katie recognised, free to be herself without worrying that others would misjudge her as Luke had; free to make her own judgements about what felt right for her and what didn't.

Once Lou had let the other occupants of the WAAF hut, to which she had been assigned a bed for the night, know that she had been in the WAAF herself, their slight wariness of her immediately melted, and before too long the whole hut, apart from its corporal, who had tactfully disappeared, were clustered together on the two beds in the middle of the hut closest to the stove, sipping cocoa generously laced with Forces-issue whisky (as one Waaf explained to Lou, her army boyfriend had told her that it was possible to swap his permitted purchase of a bottle of gin for two bottles of whisky, such was the demand for the former, so he had passed one bottle of whisky on to her).

Things had certainly changed since she had been a Waaf, Lou reflected, feeling very much like an old hand.

'There's a run on tonight,' one of the girls told Lou. 'The planes will be taking off soon, heading for Germany.'

There was a small silence whilst Lou suspected they all dwelled on the pounding Bomber Command was giving Germany's cities – and its people – destruction of property and life being a necessary evil of war. But Lou, who had lived through the Liverpool blitz, couldn't help shivering and feeling sorry for the innocents whose homes and lives would be destroyed.

Within minutes of their conversation the hut was filled with the sound of plane engines starting up. Lou could well imagine the sight of the heavy bombers queuing to take off one by one, following the lead aircraft as they headed for the South Coast and the ever-present dangers of their mission.

Automatically, without having to think about it, Lou counted the planes taking off.

'Fifteen,' the girl who had produced the whisky announced, as the sound of the last one started to fade. 'We always count them out,' she informed Lou.

'We've lost six planes and their crews already this month,' one of the other girls added quietly. 'The Luftwaffe lie in wait for them coming across the Channel if the Spits based on the South Coast aren't quick enough to force them back.'

When she was offered another splash of whisky to go in what was left of her now almost cold cocoa, Lou didn't refuse it. Now that she had flown herself, she could well imagine the vulnerability of the bomber crews in their heavily laden planes.

'Cath, didn't you say that Kieran Mallory is having to pilot Joe Stringer's plane tonight when he was supposed to be off duty?'

'Yes, poor devil. The word is that since Joe was taken off flying duties, after they were shot up so badly last week that they almost didn't make it back, his whole crew has got the jitters, and you

142

know what they say about flying with anyone like that. Some of the pilots claim that they can tell when a member of their crew can't handle it any more. They say it's like flying with someone with a death wish and that it affects the whole crew. And tonight Kieran Mallory's got a whole crew like that.'

'Well, if anyone can pull them round it's him. He's one of the best.'

'And one of the best-looking as well,' another girl chipped in, raising a laugh from everyone else.

Kieran Mallory had obviously changed a great deal since he had left Liverpool, Lou decided, listening with some surprise to the other girls' praise of him. And concern? Certainly not. There was no need for her to feel concern on his behalf. Not when there was a hut full of girls here more than ready to do that.

The dance at the Grafton was in full swing, the dance floor packed with couples. Sasha loved dancing. It was the one thing that lifted from her shoulders the fear and misery that weighed her down. When she was dancing she got forget those fears and that misery. She'd be here at the Grafton every night if she could, and Bobby, bless him, was good-natured enough to say that whatever Sasha wanted, he wanted too, except of course when it came to her wanting him to leave the Bomb Disposal unit. But she wasn't going to think about that right now, Sasha decided, not with the band in full swing. The young American GIs from Burtonwood base near Warrington were showing off their dance moves, their presence and their expertise adding excitement and energy to the evening. A lot of girls were now saying openly that they preferred to 'date' the handsome young Americans in their smart uniforms than their much less well-paid and turned-out British counterparts, but whilst she admired the GIs' dancing, Sasha had no desire to swap her Bobby for one of them.

Smiling up at him, Sasha snuggled up in his arms when the lights dimmed and the tempo of the music slowed to a smoochier number. In fact, tonight she felt happier than she had done in ages.

The dance came to an end, the lights were turned up again, and Sasha and Bobby made their way back to the table, Bobby telling her to go on ahead without him whilst he went to the bar to get them each a drink.

'I'll just nip to the ladies then. Meet you back at the table,' Sasha said, giving him a quick kiss.

The ladies was for once empty. Going into one of the cubicles, Sasha locked the door and hung her handbag on the peg.

Two minutes later, though, when she tried to unlock the door she discovered that for some reason it had jammed and she was trapped in the lavatory. Trying not to panic she called out, hoping that someone would hear her, but then abruptly all the lights went out, leaving her completely in the dark.

Now Sasha couldn't face down her panic. It seized her and gripped her, cramping her tummy and bringing her out in a cold sweat whilst her heart thumped and she struggled to breathe.

Reality slipped away from her, eclipsed by the past. Inside her head Sasha wasn't trapped in the ladies' lavatory but beneath an unexploded bomb, and she was trapped there alone, abandoned by her twin and left to die. And she would die if she so much as breathed too heavily, never mind moved.

She mustn't move, she mustn't do anything that would cause the full weight of the bomb to come down on her, crushing her into darkness and death, but despite knowing that, a small whimper bubbled in her locked throat.

The lights had come back up but Sasha was barely aware of that fact. Mentally she had slipped into a place that held her trapped by her own memories.

The door to the cloakroom opened and three girls hurried in, giggling.

'Did you hear what that Yank said to me? Called me a baby Betty Grable,' one of them told the others.

'That's 'cos he wanted to find out how old you are. The one I was dancing with promised me some proper nylons if I agreed to go out with him again. Here,' the speaker broke off, gesturing down to the floor, 'what's that?'

All three girls looked downwards.

'It looks like a shoe to me,' the third member of the trio answered, having looked round from the mirror to glance at Sasha's shoe, which was protruding from beneath the lavatory door.

'Is there anyone in there?' the girl who had first seen Sasha's shoe demanded, banging on the door and then turning the handle, telling the other two unnecessarily, 'It's locked. Here, Jenny, you're the smallest, you get down on the floor and see if there's anyone in there.'

'What? No fear. I'm not getting down there and dirtying me frock. Besides, you don't know what might be in there. In this book I read, there was a girl that was murdered in a lavvie and her body—'

'Don't be daft. Get down and have a look.'

The sound of the girls' voices brought Sasha out of the place she had slipped into inside her own head. She felt sick and dizzy, her heart thudding far too fast. She couldn't move, she couldn't do anything other than sit curled up with her arms locked round her knees, still gripped by her own fear.

Beneath the door she could see blonde hair and a girl's face, which suddenly disappeared when Jenny scrambled to her feet and told her friends breathlessly, 'There's a girl in there, sat right by the door and not saying anything.'

Pam, the eldest of the three, took charge.

Banging on the door, she asked, 'You in there, are you all right?'

Sasha blinked and shivered, the images that had been tormenting her receding and her awareness of where she was returning.

'Yes,' she called back, 'but the lock on the door's jammed.'

'Jenny, go and fetch someone and be quick about it,' Pam ordered her friend. 'Tell them that there's someone stuck in one of the lavvies.'

'What do you mean, fetch someone – who?'

'The manager, of course, you daft head,' Pam instructed her. Then, leaning towards the door she called out to Sasha, 'Don't worry, love, we'll have you out of there soon. Trapped in there when the lights went off, was you? Give us all a real shock, that did.'

'You didn't look to me like you was all that shocked when they came back on again and you was still letting that Yank kiss you,' Jenny objected, wincing when Pam pulled open the door to the ladies and pushed her through it.

'Won't be long before you're out of there,' Pam called to Sasha, only to break off when the outer door opened to readmit Jenny.

'There's a lad out there says he's looking for his fiancée.'

Pam pulled open the door and assessed Bobby. Having decided that he looked a decent sort, and safe, she told him, 'You'd better come in. There's a girl trapped in one of the lavvies. I don't know if it's your fiancée but—'

Moving past her, Bobby knocked on the locked door and called out, 'Sasha, is that you in there? It's me – Bobby.'

Relief swelled through Sasha. Once again Bobby was here to save her.

Suddenly she was sobbing and saying his name, and Bobby was telling her not to worry and that she would be free soon, before he left to go and find the manager.

'What are you crying for?' Pam demanded as Jenny burst into noisy sobs.

147

'I can't help it,' Jenny protested. 'It's just so romantic, that's all, like sommat out of a film.'

'Romantic? Being trapped in a lavvie? Don't be daft,' Pam told Jenny scornfully whilst Eliza, the third member of the trio, announced, 'Right scared, I'd be if it was me. Imagine if we hadn't come in and found her? She could have ended up locked in there all night.'

Listening to them from inside her prison, Sasha shuddered. She was so lucky to have Bobby to protect her and love her. Without him . . . A fresh fear gripped her as she contemplated how unbearable her life would be if she were ever to be left alone with her fear without Bobby to protect her from it. She wouldn't be able to live without him, she just wouldn't.

A few minutes later, freed from her prison and in Bobby's arms, Sasha thanked her rescuers between her tears before Bobby guided her tenderly towards the dance hall exit.

'I'm so glad you came and found me, Bobby,' Sasha told him.

'I'd have been there sooner,' he responded, 'but I thought you must have bumped into someone you knew and that you were having a bit of a chinwag. It was only when you'd been gone ages that I started getting worried.'

'When the lights went out it made me feel just like I did when I was trapped under that bomb,' Sasha told him emotionally.

'What? Don't be daft,' Bobby responded affectionately, adding, 'Come on, I'd better get you home.'

Once they were outside on the pavement Sasha

clung tightly to Bobby's arm. The closer they got to her home, the tighter she clung to him, and when finally they turned into her road Sasha stopped walking and told him, 'Bobby, I don't want to go home. I want to stay with you.'

'Sash, we can't do that. For one thing, my landlady wouldn't let us, and for another your dad would have my guts for garters if I were to . . . well, you know what I mean.'

Bobby was a decent young man who, much as he loved Sasha, would never dream of suggesting that they anticipate their marriage vows. Sasha's words had caught him off guard and, if he were honest, they had shocked him as well. It was so unlike her. Both of them had agreed that there would be 'no funny business' between them until after they were married. A little heavy petting on a handful of occasions was as far as they had gone, and as far as Bobby really wanted to go until Sasha was wearing his wedding ring – and not just because he knew he wouldn't be able to face either of her parents but especially her father, whom Bobby admired a great deal, if he had taken advantage of Sasha, and their engagement.

'Bobby, I want to be with you. I want you to hold me tight and keep me safe.' Sasha's voice and body both trembled, the intensity of her emotion making Bobby feel helpless. He didn't understand her in this unfamiliar mood. It just wasn't like her.

'We can't do that until we're married, Sash. You know that.'

'Then let's get married,' Sasha told him wildly. 'Let's get married now, Bobby, as soon as we can.'

'You know your dad won't let us.'

Sasha did know that. Her parents, and especially her father, had made it clear to her that he would not give his consent to their marriage until the war was over or she was twenty-one, whichever happened first.

Tears streamed down Sasha's face. Bobby just didn't know what to do. He knew that there must be some connection between her present mood and the fact that she had been trapped in the lavatory, but for the life of him he couldn't imagine what it might be. Bobby was a pragmatic young man, not given to dwelling on things or being troubled by his imagination. The fact that Sasha had told him that being stuck in the lavatory had reminded her of being trapped under the bomb was something he had dismissed as a female reaction that he was not equipped to understand.

'Come on,' he told Sasha, urging her forward, 'if we don't get back soon your mum will be worrying.'

Sasha didn't say anything. She couldn't. She was too gripped by fear and helplessness. She needed Bobby to be with her. Only he could make her feel safe. Once they were married and Bobby had left the Bomb Disposal squad then she would stop feeling like this, and everything would be all right. Why couldn't her parents and Bobby realise that? Why couldn't they understand? Once she wouldn't have needed to explain to anyone how she felt because Lou would have been there and Lou would have known. But Lou had changed, become different, forcing Sasha to be protective of her love for Bobby, and the closeness they had shared had gone. Now there was no one to understand the fear and pain locked inside her. Sometimes she didn't even understand it herself, Sasha admitted

Lou couldn't sleep, which was ridiculous, given how tired she was. She looked at her watch. Four o'clock. Surely the raid must be over now and the men would be on their way back home. Lou closed her eyes and tried to imagine what it would be like turning for home, the heavy Lancasters lighter now without their deadly loads, the night sky filled with the steady thrum of plane engines, as they crossed the darkened land below them. Each mile closer to home would ease some of the pressure, but the rear gunners would be poised and on the lookout for German planes and anti-aircraft batteries, as would the pilots, whilst the navigators kept an eye on their course. If their target had been Hamburg then they wouldn't have much land to cover, before they reached the North Sea and then the safety of English shores.

She should be trying to get some sleep, not worrying about the safety of men who had nothing to do with her, but it was impossible to do that when she was here at their base, just as it was impossible not to be infected with the mood of anxiety that gripped the other girls in the hut. It took her back to the days when she had first joined up to be back in a WAAF hut again. The other girls might be strangers to her, but she still found their presence comforting.

It was five o'clock when Lou finally heard the

151

sound for which her ears had been straining: a low barely there rumble she had to track for several seconds before she was sure it was the returning planes, and by that time the barely there rumble had intensified to a muted thrum, the sound quickly increasing.

'They're back,' came a voice from one of the other beds, and all around her Lou could hear the sound of movement of heads on pillows, lifting in the darkness and turning towards the sound of the returning planes, just as she had lifted her own.

No one was counting out aloud but Lou knew that they were all checking the numbers inside their heads as the planes came in.

One, then two, three, four, each touching-down plane easing a little more of the tension, until they had reached twelve. No one counted thirteen, just in case. Fifteen planes had gone out but for them all to return safely they would have to count to sixteen. Only they couldn't.

Number fourteen landed and then there was silence, and waiting, hoping . . . A plane could get off course, or be hit and slowed down; it might even have to be abandoned, its crew parachuting to safety if it was badly shot up. Fourteen. They needed two more to have a complete tally. Fourteen.

'Corp's chap is a navigator on one of the planes that went out tonight,' the girl in the bed next to Lou whispered to her as the door opened to the small private room occupied by the corporal, and in the dim light from that room the fully dressed figure of the corporal could be seen, smoke curling through the air as she drew heavily on her cigarette.

The minutes ticked by and became an hour.

The corporal, who had stood in silence in the doorway, stubbed out her fifth cigarette and went back into her room.

'They won't be coming back now,' the girl next to Lou told her soberly.

Two planes lost, two crews potentially lost – men with wives, and children, sweethearts and families. Men who were gone for ever. Men like Kieran Mallory. Lou's heart turned over. It was just because she knew him, that was all, she told herself sturdily. Nothing else, and certainly nothing *more*!

There was no sleep now for any of them.

TEN

'I'm still hoping that Leonard will get leave over Christmas. What about you, Katie, have you made any plans yet?' Gina asked as she and Katie walked into the office together and headed for the cloakroom.

'My parents' friends have invited me to join them for the day.'

'They live in Hampstead, don't they?' Gina asked as she unwound the knitted scarf from around her neck. Gina was wearing her lovely warm-looking camel coat and her brown beret. Her friend always looked so smart. Katie's own coat was dark grey and she had bought it just before the war.

'Yes, that's right.'

Katie wasn't really looking forward to Christmas, she admitted as she removed her own bright red scarf and hat and hung them on one of the pegs, the red making a brave blaze of colour against the dark brown painted walls.

'We'll all be going to the Manor House and Eddie's parents for Christmas dinner. Apparently it's a family tradition, with Eddie's father being the head

154

of the family. Privately, between you and me, I'd much rather Leonard and I could spend Christmas on our own.' Gina pulled a small face. 'I know that's dreadfully selfish of me.'

'No it isn't,' Katie defended her. 'It's perfectly natural. Perhaps you could suggest to Leonard that the two of you spend a couple of days in London and the rest of his leave with his family?'

'I'd love to,' Gina admitted, 'but it wouldn't be fair to the children.'

They removed their coats and hung them up.

'Come on,' Gina said firmly. 'Let's get to our desks, otherwise we'll be late.'

An air of despair and despondency at the suspected loss of two planes and their crews quite naturally permeated the thoughts of everyone at the base, including Lou, who emerged from the admin block into a morning of crisp clear air and the knowledge that she had clearance to resume her journey.

It wasn't just the thought of the two Lancasters and their crews that was weighing so heavily on Lou's heart. There was also the loss of a fellow ATA pilot, even if she hadn't actually known that pilot personally.

It had been all over the canteen when she had queued up for her breakfast that one of the Lancasters had been the one piloted by Kieran Mallory. Just thinking his name in her thoughts made Lou's heart give a fierce kick of tangled emotions, and a desire to reject the fact that Kieran and his crew were now officially posted as 'missing', which meant that it was more than likely that they were dead.

Kieran had taken her from youthful adolescence into the pain and misery of her first – and last – crush; her first taste of the bittersweetness of being 'in love'. It had been from him that she had learned about duplicity and all that went with it. It had been because of Kieran that she and Sasha had quarrelled.

His death should have freed her from all those unwanted emotions she couldn't quite escape but instead of feeling free what she actually felt was disbelief and pain, mingled with anger at this reaction.

She had no reason to mourn a man who had treated her and Sasha so badly. A man who only yesterday had infuriated her with his arrogance. And who had made her ache inside with a need she didn't want to acknowledge just by lighting her cigarette for her.

She desperately craved the comfort of a cigarette right now, Lou acknowledged, but the Spitfire had been refuelled and was waiting for her.

Her eyes stinging with unwanted tears, Lou walked to the runway, carrying her parachute with her. The morning breeze had a sharp edge to it, making her shiver slightly. A small group of mechanics were standing close to the Spitfire and outside the hangar, but instead of smoking and talking they were all standing completely still, their backs to Lou as they stared at the horizon.

Something – a frisson of sensation, an awareness of a different movement in the air – had Lou stiffening where she stood, her own focus on the empty sky, a knowing that lifted the tiny hairs at the nape of her neck filling her, even though she could neither see nor hear anything. Something was happening. The sound was so faint that she had to stretch her ears to hear it: the stuttering of a damaged engine, the growl of an injured lion, breathing his last, that had her breath catching in the back of her throat and her heart filling with hope – and fear.

Now at last they could see it, the dull grey shape no more than a smudge on the horizon, weaving its way towards them.

It didn't take one of the mechanic's grim, 'Looks like the undercarriage is gone. He'll never be able to bring her down in one piece,' to tell Lou what was happening, and how badly damaged the incoming Lancaster was.

'Mallory won't try to land her. It's a miracle he's managed to get her this far, if you ask me, but then he's a ruddy good pilot. He'll bring her down as low as he can and then give the order to the men to jump – them what can jump.'

Mallory. It was Kieran's plane that was limping home, a wounded wreck, kept in the sky only by the skill and the determination of its pilot. Her relief didn't last very long, though. Inside her head Lou could see the plane that had come down when she had been in the WAAF – with only her to witness the pilot's danger. She had acted instinctively then, running towards the crashed plane to help the pilot, her actions earning her the honour of a George Medal, which she still did not believe

157

she had really deserved. She had after all only done what anyone else would have done.

From one of the hangars the fire and 'blood' trucks came racing out onto the runway, sirens screaming as the Lancaster, tilting steeply to one side, one of its wings badly damaged, its doors open, lurched unsteadily earthwards. Lou could only imagine the cool nerve it would take to keep on flying a plane that was in that state. She could see smoke curling warningly from the plane as Kieran brought it in, skimming the trees in the field beyond the runway, and then dipping lower, almost at hedge height, so low that Lou felt sure that he was going to belly-flop and crash-land. From the open doors of the Lancaster men jumped, three, four, five of them.

'Christ, what's he doing? Why doesn't he get out whilst he can?' one of the mechanics swore, as suddenly the plane swerved fiercely to the left.

'He's trying to turn the plane so that it doesn't plough into the runway.'

'He'll never get out of it alive now,' the first mechanic stated grimly. 'Ruddy fool. He's one of the best pilots we've got. This war needs men like him. He's worth more than a ruddy runway.'

The mechanic's angrily spoken words were, Lou felt sure, shared by the rest of the small crowd, not watching and waiting, but praying, as she found she was doing herself, for Kieran's survival.

The plane hit the ground with a thump that Lou could actually feel inside her own body, gouging up the field before exploding with a dull whump of sound.

The mechanics were running towards the field, and somehow Lou was running with them, her parachute abandoned, her heart pounding. The fire truck was already on the scene, battling with the flames, whilst the ambulance crew were helping the men who had jumped out of the plane.

Kieran. She had loved him with a young girl's foolish love and then she had hated him with an equal passion, but she had never wished him dead. Emotion clogged Lou's throat. She turned away from the burning Lancaster, unable to bear looking at it, unable to endure imagining . . .

Out of the corner of her eye she saw a dark-haired figure who, despite the fact that he was limping, still managed that familiar male swagger that irritated her so much as he made his way towards where Lou was standing, by the gate in the hedge, a streak of blood on his forehead.

'You're alive,' was all she could find to say as they stood separated by the gate.

'Don't sound so disappointed.' Kieran rubbed his arm across his forehead, adding a streak of dirt to the blood.

'What . . . what happened?'

'Bomb bay door got stuck and that delayed us, so we were behind the others coming back. Jerry got us just before we crossed the Channel. Killed the rear gunner, and shot away our undercarriage. Thought I'd have to ditch in the drink, but luckily I managed to keep her going.'

Beneath the dirt and the blood, Lou could see the bleak look in his eyes belying the almost casual description he had given her of what had happened.

159

A couple of first-aiders were running towards them, carrying a stretcher.

'I'm glad that . . . that you're safe.'

What on earth had made her say that? He would think she was still the same silly idiot who had made such a fool of herself over him. The ambulance crew had reached them, obliging Lou to step back from the gate.

She wasn't needed or wanted here. She was an outsider to the base who would want to mourn their dead in private. Lou made her way back to where the Spitfire was still waiting patiently for her. Kieran was safe and alive, and she wasn't even going to think about asking herself why that mattered.

'You've got a visitor, Katie. Good-looking, and wearing a Senior Service uniform. Name of Eddie, apparently. Strictly speaking men are not allowed in female billets, but Gerry was so taken with him we had to let him in.'

Eddie. A rueful smile curled Katie's mouth as she thanked Peggy for her information.

'He's in the drawing room,' Peggy continued, 'with Gerry, and I should warn you that you'll find it difficult to evict her. She's even made him a cup of tea, or at least it was supposed to be a cup of tea. First time I've ever seen her so much as fill a kettle,' Peggy grumbled tartly and truthfully.

Gerry might have promised to mend her ways, but whilst it was true that she was no longer worrying them all to death by staying out late and

160

then returning to the billet worse for wear, she still seemed to be dating an awful lot of different young men.

Katie felt extremely sorry for her. The death of her brothers had obviously hit her hard and Katie felt she deserved their sympathy and a bit of leeway, even if Peggy Groves took a sturdier attitude and said that it was high time she pulled herself together.

Still smiling, Katie went upstairs, opening the door to the formal drawing room, which looked out into the square. Eddie was standing in front of the unlit fire, looking very handsome in his naval uniform, his mouth curling into a smile when he saw her.

'Oh, Katie. There you are. I suppose you want me to leave,' Gerry teased her with a smile.

'Oh, I don't mind kissing Katie in front of you,' Eddie assured her, with a wicked grin that made Katie shake her head reprovingly, and Gerry laugh.

'I've come to persuade you to take pity on me and have dinner with me,' Eddie told Katie as soon as Gerry had gone. 'Here I am, a chap on leave from serving his country, up in London with a table booked at the Savoy and—'

'Eddie, I'm sure your little black book is absolutely full of the names of girls who would be delighted to have dinner with you,' Katie told him.

'Yes,' he agreed simply and without embarrassment, 'but your name comes first.'

Katie didn't know quite what to say. Eddie was a charmer, she knew that, a flirt and a tease and

161

good company. His comment about her coming first was just a ploy, of course. She knew that too. But on the other hand there was really no reason why she should not have dinner with him, especially dinner at the Savoy, Katie admitted to herself. She certainly wasn't in danger of allowing herself to fall in love with him. It crossed her mind that Gerry and Eddie would be far better suited to one another than she and Eddie ever could be.

'Very well,' Katie gave in, 'but I must warn you, Eddie, I know how much of a flirt you are, and it won't wash with me.'

'A flirt? Me?' Eddie gave her a hurt look. 'How can you say that after I resisted the lures of your resident man-eater?'

Katie laughed. 'That isn't a very kind thing to say about Gerry. In actual fact she's very nice, and if you want the truth I was just thinking how much better the two of you would be suited to one another than you and I ever could be,' she told him honestly.

'Ah, but it's a well-known fact that flirts don't pair up with one another,' Eddie countered her comment, adding softly, 'You underestimate yourself, Katie. You are truly the darlingest girl, you know.'

Feeling that the conversation was getting out of hand, and well aware of the amorous look Eddie was giving her, Katie deliberately changed the subject to something less dangerous and rather more mundane.

'What time is the table booked for, only I shall need to get changed?'

'Eight o'clock, plenty of time, especially if I come and help you.'

He really was irrepressible.

'You will do no such thing,' Katie told him sternly. 'You shouldn't even be in here, never mind anywhere else. This is an all-female billet, and the rules are no men allowed.

'It's a pity Gina's taken a couple of days off to go down and see her family – she could have come with us.'

'Oh, yes, a dreadful shame that she can't. Now I shall have to put up with having you all to myself,' Eddie teased, before glancing at his watch and warning her, 'You've got just over half an hour. Are you sure you don't want me to come with you and help?'

'Perfectly sure,' Katie told him, whisking herself through the door before he could offer her any more arguments – or inducements.

Dinner at the Savoy would be a real treat. Eddie and Leonard had taken her and Gina to the Savoy for dinner the first time the four of them had gone out together, and Katie smiled as she remembered how that had been the beginning of Gina and Leonard falling in love with one another.

Now that they were into October there was a definite chill in the air and for that reason Katie decided to wear an old dress in black taffeta her mother had passed on to her, which Katie had had remodelled.

Black wasn't really one of Katie's favourite colours, but there was no doubt that the dressmaker had done an excellent job of restyling the original dress to give it a neat waist and a prettily panelled full skirt, using the spare fabric to add a new shawl collar, which showed off Katie's shoulders.

Slipping on her court shoes and grabbing her stole and her black taffeta evening bag, with its bugle bead embroidery in the shape of a flower – another loan from her mother's pre-war wardrobe, just like the long gloves she was wearing – Katie gave her appearance a final quick check in the mirror before heading for the stairs.

Eddie's impressed look and teasing wolf whistle when she walked back into the drawing room turned her face slightly pink but she still shook her head at him in reproof.

'I'll have every man in the place envying me tonight and wanting to change places with me,' Eddie told her.

'Now you are over-egging the bread,' Katie smiled, but nevertheless she was pleased by his admiration. There was nothing like having a handsome escort who was prepared to pay you compliments for boosting a girl's ego, Katie admitted as Eddie opened the drawing-room door for her.

'Do you have much contact with Leonard?' Katie asked once they were in the taxi, which Eddie had somehow miraculously managed to conjure up.

'Not since he was posted to his new destroyer.'

'Gina's hoping that he'll get leave over Christmas. She says it would be the best Christmas present she could have.'

'Would you like to know what I want for Christmas?'

Katie eyed Eddie's deadpan expression with suspicion. 'Somehow I think that is a question I shouldn't answer.'

'Ah, cautious Katie, I wonder what it would take to make you abandon that caution. Don't you sometimes yearn to find out what it's like to walk on the wild side of life?'

'No,' Katie told him promptly and truthfully. 'Being cautious is part of me and the way I am. Besides, no woman with any sense would be anything but cautious with you, Eddie. You have "Danger – charmer at large" written all over you.'

They had reached their destination and the taxi was already pulling up, depriving Eddie of the opportunity to retaliate.

Feeling femininely smug and light-hearted, Katie didn't stiffen or pull back as she would normally have done when Eddie put his arm around her as he guided her into the hotel. In fact, having the arm of such a handsome and charming naval officer holding her close to him was rather nice, Katie admitted.

'You should smile like that more often,' Eddie told her,

'Like what?' Katie pretended not to understand.

'Like you were once a very mischievous little girl who liked to have fun, and to tease the poor little boys who adored her,' Eddie told her with a smile of his own. 'Come on, I'm dying for a drink, let's head for the bar before we go in for dinner.'

Katie agreed.

The American Bar at the Savoy was perhaps not unnaturally the chosen favourite haunt of American newspapermen and women, and many of the American top brass working in London, as well as being one of *the* places that British Society and those with enough money in their pockets to afford it headed to when in the city.

In the Grill, table number 4 was always reserved for Winston Churchill, the Prime Minister, and Katie was not surprised to see that the bar was packed with men in uniform, reporters in trademark shabby raincoats, and, of course, cohorts of beautiful women dressed up to the nines, their glamorous appearance in direct contrast to the few women who were in uniform, and mostly attached to groups of very important-looking men. Katie guessed that many of them would be official drivers, stenographers, PAs and the like.

Miraculously Eddie managed to get them a table close enough to the bar for them to sit and discreetly watch the show of activity there.

The bar was very busy indeed, the majority of the voices engaged in conversation American, several smartly and expensively dressed middle-aged American wives, in clothes their British counterparts could only dream of having access to, looking askance at the pretty, young, and often a little 'too glamorously' dressed young women hanging on the arms of much older and mainly American men, who, Katie thought, it would be extremely naïve to assume were actually their husbands.

'Spoils of war,' Eddie told her in a quiet murmur, studying them with her.

Katie pulled a face. 'I hate to hear women being described in that way, even when it is obvious what's going on,' she chided him.

Eddie shook his head and informed her bluntly, 'It's the men I meant, not the girls. Would you like another cocktail?'

'No, thank you.'

'Don't worry,' Eddie teased her. 'I shan't be embarrassed if you get a little tipsy and try to seduce me.'

Katie had to laugh. 'There is no danger of that happening,' she assured him sweetly.

'Pity,' Eddie murmured in her ear as a waiter approached to inform them that their table was ready. 'I'll just have to try and seduce you instead then.'

There was no reason for her heart to give that unfamiliar little flurry of thuds that wasn't far short of a surge of anticipatory curiosity, Katie warned herself. She had no intention of allowing Eddie to seduce her, or of encouraging him to think she wanted him to. Nevertheless, it was pleasant to be escorted by someone so charmingly attentive, who seemed without any effort to ensure that things went smoothly and that, despite the crush, they were attended to as though they were regular and cherished diners.

Katie felt a little for the pretty girls in their finery with their much older men friends, an envious look in their eyes as they watched her walk past with Eddie. Perhaps their 'spoils of war' tasted a little bitter and unpalatable at times.

The Grill Room was every bit as busy as the

bar, most of the tables occupied by at least one man in uniform, if not more.

Eddie and Katie were shown to an excellent table with a good view of the room, their waiter even unbending enough to say to Eddie, 'I trust her ladyship is in good health?'

'Thank you, Joseph, and yes, my grandmother is well. I shall tell her you were asking after her.'

Rather ruefully Katie acknowledged that the waiter's comment was a sharp reminder, had she needed one, of the social gulf that existed between her and Eddie, and the very different lives they led.

It was different for Gina. For a start, Gina herself was definitely upper class and Leonard's father, whilst well-to-do, was not titled.

Menus were produced, and Katie decided on the leek and potato soup and then the fish, sole, although she doubted that it would have been caught anywhere near Dover with all the war activity taking place off the South Coast.

'This is such a treat,' she told Eddie warmly.

'Yes, it is,' he agreed, his voice for once free from its familiar teasing note and the look he was giving her so very warm and meaningful that Katie was glad that the arrival of their soup meant that they were interrupted.

With wine so hideously expensive, Katie would quite happily have done without any, but Eddie had insisted. This was luxury indeed, Katie reflected, but by far the best part of the evening was being with Eddie, who was such good company and so much fun.

She couldn't remember when she had last enjoyed an evening so much. The conversation between them flowed naturally and easily, like her own laughter, so that by the time they had finished their meal and were ready to go down to the ballroom, Katie felt so utterly relaxed and at ease with Eddie, that she actually snuggled closer to him of her own accord when he put his arm protectively around her to guide her from the Grill Room.

The Orpheans were, of course, playing, and Katie automatically looked for familiar faces amongst their number, as she and Eddie sat down at a table close to the edge of the dance floor, her foot tapping happily in time to the music.

She mustn't have been listening properly when Eddie had asked her if she wanted another drink, she decided, because she would quite definitely have refused. Now, though, with the champagne cocktail in front of her, it seemed churlish to say she didn't want it.

'See, I told you I was going to get you tipsy and seduce you,' Eddie teased her wickedly.

'That's what you might think,' Katie joked back, 'but I know otherwise.'

Of course they danced; impossible not to with such a good band and when Katie loved dancing so much. It was surprisingly easy to slip into Eddie's arms and let him guide her round the dance floor, enjoying the sensation of moving in time with the music.

'You are a very good dancer,' Eddie murmured against Katie's ear during one of the slower numbers, the movement of his lips and the warmth of his breath sending exhilarating *frissons* of pleasure sliding over her skin.

'You aren't bad yourself,' Katie joked back.

'And you know what they say about people who dance well, don't you?' Eddie demanded, continuing without giving her the chance to reply. 'They say that people who dance well, make love well.'

'They say or you say?' Katie laughed, but there was no denying that there was something very pleasurable about the confident but relaxed way in which Eddie held her, both through the fast and the slow dance numbers. And yet despite all his teasing Katie felt safe with Eddie, and as though she had known him for years, as though they had been friends and had grown up together, and knew one another so well that there was no need for any pretence between them. Being with Eddie was relaxing, Katie acknowledged, and that was because she wasn't in love with him.

Not in love with him but, to her own surprise, not averse to being kissed by him and then kissing him back, as she discovered when they made their slow way back to her billet, on foot, hand in hand, later in the evening – after Eddie had surprised her with that first unexpected kiss – Eddie's arm around her, all the better for them to draw close together to enjoy further kisses when the opportunity arose.

'It's been a lovely evening,' Katie said when they had eventually arrived back.

'It could be even lovelier, if—' Eddie began.

But Katie shook her head and told him firmly, 'No.'

'Not this time,' Eddie agreed,

'Not any time,' Katie insisted, but her rejection was given with a smile and the knowledge that she had thoroughly enjoyed their date and would be happy to repeat it.

Later, lying in bed thinking about the evening, Katie reflected on how much she had enjoyed herself. She couldn't remember ever feeling so . . . so light-hearted and ready to laugh before, the desire to laugh and be happy bubbling up inside her like the champagne she had drunk.

She felt that way in part because of Luke's letter, she recognised. Receiving it had freed her from what she now realised had been a deep-down need to prove and keep on proving to herself, and therefore inside her own thoughts to Luke, that she was the sort of girl who took her responsibilities seriously, the sort of girl who did not go out and have fun, who did not flirt and who certainly did not have lovely, fun, light-hearted evenings out with handsome charmers, with whom she then exchanged utterly delicious goodnight kisses. There was, though, now no need for her to feel guilty about doing any of those things any more because somehow that would make the cruel words Luke had written about her when he had ended their engagement true. She was free from the restrictions she had placed on herself, free from being tied to past unhappiness, and most of all free from feeling that she couldn't get on with her life because Luke had branded her as an unfaithful fiancée.

That sense of freedom was a heady and wonderful feeling, and she thanked Luke from the bottom of her heart for writing to her as he had. In a funny sort of way she almost wished that Luke was here so that she could tell him how happy she was and how grateful she was to him, because only he would understand exactly what she meant.

ELEVEN

Lying in the lovely comfortable double bed in the equally lovely and comfortable bedroom in Bella's house – the house Bella had insisted on letting her and Gavin rent for next to nothing so that they could be a proper family – Lena felt the sudden soft kick of the baby within her. Tears burned her eyes as she put her hand automatically over her body, soothing the baby, letting it know that she had felt its movement and that she loved it. Such a precious moment and one that she should be sharing with Gavin, only Gavin was already asleep, lying with his back to her, instead of cuddling up to her, and holding her in his arms.

What had gone wrong between them? Lena wished she knew, but every time she tried to say something to Gavin about his sudden coldness towards her, the words just would not come.

Because she was afraid of hearing his answers? Because she was scared silly that he might be regretting having married her and that he didn't love her any more?

Lena felt as though there was a heavy weight

of misery around her heart, a horrible burden of guilt because she had let Gavin marry her when part of her had known all along that this might happen and that he would regret being so very kind to her. He was such a wonderful man, was Gavin, strong and protective, and yet soft-hearted at the same time. She only had to see him with Janette to know that.

Janette. The thought of her daughter brought a fresh lump to Lena's throat. Janette adored the man she thought of as her father. She couldn't wait for him to come back from his work as a pilot on one of the Liverpool pilot boats that brought in the shipping over the Liverpool bar. At least Gavin hadn't turned his back on Janette like he had on her. Only this morning Lena had seen Gavin holding Janette tight, when he didn't know that she was there; a look on his face of such pain and anguish that Lena had wanted to run to him and offer him his freedom, anything just so long as he didn't look like that. But of course she hadn't, because she was too much of a coward, and because she couldn't bear the thought of losing him.

They had been so happy – too happy, perhaps. A small shiver racked Lena's body. Gavin hadn't really wanted another baby so soon, but Lena had desperately wanted to give him a child of his own and so she and nature had united against him. He had seemed so pleased when she had first told him, though, laughing and shaking his head and saying that she'd have her hands full with two little ones so close together, and then he'd kissed her and held her and she'd thought that he'd been as pleased as she was herself.

But now he never mentioned the baby. Never talked to her at all, really, retreating into silence and a place where he had shut himself off from her as surely as though there really was a door between them that he closed and locked.

Lena didn't know what on earth she was going to do. She couldn't hold him to their marriage if he wasn't happy. She loved him too much for that, but what about Janette and this new baby? Hot tears spilled from her eyes, the sound of her misery smothered against the pillow.

Gavin lay stiffly against the mattress, lying as far away from Lena as he could get. If he didn't, if he accidentally touched her, then that would be it, he would be taking her in his arms and shaming himself by begging her to love him and only him. Where was his pride? After what he had seen, his Lena with that ruddy Charlie, he had felt like giving the other man a taste of his fists and knocking him to the ground, showing him that Lena was his now and sending him packing. And if Lena had loved him she would have asked him to do that. She would have said that Charlie was trying to make a nuisance of himself, and he, Gavin, would soon have made it clear to him what was what. Instead, though, Lena had said nothing, not a single word, even though he had waited and waited, and now all Gavin could think and believe was that Lena didn't want him, she wanted that stinker who had treated her so badly, and had left her pregnant and little Janette without her father's name.

Now, much as he longed to ask Lena for her promise not to see Charlie ever again and to remind her that she had two little ones to think of – Janette, who Gavin thought of as his own daughter, and the new baby she was carrying – and that his children, like his wife, belonged here with him, he was too much of a coward to do so. A ruddy coward, that was what he was, so afraid of losing Lena that he couldn't bring himself to challenge her and to tell her what was what, and that she was staying here with him and their children, no matter how much she might want to go running after someone else. In the darkness Gavin felt the weight of his grief as though it was the heaviest of anchors pulling him down with it into the depths of despair and misery.

Luke leaned against his kitbag, enjoying the un-expected warmth of the early November sun. They were on their way to Rome, travelling along the Amalfi coast of Italy, the sparkling blue Med-iterranean to their left, below the winding road cut into the hillside, marvelling at the small villages clinging somehow to the steep hills.

He had seen so much these last few weeks, expe-rienced so much, good and bad, cruel and kind, things he could never talk about back at home to his family, things that troubled him and disturbed him and that he longed to share with someone who would understand, and so that they would not be forgotten, fading from his mind once the war was over and the world returned to normal.

Here in the sunshine it was hard to think about

Naples and all that they had found there, and yet at the same time it was impossible for him to stop thinking about it.

He reached for his cigarettes, the letter he had received from Katie crackling in his pocket as he did so.

Katie. He could tell her. She would understand.

Half an hour later Luke looked at the words he had written on impulse, his thoughts and feelings pouring from him onto the paper.

Dear Katie,
    We are now on route to an Eternal place, having passed through the hell of somewhere a person might die to see.

Would the censor allow those words? Katie would understand, Luke was sure, that he was referring first to Rome and then Naples, without naming them directly.

In that latter place there were things that it will be impossible for any of us to forget. The enemy before retreating had deliberately destroyed the city's sanitation system and water supply, and that was after having abused and starved the local population.
    The 'bad smell' I carry with me now is not due just to the filth and the stench of the place but due also to what its people have been reduced to. Boys, as young as five and six, all bones and big eyes sharp with anxiety and distrust approach us all the time, offering

us the use of their sisters in return for 'dollars'. When I think of our Italian communities at home and the ferocity with which they guard their young women, one can only imagine what these people must be going through to do what they are doing. It is a sickening aspect of war, made all the worse when I see some of our own men taking advantage of what is being offered. Not my men, though.

Before we left we gathered together what we could spare from our rations and distributed it amongst the children that came closest to us. What will happen, I wonder, to those girls who were forced to prostitute themselves to feed their families? What will happen to the children some of them are bound to have? I try to think of how I would feel if this was my country, and my family, my sisters. The thought is too unbearable to entertain. What I do know, though, is that I would still love them even though I would hate myself for not being able to protect them. This war has shown me so much, Katie. Those girls – girls who once I would have labelled as 'no good' – prepared to sell all that they have left for the sake of their families are as brave as any soldier. A soldier is praised for his sacrifice in a time of war, but these girls will be condemned and shunned for theirs.

I am sorry to burden you with such unpleasant things, Katie, but you are the only person I can talk to about them. I'm afraid of forgetting them, you see, afraid that they will be put to one side when this war is over, when they must not be.

The shame I could see in the eyes of those young boys is or should be the shame of all of us, and in some ways it is. I see it in the faces of the men who have weakened and given in to the urge to take advantage of what is being offered, and I wonder what they will tell those at home they love, and how we will all live with what this war has done, once we are no longer at war.

Luke

Having read the letter Luke folded it up, making neat straight creases as he did so with a thumb and forefinger hardened with the work of being a soldier, putting it in an envelope, carefully writing the address from the top of Katie's letter to him on it and then sealing it. Only when he had done all that did he suddenly have second thoughts. The actual weight of the letter balanced on his hand. It didn't weigh heavily but its contents did. They weighed very heavily indeed – on his heart and his conscience.

He should not send this letter to Katie, he decided. It simply wasn't fair to her to burden her with the turmoil of his own thoughts, especially now, when they were nothing more than two people who had once believed they would love one another for ever, and who had since found out that they had been wrong.

He went to tear the sealed envelope in half, only

to stop as they were given the order to move out, pushing the letter into his kitbag instead, before standing and picking up his kitbag.

'Here we go again,' Andy grimaced,

'At least we're advancing and not being held up by any ruddy Germans,' Luke reminded him.

'Not yet,' Andy pointed out, adding, 'Here, there's a letter just fallen out of your kitbag, Corp.'

Luke looked at the letter he had written to Katie. He bent to pick it up but Andy reached it first, telling him cheerfully, 'I've got a couple to get sent home. I'll take yours with mine and hand them over before we get started.'

Luke wanted to stop him and to reclaim the letter, but if he did then Andy was bound to ask him why he had written it if he didn't want to send it. Andy was the kind of person who was very open and direct – too much so sometimes, perhaps – and Luke didn't want to have to answer the questions Andy was bound to ask him if he demanded the letter back. He'd look a real fool having to admit that he had poured his heart out in the letter and was now having second thoughts about the wisdom of sending it.

In combat conditions a man saw things that made him think more seriously about the role that fate played in human lives. Why should it be that a spray of enemy fire could take out several men but somehow leave one of their number unscathed? Luke had lost count of the number of stories he had heard about men being fated to live – or die. Maybe it was the same with his letter, he thought wryly as Andy turned and loped off, carrying his letter with him.

* * *

180

Sasha was happier than she could ever remember being and the reason for her happiness was the fact that because of a nasty cut to his arm, Bobby was on sick leave from his bomb disposal work.

It was wonderful not having to worry about him, not having to worry about anything, Sasha acknowledged. Bobby walked her to work every morning, met her at dinner time and waited for her after work. There was still the awful darkness to be faced at night when she went to bed, of course, but even that hadn't seemed as bad since she'd not had to worry about Bobby's safety. Her current happiness only went to prove that she had been right when she had said that she would be much happier when she and Bobby were married and he was out of the bomb disposal unit for good.

'It's silly us not being married just because of the war,' she told Bobby now as he walked her home after work.

'There's nothing I'd like more than for us to be wed, Sash, you know that, but we've got to be practical. Even if your parents let us get married we've nowhere to live.'

'We could find somewhere. There's your billet, and . . . and, well, we could live with Mum and Dad until we found somewhere of our own.'

Bobby shook his head. 'My landlady only takes in single men, and . . . and as for moving in with your parents . . .' He hesitated and looked uncomfortable. 'Well, the thing is, Sash, we'll be a newly married couple and with them being your mum and dad, well, I just don't see how it would work, if you know what I mean.'

Sasha did, but she wasn't about to give up.

'We're bound to find somewhere,' she insisted, tugging on Bobby's arm and pulling him towards her as she told him fiercely, 'All I want is for you and me to be married, Bobby, and for you to be safe. I want that more than anything else in the world. Other girls my age get married.'

Bobby wrapped her in his arms. 'There's nothing I want more than for you to be happy, Sash, you know that. Nothing. But your mum and dad have said—'

'I don't care what they've said. I want us to be together, Bobby, always. I don't want to wait any longer.'

Bobby's arms tightened compulsively, his heart thudding into Sasha's chest at the thought of what she was saying to him. He loved her so much; there was nothing he wouldn't do for her – except encourage her to go against her parents. That simply wouldn't be right. But Bobby knew his Sasha. She'd argue and wheedle, there would be tears and recriminations. He decided to try to distract her.

'I had a letter from me mum today,' he told her. 'She's going on about us going up to Newcastle for Christmas, if I get leave. She says that you could share with our Jane, seeing as her hubbie will be away at sea over Christmas.'

Both Bobbie's sisters were married to merchant seamen. Jane lived with her widowed mother, whilst Bobby's other sister Irene and her two small children lived with her mother-in-law.

'I reckon that me mam wants to show you off a bit, with us being engaged.'

Spend Christmas in Newcastle – away from Liverpool and her own family? Sasha opened her mouth to refuse and then closed it again. Her parents were treating her as though she were still a child. Well, she'd show them that she wasn't by making her own plans for Christmas – with Bobby. Besides, Lou was bound to be coming home and Sasha knew that she didn't want to listen to her twin going on about flying and talking about people – her new friends – who Sasha knew nothing about.

'All right then,' she told Bobby, surprising him as he'd been expecting her to refuse and to insist that she wanted them to spend Christmas with her family. 'But you'll have to make all the arrangements, get the train tickets and everything.'

'But what about your mum?'

'What about her?' Sasha challenged him.

'Well, don't you want to talk to her about it first? You know, make sure that it's all right?'

'I'm not a child, Bobby. I can make up my own mind how and where I want to spend Christmas. Besides, it's time we went up and saw your family. We can talk about us getting married.'

'How are you feeling?' Seb asked Grace as he stepped in through the back door of the cottage. She'd been off colour for several days, unwilling to eat because it made her feel so sick, and Seb had been concerned enough about her to leave the Old Vicarage, which housed Y Section, a unit of the Government's covert Morse code listening operations. Officially Seb was in the RAF but he had been seconded to the Y Section early on in the war.

'I don't know,' Grace answered him. She'd been sitting down in the old rocking chair that had come with the cottage they were renting, and which Seb had rubbed down and restained, whilst Grace had re-covered some old cushions for it in the same cheerful red gingham fabric she had used for the kitchen curtains – a welcome wedding present from one of her mother's neighbours who had bought the cotton at the beginning of the war and never used it.

Grace got up, clasping her hands together, bright patches of pink colour warming her cheeks.

'I went to work this morning even though you said that I shouldn't. But then I felt so poorly, and Matron said, well, at least she thinks . . .' Her cheeks grew warmer, the words tumbling out in a rush. 'It looks like we could be going to have a baby. Oh, Seb, I'm all of aflutter,' Grace admitted. 'It's all been such a shock. You aren't cross about it, are you?'

'Cross?' Seb crossed the quarry-tiled floor and took Grace in his arms, restraining his desire to hold her as tight as he could. There was the baby to think of now, after all.

'Oh, Grace, of course I'm not cross. How could I be? I can't think of anything that I'd like more, just so long as you're happy.'

Happy to be having Seb's baby? Of course she was!

'I suppose I should have guessed,' Grace acknowledged, 'but we said that we wouldn't think about starting a baby until after the war.'

'We did say that, yes, but that was before I realised what a deliciously loving and lovable wife I was going to have,' Seb told Grace tenderly. 'If anyone's to blame for what's happened it's me for not taking more care, but you are so irresistible, my darling dearest wife, and I love you so very much.'

Laughing and shaking her head, Grace told him, 'I've been worrying ever so much, about what you'd say, since Matron asked me if it could be a baby that was making me feel so sick. I know how busy you are . . .'

'Oh, Grace, the last thing I want is for you to worry about anything. That was why I said we should wait – because I didn't want you to have to cope on your own if I got posted overseas. Now that I know I'm going to be working here until the end of war, it makes things a lot easier.' Seb kissed the top of Grace's head. He had known that he loved her before they had married, of course, but what he had not known and what had come as a delightful surprise to him had been the delicious sensuality he had discovered in his wife. To know that they were to have a child only added to his happiness. He was, Seb reflected, truly the most fortunate of men.

'Do we know when, if there is to be a baby, he or she will arrive?'

'Probably in just over six months. I'm going to have to tell Mum, of course, but, Seb, I'm not going to say anything to anyone else just yet, not until I've seen Dr Raines and he's confirmed everything. I suppose I should have realised, with me missing me monthlies, since I've always been that regular, but I just didn't think. Mum will be over the moon.' A small shadow stilled Grace's excitement and Seb could guess what had caused it. His wife and her mother were extremely close and naturally at a time like this Grace would want her mother close by her.

'I know what you're thinking,' he told her, 'but I'd miss you dreadfully, you know, if you were living at home with your parents and I could only see you when I had time off.'

'Oh, Seb, I'd never want that.'

His words had had exactly the effect Seb had hoped they might.

'Your mother will probably think it dreadfully selfish of me to keep you here with me when you could have her company if you went home.'

'My home is here with you,' Grace told him stoutly. 'Mine and the baby's.' A pretty flush stained her skin, her eyes bright with excitement and joy. 'I'm so lucky, Seb, to have you here, not just safe in England but here with me, coming home to me every day when so many other wives are separated from their husbands. Mum is bound to fuss but she'll understand that my place is here with you. I've been thinking, as well that, with the baby and everything, it might be an idea to have the family come to us here for Christmas this year instead of us going to them.'

'Well, it would certainly suit me,' Seb told her. 'Things are hotting up, and we're all being asked to work extra hours. If we spent Christmas here then I could nip in to the station to keep an eye on things and that would mean that a couple of the others could go home to their families. We could even use their billets for the family, if they all decide to come.'

'Oh, yes, that would be wonderful. I'll write to Mum tonight and tell her – about the baby and about Christmas.'

Grace put her hand on her still-flat tummy. 'Oh, Seb, I can hardly believe it. I'm so lucky to have you here, and now this as well. It makes me feel a bit guilty to be so happy when other people are suffering so badly.'

Seb put his hand over hers and bent his head to kiss her.

'I'm the lucky one,' he told her softly.

TWELVE

Emily just didn't know what to do. There'd been three letters now, all of them containing the same awful horrible words and accusations, and each one a bit worse than the last. She was just thankful that they had been slipped under her door when Tommy was walking Beauty so that she hadn't had to say anything to him about them. The reason whoever had waited until he wasn't there, of course, was because they were wanting to avoid the dog.

The one she'd found just now, this morning, was worst of the lot, saying that she should be driven out of the town and that she would be once people got to know what was going on. She wasn't fit to live amongst decent people, the letter said; she was as bad, if not worse, than the German she was consorting with. But worst of all had been words that were now engraved on Emily's heart. She didn't really need to smooth out the letter she had screwed up and put in her apron pocket to remember what they were.

'A woman like you shouldn't be allowed to bring

up a fine decent British lad. Someone ought to tell the authorities what's going on and get him taken away from you.'

The words stabbed through her mind like ice picks, chilling her, filling her with panic and dread. She couldn't bear the thought of losing Tommy and she'd do anything to stop that from happening.

Even leaving Whitchurch and Wilhelm.

Emily closed her eyes against her tears.

Yes, even that.

It was Saturday and by rights she ought to be getting ready to go to the church, since she was on the roster for doing the flowers, but she was sure that some of the other women were talking about her behind her back. She'd seen the way they looked at her, sort of knowing and disapproving. Instead of telling Ivy the truth, Emily had lied, when she'd called round yesterday evening, saying that she wasn't feeling very well and didn't think she was up to doing the flowers this week.

If she did leave Whitchurch where would she go? Back to Liverpool? Her heart sank even further. She certainly didn't want to do that, and besides, Tommy loved Whitchurch. He liked his school and he was doing so well there. And then there was Wilhelm himself. She loved him, she really did, Emily knew. They had both talked of how, after the war, they hoped they could be together, properly as man and wife. They would buy a little smallholding – Emily had the money – perhaps, Wilhelm had suggested, even set up a small market garden business. It had made her feel so happy talking about their plans, but now . . . There was no point in her giving this latest letter to Sergeant Simms. He had been ever so kind but, like he had said to her, there was no saying who might be sending them to her and they would never know unless they managed to catch that person red-handed. All Emily could hope for was that whoever it was would grow tired of persecuting her and stop doing it.

'Post's come,' Sam told Jean, coming into the kitchen from the hall, sniffing the cooking bacon-scented air appreciatively as he did so. 'Looks like there's a letter from our Grace.'

He handed the letter to her as he sat down at the table and Jean placed his breakfast in front of him. She'd cooked him what would probably be one of the last tomatoes of the year from the allotment to go with the precious rashers of bacon that had come from the pig the allotment holders had raised and fattened, adding a precious egg to Sam's plate whilst her own held a much smaller portion of bacon. It was only fair, after all, that Sam should have the lion's share of their rations, in Jean's opinion. He was the man of the house, doing a man's job in difficult circumstances, day in and day out.

Having poured them each a cup of tea and quickly eaten her own breakfast, she sat back to read Grace's letter.

Of all her children Grace was the one who wrote most frequently and at the most length. Smiling, Jean opened the envelope and lifted out two sheets of paper covered by Grace's neat handwriting.

190

She didn't need to read more than a few lines, before she had to stop and put the letter down, exclaiming, 'Oh my goodness!' And lifting her hand to her chest, as though she'd had a shock.

'What is it?' Sam asked, looking concerned.

'It's our Grace,' Jean answered. 'She's expecting.'

'Well, she is married.'

'Yes, I know that, Sam, but she said when she and Seb got married that they were going to wait until after the war.'

Sam grinned. 'Aye, well, I seem to remember you and me saying that we'd wait until we got properly on our feet and then having them knocked from under us when we found out you were carrying our Luke.'

'But that was different,' Jean protested. 'We couldn't . . . well, it's supposed to be easier these days not to have the kind of accident we had . . . and there's still a war on. How we're going to get a layette together, never mind find any decent nappies and a pram, I just don't know.'

'It will be all right, love,' Sam reassured her. 'Grace has got Seb there, doing his bit for the war but able to be at home with her, unlike a lot of young couples.'

'Well, yes, I know that, Sam, but it still doesn't seem right, what with her in Whitchurch and us here. I'd have rather they'd waited until they were back here in Liverpool and I could pop round and help Grace out.'

So now they'd got to the nub of the problem, Sam recognised. He knew his Jean. He could guess what was going through her mind. She'd always been a devoted mother, and she would naturally want to be on hand for Grace, should she need her.

Jean picked up Grace's letter. She and Sam – grandparents! It would be lovely having a new baby in the family. She was glad now that she hadn't let Sam get rid of the twins' cot, which had been dismantled and was up in the attic. It would need a coat of paint, of course, and new bedding . . .

Her mind racing ahead, Jean's concentration was only half on the rest of Grace's letter and her talk of Christmas, until she suddenly realised what Grace was planning.

'Oh, no!'

'What's up now?' Sam asked.

'Grace only wants us all to go to her in Whitchurch for Christmas instead of them coming here,' she told Sam, too put out to conceal her feelings.

'Well, what's the problem with that? It sounds like a good idea to me. Give you a bit of a rest from all that cooking and fussing around everyone.'

Sam was a good husband but there were some things important to women that even the best of husbands could not understand, Jean recognised, as she told him defensively, 'But, Sam, we always have Christmas here – always – and our Grace knows that.'

Sam could see that Jean was upset but for the life of him he couldn't understand why, and Jean couldn't explain her feelings to him. She didn't really understand them herself. She just knew that the thought of not being the one to be in charge of their family Christmas made her feel as though she was losing something, some part of herself, and that the fact that it was Grace, her eldest daughter, to whom she had always been so close, who obviously hadn't realised how she would feel made that feeling so much worse.

Of course, since such thoughts were foolish, Jean instinctively clutched at a more sensible reason for her reaction.

'Cooking a Christmas dinner for all of us will be far too much for Grace, in her condition.'

'It wasn't too much for you when you and me were first married,' Sam reminded her.

'We had the whole lot of your family round that first Christmas. I can see you now, battling with that damned turkey we could only get in the oven once I'd cut the legs off it.'

'That was different, Sam. My mother wasn't in good health, you know that.'

She had loved that first Christmas, the feeling of pride it had given her to organise everything and set a proper Christmas dinner in front of her family, and of course her new husband, taking on the role that she would make her own throughout their marriage. A role that she loved, and which Grace's letter had made her feel was being taken away from her. She wasn't ready yet to hand over the reins of family matriarch to her daughter whilst she took a secondary role, the role of an older person, loved and cherished, but to one side of things and no longer at their heart. Jean could see the future stretching out ahead of her, all the

Christmases to come when it would be someone else – Grace, or perhaps Luke's wife when he found one – who would battle with the turkey and emerge triumphant from that battle; who would be at the centre of all that was Christmas whilst she sat in a chair looking on. Tears pricked her eyes. What was the matter with her? She should be thrilled by Grace's news, and of course she was.

Grace had even written that she'd heard that poultry was going to be in short supply this Christmas so it was lucky that they lived in the country and that she'd been able to make sure of a turkey.

And she'd written to Luke and Lou, telling them both that there would be beds for them if they got leave.

> . . . And I've invited Fran and Marcus, Mum, but I'm not sure what to do about Auntie Vi and Bella. They'd be welcome, of course, and Seb says that since he has to work over Christmas so that some of the other men can have leave, there'll be plenty of spare billets for anyone who wants to come and stay.

Grace had it all planned, and without having said a word to her, or asking for her help.

Long after Sam had left for work – he worked Saturday mornings down at the depot and then spent his Saturday afternoons on his allotment – Jean continued to feel low and miserable. Grace meant well, of course, Jean knew that, and it was dreadful of her to feel like she was feeling,

194

almost as though she resented Grace for changing things.

On the other hand Jean suspected that Grace didn't realise what hard work organising a proper Christmas was. Grace and Seb wouldn't have a Christmas tree and treasured trimmings for it, like they had; Grace wouldn't have the experience of past Christmases to call on that Jean had. Of course, she wouldn't have to worry about making a cake or a pudding since it was impossible to get the ingredients for such traditional fare. But there were other things: organising stockings for everyone, inviting the neighbours in, all those little things that were part of the family tradition Jean had created over the years and which only she could orchestrate and manage.

No, it would all be far too much for Grace, especially in her delicate condition. She would have to put her foot down and tell her daughter that, thoughtful though her suggestion was, Christmas was really better spent here.

Emily couldn't settle to anything. Wilhelm was digging part of the vegetable patch, saying that he wanted to get it turned over in case they had an overnight frost. Tommy and Beauty were with him. After Wilhelm had finished digging he and Tommy were going to take Beauty's 'training' a stage further, Tommy had informed Emily importantly.

'Wilhelm reckons that with her being an Alsation, she'll be really easy to train. She's already sitting and staying, and she knows her name.'

She also knew that chewing chair legs was

forbidden but that didn't seem to stop her doing it, Emily had pointed out to Tommy.

'That's because of her ears,' he had defended his pet immediately. 'She needs to chew to make the muscles that hold her ears up work. Wilhelm told me that.'

Despite her woes, Emily smiled to herself. Beauty's ears, far from standing upright as they were supposed to do, flopped over at different angles. The puppy was all feet and growing bigger by the day, but her warning bark whenever a stranger approached the house was certainly comforting, Emily acknowledged.

She ought really to go into town. They were already in November, and with Christmas not that far away there were plenty of things she needed to do.

Tommy's cricket bat – second-hand but looking like new – and the binoculars he wanted so much – second-hand again – were already hidden away at the back of her wardrobe and she'd been busy knitting new gloves, socks and scarves for both Tommy and Wilhelm.

When the front door knocker went Emily's first instinct was to ignore it, a wash of fear rushing through her just in case the letter writer had become bolder and was about to confront her in person, but when the knocking persisted Emily forced herself to answer its summons.

The sight of the vicar standing on her front doorstep made her feel almost as anxious as she would have been had it been her unknown enemy.

The vicar's kind smile and gentle, 'May I come in?'

should have reassured her, but instead it increased her discomfort – and her guilt.

'Yes of course, Vicar.' Good manners obliged her to ask, 'Will you have time for a cup of tea, or . . . ?'

'I'd love one.'

About to show him into her pristine front room, Emily discovered that somehow or other he had followed her into the kitchen where he was now exclaiming appreciatively, 'What a splendidly warm room! My wife complains that the kitchen at the Vicarage is always cold.'

'I'm very lucky here to have the Aga,' Emily agreed. She had only been in the Vicarage kitchen once, and could well understand why the vicar's wife complained about it. It was a huge cavernous room with only one small window that let in scarcely any light, the ancient stove a sulker that was just as likely to belch smoke as produce heat.

'I'm sorry I had to let everyone down with the flowers today,' Emily felt obliged to apologise as she poured the vicar a cup of tea and offered him a slice of her upside-down apple cake, made with her own apples and a couple of rich duck eggs from the farm.

The vicar looked at her. Putting down his cup he told her quietly, 'Mrs Wilson has told me that she is concerned about you.'

Flustered, Emily went pink. She appreciated her neighbour's concern but it embarrassed her to think that Ivy had been sharing that concern with the vicar.

'Mrs Davies has also spoken to me about you.'

'Ina Davies?' Emily questioned him anxiously.

The vicar nodded. 'She has expressed to me her . . . concern that you should be welcoming a POW into your home.'

'I'm sorry if you think I've done the wrong thing, Vicar, but—'

'As Christians it is our duty to treat our fellow men with true Christian charity, which is exactly what you have done,' the Vicar surprised Emily by telling her firmly, 'and I have told Mrs Davies as much. In fact, I have spoken to all the ladies who are kind enough to arrange the church flowers, on the subjects of charity and Christianity, and the ways in which we can follow our Lord's example. The POWs work hard in our fields, helping to provide our food, often knowing that their own families in their own country may be going without food. We have a duty to show them Christian kindness, and a duty to show that same Christian kindness to one another. You may know that Mrs Davies's son was captured by the Germans at Dunkirk?'

'Yes,' Emily agreed.

'Naturally we all feel for her. However . . . I understand from Mrs Wilson that you have received a rather unpleasant anonymous letter.' Without waiting for Emily to reply, he continued, 'There was a similar incident some years ago. A pretty young teacher, who had caught the eye of Mrs Davies's son, received some rather unpleasant letters.'

Emily's startled gaze flew to the vicar's face.

'The young man came to me himself in a

198

considerable state of embarrassment, to explain to me that his mother had had plans for him to marry a girl of her own choice.'

Emily swallowed. 'You mean that Ina Davies had written the letters to the teacher?'

'Well, nothing was ever proved, and as it happened the young woman left soon afterwards to be married to a man she had known before coming to Whitchurch, so the matter died a natural death. However, it has to be said that Mrs Davies is a woman of strong emotions, and a rather difficult temperament. It is, I suspect, due to the forgiving nature of the other ladies in the parish that we do not have more problems. I have spoken very firmly to Mrs Davies this morning after your neighbour told me about your letter, and in view of the comments that Mrs Davies has already made to me herself about your POW. I don't think there will be any more letters, but if there are, please do come and tell me. We all have to make allowances for one another and to understand that those amongst us who are not as able or as willing as they might be to live as God would wish them to live, need our help to enable them to do so, but that does not mean that they should be allowed to behave as badly as Mrs Davies has behaved.'

'You are sure that it . . . that she . . . I mean, I would hate to think of her being blamed when . . .'

The vicar was smiling at her and shaking his head at the same time. 'Your neighbour is right when she says that you have a very tender heart. There is no doubt. Mrs Davies admitted to me of her own volition that she had written to you – and more than once. I think you might have found that the letters will have ceased to appear, if only because it seems that your dog has taken to looking menacingly at her whenever it sees her in the street, no doubt recognising her scent, and she is concerned that it might bite her.'

The vicar was standing up, but Emily didn't want to let him go now without making a confession of her own.

'It's true what she – Ina Davies – says about me and Wilhelm,' she told him determinedly. 'Maybe it's wrong, him being German and everything, but all I know is that I've never met a kinder, more decent man, and God willing, when the war is over him and me will be able to get married.' There she'd said it. 'If you'd rather I didn't come to church any more on account of that . . .'

'There's good and bad in every nation. I agree with you that Wilhelm is a good kind man. It is men like him, on both sides of this war, who will be needed to rebuild what has been lost when all this is over. Both of you will always be welcome in my church.'

There were tears in Emily's eyes and she couldn't speak for the emotion that filled her.

It was only after the vicar had gone that she was fully able to take in what he had told her, and to marvel at the way things had worked out. Who would ever have thought of it being Ina who had sent her those letters? Emily certainly couldn't have done so herself. Ina was always so keen on going on about other people's morals that it had never occurred to Emily to question hers. Well, at least she could sleep easily at night now instead of lying awake worrying. My, but she'd love to see Ina's face the next time Tommy walked Beauty past her. Tommy was right – the dog was clever.

There was still time for her to walk into town. She could call at the butcher's and see if he'd got a couple of bones for Beauty, Emily decided, smiling to herself.

THIRTEEN

'I've sorted out a hotel room in London for us this weekend,' June told Lou. 'One of the other ATA girls recommended it. She says it's where some of them stay, and that it's clean and respectable. It won't be the Ritz, of course,' June wrinkled her nose, 'but then beggars can't be choosers. She told me that they normally use their contacts to get into the best clubs and shows. Oh, and we've got an invite to a private party on the Saturday night – at a club where one of the top brass Americans from ATA is a member. Apparently she hosts a party there once a month and any pilots who happen to be in London are welcome. It should be good fun.'

They had both just climbed out of the taxi Anson, having spent the day collecting and delivering Spitfires from various MUs to the fighter stations, until the grey November afternoon had brought a halt to their work.

'We'll have to make the most of our weekend, especially as both of us are working over Christmas,' June continued.

Lou still felt a bit guilty about that. She'd hated writing to her mother to tell her that she wouldn't be home for Christmas but it was only fair that those of them who were single should allow the married and engaged amongst their number to have Christmas off whilst they stood in for them. Planes didn't stop needing to be delivered just because it was Christmas. What was making Lou feel even more guilty was that deep down inside she actually felt a little bit relieved to have an excuse not to go home, given the situation between her and Sasha. She had really tried her best to make things up with her twin, but Sasha just wasn't interested. Lou wondered if that was because Sasha hadn't believed her when she had tried to assure her that she no longer resented the fact that Sasha was in love with Bobby, and feared that Lou might try to come between them. How silly and selfish she had been wanting to keep Sasha to herself, but it was too late to regret that. The damage had been done and now Sasha refused to believe her or trust her.

Lou had done everything she could. She made a point of always asking after Bobby in her letters to Sasha, but Sasha's letters back to her were so obviously duty letters and not written from the heart at all that Lou was beginning to feel that she would never be able to establish an adult version of the close relationship they had once shared. It seemed such a long time ago now since they had been girls and so close that nothing and no one could come between them; a different life altogether, which, of course, it had been.

*   *   *

203

'I'd better make tracks. It won't set a good example to the other chaps if their major comes back late from leave.'

Francine gave Marcus a rueful look. 'It's my fault that you're running late,' she admitted.

They'd gone out for dinner last night, the final night of Marcus's forty-eight-hour leave, and then this morning, despite the fact that they'd made love well into the small hours, Francine had turned to Marcus again, whispering to him that she wanted him, which was why they were now running late and she was still wearing the very pretty, and totally unsuitable for wearing to make breakfast, pale peach lace-trimmed négligé she'd purchased in Egypt and worn the very first night she and Marcus had spent together.

'You call wanting me to make love to you a fault?' Marcus teased her as he drank the tea she'd just poured for him. The grey November light coming in through the window seemed to drain everything of colour rather than highlighting it, and Francine could see the new lines the war had carved alongside Marcus's mouth. Although he hadn't said – couldn't say – so directly, Francine was no fool and she had a pretty good idea why her husband was looking so tired and tight-lipped. The steady massing of troops and equipment on the South Coast, the arduous training programmes that were being put in place, the air of expectation that hung around the War Office and Whitehall, all pointed to one thing – the Allies' invasion of Northern France.

First, though, the Allies had to drive the Germans

out of Italy and that was proving hard to do, despite the Italians having surrendered.

The name Monte Cassino, with the fierce fighting there as the Allies tried to push their way forward, was on everyone's lips, especially those who had men fighting in Italy. The fighting was ferocious and the losses, so Marcus had hinted, heavy on both sides.

Francine knew that her sister Jean's son was fighting in Italy. Sons . . . children . . . was it mean and selfish of her to envy her niece Grace her coming baby? Of course Francine was pleased for Grace and Seb, of course she was, but at the same time she couldn't help feeling desperately envious of Grace. More than anything else apart from Marcus's safety, Francine longed for a child, their child, not a child to replace the son she had lost without ever really knowing him, when death had snatched him away from her.

'I'm still not sure I've done the right thing agreeing to spend Christmas in Whitchurch,' she told Marcus, thinking of how miserable she was going to be over the holiday without him.

'Of course you have. I'll feel much happier knowing that you're with your family than here alone in London.' Getting up from his chair in the once smart but now slightly war-weary Art Deco-style kitchen of their service flat attached to the Dorchester Hotel, Marcus went over to Francine and took her in his arms.

'I know what you're thinking, and there's nothing I'd like more than for us to have created a child – our child . . .'

'I keep thinking that the reason that nothing has happened is because . . . because I'm being punished because of Jack . . . because I didn't look after him properly, and because he died, all alone and thinking that none of us cared about him. I should never have let Vi send him away.'

Marcus held her close. 'You did your best for him, and you loved him – none of us can do more than that,' he reassured her. 'And as for either of us being punished – if that was the case we would never have been allowed to be together.'

Marcus's comforting words helped Fran to control her own emotions. The last thing she wanted was to send him back to his men with her face blotched by tears, and her mood full of misery.

What was the advice that was so often given to young wives and sweethearts when the time came to say goodbye: 'Be gay and smile. Let his last and lasting memory of you be of a girl who is proud of him for doing his bit and who he can rely on to hold the fort at home whilst he is away. Save your tears for after he has gone.'

'You're right,' she told Marcus determinedly, 'and I'm being very silly.'

'What do you mean you aren't coming to Whitchurch for Christmas?' Jean's normally gentle voice rose in a mixture of disbelief and irritation as she looked across the kitchen at Sasha.

'Bobby's mum has invited us both to stay with them. Bobby hasn't spent a Christmas with them for ages, and Bobby's mother wants to introduce me to all the family, with me and Bobby being engaged, and going to be married. You said yourself only the other night, Mum, that it would be a crush down at Grace's, and that you were worried about how Grace is going to manage everything, with her going to have a baby.'

Jean felt nonplussed and outmanoeuvred. It was true that she had said that she was worried about Grace being able to manage but that had been because she had still been hoping then to persuade Grace to change her mind and come home to Liverpool.

Now, though, with Francine having accepted Grace's invitation and having written to Jean to say how much she was looking forward to 'spending Christmas in the country', Jean had had to give in.

'It's not as though Lou is going to be there, with her not being able to get leave, nor Luke either, and it's only fair that Bobby should get to see his family once in a while,' Sasha emphasised.

Her daughter had a point, Jean was forced to admit, but she still didn't like the thought of Sasha not spending Christmas with the family. The speed with which things had changed, things she had somehow assumed would always be the same, like them all spending Christmas here in Liverpool, had taken her by surprise and she didn't like it. Suddenly and unexpectedly Jean thought of Vi, her own twin sister, wondering if this was how she had felt when Edwin had left her – alone; afraid; angry with herself and with her family.

Perhaps she would take the ferry over to Wallasey and go to see Vi. They weren't close and hadn't been for years, but somehow Jean felt the need to see her.

Unaware of the direction of her mother's thoughts, Sasha added determinedly, 'And besides, if we don't see them this Christmas, me and Bobby could end up married before his family have met me properly, seeing as we've decided that we don't want to wait any longer.'

Jean looked at Sasha. Her daughter was growing up, not a girl any longer but a young woman, eager to be in charge of her own life. She did understand how Sasha felt, Jean acknowledged. She hadn't forgotten how it felt to be young and in love. But still . . .

'You know what your dad said about you not getting married until the war's over, Sasha.'

'Oh, the war, I'm sick of hearing about it and of having my life ruled by it,' Sasha protested in frustration. 'It could go on for years yet, and why should me and Bobby have to wait? What difference is the end of the war going to make to us? It's not as though Bobby is going to be sent overseas or anything. I'm tired of being treated like a child. No one said that Grace couldn't get married, and no one's going to stop me and Bobby neither!'

Jean listened to her daughter's outburst with a mixture of sympathy and maternal concern, along with some anxious irritation. Sasha knew perfectly well that Grace had been older than her when she and Seb had got engaged, and that they had had to wait until Grace had finished her nurse's training and passed her exams before they got married. In the past Jean would have told Sasha this in no-nonsense terms, but Sasha had changed. She had become far too easy to rub up the wrong way, which then led to angry outbursts and upset, which did no good to anyone. Sam wouldn't be at all pleased if he came in to a house filled with the unpleasant silence of a 'bad mood'. It wouldn't do any good telling Sasha that, though, Jean recognised. In fact, it was more likely to fan the flames of her rebellion. Sasha had always been the quieter, more cautious twin, but she had changed. Right now Jean suspected that Sasha had worked herself up into such a state that it wouldn't take very much to push her into rowing not just with her but with her dad as well, and that certainly wouldn't do her any good.

So instead of pointing out the flaws in her argument Jean said instead, 'I do understand how you and Bobby feel, love, but there's a lot more to being married than having a wedding. Things like having somewhere to live, for a start.'

'Oh, Mum, we'll find somewhere,' Sasha protested, adding bitterly, 'Anyone would think that you don't want me to be happy, and that you and Dad want to keep me and Bobby apart.'

'That's silly talk, Sasha,' Jean felt bound to point out. 'Of course, me and your dad want you to be happy.'

'Then let me and Bobby get married,' Sasha challenged her.

'You know how your dad feels. He's said that you've got to wait, and you know your dad when he's made his mind up about something.'

Jean could see that Sasha wanted to continue

pleading her cause, but she knew that her daughter knew perfectly well that her father was not one to budge once he had made his mind up about something. He could be stubborn, could Sam, when he chose to be and Jean was beginning to think that Sasha took after him.

FOURTEEN

London! Lou hadn't had time to see much of the city when she had come here to be presented with her George Medal by the King, and there certainly hadn't been any partying of the kind anticipated by June, who had talked excitedly about the fun they were going to have almost non-stop since they had first got on the train, packed with other servicemen and women.

Since they didn't know their way around and it was already going dark in that grey depressing way it did in November, they agreed that it would be best to take a taxi to their hotel, although they had to wait for over half an hour to reach the head of the queue.

When June gave the cabbie the address of the hotel he nodded and then asked them, 'With that ATA outfit, are you?' looking at their uniform. 'Only I took a fare of your lot to the same address less than half an hour ago. American, they were, though.'

'Yes, we are with ATA,' June confirmed, the two of them holding tight to the seat as the driver

211

swung the cab round a sharp corner and then had to swerve to avoid a group of uniformed GIs.

'Ruddy Yanks,' the cabbie grumbled. 'City's full of them. Get more leave than our lads do, and they've more money to spend. If you two girls want a bit of advice you'll be careful how you go, especially round Piccadilly. Got a bit of a bad reputation, it has now.'

Lou and June exchanged glances.

'I suppose the driver was talking about those women they've been going on about in the papers, who target young servicemen, especially the Americans,' June commented to Lou a little later when they had paid their fare and were standing outside their hotel, a gloomy-looking building on the Edgware Road, its windows firmly blacked out.

'You mean the ones they call Piccadilly Commandos?' Lou asked, using the name by which the young women, both professional and increasingly amateur, who offered sex to the thousands of uniformed men who flooded the city on leave, were known.

Nodding, June started up the flight of stone steps that led to the hotel entrance. Once they were past the black-and-white-tiled floor of the outer hallway, and inside the building proper, the smell of cooking cabbage, and paraffin from the heaters attempting to warm the hotel 'reception' made Lou wrinkle her nose.

The bald-headed elderly man behind the desk greeted them without enthusiasm, sniffing, and then giving them a lugubrious look before demanding,

'Booked in, have you, only we ain't got no spare rooms?'

'Yes, we are booked in,' June confirmed firmly. 'Miss Campion and Miss Merryvale.'

The old man ran an arthritic-looking finger down the long list of names written into the book in front of him, the drip on the end of his nose gradually getting bigger, until just as Lou was holding her breath, expecting it to fall, he reached into his pocket to remove a handkerchief.

'One double room with single beds. Room number six. You're on the top floor. Bathroom's on the floor below. You'll have to carry your own cases.'

'We've been travelling all day. Is there any chance we could have a pot of tea and something to eat?'

'Dinner is at seven o'clock sharp,' he answered Lou, relenting a little to inform her, 'There's a Joe Lyons round the corner – why don't you take your cases up to your room and then go and have a cup of tea there? It will be warmer than it is here.'

'It looks like we're in the attic,' June announced as they puffed their way up the final flight of stairs and onto a landing with a sloping ceiling and three doors opening off it.

'This one's number six,' Lou told her, inserting the heavy key into the lock and then turning the handle.

Their room was larger than Lou had expected, with a slanting ceiling that ran down to a small barred window, with a window seat. The two single beds had matching faded satin covers and eiderdowns that could once have been either pink or blue but which now looked unpleasantly grey.

213

A mahogany wardrobe and a chest of drawers filled the wall opposite the window, whilst the space at the end of the beds was taken up by a dressing table.

'Well, this is a real home from home,' June announced. 'I'd be thinking that the girl who recommended this place to me was having a joke at our expense if it wasn't for the cabbie saying that he had brought some American ATA girls here.'

'From the way I've heard them talking whenever I've met any of them, you'd think that even the Ritz and the Savoy aren't good enough for them,' Lou said bluntly, pulling back the satin bedspread to inspect the sheets, both relieved and surprised to see that they were pristine white and clean, if a bit on the thin side.

'Well, at least we won't be spending much time here,' June told her, adding, 'Come on, I'm gasping. Let's go and see if we can find that Joe Lyons.'

Another letter from Luke? Katie picked up the letter determinedly ignoring the small kick of curiosity-cum-pleasure from her heart as she automatically weighed it in her hand. She hadn't been expecting Luke to write back. From the weight of his letter it was no mere bread-and-butter 'thank you' response.

For once she seemed to have the house to herself. Peggy had gone to Aldershot to spend the weekend with her fiance, and the other girls were either still at work or had gone out for the evening.

Making herself a cup of tea – she had eaten

earlier with Gina – Katie sat down at the kitchen table and opened Luke's letter.

She had to read it three times before she was finally ready to put it down and reflect on its contents. It was obvious from the manner in which Luke had written to her how he felt about what he had seen; Katie could feel his raw despair. She felt it herself. Those poor girls. Once to have received such a letter from Luke would have shocked her and she would have recoiled from what he had written, not wanting to recognise the reality of war and the damage it did to those who witnessed its cruelties, as well as those who suffered them, but that girl, that Katie, belonged in the past. The Katie she was now had a clearer, sharper vision of the world and knew that people could not be divided into 'good' and 'bad' or 'right' and 'wrong'.

She knew that what Luke had described to her so clearly would keep her awake not just tonight but for many nights as she contemplated the plight of those poor girls – and asked herself what she would do in their shoes.

Luke had written to her with an honesty that stripped away the convention of protecting her sex from unpleasant reality, and she was glad of that. She welcomed the fact that Luke felt that he could write to her so openly. It put them on an equal footing, somehow, in a way that they had never been as an engaged couple, and it showed her a side to Luke that she could only admire. He had not been afraid to write about his vulnerability and his doubts; he had taken her into his confidence and trusted her with that confidence, which Katie had always sensed, during their engagement, he had not felt able to do. It was as though, being freed from the convention that said there was a certain way in which the relationship between a man and a woman must be conducted, they were now able to be open with one another and to trust one another where that hadn't been possible before.

Luke was a kind man, a good man, and if her heart still ached a little because things hadn't worked out for them, well, she was mature enough to accept that ache and sensible enough not to try to turn the need of a man to tell those at home of the pitiful reality of war, into something that it wasn't.

His disclosures had shocked her, but not because of what those poor women had been driven to. Katie knew from listening to the women of the American Red Cross at Rainbow Corner, that already those in authority were expressing concern about the plight of Italy's citizens, especially the women and children, and what might be done to alleviate it. Katie knew that the unwritten rules governing those at home doing war work meant that it was not acceptable for her to question the officers of the Red Cross directly, but surely she could make a few discreet enquiries? If things had been different and they weren't all so strictly rationed themselves, Katie would have tried to organise a collection amongst the girls she worked with for spare clothes and non-perishable food for the Italian women and children who were now their allies, but the reality was that no one had anything to spare. Katie wanted to do something, though, even if all she could do was write back to Luke assuring him that she was doing her best to drop a few hints about the contents of his letter in the right ears at Rainbow Corner. Motherly Lady Irene Whittaker, a fellow volunteer who sat and sewed new stripes onto uniforms whilst the men waited and often unburdened themselves to her, would be a good person to talk to, as would Lady Charles Cavendish, another volunteer – if Katie could pluck up the courage to approach her. Lady Charles was in reality Adele Astaire, the sister and former dancing partner of the famous Fred Astaire. Both women were compassionate and friendly, and surely the right people to whom to discreetly mention the contents of Luke's letter?

Fired up by her determination to do what she could, Katie went up to her bedroom and got out her writing case, to write back to Luke.

Dear Luke,

Since receiving your letter I have been asking myself what I would do were I in the same circumstances as those poor women you described. All I can say is that since I read your letter I haven't been able to stop thinking how lucky we are in this country. Yes, we have rationing and all that goes with that, but our country has not been invaded, our children and our sick are not dying of starvation. I ask myself, if things were different, would I have the courage to make the sacrifice that Italian women are making for the sake of those who might be dependent on me? I hope that I would, repulsive though the thought is.

When I read your letter I felt so proud to know you, Luke, and proud too that you felt able to write to me as you did. I can't pretend to be ignorant of what war means. Here in London, even though women are desperately needed for war work, there are still those who prefer to ply a certain 'trade' – and with the city full of servicemen there is no lack of custom for them.

The area around Piccadilly has become notorious for the presence of these women – both professional and apparently 'amateur'. It is hard to understand what might propel a previously respectable young woman into such behaviour, when there is no need for it – unless of course one feels unable to live without silk stockings, chocolate and chewing gum. Perhaps I'm being unfair, I don't know. It isn't pleasant, though, to hear the Americans who come to the Red Cross place where I work part time joking about other British women and their availability – there's a joke currently going the rounds about utility knickers: 'one yank and they're off' – but worse than that by far, we had one elderly resident coming into us to complain about the number of 'rubbers', as the Americans call them, littering the steps down to her cellar. I can understand how a member of my own sex would sell herself for money to keep her family from starving, but for the luxuries that a few dollars can buy? That is something I do not understand, and something that to me is shameful and unacceptable, but if this war has taught me anything it has taught me not to judge others.

With your permission, Luke, I would like to mention your letter to a couple of people at Rainbow Corner. As you wrote, there are many Americans in uniform with family connections with Italy, and it may be that the Red Cross could do something to help, if they are not doing so already.

We are getting a little war weary here, complaining about our lot, envying the Americans and resenting them for looking down on us, when they have not had to go through what our men have endured, grumbling about yet another Christmas with no end to the war in sight, even though everyone is also saying that it can't be much longer before we are victorious. Your letter has shown me how little we really have to complain about and how fortunate we are that, thanks to men like you, our country has not been invaded.

Please do keep writing to me, Luke. Your letters are showing me how much more there is to this war than we can always understand here at home.

Katie paused and nibbled the end of her pen. Would Luke misinterpret her request and worry that she was trying to restart things between them? Should she cross out what she had put when the truth was that she did hope he would continue to *write* to her for the very reason she had stated. Luke's letter had shocked her but had also made her think beyond the boundaries of the everyday, sometimes aggravating, small inconveniences of her own life.

She had to make sure that Luke didn't think she was running after him, but how? Katie exhaled in relief as she suddenly knew the answer.

I had tea with my friend Gina this evening. She's missing her husband, Leonard, who is in the navy. They haven't been married very long. We met Leonard and his cousin Eddie when we went to Jane Austen's favourite city. Eddie took me out for dinner a couple of weeks ago. He is great fun – a flirt and a tease, the kind of man who is good company but who no sensible girl takes seriously, especially a sensible girl like me who has made up her mind not to get involved with anyone whilst the war is still on. Not because I'm afraid of losing someone I love to the war, although I would be, but because the war makes us view things differently, and do things we wouldn't normally do because the war doesn't give us time to think things through properly.

There, that should make it plain to Luke how she felt, and that he need have no fears about writing to her.

*   *   *

220

'Oh, Jan, I wish that your leave was longer.'

'So do I,' Jan agreed as he held Bella tightly to him. He'd arrived on an unexpected forty-eight-hour pass two days ago, and now in just over an hour he'd have to leave.

'We'd better get dressed,' Bella told him, reluctant to leave the warmth of his arms, and not just because of the cold air in the unheated bedroom. It was funny how she never realised just how much she missed him until he was with her.

'At least your mother isn't likely to come back to say goodbye to me,' Jan murmured as he bent his head to kiss her.

Bella's mother had not approved of their marriage. Not that Bella cared about that.

'We're lucky that Muriel from next door came round and took Mummy to the church Christmas fair with her.'

It had been pure heaven to spend the final couple of hours of Jan's precious leave up here in her bedroom, in bed. The room had last been decorated before the war, with pink and blue striped wallpaper overprinted with deeper pink roses, the curtains matching the wallpaper, and the pink carpet. It was a girl's bedroom, the pink sateen eiderdown looking ridiculous against Jan's tanned muscled body.

'I'm going to miss you so much,' Bella whispered to him as she kissed him. She wouldn't tell him that she feared for him. He would know that. Nor would she tell him that she still sometimes had nightmares about him being shot down and becoming a prisoner of war again. Fighting men

221

needed their womenfolk to be strong for them, so instead of crying Bella smoothed Jan's dark hair back off his forehead and told herself how very, very lucky she was.

FIFTEEN

It was only ten o'clock and the private club they'd got into, thanks to Lucky Fairweather, the well-connected and very vivacious strawberry-blonde American ATA pilot, who was holding court in one of the leather upholstered booths that filled the back wall, was seething with a mass of young men and women, all of whom seemed to have heard about the club 'from a pal'.

As she sipped her drink – a shandy, having refused the offer of an American beer to drink from the bottle – Lou, who had somehow or other got separated from June, found herself part of a group that included several American ATA pilots all trying to out-do one another, 'shooting a line' about their hair-raising flying activities.

In ATA such boasting was looked down on, as well as being against their code of practice, and Lou found herself growing increasingly irritated as she listened to one particular American pilot, who was boasting about buzzing unsuspecting ground-based vehicles.

'You should have seen the look on the face of

this farmer guy when I dropped down out of the sky heading for him. He ran for his life.'

Unable to stop herself, Lou commented coolly, 'I dare say he did. Anyone who has lived in this country through the blitz would have done the same thing. It's easy to laugh at people when you haven't been through what they have, easy, and something you Americans seem to be very good at.'

For a moment there was silence and then the girl who had been boasting threw back her head and told Lou cockily, 'Very good just about sums us up, as you Brits will find out when we win this war for you.'

'A war you didn't want to join until the Japanese pushed you into it,' Lou pointed out.

The American's face was flushed with anger. Did she think she was the only one who didn't want to hear her country or her countrymen run down and made out to be cowards, Lou wondered grimly.

The other girl took a step towards Lou, her manner openly aggressive, as she raised her beer bottle to her lips.

'Seems like you and me are going to have a little war of our own going on,' she told Lou once she had finished drinking and wiped her hand over her mouth.

Lou didn't like the direction the situation was taking but she wasn't going to back down, not with the American saying what she had about them winning the war. The other girl was plainly spoiling for a verbal fight and Lou was inwardly relieved when the girl next to her tugged on the sleeve of the low-necked dress she was wearing and told her, 'Don't look now, Patti, but that good-looking RAF flight lieutenant you were making eyes at last night has just come in, and he's looking right over here.'

Automatically Lou looked towards the entrance to the club, her heart thudding into her ribs as she realised that the 'good-looking RAF flight lieutenant was Kieran Mallory. Why did he have to keep turning up in her life when he was the last person she wanted to keep bumping in to?

The American raised her hand and called out, 'Hey, Kieran, honey, over here.'

Now was her chance to escape, Lou decided, but as she turned to move away the American turned back towards her, grabbing hold of Lou's arm and telling her, 'You and me have got unfinished business that I won't be forgetting.'

Lou tried to pull away but the other girl wouldn't let go of her, and then Kieran and a couple of other RAF pilots had joined the group, Kieran's frown in Lou's direction making it plain to her exactly what he thought about her being there.

His curt and demanding, 'Lou, what are you doing here?' caused the American girl to give Lou a narrow-eyed look of increased dislike.

Lou cursed under her breath and responded firmly, 'What do you think I'm doing here? I'm on leave and I'm having a good time, just like everyone else.'

'You two know each other?' The American's voice was cold and sharp.

'We're both from Liverpool,' Kieran answered her without taking his gaze off Lou.

Quite what would have happened if June hadn't suddenly appeared at her side, Lou didn't want to think. The American girl's hostility towards her had grown with every second that Kieran's attention was on Lou.

'There you are!' June exclaimed, plainly oblivious to the tension. 'I've been looking everywhere for you. Those two Spitfire boys we met up with earlier are waiting for their dance.'

Lou was only too glad to escape, even if it did mean dancing with a young pilot who had two left feet, both of which he kept putting down on top of her own.

'Have you seen how much some of the girls are drinking?' June asked Lou, round-eyed when they had finally returned to the table they were sharing with several other girls from their hotel, some American and some British. 'Tonight's been a real eye-opener, I can tell you. I mean, I like a good time, but some of the things that are going on here . . . I heard a couple of girls openly talking about going back to their rooms with a couple of men they'd only just met. Who was that girl you were standing with when I came over, only she's just danced past us and she was really giving you the evil eye?'

'She's an American pilot who can't resist shooting a line about her flying skills,' Lou answered June, pulling a face and adding, 'You know the type.'

Several of the other girls, who had been dancing, returned to their table, one of them, Nadine,

226

announcing, 'We're all being treated to a free drink.'

'Who from?' June asked

'An old friend of mine.'

When the drinks arrived, beer in bottles, Lou was tempted to refuse, but when Nadine told her firmly, 'This is yours, Lou: ginger beer, a special order, since you're not much of a drinker,' she felt obliged to pick up the bottle instead and thank her.

Kieran watched Lou from the other side of the room. He hadn't planned on coming to the club tonight, having discovered on previous visits to London that it tended to attract a rowdy ready-for-anything crowd that didn't really appeal to him, but the others he was with had insisted, and rather than be dubbed a spoilsport he had gone along with what they wanted to do.

He supposed he should have guessed that the loud American girl who had introduced herself to him the previous evening at another party, and who had insisted that he dance with her and return to her table with her, would be someone who would naturally gravitate towards a place like this.

He had no real idea why he should feel it necessary to keep an eye on Lou, it was just inbuilt into him to look after daft kids who couldn't look after themselves, Kieran decided. Only Lou wasn't a kid any more, she was a woman. And a very attractive woman, as well. Kieran frowned, caught off guard by the direction his thoughts were taking, and determined to stop them. There were more than enough pretty girls around for him not to need to think about Lou Campion.

Patti Beauclerk, sitting as close to Kieran as she could, watched Lou with a look of gloating triumph in her eyes.

Patti didn't like competition from other women – of any kind. The ATA pilot – Lou, Kieran had called her – was going to be very sorry indeed that she had crossed her.

It had been a stroke of luck meeting Nadine at the bar just as she was getting drinks for their table, and pretending that she owed Nadine a round of drinks. No one had seen her slip those amphetamine tablets into Lou's drink – enough to make her as high as a kite, especially with that double shot of gin she'd put into it as well.

Patti had found out, from a pilot she had got friendly with when she'd first arrived in the country, that some pilots used the amphetamines ahead of a mission, or when they had thought they might have trouble staying awake on night duty. Always eager to prove her reputation for daring, Patti had got hold of some of the tablets and had found out that they gave an added buzz to partying, as well as keeping her awake.

The pilot who had introduced her to them had told her with a wink that he reckoned they were very good for removing inhibition, 'if you know what I mean.'

She did, of course, and now she was really going to enjoy herself watching Miss High and Mighty show herself up in what she hoped would be a very spectacular manner indeed, under the influence of the tablets she had dissolved in Lou's drink.

Lou felt quite extraordinary, caught up in a rush of excitement and euphoria akin to what she normally felt only when she was flying. She couldn't stop talking, chattering away inconsequentially nineteen to the dozen, and finishing her drink despite its odd taste.

'Come on' she urged June, 'let's go and dance.'

'What's got into you?' June demanded, laughing when Lou pulled her onto the dance floor in her eagerness to be there. 'I've never seen you like this before.'

'That's because we've never been on leave in London before,' Lou told her.

'You're turning into a real party girl, and no mistake.'

Lou had stopped listening. All she really wanted to hear was the music, its beat thudding into her senses, making her whole body itch to respond to its demands.

Within minutes of them starting to dance a small space had been cleared around them, Lou's exhilaration allowing her to overcome her normal reticence as she performed some of the complicated jitterbug moves she and Sasha had learned together.

Frowning slightly, Kieran watched Lou. She was glowing with exuberance, her face flushed, her eyes shining, their pupils huge and dark. The place of the girl she had been dancing with had been taken by a young American who was twirling Lou round

229

with expertise, spinning her faster and faster, egged on by the crowd watching them.

Lou might be enjoying herself now but, as his mother had told them as children, too much excitement always ended up in tears and upset, and Lou was overexcited. Kieran had seen her dancing on many previous occasions when she and her twin had been practising for the 'competition' his uncle Con had set up, but he had never seen her behaving as wildly as she was now, throwing her head back and laughing when her partner threw her around so speedily that the full skirt of her dress flew up, revealing the long slender length of legs Kieran was forced to acknowledge were just about the best he had ever seen.

It was no business of his how Lou behaved, of course, but the way she was behaving was certainly out of character for the girl Kieran remembered.

'Looks like your friend from home has taken one too many of those pills you flyboys like to take,' Patti commented meaningfully, unable to resist drawing Kieran's attention to Lou's wild behaviour. 'She should be more careful about what she drinks.'

Patti's words, said so smugly and with such gloating delight, distracted Kieran's attention from Lou to Patti herself.

'I reckon that tomorrow morning she isn't going to feel anything like as proud of herself as she is right now. In fact, I've heard that it's a dismissal offence for the Brit ATA girls to let the side down and not behave like ladies.'

Kieran knew women – at least as much as any

man could 'know them'. He knew all about those smug secret little smiles, and the meanings that were hidden in seemingly innocuous little words. He'd grown up witnessing his sisters practising their art, and learning to be young women. He'd witnessed their squabbles, their fallouts with once 'best friends', their hostility towards other girls who had offended them in some way only under-stood by other females.

'You've spiked Lou's drink,' he guessed.

Patti was enjoying herself. Kieran's attention was focused totally on her now.

'Now why would I go and do something like that?'

'How many pills did you put in it?' Kieran demanded.

'I can't remember,' Patti lied.

'One, two?'

Patti raised an eyebrow and pouted. 'Why do we have to talk about her? What does it matter how many there were?'

There was something in the way that Kieran was looking at her now that Patti hadn't expected and certainly didn't welcome. She wished now that she hadn't let him guess what she had done, even though at the time it had seemed too delicious a secret to keep to herself.

'Tell me,' Kieran insisted grimly.

'All right, it was three,' Patti admitted sulkily, 'although why you should be making such a fuss about it and her I really don't know.'

Three? Kieran looked towards the dance floor where Lou was being swung off her feet by her

231

partner. Across the space that divided them their gazes met and somehow as her feet touched the ground Lou missed her step, and lost her balance, tumbling to the floor, and then lying there, too surprised and bemused to make any attempt to get up.

'What are you doing?'

Ignoring Patti's outraged demand, Kieran pushed back his chair and got up, striding across the floor to where half a dozen GIs had surrounded Lou and were counting her 'out' in the manner of a felled boxer in the ring, whilst Lou herself simply laughed, oblivious to the disapproving looks she was being given by some of the women witnessing what was going on.

Pushing aside the GIs Kieran reached Lou and bent down to haul her to her feet.

'Kieran . . .' Lou was uncomfortably aware of the tight line of Kieran's mouth. The look on his face rather reminded her of one her father might have given her when she was a wilful teenager.

'Show's over boys,' Kieran told the watching GIs.

'What are you doing?' Lou demanded when Kieran started almost to march her off the dance floor. 'I want to go back and dance some more. I was enjoying myself.'

'So we could all see,' Kieran acknowledged. 'But somehow I don't think you'd also enjoy waking up tomorrow morning in the bed of one of those GIs, which is what was going to happen.'

His brutal words shocked Lou out of the euphoria that had been gripping her.

'No, that's not true,' she protested. 'I'd never do anything like that.' Her head had started to ache and she suddenly felt slightly sick and dizzy, swaying against Kieran.

'Where are your friends, that girl you came here with?' Kieran demanded. The best thing he could do for her was hand her over to her friend and tell her what Patti had done, urging her to get Lou back to wherever they were staying and keep her there until the effect of the amphetamines had worn off.

'They've gone,' Lou told him. 'June wanted me to go with them but I didn't want to. I wanted to keep on dancing.'

Kieran cursed under his breath.

'I'm thirsty. I need a drink. I'll have a gin and tonic.'

'You'll have no such thing,' Kieran informed her grimly.

'Chuck will get me one,' Lou announced determinedly.

Kieran looked across at the GI who was glowering at him and reflected to himself that a drink wouldn't be all that Chuck might want to give her. Not for the first time or, he suspected, the last, he cursed the fact that his mother had seen fit to tell him every day of his growing life, 'You're the eldest, Kieran, and that means that it's up to you to look after the little ones, especially with the girls.' And had thus instilled into him an indestructible sense of responsibility.

It was no good telling himself that Lou meant nothing to him and there was no reason why he

233

shouldn't simply leave her to fate and her GI. He knew girls like Lou; he had grown up amongst them. They were the sort of girls who didn't go messing around with boys and who insisted on an engagement ring on their finger and the banns called before they permitted anything more than a few kisses. Respectable, brought-up-in-a-certain-way girls, who kept to the rules. The war might have given some of those girls a freedom their mothers had never had, but ultimately the war would end, and those who had lost their good reputations could end up regretting that freedom.

The truth was that Kieran did feel a sense of responsibility for Lou. There was no point dwelling on things that had happened in the past, though if he were honest with himself then he did still feel uncomfortable about the way he had played Lou and Sasha off against one another, manipulating their emotions and taking advantage of their naïvety when he had gone along with his uncle Con's plans to put them on the stage for his own financial benefit.

He hadn't wanted to listen then to his mother's warning to him not to follow in her brother's foot-steps. He had had to learn for himself what he really wanted from life. Joining the RAF was the best thing he had ever done. It had shown him a different kind of life, where respecting others and earning their respect in turn were more important than pulling a fast one over the naïve in order to earn a few quid.

Lou was trying to pull free of his grip and if he wasn't careful, judging from the way her GI admirer was watching them, an unpleasant scene could easily develop. The best thing he could do now was get Lou back to wherever it was she was staying, but he knew that telling her that wasn't going to be a good idea.

Instead he walked her firmly towards the exit, answering her angry, 'What are you doing?' by telling her, 'This place will be closing soon. Everyone will be moving on to another club.'

'Does it have a dance floor?' Lou demanded.

Kieran nodded.

Lou had felt so hot that she welcomed the sharp coldness of the November air against her flushed face, pulling away from Kieran as she hummed under her breath and then began to dance on the pavement.

'Come on, there's a taxi.' Kieran started to lope towards it, pulling Lou with him, forcing her to stop dancing to keep up with him.

Kieran could see from the cabbie's face that he wasn't keen to have them as passengers, but Kieran bundled Lou into the cab before the driver could protest, and then got in himself.

'Where to, guv?'

'We're going dancing,' Lou responded before Kieran could say anything. 'We're going to dance all night.'

In the mirror the cabbie's gaze met Kieran's.

'What's the address of your hotel, Lou?' Kieran asked.

'What do you want to know that for?' Lou asked indignantly. 'We're going dancing. You said so. I want to get out.' She was reaching for the door.

'Know where you're going yet, guv, only me meter's ticking away and—'

'The Montgomery Hotel, please, it's just off the King's Road, the Sloane Square end near the barracks,' Kieran answered, giving the address of his own hotel.

The taxi took off at such a speed that Lou was thrown against Kieran as they turned a corner, the taxi driver obviously eager to get rid of them as quickly as he could.

'Stop, I want to get out. I want to go dancing.'

'Carry on driving, cabbie,' Kieran contradicted Lou.

'I want to get out, and you can't stop me. You had no right to . . . to take me away from my friends.'

The cab swung onto the King's Road, the damp pavements and road glistening under the light from the moon, couples clinging together in sheltered doorways. If he let Lou get out of the cab now it would be like letting a new-born kitten cross a busy road.

'Looks like your girl has been having a good time,' the cabbie commented.

'I'm not his girl,' Lou corrected him.

'She's my sister,' Kieran fibbed, 'and not really used to London.'

'You'd better keep a watch on her, then, 'cos this city ain't the place to be these days if you don't know what's what. All sorts, we've got here, and some of them not too fussy about how they behave.' As he spoke a Jeep screamed out of a side street: the American MPs, with the white gloves

236

that had earned them the nickname 'snowdrops', no doubt on the lookout for servicemen breaking the rules.

Kieran's hotel was at the bottom end of what might once have been described as 'shabby genteel', and had, Kieran suspected, been dying a slow death until the war had increased the demand for hotel rooms. He had been meant to be sharing with another pilot, who had cried off at the last minute, leaving Kieran in sole occupation of the double room.

Lou wasn't feeling very well at all. Her heart was pounding so unsteadily and heavily that she could almost hear it beating; she felt slightly sick and dizzy and wanted to lie down, but at the same time something inside her felt as though it had been wound up tightly, filling her with an un-familiar sense of desperate, restless urgency. As she followed Kieran out of the taxi she looked curi-ously at the façade of the hotel whilst she waited for him to pay the cabbie.

'This doesn't look like a club,' she told him.

Ignoring her, Kieran took hold of her arm in a firm grip and prayed mentally that the hotel's reputation of turning a blind eye to its guests returning from an evening out accompanied by a friend, provided the doorman was tipped generously, could be relied on.

Luckily, though, the hallway was empty. It was probably too early for most of the guests to be returning, Kieran thought, as he urged Lou up the stairs and then along the landing towards his room.

They had almost reached it when Lou, who

mercifully hadn't said anything for several minutes, suddenly announced, 'I don't feel right,' and then collapsed against him.

Luckily they were close enough to his room for Kieran to be able to half carry and half drag her into it and then get her on one of the room's two single beds before turning to lock the door. When he turned back to the bed, Lou was lying there watching him.

'How do you feel now?' he asked her.

'Strange,' Lou answered him truthfully. 'Like my head's an express train with things rushing through it all the time and I can't make them stop. It's as though everything inside me is fizzing and wanting to do things, and yet at the same time I feel really dizzy and sickly.'

'Patti put some amphetamines in your drink, that's why you're feeling like that.'

'Patti? You mean your girl? The one who was boasting about buzzing some poor farmer?'

'Yes, but she's not my girl.'

'Well, she was acting like she was,' Lou pointed out spiritedly. 'Why would she put amphetamines in my drink?'

'To get even with you, I should imagine, and because she was hoping they would encourage you to throw off your inhibitions and make a fool of yourself, or worse.'

Lou was beginning to feel dreadfully weak and shaky all of a sudden, but her head was still buzzing and just trying to listen to her own thoughts was exhausting her.

'And did I?' she asked Kieran in a small voice.

'Did you what?'

'Did I throw off my inhibitions and make a fool of myself?'

Kieran paused to weigh his words. 'It depends on what you consider to be making a fool of yourself. You were certainly doing a lot of dancing.'

'Without my inhibitions?'

Kieran shrugged. 'You're a good dancer, and you aren't the sort of girl to forget the way you've been brought up, but if that GI you were dancing with had had his way, it would be *his* bed you'd be in right now.'

Lou's face burned. 'I wouldn't have done anything like that.'

'You might not have been able to stop him.'

Lou put her hand up to her head. She could remember dancing, but only in a vague sort of way. Showing off, her father would have called it. Her face burned hotter. Her father would not have approved of the way she had behaved tonight and neither would the powers that be within ATA.

'I showed myself up, didn't I?' she asked Kieran in a small voice.

'It's London, there's a war on and you're on leave – you aren't the first to let that go to your head and you won't be the last.'

'I suppose I should thank you for rescuing me.'

'Save your thanks until I've got you back to your hotel. It's a pity your pals left the club without you.'

Lou bit her lip, a memory surfacing of June's anxious expression when she had pleaded with her to leave with them.

'June, my friend, will have something to say to me, I know. At least I can tell her that it wasn't all my fault and that my drink had been interfered with.'

'You stay here. I'll go downstairs and check that there's no one around – the last thing either of us needs now is for someone to see you coming out of this hotel or, even worse, out of my room – then I'll find a taxi to take you to where you're staying. I shouldn't say anything about coming here to your pals, if I were you.'

'No. They'll be thinking badly enough of me as it is, without thinking I've deliberately gone to a man's hotel with him,' Lou acknowledged shakily, rubbing her forehead tiredly. 'My head won't stop pounding,' she went on, 'and my heart feels like it's racing, and I'm so tired.'

Classic symptoms of using amphetamine pills, from what Kieran had heard from those RAF crews who took them.

'Wait here. I won't be long,' he told Lou, going to unlock the door.

Once he had gone Lou slumped back on the bed. She felt dreadful, nauseous, tired, guilty and ashamed. How could she have behaved the way she had, dancing like she had, and speaking to June the way she had done? Was it really just the amphetamines Patti had put into her drink that had made her behave like that? Unexpectedly, Lou suddenly longed for her twin sister. Sash would have known how much of the way she had behaved was her and how much was the pills, Sash wouldn't have let her show herself up, and Sash would have defended her if she had done.

Sash. Tears welled up in Lou's eyes. She wished so much that her sister was here with her.

Downstairs in the hallway Kieran had become trapped in conversation with a fellow pilot, Robin Lewis, from the same base as Kieran, who was telling him drunkenly about his girl, who had left him for someone else.

'She never wanted me to join up. Wanted me to go into a reserved occupation like her dad, but a chap has to do his duty, doesn't he?'

'I should go and get some sleep, old chap,' Kieran suggested. 'You'll feel better in the morning.'

'No. Tried that before. Doesn't work. Drink works, though. Want you to have a drink with me. Shouldn't drink alone. Got a bottle . . .' He waved a half-empty bottle of gin in front of Kieran.

Lou would be wondering where on earth he was. Kieran just hoped that she wouldn't take it into her head to come looking for him. The last thing either of them needed was for Robin Lewis to start telling everyone that Lou had been in Kieran's room, once he'd sobered up and they were back at their base. Word spread fast in the small community pilots inhabited, especially when it was gossip.

She was so tired. Where was Kieran? Lou stretched out on the bed. It wouldn't hurt to close her eyes for a few minutes. They felt gritty and strained. Her heart was still racing, thudding into her chest wall, its fast pace wearying her. Lou closed her eyes. Inside her head she could still hear the beat of the music she'd danced to earlier. The GI had been a good dancer, but dancing with him hadn't been as much fun as dancing with Sash. A small smile softened Lou's mouth.

Sash. As girls sharing a bedroom their beds had been so close together that they could reach out and hold hands.

Sash. A tear rolled down Lou's cheek from beneath her closed eyelids, followed by another. Her heart was still racing. Lou put her hand on her chest, wanting somehow to slow it down.

She was so tired. She yawned and then settled herself more comfortably on the bed, giving in and letting sleep claim her.

Kieran exhaled in relief as he finally managed to extricate himself from Robin's drunken grip, mainly by redirecting his attention to a group of equally inebriated pilots and assorted crew members who had just returned from their evening out.

Now, though, the hallway was crowded with them, and it was going to be next to impossible for him to get Lou out of his room and safely into a taxi without anyone seeing her.

The first thing Kieran saw when he opened the door to his room was Lou flat out and dead to the world, and making that small snuffling sound as she breathed that he remembered his sisters making as children.

Kieran looked back towards the stairs. From the sound of male voices sharing ripe descriptions of their evening's entertainment, the hallway was still packed and likely to remain so for the foreseeable future.

He looked back at the bed where Lou was fast asleep. There was nothing else for it now, he decided reluctantly. Lou would have to spend the night in his room. Then he'd have to wake her and get her out before any of the other hotel guests were up and about.

SIXTEEN

'Lou, thank goodness. I've been so worried about you. Where have you been? You've been gone all night.' June was sitting up in bed as she spoke, rubbing a tired hand across her eyes, and looking rather disapproving.

Lou forced what she hoped was a reassuring smile as she sat down on the bed in the hotel room she and June were sharing – the unslept-in hotel bed, because last night – but no, she must not think about that. Kieran had said and she had agreed that last night was something it would be best if they both pretended had simply not happened. Not that they – she – had done anything wrong. When Kieran had woken her just over an hour ago she had been shocked by the sight of him standing over her, and then horrified when the events of the previous evening had come back to her.

They had agreed, reluctantly on Lou's part, since June was her best friend and closest confidante, that all she would tell June was that when she had realised they had left the club, she had felt so unwell and alarmed that she had taken a taxi to her aunt's apartment at the Dorchester, where she had spent the night.

It had been unfortunate, though, that one of the occupants of the other rooms had seen her leaving Kieran's room this morning before Kieran had hurried her downstairs and then found her a taxi. Lou's face burned as she remembered the leering, knowing look he had given them both. A man's reputation would not suffer any harm because a girl had been seen leaving his room, but her reputation would certainly suffer if it became known that she had spent the night in a man's bedroom. Working with so many men as they did, it was essential that they were able to command the respect of those men. A girl with a reputation for spending the night in men's rooms would certainly not command any respect.

'I know. I'm sorry if you were worried about me. I should have left the club with you when you said you were leaving,' Lou admitted penitently, avoiding looking directly at June in case her guilty expression gave her away, as she added, 'When I realised you'd gone I was feeling so off colour that I got in a panic and decided the best thing I could do was take a taxi to my aunt's – you remember I told you about her? She was with ENSA but she's married now to a major and they live in an apartment at the Dorchester. Luckily she was at home. I should have asked her to ring the hotel and leave a message.'

'Yes, you should,' June agreed, obviously not entirely placated, which made Lou feel even worse

245

about lying to her, but Kieran had been insistent that a confidence shared with even one person was potentially no longer a confidence.

'How are you feeling now?' June's initial coolness had thawed and she sounded genuinely concerned as she drew her knees up under the bedclothes and rested her arms on them, leaning forward to listen to what Lou was saying, her concern making Lou feel even more guilty about lying.

'Tired,' Lou told her truthfully, adding equally truthfully, 'I'm really sorry that you've been worrying about me, June.'

'That's OK. I'm just relieved that you're all right.'

The truth was that she was far from 'all right', Lou acknowledged later, breakfasting in the crowded ground-floor room along with June and some of the other girls. Whilst they were exchanging banter, raising their voices so that they could hear one another above the clatter of breakfast activity and talking about their night out, her mind was on the horrible situation she was in. She hated being deceitful, especially to such a good friend as June, but she had had no other option. Good friend though June was, Lou had been forced to admit to herself that if she knew where she'd been June would be bound to wonder if Lou's night in Kieran's bedroom was as innocent as it truthfully had been, because in June's shoes she would probably have asked herself that question. Kieran was, after all, a very good-looking man, the kind of man who women noticed, the kind of man who a girl was highly unlikely to fall asleep on, should he take her back to his room. But it was different for her. For her, Kieran was part of Liverpool and home, and his behaviour towards her over the last twenty-four hours had reminded her of the elder brother superiority and bossiness that she remembered from her own brother, and that Kieran himself had so often exhibited towards both her and Sasha when they had both been desperately keen to have him think of them as dashing young women, not silly young girls.

Kieran's parting words to her had been a groaned comment that she was causing him more trouble than all his own four siblings put together. Confirmation, had she needed it, of exactly how he thought of her. Not that she wanted him to think of her in any other way. Not for one minute. And if for some silly reason it had made her eyes sting with tears to wonder what it might be like to have Kieran treating one with the tenderness and adoration of a man towards the girl he loved, well then, that had just been silliness and obviously something to do with the pills in her drink.

'Oh, Lena, he's so beautiful. His little nose is just like Gavin's, but otherwise he's the image of Janette.'

Bella's voice softened with emotion as she looked down at the three-week-old baby nestled in her arms, whilst Lena looked on in silence.

Little David Gavin was a lovely baby – David for Gavin's late father and Gavin for Gavin himself. Lena had insisted on that, even though Gavin had protested, saying it would cause confusion. Lena had been so proud of her son, and so proud of the fact that Gavin was his father, that she had wanted the world to know it. That had been in the euphoric aftermath of the birth when she had managed to convince herself that everything was going to be all right and that it was just her imagination that things hadn't seemed right between Gavin and herself. Then she had been remembering how Gavin had reacted to Janette's birth, how tenderly he had looked at her, how wonderfully he had taken control, said that they were to get married and that Janette was to be his. Now with the new baby, his own baby, he had barely seemed to look at him. In fact, Lena had hardly seen him at all.

'Work,' he had told her brusquely, when Lena had made herself ask him why he was spending so much time away from the house. The port was so busy with incoming and outgoing convoys that they were all having to do overtime.

'It isn't because of the baby, is it?' Lena had asked him worriedly. 'I don't want you half killing yourself with too much work because we've got an extra mouth to feed.'

Of course she had been hoping that he would laugh and say she was talking nonsense and that there was nothing he wanted more than a row of little mouths to feed, and their mother along with them, and she had been hurt when he hadn't.

Even his mother had remarked on the change in him, putting it down to the war and the pressure it was putting on everyone.

Lena, though, knew better. *She* was the cause of Gavin's grim manner and withdrawal into himself, she was sure. It was because of her that he came in late and went out early and hardly looked at little Davie, because he wished that he hadn't married her.

Lena had always feared deep down inside herself that being loved by Gavin was too good to be true, that somehow there had been a mistake, that one day she would wake up and find out that he didn't love her after all. Why should he? How could he when she was what she was: unwanted by her father's Italian family, despised for her Italian blood by her mother's side, thrown out by her mother's sister because she had let Charlie have his way with her. Pregnant and unmarried. As an adult the spectres of what her life might have become if Bella hadn't taken pity on her and rescued her were always there at the back of her mind, and Lena knew she would fight tooth and claw to protect her own daughter from the fate that could so easily have been hers. When she had fallen in love with Gavin, with his respectable family background, his decency and kindness, his good looks and sense of humour, she had hidden that love, feeling that he could only despise her. But then had come the miracle of him telling her that he loved not just her but baby Janette as well.

She had been so happy. Too happy?

She looked down at Davie. When Janette had been born Gavin had been besotted with her – her cot had been the first place he had gone when he came in from work – and Janette had returned his love, her first smile for him, her daddy, and not for Lena. Janette was a real daddy's girl. Tears burned the backs of Lena's eyes. She had been so thrilled to be carrying Davie, secretly hoping all along that she would have a boy, her gift to Gavin for his love for her and Janette, but Gavin scarcely paid any attention to Davie.

Reluctantly Bella handed Davie back to Lena. He was a strong and sturdy baby and in due course Lena would come back to work at the nursery, bringing both Janette and Davie with her. Lucky Lena to have two children. Bella opened her arms to Janette, who had decided that her new baby brother had had enough adult attention.

Just because she and Jan had not started a baby yet, that did not mean that there was anything to worry about, Bella reassured herself. They had scarcely had any time together, after all. And just because she had lost that first baby when she had been married to Alan, that didn't mean that there would not be other babies, despite her mother's old wives' tales about 'some women just not being able to carry a baby'. She wasn't worried at all, really, Bella assured herself. It was just that seeing Lena with Davie made her feel a little envious, that was all. There was plenty of time for her and Jan to start a family. But what if there wasn't? What if the unthinkable should happen? Jan was a Spitfire pilot who had already been shot down and taken prisoner once. What if . . . ? But no, she must not think like that otherwise she'd start getting like her mother, who couldn't so much as listen to a wireless news bulletin without working herself up into a dreadful state because Charlie was in action in Italy.

It wasn't long now until Christmas, and Jan had written that he hoped to have some leave then. Mentally, Bella imagined the two of them sharing an intimate Christmas alone together, in a remote and romantic cottage, thatched and beamed, perhaps close to the South Coast, where Jan was based. There would be an open fireplace in the bedroom so that they could lie snuggly in bed in one another's arms. With any luck it would snow, heavily, and she and Jan would be snowed in . . .

That, of course, was just a dream. The reality was that, if Jan did get leave, they would spend Christmas at her mother's, with her mother, who would allow them no privacy whatsoever, and of course they would have to make time to see Jan's mother and sister as well – not that Bella objected to that. She liked her mother- and sister-in-law. It was just that the time they had together was so precious and so short-lived, and she so longed to be able to hold their own baby in her arms, a baby with Jan's eyes and dark hair and Jan's nose and mouth, and . . . Oh, Jan. She missed him so much.

SEVENTEEN

'Marcus!'

Dropping the small last-minute extras she had gone out to buy ahead of her Christmas Eve journey to Whitchurch tomorrow morning, to spend Christmas with her family, Francine ran into her husband's arms, her eyes shining with love and delight.

'I wasn't expecting you. Why didn't you ring?' she asked him. 'I wouldn't have gone out. How long—'

'I didn't ring because I found out only this morning that I'd be able to take some Christmas leave after all,' Marcus interrupted her in a tender voice. 'And as for how long – well, four days—'

'Four days. Oh, Marcus, and I've gone and agreed to spend Christmas in Whitchurch, when we could have been together, just the two of us. I'll telephone Grace and tell her that you've got leave and I won't be going. She'll understand.'

'No, you can't do that,' Marcus told her, shaking his head as he kept her close to him, his arm wrapped around her slender waist. 'Didn't you say originally that Grace said there was room for us both?'

'Yes, in the digs where one of Seb's colleagues normally stays – he's gone home for Christmas. Apparently, it's a double room, and the landlady doesn't mind because I'll be eating at Grace's.'

'There you are then – a double room – what more could we want?'

'We've got a double room here,' Francine pointed out. 'And a sitting room, and . . .'

She couldn't say any more because Marcus was kissing her and murmuring against her ear, 'Never mind the sitting room . . .' making her laugh and sigh, and then hold him close when he kissed her fiercely, not minding the rough scratch of his unshaven jaw against her own skin. This was Marcus, her husband, her love and the fact that he had not shaved only showed his impatience to be with her.

'I need a shower and a shave,' he told her. 'The car's low on petrol so I had to grab the first transport I could, with some Royal Engineers and their lorry.'

'I'm so glad you're here and so glad you aren't in Italy.'

'There's going to be worse than Italy to get through,' Marcus warned her.

Francine looked at him. 'When?'

'Not yet – Churchill would never countenance a winter invasion. The simple logistics of getting enough men and equipment over there make it a necessity that he waits for good weather. And besides, the men aren't ready yet. We're having to try to train them on the South Coast whilst pretending to Hitler that we aren't. Not easy with God knows how many thousand troops going to be encamped down there, come the spring.'

'I really wish we could stay here and not go to Whitchurch,' Francine repeated.

'Whitchurch will be wonderful,' Marcus assured her, kissing the tip of her nose. 'A family Christmas in the country? What could be better?'

'Do you really want me to answer that?' Francine asked him ruefully.

'Oh, Mum, I just don't know what I'm going to do. The turkey won't fit in the oven.' Grace was in tears as she hugged her mother.

Seb had just collected Jean and Sam from the station, and now as she looked round the pretty country kitchen and listened to her daughter's tale of woe, Jean suddenly knew that Christmas was going to be Christmas after all, and that all her worries and misery had been for nothing. Grace had a discreet little bump under her soft cherry-red wool dress, her cheeks flushed and stained with tears, the cause of her despair sitting in the middle of the kitchen table, and Jean was filled with maternal love for her, and the confidence that came from managing over two decades of Christmases.

Mind you, it was certainly a very large turkey, Jean acknowledged, assessing it with an eye experienced by many years of assessing those birds that had gone before it, then turning to look at the Aga.

254

'I told the farmer's wife that the oven was only big enough for a medium-sized turkey and that this one is a large one, but she said that this is only a medium one,' Grace wept. 'I'm sure she's given my turkey to someone else and that's why I've got this one. Mum, what am I going to do? We can't have Christmas without a turkey, and now Francine and Marcus are going to be here and I'm going to look such a fool, when I wanted everything to be just right.'

'And it will be,' Jean assured Grace. 'It's got two ovens, has it then, this Aga?'

'Yes,' Grace agreed. 'One for slow cooking and the other for faster.'

'Well then, what we'll do is, we'll get your dad, or Seb,' Jean added hastily, remembering just in time that she and Sam were merely guests, 'to cut off the legs and then we'll see what can be done. First, though, love, how about putting on the kettle?'

'Oh, Mum, I'm sorry . . . I was that upset about the turkey I forgot . . . I've been worrying about it all morning since the POW from the farm delivered it along with my veggies and that.' Fresh tears rolled down her face. 'I'd got it all planned so carefully, and when you arrived we were going to go into the sitting room and have tea with a tea table properly set, with that lovely tablecloth and them napkins you got me before me and Seb were married – do you remember?'

Jean nodded.

'And we were going to have mince pies and everything, and now I haven't even cooked them because I got in such a state over the turkey.'

'Well, then, it's just as well I've brought a few mince pies of me own with us then, love,' Jean said comfortingly, welcoming the relieved and grateful smile Grace was giving her. 'Now why don't you let me get me coat off, and then you can sit down and I'll put the kettle on. Your dad's been looking forward to seeing this garden you've been telling us you're going to have a vegetable patch on, so perhaps him and Seb can go and have a look at it after we've had our tea, and then you and me can get things sorted out a bit.'

'Oh, Mum!' Grace threw herself into her mother's arms. 'I wanted everything to be just right so that you'd be proud of me and you could have a lovely restful Christmas, and now everything's spoiled.'

'Of course it isn't, and we will have a lovely Christmas.'

And so they would, Jean decided. They would have a wonderful Christmas.

'I'm so glad you're here, Mum.'

'So am I,' Jean told Grace as her daughter hugged her.

'. . . And then Francine rang and said that Marcus had got leave and would be coming with her after all, and Seb will meet their train and take them to Mrs Wilson's, where they'll be staying, and then he'll bring them here, and we can have a bit of supper together, and then go to Midnight Mass. We can walk to the church, and Francine and Marcus will be able to walk back to their billet.

It's a shame that Sasha and Lou can't be here, and Luke, of course.'

'Well, we don't want you over-doing things, Grace. Not in your condition.'

Mother and daughter exchanged smiles.

'Newcastle?' Lou looked at the chit she had just been given.

It was Christmas Day and all those working at the base had been given a special Christmas breakfast, but as Lou had said to June, it didn't really compare with her mother's Christmas breakfasts, or being at home.

'Never mind, at least we've got our New Year's Eve dance to look forward to,' June had reminded her.

Typically perhaps, the nearby American Air Base had sent out invitations to all those ATA pilots who could make it to attend a real American New Year's Eve 'party', which they were hosting. 'Forget Times Square,' the invite had run. 'Our base is where it's going to be at this New Year's Eve.'

It wasn't New Year's Eve that Lou was thinking about right now, though, but Newcastle. Sasha was in Newcastle. Lou had been thinking a lot about her twin recently. The lies she had had to tell June about her night in Kieran's room had left Lou feeling very uncomfortable and guilty, and a little to her own surprise she had started wishing that she and Sasha were still close enough for her to be able to tell her twin how she felt. Now she had a ferry job up in Newcastle. Lou was tempted to telephone her sister Grace and ask if she had Bobby's family's address, but then common sense reminded her of the reality of the situation between her and Sasha. Her twin probably wouldn't like it one bit if Lou suddenly appeared when she was with Bobby and his family. She might even take Lou's appearance as an indication that Lou was once again trying to come between her and Bobby. And besides, she probably wouldn't even have time to see Sasha, Lou acknowledged. They were short-staffed, with so many people wanting to take Christmas leave, and Lou suspected that virtually the moment she put down the Spitfire she was delivering she would be given another job.

She was by far the youngest person sitting round the lunch table at the house in Hampstead, Katie acknowledged ruefully, feeling guilty that she wasn't more grateful to her parents' friends for inviting her to join her parents and them for Christmas lunch.

The heavy faded dark red velvet curtains, with their fringe trimming, had already been closed against the feeble winter daylight, casting a dull red glow over the room that was more gloomy than cheering, thanks to the poor quality and wattage of the wartime light bulb suspended from a bare cord to dangle over the Victorian mahogany table. The chandelier that had apparently once graced the dining room had been removed and packed away for safekeeping, Katie's mother had told her, their friends living in dread of their good things being damaged by Hitler's bombs, although they were still using their lovely elegant Spode dinner service.

'I simply can't bear the thought of not drinking tea out of a china cup,' Lavender Hillbrook had told Katie earlier in the day when Katie had asked what she could do to help with the preparations for their Christmas lunch and had been told that she might lay the table.

Katie knew what she meant, and could sympathise with her. Jean Campion would have loved the Spode, with its hand-painted gilt borders.

The Hillbrooks had done well for themselves, as the saying went. Gerald Hillbrook had been an impresario before he had retired, whilst Lavender had sung in the same revues as Katie's mother. The Hillbrooks didn't have any children, and their favourite form of entertainment was talking about the past, retelling the same stories that Katie had already heard many times before, although of course she was too polite and kind to spoil their stories by saying so.

This morning, when she had woken up in her narrow bed in a small boxroom, there had been no stocking for her to investigate as there had been last year, sent with her to Hampstead by Jean Campion, who loved her own family traditions. There wasn't any of the laughter and shared fun of the Cadogan Place house. Nor should Katie compare the happy chatter of a Campion Christmas lunch with the silent concentration on eating favoured by her parents' friends. The Hillbrooks were quite elderly, older than her parents, and so very kind that Katie felt guilty for making comparisons.

Lunch was turning out to be a solemn affair, with little conversation other than the Hillbrooks' views on the merits of the new vicar's sermon and the preponderance of people in uniform at the Christmas morning service.

They had already had their first course, a thin watery brown Windsor soup, and now they were on their main course, thin slivers of roast goose, carved by Gerald Hillbrook and placed with due pomp on each plate. One each for the women and two for the men. The goose had, as Katie's mother had already confided to her, to last them until New Year, when they would be having a pressed tongue.

After lunch her parents and their hosts would 'retire' to the drawing room, with its small smoky fire, its draughty bay window and its dark brown hide suite decorated with cream antimacassars, to sit down to listen to the King's Christmas message.

After the King, it would be time for afternoon tea, following which they would play cards before falling asleep in their chairs. Katie's heart sank a little, but then she reminded herself of poor Gerry, who had travelled home yesterday to spend Christmas with her parents, and who had been dreading doing so because of the loss of her brothers.

The best thing she could do would be to take herself out for a brisk walk, Katie decided. She would welcome some fresh air after the stuffiness of being inside. At least this Christmas she wouldn't have to cope with the misery of receiving a letter from Luke breaking off their engagement. Kate ate another mouthful of rather hard roast potato and tried hard not to think of the delicious outer crispness and inner fluffiness of Jean's roasties.

She did have something to look forward to, though, Katie reminded herself. She had agreed to partner Eddie to a dance on New Year's Eve, and a little to her own surprise she was rather excited about that. She didn't love Eddie. There was certainly nothing of the sometimes frightening intensity in her affection for him that there had been in those feelings she had had for Luke. She did like him, though, and she knew that the evening would be fun, filled with laughter, and perhaps even a few shared but non-serious kisses of the kind that New Year's Eve encouraged.

It had been a relatively easy flight from the maintenance unit where she had picked up the Spitfire, to the small RAF base just outside Newcastle – a single delivery rather than one of several shared with other pilots, all of them flying carefully under the cloud cover as they made their way to their destination. Nothing had been said at the maintenance unit, but it didn't take much to work out that the plane must be a replacement for one lost or damaged in action. Lou hoped that its pilot had made it. They'd been discussing the current on-going bombing raids over Germany at the maintenance unit and commenting on how many planes – and their crews – were being lost. Lou had thought automatically of Kieran, and had then made herself stop thinking about him as her continuing guilt over her behaviour in London took hold of her. Up ahead of her she could see the airfield. Beginning her descent, she headed for the airstrip.

Christmas in Newcastle wasn't at all what she had been expecting, Sasha acknowledged unhappily. She had tried to fit in and enjoy herself but the truth was that she missed her own family and their traditions, and somehow the fact that it was Christmas only underlined that feeling.

Bobby's mum had made her welcome enough last night, Christmas Eve, when they had arrived late after a cold stop-start journey on a packed train, greeting Sasha with a jolly, 'Why aye, Bobby lad, she's a bonny lass.' But adding to Sasha herself, 'But you're a bit on the thin side, pet.'

Sasha could understand why her mother-in-law-to-be thought that. She and her two daughters, Bobby's sisters, were all comfortably upholstered and sturdy-looking. The three of them shared the same warm-hearted manner, and Bobby's sisters, Irene and Jane, were both jolly young women who laughed a lot and ribbed one another good-naturedly whilst they talked about their work at the fish market where the fishing fleet brought in their catches.

They had all made her feel welcome but their customs and their way of life were not hers and felt more alien to her than Sasha had expected.

Now with Christmas afternoon fading into grey darkness Sasha was beginning to feel extremely sorry for herself. This morning, for instance, there had been no Christmas stocking hanging on her bed, carefully prepared by her mother, and no Lou either to share that special Christmas morning excitement with. No delicious Christmas lunch cooked by her mother either – Bobby's mother meant well, but she didn't share Sasha's mother's domestic skills. Not that Sasha felt particularly interested in food. She had so looked forward to spending Christmas with Bobby as his fiancée, the two of them an acknowledged couple, but nothing was turning out the way she had envisaged.

Take this morning. After church they had gone round to Bobby's mother's cousin's, whose husband ran a pub close to the docks. This, apparently, was one of their family traditions and the pub had been packed with family, all eager to meet Sasha. The pub had, of course, been closed for Christmas Day, but Sasha had had a horrible shock when their hostess had summoned Sasha herself and Bobby's sisters, and instructed them to go down into the cellar to bring up some more bottles of beer.

'There's no light working down there – the bulb went last night and I haven't had time to replace it – so mind how you go. I'll leave the door at the top open for you,' she had told them.

Frozen with fear at the thought of descending into the unknown darkness, Sasha had made the excuse that she needed the toilet. After that she hadn't been able to relax for fear of having to go down into the cellar.

Sasha had never given much thought to Bobby's

life at home in Newcastle before the war, but now, their Christmas Dinner over, sitting in the small cramped front room with its leatherette furniture, and squashed in the middle of the sofa between Irene and Jane, Irene's two children sitting on the floor, the coal fire hissing, and listening to his sisters ribbing Bobby about being seasick and therefore unsuited for the life of a fisherman, Sasha suddenly realised with a sharp thrill of dismay that his family were expecting them to make their home in Newcastle once the war was over and they were married.

The very thought of doing that filled Sasha with panic. She couldn't live up here so far away from her family and everything she knew. What little she had seen of Newcastle on their walk from the station and their trip to the pub this morning had shown her a city as war weary and indomitable as her own home city of Liverpool, but whilst Liverpool might also have its rows and rows of terraced houses without any greenery to be seen, her parents did not live in that kind of environment. The part of Liverpool where Sasha had grown up was on the border with Wavertree, an area that had been developed by builders to provide comfortable homes in a pleasant suburban environment for families. They might only live on the western edge of Wavertree, but they had lived within easy walking distance of its park, and its tennis club, Sasha's home was on an avenue, not on a street, and that avenue was planted with trees. Bobby's mother's house opened straight onto the pavement, and at the back of the house all there was, was a yard with a privy in it. The house did not have either an inside lavatory or a bathroom, and now it seemed that Bobby's mother was expecting them to set up home here.

'Give over, you two,' Bobby's mother told her daughters, getting up to cuff Jane, who was closer to her, good-naturedly with a large hand – Bobby's mother was twice the size of Sasha's own mother. 'You'll have poor Sasha here thinking that our Bobby won't be able to provide for her, telling him he won't get a job on a fishing boat. Don't you listen to them, pet. Our Bobby's got a job waiting for him on dry land, down at the fish market, once this lot is over and Hitler's bin sent packing. Me cousin Frank wot runs a stall down there, he's promised to see Bobby right. Of course, it won't bring in as much as he's getting now from the army. I dunno what I'd have done without him sending me half his wages every week. Still, we'll manage, eh, pet? I'd have liked to have you living here wi' me 'cos that would be more comfortable for you, like, but there isn't enough room. Our Irene's had to go and live with her in-laws, but then they've got two spare rooms, which means that there's one for the kiddies as well as one for Irene and her hubby.'

'Our gran's on her own now, Mam, since our granddad died. And she's got a spare room, Mam,' Jane chipped in. 'Bobby and Sasha can move in with her and then, wi' Sasha being there to keep an eye on our gran, you won't have to go running round there with Gran's dinners and that. You'll have to watch Gran, though, Sasha,' Jane confided.

'She's gone a bit forgetful and there's a couple of times when she's bin found wandering in the street in her nightclothes.'

Sasha had heard enough. In a panic she got to her feet and told them, 'No. When me and Bobby get married we'll be living in Liverpool, not here.'

The silence that filled the small room as Bobby's mother and sisters looked first at her and then at one another made Sasha's face burn. She knew full well that had her own mother been there she would have had a sound telling-off for her lack of manners and tact, and now she felt very alone and very close to humiliating tears.

'Had any Christmas lunch, have you?' the officer temporarily in charge of the order room asked Lou after he had cleared the paperwork for the Spit she had just delivered.

Lou shook her head.

'Well, since we've just had a report that the weather is about to close in, and we're going to have to close the airfield until tomorrow morning, why don't I see if the mess can manage an extra meal?'

She was going to have to spend the night here? It wasn't unusual for ATA pilots to be grounded because of the weather during the winter months, but that wasn't the reason Lou's heart suddenly beat faster.

'Could I possibly use the telephone?' Lou asked the ops officer. 'Only my twin sister is up here in Newcastle visiting her fiancé's family, and since I haven't seen her for months, if I can't pick up another ferry until the morning I'd like to try and meet up with her, but I shall have to ring my family in Whitchurch to get her address.'

'Help yourself,' the ops officer smiled.

EIGHTEEN

It was just as well that the people of Newcastle were so very friendly and helpful, Lou decided, as she stood on the step outside Bobby's mother's house, giving her careful directions whenever she had asked if she was going the right way. She just hoped that Sasha's reaction to her would be as warm. Their mother had certainly approved of what Lou was doing, and had said so when Lou had telephoned to Grace and Seb's cottage to get Bobby's mother's address.

Someone was coming to answer the door. The nervous butterflies in Lou's tummy grew in intensity.

Sasha was upstairs, lying on the bed in the room she was sharing with Jane, when Lou arrived, and feeling guilty and miserable, and wishing she had not rushed out and up to the bedroom in the way that she had, but not knowing how she could make amends for her behaviour.

Then Jane came pounding up the stairs to open the bedroom door and announce breathlessly, ''Ere, you'd better come down, 'cos your sister is here. Looks just like you, she does, an' all.'

All Sasha could do was stare at her. 'Lou's here?' she demanded in disbelief. 'But . . .'

'Come down and see for yourself,' Jane told her.

A little shakily Sasha got up off the bed and followed Jane out of the room and down the dusty stairs with their threadbare runner of discoloured carpet.

Bobby's mother, Jane and Bobby himself were standing in the narrow hallway, with Irene's two small children clinging to their mother's side, Bobby's mother and Irene both talking at the same time, and then as they turned towards her, she could see her twin standing there looking up at her.

'Lou!'

Sasha's voice caught on a small sob as she covered the short distance between them.

It was going to be all right. She had done the right thing, Lou recognised with relief as Sasha hugged her and she hugged her twin back.

'I can't believe that you're really here,' Sasha said for the umpteenth time later as she and Lou sat together on the leatherette sofa.

'I was a bit worried that I might be intruding,' Lou admitted. 'But it just seemed too good an opportunity to miss, especially with it being Christmas. Mum and everyone send their love, by the way.'

'You've spoken to Mum?' Sasha's voice was wistful.

'I had to ring Grace to get your address,' Lou

answered her matter-of-factly, before adding, 'The people up here are ever so kind, aren't they? I had to keep stopping to ask for directions once my lift had dropped me off at the station.'

'Oh, Lou, I'm so glad you're here,' Sasha told her twin, looking a bit teary.

'What is it? What's wrong?' Lou asked. 'You and Bobby haven't had a fall-out, have you?'

'No, but, Lou, Bobby's mother seems to think me and Bobby will be living up here once we're married. She wants us to move in with Bobby's gran.' Tears glistened in Sasha's eyes. 'I don't think I could bear it. I want to stay in Liverpool.'

'Well, you'll just have to tell Bobby that. Anyone can see that there's not much he wouldn't do to make you happy, Sash,' Lou assured her twin.

Sasha managed a slightly watery smile. Lou had always had that way of making problems seem unimportant.

Sasha took a deep breath. The unexpected arrival of her twin had broken through the barriers Sasha had erected between them and now she had a longing to unburden herself to Lou.

'I was thinking about you this morning,' Sasha agreed. 'And about Christmas.'

'I was doing the same,' Lou admitted. 'I love being in ATA, just like you love being with Bobby, but that didn't stop me feeling a bit sorry for myself this morning because I wasn't at home.'

Sasha gave Lou a grateful smile. 'That's exactly how I felt.' She added shakily, 'Lou, you know the last time we were at home together, and I had my torch? Well, it wasn't so that I could read in bed.

Lou, don't laugh at me but . . .' Sasha took another deep breath, 'sometimes I have these terrible nightmares that I'm back in that crater with the bomb. You're there too and you're holding my hand, stopping me from falling under the bomb, just like you did, but then you let go.' Sasha managed a weak smile. 'You don't say why but I sort of think it's because of Kieran and you wanting to get back to him 'cos you'd left him to find me. Anyway, you let go and then I'm falling. I can't breathe and it's dark and the bomb's there and I know that I'm going to die.'

'Oh, Sash!' Emotion dampened Lou's eyes as she hugged her twin fiercely. 'I would never let you fall, never, not for anyone, and least of all for Kieran Mallory. You and me, we're a pair. You're part of me and I'm part of you. If you were going to die under any bomb – which you aren't 'cos your Bobby rescued you – then I'd be there with you.'

This was why Sasha had been so withdrawn and had seemed so distant with her for so long, Lou recognised, and her heart ached for all that her twin must have endured, at the same time as she felt guilty because she hadn't known, and because Sasha obviously hadn't been able to tell her how she felt.

'You should have told me before,' she rebuked her gently.

'I should have done,' Sasha agreed, 'but I was so mixed up inside myself, Lou, that I couldn't. I knew you'd stayed with me but then in my dreams, when you left me, it made me feel . . . angry inside and hurt, and frightened. I couldn't tell anyone what it was like, not you and not even Bobby. I feel ever so much better now that I've told you.'

'And I feel better for knowing. I've been worrying, wondering what it's been that has made you so unhappy.'

'Oh, Lou, I'm so glad you came today,' Sasha told her. 'I've missed you so much.'

Lou knew that Sasha wasn't just talking about missing her because it was Christmas.

'I've missed you too. We've had our misunderstandings,' Lou said gruffly, 'but that doesn't mean that we don't still . . . well, we are still us, Sash, and I mean that promise I made you. You can trust me never ever to do anything that might hurt you.'

'I know. I knew that all the time really, but my bad dreams just kept getting in the way of me believing it.'

As they hugged one another tightly, Lou made a silent prayer of thankfulness that the gulf between them had finally been bridged, and promised herself that she would never let anything come between them again. She could only imagine what poor Sasha must have gone through in that bomb shaft. She knew how terrified she had been that she might lose her grip on her twin. It was no wonder the experience had had such a misery-inducing effect on her twin.

They were laughing together when Bobby's mother returned with the tea she had gone off to make, accompanied, of course, by her daughters, her grandchildren and by Bobby, who had tactfully left the sisters to have a few minutes together on their own.

'Well, I just can't get over how alike the two of you look. Got a young chap, have you yourself, Lou? Only if you had you and Sasha would look ever so lovely having a double wedding,' Bobby's mother commented.

'No. I'm single and fancy-free,' Lou answered her.

It had been a funny Christmas, Sasha thought sleepily later that night as she lay in bed. She had been so miserable earlier, but once Lou had arrived everything had changed. She'd got Bobby's mother and sisters holding their sides laughing when she'd told them some tales of their childhood antics, and then somehow or other, the turkey carpet had been rolled back and she and Lou had given them a demonstration of their dancing. This had led to Lou trying to teach Irene and Jane how to jitterbug, which had everyone breathless and giggling. Then they'd walked round to another relative of Bobby's mother's and there'd been a singsong round the piano, which Sasha had joined in instead of hanging back, thanks to Lou being there.

Having everything right again between her and Lou had lifted a weight from her shoulders she hadn't even known was there, Sasha admitted, and there'd even been enough time on the walk home, when Lou had linked up with Irene and Jane so that Sasha could fall behind everyone else with Bobby, for her to tell Bobby how much she wanted them to stay in Liverpool.

To her relief he had immediately reassured her,

telling her ruefully, 'The truth is that I've never fancied spending the rest of my life gutting fish, which is one of the reasons why I joined the army in the first place. If I could choose a job for meself when this war is over I'd go for summat like your dad does,' he had confided. 'He's a grand man, your dad, Sash, one of the best.'

'And so are you, Bobby,' Sasha had responded.

After that they had had to run to catch up with the others on account of Bobby taking advantage of their turning a corner to hold Sasha back so that he could kiss her and whisper to her, 'Happy Christmas.'

NINETEEN

'Go for a walk?' Emily looked reluctantly at the grey sky beyond the window, but Tommy was insistent, and Beauty was rushing to and fro, having heard that magic word 'walk', whilst Wilhelm was smiling at her and telling her that some fresh air would probably do them all good before they sat down to their Boxing Day tea.

'Go on then.' She gave in. 'But not too far.'

'We could walk as far as the Llangollen canal,' Tommy suggested eagerly. The canal, with its flight of staircase locks at Grindley Brook, was about a mile from the town and slightly less from Emily's house on the outskirts. The locks fascinated Tommy.

'All right then,' Emily agreed.

'Happy?' Marcus asked Fran as they walked hand in hand through the winter landscape of bare turned earth and leafless trees. They'd both agreed on how much they liked the small market town.

Marcus had been particularly interested in the history of J. B. Joyce & Co., a firm of tower clockmakers said to be oldest in the world, whilst both Fran and Grace had agreed that knowing that the heart of Sir John Talbot, Earl of Shrewsbury, had been buried under the porch of St Alkmund's church gave them goosebumps.

'Very happy,' Fran smiled in response to Marcus's question. 'Do you think it was just coincidence that our landlady decided to spend Christmas with her sister, or do you think she was being tactful in leaving us alone in the house?'

'I don't know, but whatever the cause I very much enjoyed its effect,' Marcus teased her, referring to the long leisurely lovemaking session they had enjoyed before finally getting up. After a very late breakfast-cum-early lunch they were now on their way to Grace and Seb's to spend the afternoon with the family.

Up above them the sky was a clear shade of winter blue, and in an adjacent field were sheep with coats so similar in colour to the frost-rimed grass that it was only possible to see them because of the black markings on their faces. The sight of a robin hopping from twig to twig in a nearby hedge made Fran pull on Marcus's arm to draw his attention to it, leaning her head against his shoulder as they paused to watch the robin's busyness, before continuing on their walk.

'Being here, it's almost possible to forget that there's a war on,' Fran told Marcus.

'If you disregard the work that the Y Section are doing, and the fact that there's an American hospital and an American base not all that far away,' Marcus agreed, 'although I do know what you mean. This is the England that we're fighting this war for, the England we all carry in our hearts when we're away from it.'

Fran shivered. She didn't want the reality of the war to intrude on their happiness – not today, not for a few precious hours, when Marcus was safe here with her, and everything was so peaceful.

'I really didn't want to come here once I knew you'd got leave, but I really enjoyed spending Christmas Day with the family.'

'And is that all you enjoyed?'

'Marcus,' Francine objected, but she was laughing when he stopped walking and turned her towards him, taking her in his arms.

With Tommy and Beauty running on ahead of them, Emily and Wilhelm were walking companionably together along the country lane that led eventually to the path to the canal, all three of them wrapped up warmly against the chill of the fresh winter's day, its thin sunshine doing more to make the frost sparkle and glitter than it did to give off any warmth. To the west of them the Welsh Marches and the hills lay against the horizon in blue-grey smudges topped with white, a pair of reconnaissance planes leaving white vapour trails across the sky.

She had never felt happier, Emily reflected. This morning in church, after joining in the public prayers for the fallen and for those who were still fighting, she had added a special prayer of thanks of her own for the happiness Tommy and Wilhelm had brought into her life. She gulped in some of the fresh cold air, sniffing back her own silly tears.

A sudden bend in the lane hid Tommy and Beauty from them, and automatically Emily started to walk a little faster to catch up with them, but when they too turned the corner, instead of still racing on ahead of them Emily could see Tommy standing stock-still in the middle of the path, looking at a couple who were walking towards him. Since his hand was on Beauty's collar, Emily supposed at first that he was simply holding on to his dog so that she wouldn't run up to them, but then suddenly the woman pulled away from her companion and started to run towards Tommy, crying out, 'Jack!' and immediately Tommy turned and ran, not towards Emily, but across the field, fleeing as though for his life, his dog at his heels.

It was even worse than her worst nightmare, Emily recognised. The woman was standing white-faced, and in shock, staring, the man with her trying to comfort her, whilst Wilhelm had gone after Tommy, leaving Emily standing alone to confront what she had always dreaded.

'That boy,' the woman begged Emily. 'Who is he? Only he looks so like . . .'

In the distance across the field Emily could see that Wilhelm had caught up with Tommy. She had had a chance to look properly at the woman now. She was very pretty and somehow familiar, her expression, a mix of shock, disbelief and hope, turning a knife in Emily's heart.

The man was speaking, his voice calm and firm

as he explained, 'My wife lost her . . . a close relative in tragic circumstances. He'd been evacuated to Wales and the farm where he was staying was bombed, and the boy—'

'I should never have let Vi send him away again. I should have stopped her.'

Francine's eyes were huge with shock, her heart still pounding from the moment when the boy had come running towards them, running exactly as Jack had run, and looking so like her dead child that her heart had immediately reached out to him, just as her arms had wanted to do. Then he had seen her and he had looked at her and in that second, when their gazes had locked, Francine had known that, incredible though it was, the boy was Jack.

'It is him. I know it is. He recognised me, Marcus. He looked at me and . . .'

The woman looked close to collapsing, Emily recognised. She, on the other hand, felt as though she had been turned to stone, as though she was incapable of doing anything other than just standing there.

'His name's Tommy. Not Jack,' Emily told the woman. She could see Wilhelm and Tommy making their way back towards the cottage, but keeping well away from the lane. 'I'm sorry you've had such a shock. It can't be easy – losing a child.' Emily turned round, not wanting to prolong things; not wanting to give the woman the opportunity to tell her any more. She didn't want to know any more. She didn't want to know about her heartache, her heartbreak over the loss of her son, she didn't want to hear anything that might tell her that that son was her Tommy.

She didn't want to hear, but she had to ask, for Tommy's sake, Emily acknowledged later that night, sitting beside Tommy's bed whilst he slept, Beauty for once allowed to sleep on the floor beside him.

He hadn't said a word when they had all got back to the cottage, but his face had been white and his eyes filled with dread.

Emily had tried to behave as normally as possible, not asking him anything, just going about their normal routine, and gradually the stiffness and the fear that had him constantly looking towards the door had eased out of him.

They had talked about what happened, her and Wilhelm, after Tommy had gone to bed.

'What shall I do if Tommy is hers, and she tries to take him from me?' she had asked, but Wilhelm had not been able to answer her.

Now, though, looking down at Tommy's sleeping face in the faint light from his nightlight, Emily understood that she already knew what she must do. Tommy's happiness was far more important to her than anything else, far more important than her own. She tried to think how she might feel were she a child who had thought its true mother lost and who had gone through all that Tommy had gone through. Surely such a child would be overjoyed to be reunited with its mother, and not run away from her? If the woman tried to take Tommy away, she would not let him go until and unless she was sure he wanted to be with her, Emily decided fiercely. If she was his mother and he wanted to be with her then she would have to let him go, but even if she was his mother and he didn't – then she wouldn't. But how would she know what he really wanted? Tommy was a loyal little soul who knew how much he meant to her.

She was going to have to talk to him properly Emily realised, no matter how painful that was for both of them.

'Mum?' The sound of Tommy's voice brought Emily from her light sleep in the chair beside his bed. His hand was clutching hers, his voice anxious.

'Yes, I'm here, love,' she reassured him.

'You won't let anyone take me away from you, will you, and go and live with them?'

'I won't let anyone make you do anything you don't want to do, Tommy. Not anyone,' Emily stressed.

Tommy exhaled and went silent.

'Why don't you tell me all about what happened before you and me met, Tommy?' Emily suggested gently.

'You won't send me back to them, my mum and dad?'

'I won't do anything ever that you don't want me to do, Tommy,' Emily told him truthfully. 'But that lady we saw today – your mum was she—'

'No. Not my mum, she's my auntie. I liked her. She was kind to me, but she promised . . . They never wanted me, my mum and dad, they were always saying what a nuisance I was. When the war started they sent me away to this farm. The farmer made us work hard and there was never enough food. I ran away, but they made me go back. They said I had to be evacuated and that I was making a fuss over nothing. They said that because the farmer had told them that I'd caused him a lot of trouble I'd be going to another farm. They said it would be best for me on account of the war, but really it was because they didn't like me and because I was a nuisance. My mother said that she wasn't surprised that the farmer got angry with me and my father said that I deserved a good hiding.'

Emily's hand tightened around Tommy's, maternal fury burning inside her chest at the thought of such inhuman cruelty to her precious boy.

'So you ran away, did you, after you'd been evacuated again, and came back to Liverpool?'

Tommy nodded. 'There was a bomb. It hit the farm. I was frightened that they'd send me to another farm if I stayed, so I left.'

Emily had always known that he must have a family somewhere but she'd assumed that he had either become separated from them or they had been killed, never dreaming that he had been treated with such unkindness that he had preferred to live rough rather than go home. The story Tommy had given her, though, was a child's story told from a child's perspective. His parents might in reality be desperately grieving for him. That woman today had looked at him with so much yearning in her eyes, and according

282

to Tommy she was only his aunt. She would be back, Emily knew, and when she came she would try to take Tommy from her.

'Your mum and dad—' she began.

But Tommy stopped her, insisting emotionally, 'You're my mum now, not her. I won't go back to them, I won't.' His voice rose and filled with a panic that caused the dog to get up off the floor and move protectively towards him.

She felt so much happier now that things were back to normal between her and Sasha, Lou acknowledged as she sat down on the edge of her bed back at her base at Thame, to read her mail.

The sun coming in through the narrow leaded window of her room threw small oblongs of light across the oak floor, the now familiar smell of old house and dust making her nose itch. As her room was at the end of the corridor the comings and goings of the other girls who shared the accommodation were muted to her, the sounds of footsteps on the bare wooden stairs, the opening and closing of doors, the voices of her fellow ATA pilots only just audible on the still air.

Her room felt cold after her absence. They weren't allowed to light fires in the huge fireplaces in their rooms because of the risk of the old wing of the house catching fire, but it was tempting to imagine just how cosy the room would have been with a fire burning in the grate. In your dreams, Lou mocked herself. Even if having a fire wasn't banned, coal itself was rationed. She looked back at the post she was holding, frowning slightly at the unfamiliar writing on one of the envelopes. Curiously, she opened the letter.

> I need to see you a.s.a.p. I've got a pass for 20 Jan, and I think I can borrow a car from a pal so I'll drive over and pick you up, hopefully just before lunch.

It was signed 'Kieran'.

What did Kieran mean, he 'needed' to see her? Lou felt both irritated and anxious. Why hadn't he explained why he 'needed' to see her?

'Have you decided what you're going to wear on New Year's Eve yet?' The sound of June's voice had Lou stuffing Kieran's letter into her pocket out of sight, guiltily reminded of the way she had deceived her friend.

'I don't think Jean really approves of what I'm doing,' Francine told Marcus as they walked towards the pretty row of cottages where Emily – and Jack – lived.

It hadn't taken long for Francine to find out Emily's address. Whitchurch was only a small place, and when she'd telephoned this morning to say that she wanted to talk to her, Francine had got the impression that the other woman hadn't been surprised.

Of course, she'd told the others what had happened the minute they'd arrived at Grace and Seb's, and Grace herself had then admitted that she had thought that she'd seen a boy in Whitchurch who looked uncannily like Jack.

'I wouldn't get your hopes up, Fran,' Jean had cautioned her. 'This boy probably just has a look of Jack, that's all.'

'No, it was Jack. I could tell from the way he looked at me before he ran away that he recognised me.'

'She just doesn't want you to be disappointed, or hurt,' Marcus told her.

'Hurt?' Fran looked at him.

'The boy ran away when he saw you, Fran,' he reminded her gently. 'You've said yourself that he had a rotten life with your sister and her husband. He's old enough to have been able to say who his family are and where they are, but obviously he has chosen not to do so.'

'But, Marcus, he's my son. My son, and not hers. My son, who I thought was dead.'

As she spoke Fran's voice trembled with pain and anger. How could another woman have claimed Jack? Had she no pity, no compassion, no understanding of how she, Jack's real mother, might be feeling, believing that her child was dead? But underneath her anger Fran was battling not to listen to the critical inner voice telling her that she had never been a proper mother to Jack and that she had let him down. This was a voice she didn't want to hear.

'Jack's mine. He belongs with me. With us, Marcus,' she insisted.

Marcus squeezed her hand, but did not make any response.

* * *

285

Emily hadn't been surprised when Francine had rung to say that she would like to talk to her. She'd been expecting her to make contact, and, of course, dreading it. Emily knew in her bones that Tommy's auntie would want to make a claim on her nephew. Emily had seen it in her eyes when they had met in the lane. Emily had no proper legal right to Tommy, not really, even if she did have those false papers she had managed to get when she had first taken him in, claiming that he was the son of her dead cousin. They wouldn't stand up in a court of law if things were to get nasty. Emily's stomach was twisting itself into painful knots. She hadn't said anything to Tommy about her fears. The poor lad was upset and worried enough.

'Your auntie wants to come and see me,' she had told him after the phone call, and immediately he had got all upset.

'She can't take me away. I won't go with her,' he insisted in a panic.

'No one's going to take you away from me, Tommy, unless you want them to,' Emily had tried to reassure him, forced to acknowledge deep inside herself that whilst Tommy was saying now that he wanted to be with her, he might change his mind. His auntie was his own blood, after all, even if she, Emily, hated having to acknowledge that fact.

Determined to put him first and do her best for him, she had told him, 'Listen, I'm going to make you a promise now and then I want you to make me one, all right?'

He had nodded and waited.

'I promise you that whatever you want to do, whoever you want to be with, I will make sure that you can. Whatever you want to do, Tommy, do you understand? And in return I want you to promise me that you will tell me honestly what it is that you want. Not now . . . not just yet . . . but you'll know when the time is right. Promise?'

When he flung himself into her arms and replied gruffly, 'Promise,' Emily had held him tightly. Parting with him would break her heart, but far better that her heart was broken than his.

However, she certainly wasn't going to have his auntie crying all over him and making him feel bad, so she'd sent him out of the house with Wilhelm and the dog – for his own sake – whilst she heard what his auntie had to say.

'This is the house.'

Francine looked at the pretty Georgian building, and then took a deep breath. Jack was her son. Twice now she'd allowed others to overrule her and to take him from her. Well, she wasn't going to let it happen a third time.

Francine looked round the warm comfortable kitchen, a proper family kitchen, her critical inner voice pointed out, not like the cold clinical kitchen of Vi's house.

She looked at Marcus. She was so thankful that he was here with her and that this hadn't happened whilst he had been away on duty. He was holding her hand firmly in his own, his presence helping her to stay calm.

Emily had intended to take them into the front room after she had let them in, and he, Tommy's auntie's husband, had introduced them both, but then she had told herself that she had nothing to hide from Tommy's auntie and that she certainly wasn't going to put on airs and graces for her.

Tommy had told her already that he didn't know the man who'd been with his auntie, so Emily guessed that they couldn't have been married that long.

'I've sent Tommy out whilst we have our discussion,' Emily told Francine, lifting her chin determinedly. 'Proper upset, he's been, begging me not to let you take him back to those parents of his who don't seem to have cared tuppence about him, from what he's told me.'

Francine looked at Marcus. They'd discussed the necessity for her to reveal her real relationship with Jack, and that it was his mother that was claiming him and not merely an aunt, but now that the moment had come to do so, Francine was uncomfortably aware of how her past would appear to another woman. Her heart was thudding into her chest. Emily's blunt accusation made her feel so guilty.

'There's no question of Jack going back to live with Vi,' she told Emily immediately. 'He will be living with us in London, won't he, Marcus?' she appealed to her husband.

Emily wasn't having that. 'An auntie he barely

knows and an uncle he doesn't know at all? Where's the sense in that? It's bad enough that the poor lad was treated the way he was by his mum and dad. Begged me to promise him that he wouldn't have to go back to them, he has. Not that they seem to care much about him. If they did then they'd be here, wouldn't they?' Emily demanded with irrefutable logic, which Francine could only contradict by bursting out, 'The reason they aren't here is because they aren't really his parents.'

This wasn't how she had intended their discussion to go, but it was important that this woman, who was behaving as though she had the maternal right to protect Jack, should know what the real situation was, Francine defended her outburst to herself. She looked silently at Marcus for his support.

He gave it promptly. 'What my wife has said is the truth. The Firths are not Jack's real mother and father, even though they brought him up as their son.'

'Then whose son is he?' Emily demanded, even though she had already begun to suspect the truth. No mere auntie would behave as the woman in front of her was doing.

'He's mine,' Francine answered. 'Jack is my son, although of course he doesn't know it.'

Emily was trying desperately not to let the couple see how afraid what she had just learned made her feel.

'A mother who turned her back on him and let him be treated badly,' she couldn't stop herself from accusing Francine.

Immediately Marcus leaped to Francine's defence, saying firmly, 'My wife didn't know—'

But Francine stopped him, shaking her head and telling him determinedly, 'No, Marcus, let me explain. She's got a right to know the truth, and so, when he's ready to hear it, will Jack.'

Lifting her head Francine looked Emily in the eye and told her unsteadily, 'I was only a girl when Jack was born. A girl without a husband who'd got herself into trouble. My mother was ill. There was no one for me to turn to except my sister Vi. When she begged me to let her and her husband adopt Jack, saying that they'd love him and look after him, I agreed because I thought I was doing the best thing for him.'

She mustn't allow herself to feel sympathy, Emily determined, ignoring the tears shining in Francine's eyes.

'You thought but you didn't bother to find out, did you?' she demanded briskly. 'You didn't care enough to see that your sister and her husband were making him unhappy and treating him badly, poor little lad. Scared to death of your sister's husband, he was, and always being sent to bed supperless and made to feel he wasn't wanted, from what he's told me.'

'Do you think I'd have let that happen if I'd known?' Francine demanded, white-faced. 'Vi made me promise not to have any contact with him. She said it was for his sake. I thought that Vi would love him. I went to work in America. Vi encouraged me to go.'

Marcus put his arm round her to comfort her.

This was awful, Fran thought. So much worse than she had anticipated it was going to be. This woman was behaving as though she had deliberately abandoned Jack, and that wasn't true.

'I missed him dreadfully. I thought about him every day, imagining him growing up. I wanted to be with him. It was only when I came back that I found out what was going on. Vi had had Jack evacuated, even though Jean, my other sister, had tried to persuade her not to.'

Francine paused to take a deep breath and steady her voice. 'When he ran away and turned up at Jean's, too afraid to go home, I thought it must have been meant to be. I wanted to tell him then – I wanted to – but Jean said that I shouldn't, that it wouldn't be fair to him, and then Vi started creating and I knew that if I tried to do anything it would only make things worse for Jack, so I had to let him go . . . again.' She had to turn into the loving protection of Marcus's arm as the memory of that awful time came flooding back to her.

When she had herself back under control she turned to look at Emily again. The other woman hadn't moved. Her face, set and bleached of colour, was devoid of any expression, but Francine knew how Emily would be judging her, and finding her wanting.

'I couldn't bear it. I wanted to be with him so much. I tried to see him. I drove out to the farm where he'd been evacuated to, but it had been hit by a bomb. There was nothing left of it . . . and I thought . . . that is, everyone said . . . that Jack would have been killed along with the farmer and his wife.'

Emily said nothing. The truth was that she dare not speak. The story Francine had told her would surely tear at the coldest stoniest heart, and her heart was far from that. Just because she felt sorry for the woman that did not mean that she should give Tommy up to her, Emily told herself. It was what Tommy himself wanted that mattered, not anyone else.

'I don't know how my Jack came to be with you, but you must have realised that he had a family,' she accused Emily.

'What I realised was that he was like a little starving animal, creeping out of the shadows behind the Royal Court Theatre to live off scraps of food,' Emily told her, her sympathy for Tommy's mother vanishing as she remembered the poor little boy's plight. 'Couldn't even speak then – not so much as a word, and so thin that . . . It took me a good while to coax him round, and with my late husband's favourite salmon sandwiches as well. Con would have had a fit if he'd known. Well, he did have a fit when I told him that Tommy was coming to live with us, but I soon told him what was what.'

'Con?' Francine demanded, white-faced.

Emily looked at her, and suddenly realised why her face had seemed so familiar.

The two women stared at one another, the silence in the kitchen broken only when Emily gave a small sigh.

'I remember you now,' she told Francine. She

292

did remember her, a very pretty, very young girl working at the theatre, one of Con's girls. Tension replaced the earlier silence. Emily took a deep breath, putting two and two together. 'So it was Con who got you into trouble, was it?'

Con, Tommy's father. The thought gave her quite a turn, and oddly, made it seem all the more right and proper in a way that Tommy should have found his way to her, Emily thought.

'Yes,' Francine admitted. 'I loved him and I thought he loved me.'

'Con never loved anyone but himself,' Emily told her matter-of-factly, before adding, 'You'd certainly never have known that Tommy was his. Tommy doesn't take after Con, thank goodness. Never did have much patience with him, Con didn't, especially when I first took Tommy in and he couldn't speak.'

Emily looked directly at Francine, so elegant and smartly dressed, and so ladylike too, with her expensive clothes and her officer husband, who plainly adored her and who equally plainly knew all about her past, Emily acknowledged with grudging respect. It couldn't have been easy, admitting what she'd done.

'I'd never have put you down as one of them that were daft enough to be taken in by Con,' she felt obliged to say. 'Not looking at you now.'

'I thought he loved me. I was young and silly.'

'And he had a smooth tongue and a handsome face,' Emily supplied for her. 'Well, you weren't the first and you certainly weren't the last. You know he's dead?'

'Yes. My sister mentioned it.'

'There was no real harm in him, just weak, that's what he was,' Emily felt bound to say, although there was no real reason why she should defend her late husband, she told herself. 'Weak and too good-looking for his own good, that was Con. They were the death of him in the end – that weakness and his good looks.'

'I want my son and I mean to have him,' Francine told Emily, gathering strength from having told Emily of her claim on Jack. She would never have recognised this trim determined-looking woman as the same worn-down creature she remembered Con's wife to be.

'I love Tommy just as much as though I'd given birth to him myself,' Emily responded. 'Him and me, we've been happy together. He loves it here in Whitchurch. Doing ever so well at school he is too, and the headmaster reckons he could go on to university if he applies himself.'

Francine could hear the love and pride in Emily's voice. She was still trying to come to terms with the fact that Emily had been Con's wife, almost as though fate had decided that Jack should grow up living with one of his real parents. She pushed the thought away.

'A boy needs a father,' she told Emily, 'and Marcus—'

'When this war is over, me and Wilhelm will be getting married. Thinks the world of Wilhelm, Tommy does, and Wilhelm's been like a proper dad to him,' Emily immediately defended her own position.

'He's my son.'

Emily took a deep breath. 'You can say that all you like and it won't make a bit of difference to me, but I've made Tommy a promise that I'll make sure he gets to do whatever he wants, and be with whoever he wants, and I aim to keep that promise. I won't stand aside and see him dragged away from here if that isn't what he wants. I know what you're thinking and you're right. Of course I want him to stay with me, but I won't stand in his way if he decides he wants to go back to his family. What he wants matters more to me than what I want.'

Francine's eyes stung with tears. She felt humbled and helpless, filled with remorse and longing, recognising that this woman truly loved her son, and had probably saved his life when she had taken him in.

But he was her son.

'What I'm going to suggest,' Emily continued, 'is that you leave him here with me for now, to give him time to decide what he wants to do. You can come and see him whenever you want. You can tell him the truth or you can keep it from him, but what I will not tolerate is you or anyone else trying to make up his mind for him. If, at the end of six months, he wants to leave here to be with you then I won't stand in his way, and by the same token, if you love him only half as much as I do, you'll feel the same if things are the other way round.'

'I think that's a very fair suggestion.' It was Marcus who spoke, his arm around Francine's shoulders as he pulled her close to him. 'My wife loves her son every bit as much as you do, and, like you, all she wants is for him to be happy.'

'That's that then,' Emily said firmly, her gaze turning to the back door as they all heard it opening.

The dog came in first, followed by Tommy and then Wilhelm, both of them removing their boots and then their coats, standing the boots neatly side by side and then hanging up their coats on the pegs behind the door.

Watching them, Francine felt her heart ache with longing and with a small pang of sadness when she saw how Jack, her Jack, echoed the actions and mannerisms of the big German. It should have been Marcus Jack was mimicking, Marcus who he was looking up to.

Jack hadn't looked at her at all, not properly, and now he skirted round her, rushing to Emily's side and burying his head against her as he said fiercely, 'I want to stay here with you. Don't let them take me away.'

Once again Marcus stepped in, saying gently, 'No one's going to take you anywhere you don't want to go, son.'

'Your auntie's going to come to Whitchurch every now and again so that you and she can catch up with one another,' Emily told Tommy calmly.

She knew what Francine was hoping for. She was hoping that Tommy would change his mind once he got to know her. She was hoping that blood would be thicker than water. And maybe she would be right. Maybe Tommy would start to want to be with her and his family. But that was a chance she had to take, Emily knew, for Tommy's sake.

TWENTY

'So, do tell, sweetie, was Kieran Mallory as good at you-know-what as he looks as though he is. You must know. After all, you spent the whole night in his hotel room with him. Ah, don't try to deny it. You were seen leaving by a very old friend of mine who just happened to be staying in the same hotel, when Kieran hurried you out of his room.'

Lou went white and then red. The gaze of all the other girls sitting round the table was fixed on her, she knew, but most especially June's.

This was worse than her worse nightmares. She hadn't been particularly pleased when she and June and the two other girls from their ferry pool had ended up on a table in the makeshift 'ballroom' at the large American base where the dance was being held with a crowd of American ATA pilots, but she had never envisaged something like this happening. She'd recognised Nadine straight away, of course. After all, she had been the one who had given them their free drinks. It was quite plain to Lou that Nadine was enjoying the embarrassment and discomfort she was causing her. Did she know about the amphetamine that had been put in her drink, Lou wondered bitterly.

'And to think we thought you Brits were staid and a bit on the prim side. Mind you, he is a honey. You've really got Patti's back up, you know. She'd had her eye on him for ages before you popped up and got in first, and Patti doesn't like being upstaged by other girls.'

'I think there must be some mistake,' was all Lou could manage to protest, but the American girl merely laughed.

'Honey, the big mistake was yours when you didn't take more care not to be spotted when you left. I can tell you that the gossip is buzzing everywhere, and we girls are all fearfully envious of you for being so . . . well, so daring when it comes to the conventions. We didn't think you Brit ATAs did things like that. We thought you were all prim lips and firmly crossed legs. My friend says there's a gang of bomber pilots all waiting to queue up to offer you a room the next time you're on leave.'

Lou's face burned with shame.

'The next thing we know you'll be challenging one of us to a race to see who can fly fastest and lowest under the Severn Bridge, although I should warn you that Patti is an ace at doing it. She's even beaten a couple of your Spitfire boys.'

The bridge in question was notorious for attracting show-off pilots and equally notorious for the number of pilots who had lost their lives because of it.

She was in trouble, Lou recognised, and the truth was that she didn't know how to get herself out of it. She suspected that even if she had gone public from the start and had explained what had happened there would still be those who would have chosen not to believe her and to make the same assumptions about the nature of her night in Kieran's room that were being made now.

Of course, whatever enjoyment she might have found in their New Year's Eve dance was now ruined – along with her reputation, Lou acknowledged. From now on she would have to wonder if every man who so much as asked her for a dance was secretly doing so because of the gossip that would spread about her; and it would spread – like aero fuel deliberately spilled and set alight, exploding in a sheet of fire that would devour everything it could. Only in her case what would be devoured and destroyed would be her reputation.

She glanced at June, her heart turning an uncomfortable somersault when her friend quickly looked away. June had every right to be angry with her, Lou knew, and she had never needed the support of a good friend more than she did now.

The room had been decorated for New Year's Eve with bunting in red, white and blue, and Stars and Stripes, and that theme had been followed with the food – American food made from American supplies shipped over to stock the American bases' PX stores and canteens – luxuries such as cakes with proper icing, plates full of Hershey bars rewrapped in Stars and Stripes paper, and of course hot dogs and 'sodas', along with plates heaped with chicken, and bread that tasted of proper bread and not the horrible 'national loaf' that Britain was obliged to eat because there was nothing else.

Prizes handed out to the winners of the games played by the Tables – pass the parcel being one of the favourites – were pairs of stockings for every girl seated at that table, and were received with delight. But when Lou and June's table won, all Lou could feel was a tight numbness that isolated her and prevented her from joining in the fun and laughter.

The band was excellent, but the last thing Lou felt like doing was dancing. When midnight came, instead of singing 'Auld Lang Syne' with everyone else whilst the lights were dimmed and the nets holding up the balloons above the dance floor were released, Lou was on her own in the ladies' lavatory, feeling wretched and worrying herself sick about what the outcome of the gossip about her was going to be.

June hadn't spoken a single word to her since the American girl's revelations.

The evening was ruined, of course, and with it Lou's composure.

It was only when they had been dropped off at their base in the early hours of the morning and the two of them were trudging in silence towards their dormitory that June finally spoke to Lou, saying bitterly, 'Well, I never thought of you as a liar, Lou. I thought you and me were good pals but it seems I was wrong.'

301

'June, please let me explain,' Lou begged her friend.

'Explain what? If what Nadine said wasn't true and you really did spend the night at your auntie's, like you told me, then why didn't you say so at the table?'

'It isn't as simple as that.'

'It seems pretty simple to me. Either you spent the night at your auntie's or you lied to me.'

'I did spend the night in Kieran's room,' Lou was forced to admit. 'No, wait, June,' she pleaded as her friend made to walk away from her, Lou reaching out to grab her arm to stop her. 'There was a reason why that happened.'

'And we all know what that reason was.'

'No!' Lou denied forcefully. 'No. It wasn't like that at all. Me and Kieran go back a fair way. Me and my sister Sasha knew him in Liverpool. We were a couple of daft kids with stars in our eyes wanting to be on the stage. He was working for his uncle who worked in the theatre.'

'So you were old friends and now you're—'

'We aren't anything,' Lou denied. 'It wasn't like that. Do you remember how I was dancing when we were at that club?'

When June nodded, Lou went on quietly, 'Kieran reckons that someone probably slipped a couple of those amphetamine pills into my drink.'

June pursed her lips, looking far from convinced. 'Amphetamines? You mean those pills some of the pilots take to help them stay awake?'

'That's right.'

'Who would want to put something like that in your drink?'

'That pilot Patti. You heard what Nadine was saying tonight. Kieran reckons she did it out of spite and to have a laugh at my expense when I made a fool of myself. And I *was* making a fool of myself before Kieran stepped in and stopped me, acting like a know-it-all older brother.'

'Oh, a brother, is it? But he isn't your brother, is he?'

'Please don't be like that, June,' Lou begged. 'I know I should have told you. I wanted to, but Kieran said it was better not . . . that it wouldn't be fair to involve you.' There was no point in making a bad situation worse by telling June that Kieran had suggested she might be tempted to gossip.

'All Kieran intended to do was see me safely back to our hotel but I couldn't remember the address and so in the end he took me back to his instead. Nothing happened between us, nothing at all. June . . . June,' Lou protested as her friend pulled away from her and started to walk towards their dormitory without saying anything.

Helplessly Lou began to follow her. It was plain that June didn't believe her and if she didn't then what chance was there of anyone else doing so?

'I shouldn't have left him with her, Marcus. He's my son. I should have been firmer.'

'No,' Marcus told Francine as she paced the floor of their London apartment, her beauty only enhanced by the emotion gripping her. 'No, you did the right thing, and I'm proud of you for doing that, for putting Jack first.'

'He looked at me as though . . . as though he was afraid of me, and he looked at her . . .' Francine's voice broke on a sob. 'I'm his mother but he ran to her as though she was the one who . . .'

'He's a boy, Fran. A boy who had a pretty miserable life with your sister and her husband, from what you've told me – no, that wasn't your fault,' Marcus went on when Francine would have interrupted him. 'You did what you believed was best for him and out of love for him, when you were still only a child yourself. But it's only natural that he has become attached to the person who, in his eyes, has given him the love he never had before.'

'She said that she first saw him at the Royal Court Theatre. That's where I told him he could find me, when . . . when Vi insisted on having him evacuated again. He had gone there looking for me, Marcus, for me, not for her. I should have been there. I shouldn't have run away like I did, joining ENSA because . . . That's twice now I've run away and left him. I shan't do it a third time. This time I shall stay and I'll prove to him that I love him. His place is with us, Marcus. Surely you agree with me. After all, you know what it's like to lose a child . . .'

'We both know that, but does either of us know what it's like to be a child who is forced away from the one person he believes loves him, the person who has given him security, who has put him first? And Emily has done all of those things for him, Fran. You only have to look at the boy to know that.'

'You're taking her side.' Francine's voice was filled with despair.

Marcus shook his head. 'No. If I'm taking anyone's side, it's his, Jack . . . Tommy.'

'He looked so frightened when he saw me. He looked at me the same way he looked at Vi when she came to Jean's to take him away from me. I can't bear to think of how awful things must have been for him, the farm being bombed and everything, and then him finding his way back to Liverpool to find me, but me not being there.' She was crying in earnest now.

Marcus took her in his arms and rocked her gently. 'I do understand how you feel,' he told her, 'but we're adults, Fran, and Jack is only a boy. We have to think of what's best for him and not what we want.'

'And you think that it's best for him to be with her – Emily.'

'No. What I'm saying is that I'm proud of you for holding back and for not forcing the issue, and that I think that the best thing you can do for him is to give him time to get to know you. Ultimately he must be the one who decides where he wants to be.'

'How can he make that decision when legally Vi and Edwin are his parents?'

'Without the boy's co-operation there's no way of proving that he is Jack, and he's not going to give that co-operation if he thinks he'll be forced to go back to your sister. Give him time, Fran, time and the confidence to know that he won't be forced to do anything he doesn't want to do.'

'Time to recognise that I am his mother and that he should be with me . . . with us. Yes, you're right, that is what I must do.'

TWENTY-ONE

Katie paused to laugh out loud in the middle of reading Luke's latest letter in which he described the delights of the army rations Christmas dinner 'enjoyed' by him and his men.

'Even the stray dogs that have attached themselves to our camp turned up their noses at it,' Luke had written.

It took courage and fortitude to write so amusingly about the hardships of their situation, Katie reflected. Luke didn't give any detail about the danger he and his men faced, but Katie had become avidly attentive to everything she could read and hear about the Italian campaign, her heart in her mouth every time there was any mention of the combat with the enemy.

The Allied Forces were having to fight for every single advance they made towards Rome, through the rugged terrain of the Apennines, both from the east and from the west, where Katie had decided that Luke must be.

She tucked his letter into her handbag as the train reached her underground stop.

307

The January weather was cold and damp, and streets busy with people hurrying back to work after their lunch break, as she was doing herself.

She had enjoyed herself with Gina and Leonard, and of course Eddie, on New Year's Eve. With the threat of an invasion now over and Hitler no longer bombing the city, the atmosphere at the Savoy had been one of optimism mingled with an impatience for the war to be over.

'We've got a long way to go yet,' Leonard had cautioned. 'The only way we can win is via an invasion of the north coast of France. We know that, and so too, you maybe sure, does Hitler.'

'We'll win. I'm sure of it,' Gina had forecast determinedly, and that had been their toast when the bells of London – no longer forbidden to ring – had rung out to welcome in the New Year.

At the Postal Censorship Office, the large room in which everyone worked smelled of damp clothes and stale air, but at least it was relatively warm stale air, Katie acknowledged as she made her way to her desk. However, before she could sit down the girl in charge of her desk tapped her on the shoulder and told her quietly, 'Miss Pearson wants to see you in her office.'

Since Miss Pearson, who was in charge of them all, rarely summoned anyone to her office, Katie tried to think of anything she might have done wrong, as she hurried into the corridor.

To her astonishment, Miss Pearson herself was waiting just inside the open mahogany door, with its scrolled and etched glass upper half, through which one could only see the shadowy outlines of anyone inside.

'Katie. Good. Come in and sit down.' Ushering her inside, Miss Pearson closed the door behind them, reducing the busy hum from the main office to a faintness that only intensified Katie's tension.

'We haven't got much time because Gina will be here in a second. You know one another very well, I understand.'

'We're good friends, yes,' Katie agreed, bewildered by Miss Pearson's questions.

'You attended her wedding – you knew her husband?'

In her confusion Katie almost missed it – that significant and horribly meaningful use of the past tense, but when she realised what was actually being said, her heart started to thump heavily with dread.

'I . . . yes. I was there when Gina and Leonard first met.'

'She is going to need the support of a good friend, I'm afraid, which is why I've asked for you to be here. Ah . . .' Miss Pearson looked up from her desk and over Katie's head towards the door. 'Here she comes now.'

Gina looked as bewildered as Katie had felt when she had first been ushered in to Miss Pearson's office, giving Katie herself a look of enquiry before taking the chair next to her.

'I'm really sorry to have to be the bearer of bad news, my dear. There really is no easy way to tell you this,' Miss Pearson announced without any preamble. 'This office received a telephone call half an hour ago from your father-in-law.'

Katie reached for Gina's hand and held it tightly.

'One of the children?' Gina asked, anxiously half rising from her chair. 'Something's happened . . . ?'

'No, it's not the children. The authorities have been in touch with your father-in-law to advise him that his son, your husband, is missing in action, presumed—'

'No!' Pulling her hand free of Katie's, Gina stood up, her denial as sharp as a burst of gunfire.

'I really am sorry. Your father-in-law has asked that you be granted compassionate leave in order that you can return home, and that of course has been granted.'

'No. I won't believe it.' Gina overrode her superior. 'Leonard can't be dead. He can't be. He mustn't be.'

'I'm so sorry, my dear.'

Miss Pearson stood up and looked at Katie. 'Perhaps you would be kind enough to assist Gina with making her preparations to return to her husband's family home. I understand that her father-in-law is concerned for the health of his wife, and that as yet the news has not been broken to the children.'

Katie nodded.

They were alone in Miss Pearson's office. Gina was sitting staring blankly at the wall, the silence of the room thick with emotion.

'It isn't true. I won't let it be true,' she told Katie.

Katie reached for her hand. It felt cold, Gina's

310

wedding ring gleaming dully in the thin office light.

'It can't be true, Katie.' Gina's voice had started to rise, tears filling her eyes and spilling from them as she begged, 'Please, God, don't let it be true. Not Leonard.'

More silence and then Gina said fiercely, 'It isn't true. There's been a mistake. There's got to have been a mistake. Leonard can't be dead. Not my Leonard. It's too soon for me to lose him, Katie. God couldn't be so cruel.'

'Lou?'

June's hesitant voice had Lou turning round to look at her former friend, as she headed towards the house. She'd had an unexpected day off after her collections had been cancelled, due to a hold-up at the factory, so she'd walked into Thame, along the pretty Buckinghamshire lanes. It had been market day – not that there was much on the market stalls, thanks to rationing. After a cup of tea in a small teashop she had walked back. It was the kind of thing she would normally have done with June, had they still been friends. She and June had barely seen one another since she had tried to tell June the truth and June had walked off, because of the heavy workload the ferry pool had had to deal with, something for which Lou had been grateful. It was horrible knowing that the reason for the silence whenever she walked into a room where other pilots were gathered was because they had been talking about her.

Like June, this afternoon she was wearing her

uniform skirt and jacket, and, of course, her red lipstick – applying it automatically now.

Uncertainly she waited for June to catch up with her, astonishment widening her eyes when June said uncomfortably, 'I've been thinking about . . . about what you told me, Lou, and . . . well, perhaps I was a bit hard on you, flaring up at you the way I did.' She smoothed down the skirt of her uniform, looking embarrassed.

'That's all right,' Lou answered. 'I shouldn't have lied to you about what happened.'

They exchanged uncertain looks, neither of them paying any attention to the comings and goings around them.

'Kieran's coming to see me.'

Now it was June's eyes that widened as she moved out of the way of two other girls who were obviously heading for the girls' wing of the house.

'So the two of you *are* an item—' she began, but Lou shook her head, squinting into the sunlight.

'No. What I told you about him and me was the truth.'

'Then why does he want to see you?'

'I don't know for sure, but I suppose he's heard the gossip.'

'He's bound to have done. When are you seeing him?'

'Tomorrow. I've booked a day's leave. I'm owed some for working over Christmas. I just wish I had never touched that drink,' Lou sighed heavily.

'That wasn't your fault. How were you to know? It's that Patti who's the one to blame, for ruining your—' June broke off and looked flustered.

312

'It's all right, you can say it,' Lou told her. 'After all, it's the truth. My reputation *is* ruined.'

'There's a lot of talk still about the whole thing,' June acknowledged reluctantly. 'I think that some of the Americans are deliberately stirring the pot and keeping it going. Has anyone higher up said anything to you about it?'

'No, but some of the senior girls have been pretty cool with me.'

'Oh, Lou, I'm so sorry, but people are bound to forget about it in time,' June tried to console her taking a step closer to her and putting her hand on her arm.

Lou looked down at the grass. It wouldn't do at all to start blubbing, even if June's kindness was such a relief that she did feel like crying.

'In time,' she agreed, 'but in how much time – before the end of the year? Before the end of the war?' She tried to smile. The last thing she wanted was for June to think her self-pitying.

'You'd think we all had more important things to talk about,' she went on, 'with all the losses sustained by Bomber Command. I heard someone saying in the mess this morning that she'd heard that when the men were told in their briefing that Berlin was to be their target again, the other night, there were gasps of horror. Twenty-eight Lancasters were lost in the first raid, and twenty-seven in the second, that's seven per cent of all the planes dispatched lost.'

June shuddered. 'I'd hate to be involved with a chap flying with Bomber Command.'

'Me too,' Lou agreed fervently.

'Are you going back to your room?' June asked.

'I was.'

'We may as well walk back together then,' June told her, linking arms with her.

Christmas hadn't been anything like as bad as she had expected, Jean admitted, as she rubbed a shine into the enamel of her cooker with a duster made from one of the twins' old liberty bodices with the buttons taken off.

Of course it had been a shock when Francine had announced that she'd seen the son they'd all thought was dead. Sam reckoned that it would have been better for all concerned if Francine hadn't seen him. By all accounts the lad was happy where he was, and very much loved by the woman who had taken him in. Jean felt for her younger sister, but there was no denying that it was demanding a lot of a young lad to expect him to take on board the fact that the woman he had thought was his auntie was really his mum. He was settled now and happy, even Francine had admitted that. But she was determined to win him round and to claim him.

She'd have to have a word with Bella, Jean decided, and put her in the picture, although it was probably best not to say anything to Vi, not after the upset she'd already caused over the way she'd treated the poor little lad, making him so unhappy that he'd never said a word to the woman who'd taken him in about his family.

'So what is it you wanted to see me about?' Lou asked Kieran.

They were sitting at a table in the corner of the centuries-old Buckinghamshire pub with its cavernous fireplace and its beams, the walls yellow with smoke, both from the fire and cigarettes.

Both of them were in uniform, and Lou so nervous that she was smoking.

'You were seen leaving my hotel room.'

'Yes, I know. One of Patti's friends told me on New Year's Eve, so you needn't have driven all the way over here just to tell me that.'

'I haven't done.'

'Then why are you here?'

'We've both got our good reputations to think about. It won't do either of us any good to have everyone gossiping about the fact that we spent the night together. Questions are bound to be asked. Has anyone said anything to you officially about it?'

'Not officially, although there's been plenty of gossip,' Lou admitted, telling him when she saw his frown, 'I'm the one who's going to get the worst of it, not you. After all, you're a man, and spending the night with someone doesn't count against men like it does women.'

Kieran shook his head in emphatic rebuttal. 'I want to make a career for myself in flying after the war, and I'm not going to be able to do that if I've got the kind of reputation you're talking about hanging round my neck. There'll be money to be made and jobs to be found flying freight, after the war, and it will be pilots with good reputations, who are reliable and trustworthy, who'll be taken on.'

Lou was grudgingly impressed that Kieran had

obviously given so much thought to his future. All those who flew knew that wartime flying had brought a new dimension to transport, but Lou hadn't heard anyone else talking about transferring that knowledge to a peacetime job.

'The war isn't over yet,' she reminded Kieran, 'and by the time it is everyone will have forgotten about us.'

'Not the kind of people I'm talking about,' Kieran contradicted her. 'I've got a suggestion to make – something that will benefit us both.'

'If you're talking about us telling the truth, then I wouldn't bother. I've already tried that with my best friend and—'

'No, it isn't that,' Kieran cut her short. 'What I think we should do is let it be known that we're an item and that we're planning to get engaged.'

'What? That's ridiculous,' Lou protested, almost knocking her glass over in her agitation. 'Anyway, no one would ever believe that we would want to get engaged to one another.'

'Why not?'

'Well . . . we don't act like . . . like a couple.'

'We spent the night together,' Kieran reminded her.

'No. It wouldn't work. Everyone would know that we were pretending.'

'Would they? Are you sure?' As he spoke Kieran reached across the table and took hold of her hand, lacing his fingers between hers with a lazy intimacy that made Lou's heart skid into her ribs. The pub door opened, and two RAF men walked in, bringing with them a surge of cold air.

316

Lou could see them looking towards her and Kieran, and then one of them nudged the other.

'We're being watched,' she warned Kieran, who was sitting with his back to the bar.

'I know,' he responded. 'I saw them walk past the window.' He lifted her hand to his lips and kissed her fingers, his gaze fixed on hers, his voice low but perfectly audible as he told her, 'So it's agreed then: as soon as this ruddy war is over, you and I are going to be married.'

'Stop it,' Lou demanded, but it was too late, the men standing by the bar had heard him and were exchanging grins.

'There's a dance on at our base this Friday. I've got tickets. We'll go there together, as a couple and make it plain that we *are* a couple.' Now Kieran's voice was lower, so low that Lou had to lean closer to him to hear what he was saying.

'No,' Lou protested, in a frantic hiss.

'We haven't got any choice, unless you want your reputation to be completely ruined.'

'Of course I don't. But we can't pretend to be planning to get engaged for ever.'

'We won't have to. Engagements are broken every day. It's part and parcel of being at war.'

What Kieran was saying made sense, Lou had to admit. A soon-to-be-engaged young woman could be forgiven for letting her feelings get the better of her, even if, strictly speaking, what she had done wasn't 'allowed'.

'People will ask why we didn't say we were an item straight off,' Lou pointed out.

'Then we'll tell them that we wanted to wait

until I'd had the chance to speak to your dad,' was Kieran's prompt response.

Kieran watched the expressions chasing one another across Lou's face. He hadn't been best pleased when he'd heard the gossip about the two of them. Like Lou, he suspected that Patti had had a hand in keeping it stirring and of adding in a few ingredients that were pure fiction, but he had meant what he had said to Lou about his plans. The RAF had opened his eyes to the possibilities of the future and had given him ambitions that meant he would need a clean record, and a reputation for being morally responsible. And that was why he was doing this. No other reason. Certainly not because he felt he had any obligation to protect Lou Campion's reputation, and to keep her safe from the predators who would now be on the prowl, given the gossip about her.

'So it's all sorted then,' Kieran announced. 'You're officially my girl and the two of us are planning to get engaged, and from now on, the only man you'll be dancing with is me.'

It *would* quell the gossip if people thought that she and Kieran were serious about one another, Lou knew.

'All right then,' she agreed, and then gasped in shock when Kieran leaned across the table and kissed her briefly full on the mouth.

Emily had always tried to be honest with Tommy and to talk openly with him, but she had no idea what to say to him about what had happened.

He had gone all quiet and had withdrawn into himself, and Emily was relieved when the school holidays were over. She hoped that being with his school friends would cheer him up and take his mind off what had happened. Not that she could take her own mind off it.

She couldn't sleep for her misery and anxiety at the thought of losing him. But she had given her word and she meant to keep it – for Tommy's sake.

It had given her a real turn to learn that Con was Tommy's father. He had never shown the slightest interest in Tommy, and had in fact demanded that she hand him over to the council, saying that she had to choose between him and Tommy. Well, she had, and she had chosen Tommy.

Everything had seemed so easy before she had known who Tommy really was. She had managed to convince herself that he was all alone in the world and that he was hers. She had told herself that one day he would talk to her about his family and tell her what had happened to them. She'd envisaged comforting him because he'd lost them, and listening whilst he told her about them, imagining that he'd had parents who were married to one another, a decent loving couple who'd been taken by the war, not a sixteen-year-old girl and her own husband. How was she to explain that to him? Con had been unkind to him and he certainly hadn't been a father a boy could be proud of. In Emily's opinion Tommy was better off with the fictional parents she had mentally created for him and not knowing who his real mother and father had been, but the decision to keep that information from him might not be hers to make.

Wilhelm had looked grave and concerned when she'd told him all about Tommy's past.

'These parents who were not really his parents, they will not want him back,' he had tried to reassure her, but as Emily had told him, it wasn't them who were trying to claim him, but his real mother.

She pinned a bright smile to her face as the back door opened and Tommy came in.

'I've just put the kettle on,' she told him. 'You get your coat and scarf off and we'll have a bit of toast.'

When Tommy didn't make any response, Emily put down the loaf of bread she had just been about to cut and looked at him. He looked thinner and unhappy.

'Why did she have to come here?' he burst out, fighting back tears. 'Why did she have to come here and spoil everything? I won't go back to them. I'll . . . I'll run away if anyone tries to make me.' His hands were balled into tight fists, coins of flushed colour staining his cheeks.

Emily's heart ached for him, as the same time as it thumped with anxiety at the thought of him running away. He was frightened, she realised, and that was her fault. It was up to her to reassure him and to protect him.

Taking a deep breath she told him firmly, 'Run away? You'll do no such thing, young man. No son of mine goes doing something daft like running away, especially when he's got no reason to.' Pretending not to be watching him, Emily sliced the bread. That was better. He was looking a bit more relaxed now. 'And as for anyone making you go back, that's daft as well. When I took you in, Tommy, I told the authorities that you were my cousin's lad and I got the papers sorted out to say that you were, so until you say otherwise, your place is here with me.'

'And no one can take me away?'

'No one,' Emily assured him, 'not unless you want to go.'

Katie hadn't forgotten her promise to Luke but she had had to wait until the right opportunity to mention it had created itself, and tonight she was hoping that it had, as she sat with Lady Irene Whittaker, helping her with her sewing.

'You are a kind girl, Katie. I know perfectly well that you were due to finish your spell of duty in reception over an hour ago, but here you are, helping me out.'

Lady Irene's praise made Katie feel a bit guilty, her manner so warm and friendly as Katie sat close to her, sewing stripes onto the jacket a newly made-up sergeant had left with her whilst he went to get himself a 'soda' – the stripes to be sewn on 'upside down' in the American manner – that Katie felt obliged to tell her the truth.

'Well, I do have an ulterior motive.'

Lady Irene gave her an encouraging smile. 'Which is?'

Unable to see any scissors, Katie bit the thread

with her teeth, before responding, 'I had a letter from . . . from a friend in the army a little while ago. He was in Italy, Naples. He wrote about how awful things are for the women and children there, and . . . and what some of the women are having to do.' Nice as Lady Irene was, Katie couldn't bring herself actually to say what Luke had told her, but it seemed that Lady Irene knew what she meant, because she sighed and put down the shirt she was mending.

'Those poor people. One feels for them. We sometimes feel sorry for ourselves here in this country because of rationing, but when one hears what others are having to bear . . . Mind you, I'm not sure that your young man should have burdened you with—'

'Oh, Luke isn't my young man. He's just . . . just a friend,' Katie corrected her hastily, pausing before finding the courage to add truthfully, 'and I'm glad that he has told me. After all, we know all about our boys being killed and injured. We aren't sheltered from that, and to think of children starving . . . What I was wondering was if it was worth saying anything here, to the American Red Cross. The Italians *are* our Allies now.'

Lady Irene patted Katie's hand. 'Your compassion does you credit, my dear, and if it puts your mind at rest then let me assure you that the plight of those in Europe left homeless and destitute by this war is one that already has the attention of those in authority, and not just from the Red Cross, but from the United Nations authorities as well.'

She gave Katie another kind smile. 'You may not have heard of this, but I can give you my word that it is the truth. These things take time to arrange and organise properly but you can tell your . . . friend not to worry. Those who need to know such things are aware of the situation and intend to do something about it.'

Katie smiled at Lady Irene with grateful relief, and then returned to her task as she saw the new sergeant making his way back to her.

'So what did Kieran want to see you for?' June asked Lou as they sat down to eat their supper together.

'He wants us to pretend to be an item and planning to get engaged,' Lou answered. 'He says that it will stop the gossip if people think that we're properly together.'

'He's right,' June pronounced approvingly. 'I thought all along that he was a decent sort.'

'He says that we'll have to be seen together, at dances and that kind of thing.'

'Well, I'll do what I can to help,' June offered generously, 'like telling people that you're together, if they start talking about the two of you.'

Lou tried to look grateful but the truth was that she wished desperately that they could have found another solution to the problem. Kieran kissing her like that had given her ever such a shock, and he hadn't just kissed her the once either. He hadn't driven off straight away after he'd brought her back, and of course they had been seen together, and then he'd kissed her again before he'd finally left.

There was no use pretending to herself that she hadn't been affected when he'd kissed her, or that there hadn't been all those times when they'd first met him when she'd longed with girlish fervour to be kissed by him. She wasn't a girl any more, though.

The last thing she wanted now was to go and make a fool of herself by letting him see what kind of effect he could have on her. Not, of course, that she would do that. But just to be sure she'd have to tell him that they could act like a couple without him kissing her.

Marcus had gone back to his men, after a brief leave of twenty-four hours, but their bed still smelled comfortingly of him. Francine buried her face in his pillow, breathing in the scent of him.

She must get up; there were things she had to do. Marcus hadn't been very keen when she had told him about her plan to rent a house in Whitchurch so that she could go there to be with Jack whenever possible. It would hurt Emily to part with him, she knew, but *she* was his mother. She would make it up to him for all that he had suffered, all that they had lost as mother and son.

But Jack thought that Vi was his mother. Francine pushed away the bedclothes and reached for her dressing gown. She would find a way of telling him the truth.

About Con, as well as about herself?

There was no need for her to think of that now. She must win Jack's trust again and his love first, before she started telling him just why he was so important to her.

TWENTY-TWO

'Katie?'

Katie gripped the telephone receiver tightly as she heard Eddie's voice, before saying, 'Yes, it's me, Eddie.'

'I'm in London. I want . . . Can I see you? I . . . I need to talk to you. You've heard about Leonard, of course?'

'Yes.'

'I can't believe that he's gone. It's so ruddy unfair. A good decent chap like Leonard. They should have taken me instead. I wish they had . . .'

Katie didn't try to stem his emotional outburst. She knew how close the two cousins had been.

'I really need to see you, Katie,' Eddie continued. 'We could meet at the Savoy. I'm staying there.'

'Yes, of course,' she agreed. 'What time?'

'Now. As soon as you can make it. I'll be in the American Bar.'

She'd only just got in from work but Katie could hear the strain in his voice.

Leonard's Memorial Service had taken place earlier

in the month. She hadn't attended it herself; it had been a strictly family affair, held in the private chapel on Eddie's parents' estate. She had thought about Gina, though, all day, glad that her friend would have the support of her own parents and Leonard's family, but at the same time knowing that no amount of support could possibly take away the pain of her dreadful loss. Eddie would have had leave to attend the Memorial Service, and it had been plain from the emotion in Eddie's voice just how much he had been affected by the death of the older cousin he had admired. So many lives were damaged by every single lost life. Like ripples in a pool the effect spread outwards. There was no point in trying to make sense of why one man should die and often the man standing next to him should not. Leonard had been such a good man. In Leonard's case, though, it did seem particularly unfair. He and Gina had both known loss and suffering before they had met. They had been so happy together. Katie remembered the small secret smiles she had seen Gina and Leonard sharing on New Year's Eve; the smiles of a couple totally at ease with one another, and very much in love. Now Gina had been left a widow and two small children had been left without a father.

It was because of her own low spirits as much as out of respect for Leonard's death that she changed quickly into a dark grey wool dress, before she left Cadogan Square, less than half an hour after Eddie had telephoned, in a taxi she was lucky enough to find on Sloane Street.

Eddie had sounded so desperate, poor boy, and rather as though he had already been drowning his sorrows a little. Who could blame him for that? Eddie wasn't a heavy drinker, by any means. Katie didn't want to think about how grim it must have been to stand there at Leonard's memorial service. January was such a depressing month at the best of times, with spring so far away.

The bar in the Savoy was crowded as usual, but Katie quickly spotted Eddie and made her way towards him.

He looked haggard, as though he had lost weight, his eyes red-rimmed and bleak with emotion, the pain she could see in them briefly replaced by relief when he saw her.

'Katie.' Eddie hugged her so tightly that his grip almost hurt, his face buried in her hair, his voice muffled.

'I came as soon as I could,' Katie told him, gently pushing him away. 'Are we eating here?'

'We can do. I hadn't thought about food. I haven't thought about anything really except Leonard.'

Katie put her hand over his, feeling almost maternal towards him.

'Why don't we find a table and sit down?' she suggested.

A couple of minutes later they were seated at a table that gave them a bit more privacy, away from the busy bustle and jovial atmosphere around the bar. It was hard not to think about the last time they had come here, with Gina and Leonard.

Then they too had been in the same celebratory mood as those grouped around the bar tonight. Poor Eddie. Katie reached for his hand again.

'I'm so sorry about Leonard, Eddie,' she told him gently. 'I know how close the two of you were.'

'He was one of the best, Katie. One of the very best. My best friend as well as my cousin. Now he's gone. He was more than a cousin to me, always there to set me straight and help me out, the brother I never had. Whilst he was there . . . Now it's all down to me, Katie. I'm feeling very much like my parents' only child, and if I go, then the whole family will go.'

'Don't, Eddie. Please,' Katie begged him. 'You mustn't think like that.' She had never heard him talk like this before, with such obvious desperation and despair in his voice. All the teasing insouciance that she always associated with him had been stripped away, leaving the bare bones of what he really was, Katie recognised. Now his upbringing and its traditions truly showed. Katie felt desperately sorry for him.

He turned to her with a faint echo of his normal smile. 'Oh, but I must, Katie. That is exactly what I must think about and why I'm here.'

Katie was still holding his hand and now he put his other hand on top of their clasped hands and looked directly at her.

'Losing Leo has made me see things differently. Of course I've always known that ultimately it's up to me to marry at some stage and produce a son, but I've always thought of it as something to do after the war, not during it, when there are so many . . .'

'Pretty girls to flirt with?' Katie supplied for him, trying to lighten his mood, but instead of smiling he simply shook his head. 'Leonard was the one who always looked out for me, when I first learned to ride, when we went to school and then later when we both joined the navy. But now he's gone. It seems impossible, but it isn't.'

Katie squeezed his hand in silent sympathy.

'The parents haven't said anything, that isn't their way, but it's pretty obvious that for as long as this war goes on there's going to be the risk that I won't get to see the other side of it. Somehow I never thought of that whilst Leonard was alive. But now . . . I had a long talk with my grandmother after the memorial service and it's like she says, eleven generations of our family have passed on the estate and the title to the next, and now it's down to me to do the same thing before it's too late.'

Katie was horrified.

'She said that to you?' Eddie's grandmother, a graceful straight-backed individual in her late seventies, with snow-white hair she wore in an elegant chignon, was very much the matriarch of the family, Gina had told her, adding, 'She's very old school – you know, keen on one doing one's duty and that sort of thing. The whole family is a bit in awe of her. Luckily she approved of me otherwise I doubt that Leonard would have dared to propose to me.'

Katie had laughed, knowing that Gina's last comment had been a joke, but sensing at the same time the importance the whole family placed on the Dowager Lady Spencer's views.

Katie, who had only met her once, at Gina and Leonard's wedding, had found herself contrasting Eddie's grandmother's strict view on protocol and the right way of doing things to her own parents' more bohemian way of life, and she hadn't envied Gina having such a stern presence in her life. Not that Leonard and Eddie's grandmother had been anything less than gracious to Gina. But then Gina's family, whilst not ennobled, still had a recognisable pedigree so far as the dowager was concerned.

Eddie was giving her a serious look. 'She only said what needed to be said, and the truth is that I'm glad that she did. She made me think, and what she made me think is that I can't imagine anyone I'd be happier married to than you, Katie.'

Now Eddie had shocked her. A proposal from him was the last thing she had expected – and the last thing she wanted? Feeling guilty, Katie reminded herself that Eddie had just lost his cousin and best friend and that that was enough to make anyone think about their own future. In Eddie's case that future included the need to marry and have a son to continue his family line. It was therefore only natural that marriage should be very much to the forefront of his mind. But surely not to her?

'I'm very flattered, of course, Eddie,' Katie told him, groping for the right words. 'And I do understand how you feel, but I can't help thinking that your family, your grandmother, will expect you to marry, well, someone from your own background.

Someone who would be far more suitable than me.' Someone far more suitable and thus, far more acceptable.

'The thing is that I may not have much time.' The bluntness of Eddie's honesty tore at Katie's tender heart. 'And besides,' he added, 'no one could make me a better wife than you, Katie. You are the best of the best. Leonard always thought so. And you don't need to worry about all that lady-of-the-manor stuff. There'll be plenty of time for you to pick it up from m' mother. In fact, I'd say she'd welcome having you with her, and get you trained up for taking over from her when the time comes.'

So, privately Eddie knew himself that she wasn't the ideal choice. Katie didn't know whether to laugh or take offence. On balance, laughing would probably make things easier, she acknowledged, as she told him firmly, 'Eddie, I can't marry you. It wouldn't be right.'

'Why not? Because you're still in love with that corporal who treated you so badly and let you down?'

Gina must have told him about Luke.

'Certainly not,' she denied. 'Luke doesn't mean anything to me any more.'

'Prove it then, and marry me,' Eddie responded promptly.

'Eddie—' Katie tried to stop him, but he shook his head and held her hand tighter.

'I know what you're going to say, but don't say it yet, Katie. Hear me out, please. Leonard always warned me that I should think more about my duty to my inheritance and less about having a good time. I used to laugh at him. I never thought . . . I thought we'd both see this ruddy war through. I thought if anyone deserved to live it was Leonard, but now he's dead and the future of everything my family has fought and worked for is dependent on you, Katie.'

'That's not fair,' Katie objected shakily. 'It's emotional blackmail.'

'I know,' Eddie admitted, 'but I have to use whatever means I can to persuade you to agree, and I haven't much time. We're almost in February now, and once we get into spring it won't be long before the Allied Command gives the orders that we've all been waiting for and the invasion of Northern France begins. I can't say any more than that, but I know you'll understand what I'm trying to say.'

'I do understand,' she agreed, 'but . . .'

'Don't turn me down, Katie, please. I'll make you the happiest you could imagine being, I promise you.'

'I know you think we could be happy together, Eddie, but marriage is such a huge step, and for us to marry under such circumstances . . .' Katie paused, wanting to let him down gently. She thoroughly understood what was motivating him, but even if she had loved him in that way and not as a friend, and had wanted to marry him, she wouldn't have wanted to agree to such a rushed marriage. The war made people do things they wouldn't do in peacetime. It gave things an urgency and an immediacy that propelled people into rash decisions, and rash emotions. She knew that from her engagement to Luke. She had already told herself that she wouldn't get heavily involved with anyone until after the war had ended and things had returned to normal, when people could see one another clearly without the threat of war colouring their vision.

'Please don't turn me down, Katie. I owe it to Leonard and to my family to do my best to provide an heir – and the sooner the better. I know how unromantic and selfish that must sound, but I promise you that it doesn't mean that the only reason I want to marry you is because of that. I do love you, Katie, and I think that if you put your mind to it you could very easily love me. Couples get married every day with less to bind them together than we have.'

Katie felt desperately sorry for him, but she had to stop him.

'Eddie, we can't get married,' she told him gently. 'Your grandmother would never approve.'

If she had hoped to bring the discussion to an end by mentioning Eddie's grandmother, she quickly discovered her mistake.

'Of course she will,' Eddie insisted. 'Why shouldn't she? Oh, I know she's dropped a few hints about some girl whose grandmother she was at school with, but I dare say she's plain and as dull as ditchwater. Not like you, Katie. No,' he shook his head, 'you're wrong; I shall prove that to you. And when I do, Katie, I shall expect you to say yes.'

He was cutting the ground from under her feet,

although thankfully it sounded very much to Katie from what he had let slip that his grandmother had already selected a possible bride for him.

However, before she could say so he continued, 'I'm on leave at the moment, but I've got to go down to my ship tomorrow morning for a meeting. I could be tied up there for a couple of days or so, but as soon as I can I shall go home and tell my parents and my grandmother that I want to marry you.'

'And if they disapprove—'

Then you'll drop the whole idea, Katie had been intending to say, but before she could finish her sentence Eddie cut in determinedly, 'They won't disapprove. The next time I see you, Katie, it will be to put an engagement ring on your finger, with my family's blessing and approval. We won't want to wait long to get married. The sooner the better, in fact.'

'Eddie . . .' Katie tried to stop him, before giving a small sigh, and reflecting that there was really no point in her trying to make him see reason when he was so determined not to listen to her. He would, though, listen to his grandmother and his parents, and they would, Katie felt sure, make it plain to him that they would not want him to marry her.

'Let's make a date for Valentine's night,' he told her.

What could she say? How could she refuse?

'Very well,' she agreed, but she felt very cowardly for not telling him straight that she didn't want to marry him, and letting his family be the ones to make him see that a marriage between them would never work.

'Of course it would be much better if you said "yes" now,' Eddie told her. 'Then we could buy your ring, and we could tell the family together. Present them with a *fait accompli*. I've got a room here – we could have celebrated our engagement there, in a very special way. What do you say, Katie?'

She said 'no', of course, and something in the look Eddie gave her told her that it was the answer that he had expected.

It was only as they were leaving that he said something that really did weaken her resolve, holding her hand in the hotel foyer as he drew her to one side and told her emotionally, 'It will work out for us, Katie, I promise you. I'll do everything I can to make you happy. Our children will play in the fields where Leonard and I played as boys, they'll explore the same woods, and laugh at the same dull family portraits in the long gallery. They will be the promise I made to Leonard in church on the day of his memorial service. Help me keep that promise.'

Listening to him, Katie had to blink away her tears. The picture he drew of the children had really touched her heart.

It was an intrinsic part of her nature to want to help others where she could, and Katie could feel herself weakening. She couldn't marry Eddie, of course. She didn't love him in that way but she simply didn't have the heart to refuse him outright when it was so obvious that he was desperate to do the right thing by his family.

There was no harm, after all, in allowing him to think that she would agree to marry him, not when she was pretty sure that his grandmother already had a prospective bride, who, Katie suspected, would be produced in double-quick time once Eddie had informed his family of his desire to marry her. Eddie was an easy-going young man, who would soon see the sense in marrying someone his family thought suitable. Was it selfish of her to wish that she could turn to Gina to confide in her? Of course that was impossible with Gina so newly bereaved, even if her friend had not been on compassionate leave and staying with Leonard's parents. Gina might often have teased her about Eddie being sweet on her but Katie knew that Gina would feel as she did herself: that a marriage between them was out of the question. There was no one else she could discuss the situation with. She got on well with the ATS girls but she wasn't close enough to them to want to confide in them. Her parents, especially her father, for all their bohemian friends and way of life, would be outraged at the idea of her not being considered good enough to be someone's wife. Of course, had she loved Eddie it would have been different. But she didn't. She liked him, but liking wasn't love. Even so, she couldn't help feeling a sense of responsibility towards him.

'Very well,' she agreed. 'We'll have dinner together on Valentine's Day.'

Was it wrong of her not to refuse him outright? Katie didn't know. She only knew that she couldn't turn him away with a flat refusal when he was so obviously in so much despair and need.

'I've found somewhere to rent in Whitchurch, it's only a small cottage, but it does have two bedrooms, so that Jack can stay overnight . . .'

Jean gave her younger sister a troubled look. She could understand how she felt, of course she could, and she was glad that Francine had taken the trouble to stop off on her way back from Whitchurch to bring her up to date with her plans but in her heart of hearts Jean couldn't help but think that it might have been better for everyone if Francine had never learned that Jack was still alive. Not that she could say that to her, of course. She knew too how she would have felt had she lost one of her children and thought them dead, only to discover that they were still alive. She wouldn't have been able to rest until they were home again with her.

'Why are you looking at me like that?' Fran asked. 'You don't really approve of what I'm doing, Jean, do you?'

Jean picked up one of the delicate teacups she had just washed – she had got out the precious teaset in honour of Francine's visit – and started to dry it slowly and carefully, finding comfort in the familiar chore.

'It isn't a matter of me not approving, Fran. It's just that . . . well, Jack's settled now, by all accounts, and doing well, and I can't help thinking that being uprooted all over again after everything he's been through won't be easy for him. You see, children like

338

things to be the same.' Jean groped for words that wouldn't hurt her sister. 'They don't like things that are important to them changing.'

'You mean that Jack won't want to leave Emily? But I'm his mother, Jean. He's my son.'

'You and I know that, Fran, but Jack doesn't. It seems to me that it's the *kind* of mothering they get that's important to children – not the person who gives it. You love Jack, of course you do, but you don't know him, Fran, not really. Not like she will know him, and that's important to youngsters. He's a bright boy, a clever boy, since he's at grammar school, but he's never said a word to anyone about who he really is and it seems to me that he's done that for a purpose.'

'Because he doesn't want to go back to Vi and Edwin, and I wouldn't let that happen, Jean. I'm not a child any more, I'm a married woman. Marcus and I can give him so much. Marcus can be a proper father to him, not like Edwin was.'

'You said yourself that he's very attached to that German POW,' Jean pointed out.

'Yes, but that just shows how much he needs a father.'

'It will be hard for her to give him up, loving him like she does, and thinking that no one would ever claim him.'

'Don't you think it's been hard for me, thinking that he's dead, and now seeing him with someone else? He's my son, Jean.' There were tears in Fran's eyes and her voice was shaking.

Jean put down her precious teacup and her cloth and went over to her younger sister, putting her arms round her. 'I know it's hard for you, love,' she tried to comfort her. 'It's hard for all of you. That's the trouble. In the end someone's going to be badly hurt.'

'I just want the best for Jack, Jean. I just want the chance to show him how much I love him and to make it up to him for letting Vi and Edwin have him.'

Jean nodded. She could see that Francine had made up her mind.

Katie looked at her watch. Eddie should have been here by now. Seven thirty, they'd said they'd meet here in the American Bar, and now it was almost a quarter to eight.

It wasn't like him to be late, but maybe his train had been delayed or he'd been unable to get a taxi from the station. If he'd been delayed for some reason in Dartmouth he'd have found some way of getting a message to her, Katie knew. She had actually been half expecting to receive a letter from him, telling her that she had been right and that his grandmother did not want him to marry her. Perhaps she was too used to reading 'Dear John' letters, Katie thought ruefully, thinking of all the letters they had to read and then pass on, from men and women who had found out that they had made a mistake and wanted to end a relationship. Just like Luke had ended theirs . . .

This was no time for her to be thinking about that, Katie told herself sternly, switching her thoughts from her own situation to Gina's. Her friend was still on compassionate leave and Katie missed her. Katie had written to her but as yet had not received a reply, which was unlike Gina, but Katie had told herself that her friend would write back to her as soon as she felt able to do so.

As usual the bar was busy, filled with couples, since it was Valentine's night, the meaningfulness of the date, in the midst of war, being even more poignant and precious for those couples who were lucky enough to be together to celebrate it, Katie suspected.

However, she was beginning to feel slightly self-conscious sitting at a table on her own, on such an evening. She'd seen the speculative looks one or two of the handful of men unaccompanied by women and standing by the bar had given her, and she was praying that none of them would take it into his head to come over to her, thinking that she was here on her own because she was hoping to be picked up.

She'd dressed carefully for the occasion – more because she felt morally obliged to do so than for any other reason, in the dress she had bought in Bath the weekend she and Gina had first met Leonard and Eddie. She felt such a fraud, though, being here amongst so many couples who were quite plainly in love with one another. It felt horrible being what, to Katie, was really quite deceitful, and all because she had been too much of a coward to refuse Eddie outright. What was she going to do and say to him if by some awful chance his grandmother did not object to his plans to marry her? That wasn't going to happen, Katie reassured herself, but knowing that only made her feel worse. Poor Eddie. She really ought to have spared him the upset of incurring his grandmother's rejection of his plans. Eddie was charming but immature, really. She couldn't imagine Luke allowing anyone to tell him who he should and should not marry.

Luke. Katie's heart gave an unsteady thump. Luke would understand how she felt, even if he might not approve of what she had done. It would be a relief to confide in him as well. He had mentioned Eddie in his latest letter and asked if she was still seeing him.

Eddie? Where was he? Katie was beginning to feel not just self-conscious because she was on her own but also slightly angry. She could understand that Eddie might be embarrassed about telling her that he didn't want them to be engaged after all, but that was no excuse for standing her up and leaving her here on her own. What did he think she was going to do? Make a silly fuss? Men didn't like that, of course. Perhaps his grandmother had insisted that he take her friend's granddaughter out for the evening. Katie's face began to burn with righteous indignation. At the very least Eddie could have written to her, even if he hadn't felt up to telephoning her. She hadn't heard a word from him since he'd telephoned her from Dartmouth three days ago to say that he was leaving for his home in the morning and that he'd see her tonight.

A waiter approached Katie's table, coughing discreetly and bending his head towards her to inform her that a 'gentleman' by the bar would like to buy her a drink.

Embarrassed, Katie shook her head. 'No. I'm waiting for . . . for someone,' she told him, feeling horribly self-conscious.

Why wasn't Eddie here?

She would wait until nine o'clock and if Eddie hadn't arrived by then, or sent her a message, then she would leave, Katie told herself, feeling decidedly cross with him.

TWENTY-THREE

'There's no need to look at me like that,' Lou hissed at Kieran as he handed her her drink. 'No one's watching us.'

They were in the same pretty thatched pub where Kieran had told her that he thought they should become a couple, but this evening the bar was filled with airmen and their partners, who had come, like Kieran and Lou, to celebrate Valentine's Day.

'I'm just getting in some practice,' Kieran told her, 'and making sure that if anyone is watching they know that you are my girl.' As he finished speaking he leaned closer to her as though he was going to kiss her, making Lou edge back apprehensively, the look in her eyes giving away more than she knew.

'Keep still,' Kieran told her. 'You've got a piece of twig in your hair. If anyone sees it they'll be ribbing us about indulging in a bit of al fresco lovemaking.'

Lou tensed as she felt his fingers in her hair, wondering why such a mundane task as him removing a twig from her curls should send such an intense zigzag of sensation racing down her spine. She could feel the warmth of his breath on her forehead. Her gaze was on a level with his throat, his skin a warmer tone than her own. She had a sudden desire to reach out and touch it, to see if it felt as warm as it looked and she had to curl her fingers into the pocket of her jacket to make sure that she didn't.

What was wrong with her?

'Come on, you two, that's enough of the sweet nothings, even if it is Valentine's Night,' Hilary, the senior ATA pilot who had befriended Lou, told them, taking one of the empty chairs at their table.

'I'll be back in a minute. Don't forget to miss me,' Kieran told Lou, dropping a kiss on the end of her nose before heading back to the bar.

'Cigarette?' Hilary offered Lou, but Lou shook her head, leaving Hilary to light up, inhale slowly and then exhale.

'Been meaning to have a word with you,' Hilary continued, 'just to say that I'm glad the two of you decided to go public and scotch certain rumours that were doing the rounds. We all know that there are girls who go off the rails in wartime, but in ATA we like to think that our girls are above that sort of thing.' She gave Lou a friendly smile and stood up.

'Better go and join the others. I'm on taxi duty tonight. Oh, and jolly good show on completing so many ferries – top of the list, weren't you, for Spits? It isn't easy flying in the winter months.

It takes guts and strong nerves as well as good training and sound sense.'

Lou's hands were trembling as Hilary walked off. She knew perfectly well that the older pilot had been making a point to her, making it plain that the approval she had just given her would not have been forthcoming if Lou and Kieran had not been legit.

A burst of laughter from the bar had her looking towards it and straight at Kieran. He was doing it again, she recognised, as the heat crawled up her throat and burned her face: he was looking at her like *that* – as though . . . as though they shared something special and private and, well, *intimate.*

Standing at the bar, Kieran watched Lou, telling his companions without taking his gaze off her, 'Scuse me, chaps, but I've just remembered something very important,' ignoring their bantering as they followed his gaze, to leave them and lope speedily back to Lou.

'Give us the thumbs up, did she?' he asked, nodding in Hilary's direction.

'How long are we going to have to do this for?' Lou demanded, ignoring his question.

'As long as it takes,' Kieran told her, pulling out his cigarettes and smiling at her. 'Why? Not found someone to replace me already, have you?'

'Don't be silly. That's the last thing I want to do.'

'I'm flattered.'

Lou shook her head and objected crossly, 'I didn't mean it like that. I meant that after all the

346

fuss this has caused, the last thing I want is to get involved with anybody.'

'Apart from me.' He'd lit his cigarette now, knowing that Lou wouldn't want one, but suddenly he put it down and reached across the table to cup her face in both his hands and kiss her – very fiercely.

Kieran's kiss tasted of freshly lit cigarette, warm beer, and something else, something that had Lou's heart thudding into her ribs and her pulse racing. She badly wanted to pull away from him but she also equally badly wanted to stay where she was, and that was dangerous. Quickly she made herself pull free, demanding, 'What was that for?' looking and feeling red-faced and on edge.

'It's what promised-to-one-another couples do, especially when it's Valentine's Night,' Kieran answered her unrepentantly before changing the subject.

'We've got a new op on tomorrow night.'

Now Lou's heart bumped into her ribs for a very different reason. Everyone knew how many crews and planes Bomber Command were losing, and how dangerous their bombing missions on German towns were.

'France. Dropping supplies for the Resistance. Safer than bombing German cities, at least if we manage to avoid the Luftwaffe.'

Lou's eyes widened. 'You aren't supposed to tell me things like that.'

'I didn't want you to worry about me.'

'I wasn't.'

'Every girl worries about her chap.'

347

'You're not my chap. Not really.'

Kieran was looking at her in a way that Lou didn't like, as though he knew something that she didn't, as though he knew how she felt when he touched her and when he kissed her, as though he knew what she didn't want to allow herself to know.

Quickly Lou made herself think about something else.

'Jack, surely you remember me, don't you? We had such fun together.' Francine could hear the note of panic and pleading in her voice as she tried to coax Jack to respond to her.

She'd been so full of hope this morning when she'd called at Emily's, as they'd arranged, so that they could have some time together, imagining the two of them getting on, and Jack beginning to relax with her, but instead her son had made it plain that he didn't want to be with her and that he resented having to do so.

'Do I have to go?' Francine had heard him asking Emily as the other woman fussed over him, tying his scarf, and tucking what had looked like a packet of sandwiches into the pocket of his coat.

Did Emily really think that she wasn't capable of feeding him, Fran fumed now. She was Jack's mother, after all. She'd brought some special treats down from London with her, cajoled from the Dorchester's chef, only to discover that the range in the kitchen of the cottage she was renting billowed out smoke the minute she tried to light it.

348

'Jack, speak to me, please,' she begged. Nothing was turning out as she'd expected. She'd planned to take Jack round to Grace and Seb's, thinking that that might help to break the ice between them, but then Seb had telephoned and said that Grace was feeling a bit under the weather and not really up to visitors, and now she was going to have to take Jack back to her cold cottage or spend the day walking round Whitchurch with him trailing behind her, and obviously wishing that he wasn't with her.

She would have to be patient, Fran reminded herself. She'd have to win his trust slowly and let him take his time to get to know her instead of trying to rush him.

'It's rather cold in here,' she told him as she unlocked the door to the cottage. 'I think there's something wrong with the range.'

The cottage was so small that there was only one room downstairs, which was both the kitchen and the living area. Despite her sheepskin-lined boots, Francine could feel the cold coming up from the stone-flagged floor. She could see Jack looking round and suspected that he was comparing the bare chilliness of the cottage to the comfort and warmth of the home he shared with Emily.

Her kitchen smelled of baking and warmth, whilst the cottage smelled of emptiness and damp.

Fran sank down onto one of the dilapidated chairs at the kitchen table. She refused to touch the ancient sofa, with its ominously worrying holes through which loose horsehair poked. The cottage was a world away from the comfort and elegance of the London apartment she and Marcus shared.

Marcus. She wished that he was with her now. He would have known what to do, how to make Jack relax and smile at her instead of refusing to look at her. Jack was her son, she reminded herself. They shared the same blood. They . . .

'I know this isn't easy for you,' she told him. 'It isn't easy for me either.'

She saw the movement of his head as he turned to look at her.

'You love Emily.' How hard it was for her to say those words. 'And she loves you. But we love you as well, Jack. We are your family.' She reached impulsively towards him.

Immediately he recoiled from her, asking, 'Can I go home now, please?'

Home. His home should be with her, not with Con's wife, however good to him she had been or however much she loved him.

Emily couldn't settle to anything. She'd cleaned the kitchen from top to bottom, but she still felt too restless to sit down. The back door opened and she turned round anxiously, giving a small sigh when she saw Wilhelm. Not that he wasn't welcome. She'd tried to explain as vaguely as she could to her neighbour about 'some of Tommy's family turning up and wanting to get to know him,' but it was only with Wilhelm that she could truly express her feelings – and her fears.

'I know she's his real mother and that she's every right to want him,' she told Wilhelm now, 'but when I had to stand here and watch her walk out with him this morning, Wilhelm, I could hardly bear it, I really couldn't. I don't know what I'm going to do if he decides that he wants to be with her. I love him as though he's been mine all along, as though . . .'

She tried to smile through her tears as Wilhelm took hold of her hand.

'It is for Tommy that you must do what is right, and because you love him. I know that that is what you will do.'

Jack/Tommy couldn't wait to get home to Emily. It had made him feel funny inside hearing her, his aunt, talking to him in that cracked, upset voice, and he wanted to put his hands over his ears and not hear her.

He could remember the bedroom he had had at the house in Wallasey, the small back bedroom, which his mother had said was good enough for him, and where he had never been allowed to have any toys in case he made a mess. Now he had a great big room, with a deep chest of drawers where he could keep his Meccano and his jigsaws. He had a special shelf for all his annuals, and his bird book, and best of all, upstairs in the attic, Wilhelm had helped him to lay out his railway set.

He shivered, remembering too the pursed-lipped crossness of his mother's face; the bad temper of his father, and the brother and sister who had always seemed alien to him. He didn't want to go back to that or to them. He wanted to be with Emily.

'You want to go home?' Auntie Francine asked him. Her voice had that funny cracked sound to it again.

Tommy nodded. 'Yes please,' he told her.

TWENTY-FOUR

It was a shock to realise that it was now officially spring Lou acknowledged, as she climbed out of the taxi Anson at Thame after a very long day's work, during which she'd moved seven Spitfires from their maintenance units to their new RAF bases. They'd been so busy these last few weeks, picking up and delivering planes, in the build-up towards the expected invasion of Northern France, that she'd hardly had time to notice how quickly the days were slipping by. Impossible not to notice now, though, with double summer time coming into force, making the days longer and the evenings so much lighter, the fields beneath her busy with land girls, POWs and farmers all doing their bit to help feed the country.

When she removed her helmet the evening breeze smelled of fresh air, and the last of the day's sunshine. The sun was dying into a red sky, promising good weather, which, allied to the full moon – a bomber's moon – meant that it would be a busy night for Bomber Command, still flying raids on Germany, and dropping guns and other supplies in France for the Resistance – work in which Kieran was heavily involved.

The gathering dusk, waiting beyond the blazing glory of the sunset, meant that there would be no more flying for her until the morning, which was probably just as well, Lou acknowledged. Beneath the adrenalin rush of non-stop pick-ups and deliveries, working always against the clock and praying for good flying weather, she was tired. They all were. It was rarely voiced but there was always the knowledge that men's lives and the ultimate success of the war for the Allies rested in part on the delivery of much-needed planes to replace those lost in action, and to replenish those RAF bases desperately in need of more.

Lou had just signed off for the day and was about to leave the ops office when the relief ops officer called her back.

George Simmonds was ex-BOAC, a kindly avuncular man, with a wide warm smile, whom all the girls liked. Right now, though, his smile had been replaced by a more serious expression, his hand on Lou's arm, obviously intended to be comforting as he drew her to one side and told her quietly, 'Officially I shouldn't be doing this but I thought you'd want to know that part of 184 Squadron were doing a French Resistance drop earlier today, and they ran into a spot of trouble from the Luftwaffe on the way back.'

Immediately Lou's stomach muscles clenched. In fact the whole of her body was rigidly tight with apprehension whilst her heart hammered too fast and too hard as she anticipated what was to come.

'Kieran?' she managed to ask stiffly. But even before George Simmonds shook his head, she knew the answer.

'Posted missing. He'd dropped back to protect the rest of the squadron. One of the other pilots saw his plane go down over the Channel.'

Lou nodded, too choked up to speak, her throat muscles as tight and strained as though she'd been screaming.

Kieran gone . . . dead. Kieran, who meant nothing whatsoever to her. Kieran, whose 'girl' she was supposed to be, but who would now never ever hold a girl he really loved in his arms ever again.

Kieran.

Dead.

Unsteadily Lou walked out of the office, her vision blurred by the tears she was determined not to cry.

Spring already and she felt ever so much better than she had done, Sasha acknowledged. Had felt better ever since they had made things up, Lou and her, and were close again. She still hated dark places, and she still sometimes had nightmares, but these days, in those nightmares, Lou was there to hold on to her.

She still wished that Bobby would get a transfer, but with her parents adamant that she and Bobby must wait for the war to be over to get married, Sasha had accepted that she would have to learn to live with her anxiety. Bobby's safety and their marriage aside, all she really wanted now was for

Lou to meet someone and settle down so that the two of them could share looking forward to the future. Lou's letters, though, never mentioned men or dates. Sasha sometimes wondered if her twin had really got over her crush on Kieran Mallory. Sasha could smile now at her own adoration of him, safe in the knowledge that now she understood what real love was, thanks to Bobby. It had been daft, her and Lou falling out the way they had, first over him and then over her getting together with Bobby, but Sasha recognised now that they had perhaps needed that separation in order for them both to become young women in their own rights.

Now that they had made up their differences, though, there was no way that Sasha wanted them to fall out like that again. It was lovely being able to write to Lou openly about how she felt, able to tell her twin how much she had missed her. She thought about Lou every day but today she'd been thinking about her almost all the time.

Humming to herself, Sasha brushed her hair sitting down at the dressing table she and Lou had shared. Bobby was on duty tonight, but she would be seeing him on Friday.

She heard the knock on the front door and the sound of her father going to see who it was, but she didn't pay much attention. It would probably be one of her father's allotment pals or one of their neighbours

Only it wasn't, and when her father called upstairs to her to come down she knew the minute she saw the grey-faced officer from Bobby's unit standing in the hallway why he was there, her fiancé's name escaping from her lips on a plea, as she begged, 'Bobby?'

'Gina.' Katie hurried between the tables of the large sorting room to greet her friend's unexpected appearance. 'I thought you were still on extended . . . leave, otherwise I'd have made sure I got here earlier this morning. How are you?'

'I'm not coming back, Katie. I've only come in to collect my things.'

Gina had lost weight. There were dark circles beneath her eyes and her eyes themselves held the brutal reality of her loss and her grief.

'They need me at home. Losing both Leonard and Eddie has been terrible for both families, and—'

'Losing Eddie?' Katie couldn't conceal her shock.

After she hadn't heard from Eddie on Valentine's Day, Katie had decided that she had been right to guess that he had had a change of heart and had been unable to face her with it, so of course she hadn't made any attempt to get in touch with him, just as she'd felt it best to allow Gina to make contact with her when she felt ready to do so, rather than bombard her with letters at a time of such personal grief. That hadn't stopped her from ending up thinking rather less of Eddie, though, and feeling that he should have had the decency to get in touch with her, even though she had known all along what would happen.

Now, though, Katie felt as if her heart had been gripped in a giant vice of guilt and shock.

'Yes,' Gina told her wearily. 'I would have let

you know only, well, it's all been so dreadful. Eddie's father collapsed with a heart attack when we heard the news. We were expecting Eddie, you see. He'd telephoned his parents to say he was coming, and that he'd got something important to tell them. We'll never know what it was now.'

'What . . . what happened?' Katie's mouth had gone dry and her heart was hammering. How awful to think she had felt so cross with poor Eddie for not keeping their date.

'No one's really sure. It seems that a fight broke out in a pub down by the docks between two sailors, and Eddie stepped in to intervene and break it up, only instead he ended up bleeding to death after one of the sailors turned on him with a broken bottle. First Leonard and now Eddie. It's so hard to believe, and it seems so . . . so bloody unfair.'

'Oh, Gina, I'm so sorry.'

Katie went to hug her friend. Gina's rigid body felt so thin. Katie's was filled with sorrow. Poor Eddie. What a dreadful thing to have happened.

'We've buried him.' Gina's voice was muffled against Katie's shoulder. 'Oh, but Katie, it's all so awful. Eddie's grandmother had hoped to get Eddie interested in the granddaughter of a friend of hers. She desperately wanted him to get married and have a son. She's taken his death very badly, as you can imagine.'

'Yes,' Katie agreed bleakly. She felt all trembly and sick inside. There was no point in saying anything to Gina about Eddie proposing to her. What was the point? But what part had her relationship with Eddie played in his death? Was she in any way to blame? Had he realised that his grand-mother wasn't likely to agree to him marrying her? Had that been on his mind when he had been struck down so that he hadn't been concentrating properly on protecting himself? It was too late now to wish that she had been honest with him, Katie told herself.

Gina straightened up and gently freed herself from Katie's concerned hold.

'My place is with the family now, Katie. Leonard's children need me. I'm all they've got, and . . . little Adam looks so like Leonard. Having them to look after helps, and I know it's what Leonard would want me to do. You are so lucky not to be involved with anyone. Take my advice, my dear, and stay that way, at least until this dreadful war is over.'

Katie hugged Gina tightly, filled with admir-ation for her friend's courage and steadfastness at the same time as she was struggling to come to terms with the shock of Eddie's death, and all that it meant.

Had she in any way contributed to his death? That fear would haunt her, Katie knew.

Whilst the entrance to the hospital smelled of carbolic and starch, on the ward those smells were overlaid by the scent of blood and the other odours of damaged flesh and pain-filled bodies.

Sasha had wanted to come here last night the moment she had been told the news that Bobby was still alive but badly injured, but both Bobby's commanding officer and her parents had insisted that she wait until the morning.

She hadn't slept, of course, watching the dawn break, praying with all her might for Bobby's life.

The bomb had gone off unexpectedly, killing the young sapper who had been tunnelling alongside it, and injuring Bobby, the officer had told them.

'How badly?' Sasha had asked, but the officer had said that he was unable to say.

Now, though, she knew. Both her parents had come with her, and the matron, remembering Grace, who had trained at the hospital, had waived the rules to tell them that Bobby had sustained several severe cuts to his arms, but that the worst injury had been to his left leg, which had been pierced by shrapnel.

'He will live, won't he?' had been Sasha's immediate anxious question.

'We hope so,' the matron had replied, but there had been a look exchanged between her and Sasha's parents that had alerted her to something being concealed from her.

'What is it? What aren't you telling me?' she had demanded.

It had been her mother who had given the matron a small nod of her head, and then reached for Sasha's hand, holding it tightly as the matron told her quietly, 'I'm afraid the leg has had to be amputated. It was damaged so badly that to leave it would have risked gangrene setting in and Bobby losing his life.'

Sasha hadn't said a word but she knew that she

360

had dug her nails into her mother's palm because she had seen the marks later when she had released her mother's hand.

'I want to see him,' she had begged the matron when finally she had been able to speak. 'I want to see him and I want him to know that . . . that nothing's changed between us, because of what's happened.'

The matron had given her a small nod of approval then and that had helped Sasha to refuse her mother's offer to go onto the ward with her. She wasn't a little girl any more. She was a woman, a fiancée of a young man who was going to need her to be brave for both of them.

The ward was quiet, the silence broken only by the squeak of trolley wheels and nurses' shoes on the shiny linoleum-covered floor.

This was, Sasha had understood immediately without having to be told, a ward to which only the most poorly of patients came. Each bed contained a patient, and contraptions and cages protecting damaged limbs and bodies.

Bobby was in a small separate room close to the doors to the ward – rooms reserved for the most poorly patients of all, as Grace could have told her.

He was deeply asleep – 'because of the anaesthetic he was given for his operation,' the nurse who had shown Sasha to his bed told her.

Beneath the bedclothes, it was easy to see where Bobby's leg had been removed because from his thigh downwards on the left side of his body there was nothing. No shape to match the right-hand side, just a flat sheet, empty of anything beneath it. Sasha forced back a sob. She must be brave – for both of them. She thought of Lou and drew comfort from thinking of her twin and of knowing that, more than anyone else, Lou would understand all that she was feeling right now. Even the mean nasty things that she was trying desperately to push to one side; the bits that said— But no, she must not think like that.

'I want to stay with him so that I can be here when he wakes up,' she told the nurse. 'I want him to know the minute that he does that I'm here and that I love him, and that nothing matters to me except that he's alive.'

The nurse's expression softened. She patted Sasha's arm. 'I'll go and see if I can scrounge you a cup of tea.'

What she had dreaded had happened; but Bobby was still alive and he would be safe now from having to go back into danger. If he lived. The tears she was trying to hold back made Sasha blink fiercely. He *must* live. She loved him so much.

His family would have to be told, of course, and his mum would want to come and see him, but for now Sasha wanted to keep him to herself. The only other person she could bear to share this time with, the only person she wanted here to support her, was Lou.

It had been another busy day. Lou had been asked if she wanted to work, given the news about Kieran, but working was preferable to sitting alone thinking about him, and having to think too about

362

how desperately she ached for him still to be alive, and just what that meant.

Unusually, and because they were so busy with the impending invasion, she'd got a Spitfire to deliver down to the South Coast – a job that would normally have fallen to Hamble ferry pool – an emergency delivery, with Lou having to stand in for another ATA pilot who had gone off sick at the last minute, which had meant that she'd flown wearing her uniform skirt and blouse instead of her Sidcot flying suit. Of course, the most difficult part of the flight had been clambering down off the wing without her skirt riding up.

She was halfway towards the ops office when she saw him, standing outside the office, his hands on his hips, his cap pushed back.

Kieran – but it couldn't be.

She must be hallucinating. But he started to walk towards her and suddenly she was running towards him, and then she was being scooped up into his arms and the way he was kissing her was way beyond the powers of any hallucination, Lou decided dizzily, as she wrapped her arms round him and kissed him back.

'You're alive. I was told that you'd been shot down.' She was breathless, kissed breathless, her heart pounding like a drum as Kieran kept her close to his side, his arm around her waist.

'I know. They told me when I rang Thame to speak to you. We did have to ditch after the Luftwaffe got us, but luckily the old girl stayed afloat for long enough for us all to get out. And even more luckily, a vessel on coastal defence duty

363

saw us and picked us up. When I learned you were due down here I cadged a lift to the base.'

'Oh, Kieran.'

'Oh, Louise.'

The way he said her name might be teasing, but the way he was looking at her was anything but.

'I've been given a temporary billet in a cottage less than five miles away, and you've been given leave, so how about I take you there so that you can change into that pretty frock you ATA girls are rumoured to carry around with you, and then we go out for dinner?'

Dinner? Dinner was the last thing on her mind, Lou acknowledged, blushing slightly as she realised what *was*, but she nodded, still trying to take in the fact that Kieran was actually alive.

RAF transport took them into the small village set back from the coast and from there they walked the mile that separated the village from the tiny farm labourers' cottages that the War Office had requisitioned.

It was a long mile when walked hand in hand, and then tucked up against Kieran's side with his arm around her, but Lou didn't have any complaints. Not even when Kieran stopped walking to kiss her. Nor even when his kisses grew far more passionate than she had previously known them and his hand cupped the rounded curve of her breast over the fabric of her blouse.

'I couldn't die, Lou,' he told her. 'Not yet.'

'Not ever,' Lou answered fiercely, making him laugh.

'We all have to die sometime, you know,' he teased, before twining his fingers with hers and tugging her in the direction of the cottages.

Tiny and low, with thick thatched eaves, upper storey windows under them like eyes beneath bushy eyebrows, the cottages drowsed quietly in the spring sunshine.

'Who else is staying here?' Lou asked Kieran as he used a heavy iron key to unlock the door.

'No one.'

Beyond the door the sunshine slatting into the small sitting room, with its huge fireplace, its wattle and daub walls and its stone floor, picked up speckles of golden dust in its beam. Lou stared at them as though her life depended upon doing so before finally looking up at Kieran. There was nothing in his expression to give her any clue as to what he was thinking. Her heart hammered heavily into her ribs – with apprehension, or with hope and expectation? That was a question Lou didn't want to answer.

The door swung closed, shutting out the sunlight. The room smelled of beeswax and lavender. Curtains had been closed over the windows, no doubt a precaution in case the cottage was empty at night. A sofa, covered in faded chintz patterned with fat deep pink cabbage roses against a cream background, was drawn up invitingly in front of the fire, a sturdy-looking armchair set either side of the large inglenook fireplace.

'I thought I would never see you again.' The admission whispered from Lou's lips like a sigh.

Without understanding how she had come to

do so she discovered that she had lifted her hand and placed it against Kieran's heart as though she needed to convince herself that it was actually beating.

'When I knew I was going to have to ditch the plane, I thought of you and this,' Kieran responded, cupping her face and kissing her slowly and oh so deliciously.

'I'd better go and get changed, if we're going out for dinner.'

Kieran nodded. 'Bedroom's on the left at the top of the stairs, bathroom's on the right. I'll make us both a drink whilst you're getting ready.'

The stairs, narrow and twisting, led up from a small inner hallway onto a narrow landing.

In the bathroom Lou washed quickly, trying to avoid noticing the male 'things' – a razor, male cologne, a shaving brush. All familiar from her own home and her father and brother, but somehow so very different seen here, because they belonged to Kieran.

She'd left the overnight case, which all the girls flew with 'just in case' they had to spend the night away from their ferry pool base, in the bedroom, so she made her way back there carrying her uniform and wearing only her underwear. The bedroom was as cosy as the room downstairs, dominated by a large iron-framed bed covered by a quilt made from patches of pretty coloured fabrics in pinks and blues. A rag rug covered the bare floorboards in front of the fire, the rest of the space in the room taken up by a large mahogany wardrobe and a matching tallboy.

Putting her case on the bed, Lou was just unfastening it when the bedroom door opened and Kieran announced, 'I've brought you your drink – a G & T – very weak. Is that . . . Oh.' He stopped abruptly when he realised that she wasn't dressed, putting down the glass he had been holding, his gaze moving swiftly over her body and then averted, as he said thickly, 'God, Lou,' and reached for her.

Lou didn't make any attempt to stop him. She didn't want to stop him. Not one little bit. In fact, what she wanted . . . what she wanted, she admitted, as much as she was capable of thinking logically about anything whilst Kieran was kissing her in the way that he was, was Kieran and exactly this.

Somehow it all seemed so natural and right, from lying on the bed in Kieran's arms, to lying watching him whilst he undressed and then later watching him whilst he slid her underwear from her body and then kissed her so tenderly that her emotions filled her heart.

It was all wonderful and utterly perfect, from Kieran's first passionately tender kiss to the moment when he had held her and watched the shock of her own pleasure seize her, and then beyond that, when they had finally been one and he had told her how much he loved her. So much more, in fact, than her naïve senses had longed for and thought she would ever know, that afterwards, when Kieran had fallen asleep, Lou propped herself up on her elbow and leaned towards him, studying the way his dark lashes shadowed his skin, the way he breathed and the way he turned in towards her, one leg thrown across her body as though to secure her close to him, just for the pleasure of knowing how much she loved him.

They had the evening, the night and the early morning in which to affirm and reaffirm their love for one another, with words and kisses, the feel of Kieran's hand on her body and the feel of his skin beneath her own touch. It was heaven, an oasis of joy so deep and complete that Lou knew it had changed her for ever.

'Now you'll *have* to marry me,' Kieran told her as they locked the cottage and walked back down the lane towards the village, with luck to find some transport to get Lou back to the Hamble ferry unit.

Lou turned her face up toward Kieran's. There was nothing she wanted more.

'I've got to stay down here for a couple more days whilst all the reports are filed but once that's done, you and I are going to go shopping – for an engagement ring.'

It had been a nerve-racking twenty-four hours whilst they waited to see whether or not the wound from Bobby's amputation would remain free of infection, but now the surgeon had said that he was pleased with the way things were progressing.

Bobby had told her over and over again just how much it had meant to him to open his eyes and see Sasha sitting beside his bed, but then he had started to talk nonsense about not wanting to hold her to their engagement because of his injury.

Sasha had soon put a stop to that, by bursting into tears and accusing him of not loving her any more, and had been delighted when her small ploy had worked and had had Bobby insisting vehemently that she was wrong.

The truth was that Sasha couldn't remember when she had last felt so relieved and determined – relieved that Bobby would never be able to go back to active service, and determined that she was going to look after him and love him so much that he would never even miss his leg. But of course she couldn't say that to anyone, especially not Bobby himself, because they wouldn't understand.

She paused in the middle of the letter she was writing to tell Lou what had happened. Lou would understand.

Lou's happiness lasted for just over forty-eight hours – the length of a weekend pass – destroyed by the two letters she received the day after her return from Hamble, one from her mother and one from Sasha, both of them telling her about Bobby's accident and the subsequent amputation of his leg.

Sasha. How could she have overlooked the effect her engagement to Kieran might have on her twin, especially now, with Bobby so badly hurt. Sasha had originally fallen for Kieran every bit as much as she had done herself. She had told Lou that she never wanted to hear his name mentioned again, she had asked Lou to promise her that nothing would ever come between them again, and Lou had given her that promise.

How could Lou break that promise and let Sasha down, after the things Sasha had told her at Christmas?

How could she give Kieran up?

Lou closed her eyes against the tears burning behind them.

She had seen how hurt her mother had been by the distance that existed between her and her own twin sister, Lou's auntie Vi. Her mother had often said that she didn't want that happening to Lou and Sasha, but if Lou married Kieran it was bound to happen, because Sasha would never forgive her. She would think that Lou was deliberately going against all they had said to one another.

Sasha had written that she missed her, asking if there was any chance of Lou going home. Sasha needed her, Lou recognised, because of what had happened to Bobby. Lou couldn't let her down. She mustn't. She only had to think of the effect that fearing Lou would leave her to die in the bomb shaft had had on Sash to know that. No matter how much she loved Kieran – and she did – Sasha had to come first, at least for now, until Lou had had a chance to see her twin and assess the situation.

'So when is it to be, this invasion?' Francine asked Marcus anxiously.

Marcus looked at her and shook his head. 'You know I can't tell you that, but soon.'

'And you'll be going in when it does happen?'

'Yes.'

'I'm such a coward,' Francine told him from the comfort of his arms as they lay together in bed in their apartment at the Dorchester, with the spring sunshine pouring in through the windows, 'and so afraid of losing you, Marcus.'

'You won't lose me, not ever. You and I are bound together for eternity, through this life and beyond it.'

Francine's powder-blue satin négligé, with its swansdown trimming, lay across the chair where she had dropped it when he had taken her in his arms.

When he was away from her he always pictured her here in this room with its high ceiling and elegant plasterwork, the walls painted a soft silver blue that matched the heavy silk curtains.

'Will you get any more leave, before . . . before it happens,' Francine asked. She wished desperately that she could keep him safe here with her for ever. Their happiness was so precious and so fragile with the thought of Marcus going into action any day always to the forefront of her mind.

'Probably not.'

Francine exhaled and looked at him, smoothing the blue satin of the bedspread in her fingers.

'There's something I want to tell you. I've been thinking . . . about Jack. He's such a lovely boy, Marcus, and he can sing – he's inherited that from me. He's clever too, and he's unbending a little towards me. The last time I went down to the cottage, he'd actually asked Wilhelm to look at the range for me. Apparently the chimney needed sweeping and now that that's been done it doesn't smoke any more. He's very protective of Emily.'

Marcus smiled at her and stroked her hair back off her face. She was so beautiful, inside and out. He wished he could wave a magic wand for her and give her what she wanted.

'He really loves her, Marcus. *Really* loves her,' Francine told him painfully.

Marcus drew her against his side, holding her tightly. He knew how much she loved her son.

It was no use, there was no point in her trying to deceive herself or keep hoping. It was too late for that, and had been too late, Francine suspected, from the minute Emily had taken Jack in, giving him the love that had previously been denied him.

She swallowed against the pain constricting her throat and then raised her head so that she could look at Marcus.

'I've made up my mind what I'm going to do about Jack . . .' She took a deep breath. 'You were right, Marcus. It wouldn't be fair to him to separate him from her. If I took him away from her, no matter how much I love him I couldn't ever replace what he'd feel he'd lost. He'd be hurt and he'd miss her. I can't do that to him. I've tried to convince myself that he'll be happy with us, but when I see him with Emily it's obvious how much he loves her.'

Marcus's arm tightened around her.

'I haven't said anything to Emily yet. I'm going

to go down this weekend – but . . . I wanted to tell you now just in case I don't see you again before "it" happens and just in case . . .' She had to stop speaking as her emotions caught her by the throat, suspending her voice.

'I don't want you having to worry about me doing the right thing – or rather, doing the wrong thing. If anything should happen and we don't . . . well, I want you to have only good thoughts and memories of me, Marcus.'

Her tears wet his shoulder as Marcus held her tightly in his arms.

'I never doubted you for a minute,' he told her emotionally. 'I know how hard it's been for you, and how much you love Jack, but I know too that you loved him enough to put him first.'

'It hurts so much to have found him and to know that I have to lose him again, but I have to do it – for his sake and for my own. I couldn't live with the guilt of taking him away from where he wants to be. I'm such a coward too because I don't want you to disapprove of me for being selfish.'

'You aren't a coward. You are one of the bravest people I have ever met. You've faced and come through so much, Fran, things that other people have never had to face. You've been tested and you've won through. For this, for what you are doing now I am more proud of you than you can possibly imagine. And let me tell you that no matter what you had decided, my love for you couldn't change because I know your heart and your goodness.'

'You make me sound so much better than I really am,' Francine tried to smile. 'Just hold me, please, Marcus. Hold me and help me to have the courage to do what I know I have to do.'

TWENTY-FIVE

Katie looked down at the letter she had just finished writing, an outpouring of guilt and misery, written to the one person she knew she could trust to understand how she felt.

Luke.

Others might think it odd that she should write about Eddie to her ex-fiancé, but Katie could not think of anyone whose judgement and opinion she valued more. The letters they had exchanged over the months had shown her a Luke who had grown and matured to become a man who thought deeply and carefully about life and other people, a man who cared about those under his command, and those who were suffering because of the war.

Since Gina had told her about Eddie's death Katie hadn't been able to stop thinking about him. Nor could she stop worrying and feeling guilty, questioning whether, if she had refused him straight away, that could have made a difference and saved his life. Her guilt kept her awake at night and had now finally compelled her to unburden herself to Luke, holding nothing back of what had happened, how she had felt when Eddie had proposed to her and why, and how she now felt in the aftermath of his death.

In her final paragraph she had added an apology to Luke for bothering him with her problems when he had so much to face, and then added an extra few words, having remembered that she hadn't told him yet about what had been said at Rainbow Corner, about the Allies already being aware of the plight of the Italian population and that steps were already being taken to help them.

She had guessed from his last letter that they were advancing on Rome. She hoped he would find the people there in less dreadful circumstances than the people of Naples, and reflected not for the first time that she was glad that Luke wasn't involved in the assault on Monte Cassino, which was costing so many Allied lives.

'What do you mean, we can't get engaged?'

They were in the pub where Kieran had taken her to discuss their pretending to be planning to get engaged. Outside its doors, spring flowers were blooming in the hedgerows and on the banks of the stream that flowed through the village, where Lou had seen a duck and her ducklings as she cycled past on her way to meet Kieran.

'It's because of Sasha. I should have thought, but I didn't, and now it's even worse. The most dreadful thing has happened. Bobby, her fiancé, has had to have his leg amputated, and Sasha's written to me asking me if I've got any leave due. She needs me, Kieran.'

'Yes, I can understand that, but how does her needing you affect us getting engaged?'

'When we first met you, she loved you, Kieran, just like I did, and well, I don't know if she ever really stopped loving you. Don't you see how impossible it is for me to tell her that you and I love each other, when she's there with Bobby so badly injured? We quarrelled dreadfully over you, Kieran, and I made it worse when she first got engaged. It was only this Christmas that we finally made things up. She asked me to promise her then that I'd never let anything or anyone come between us again and I agreed. Now if I tell her that we're engaged, she'll think I'm breaking that promise. We need to wait until . . .'

'Until what? Until when, exactly? You said you loved me.'

'I do,' Lou insisted. She could see that Kieran was angry, and of course she didn't blame him.

'Well then, it's you and me you should be putting first, not your sister. You're acting like a kid – the kid you were when I first met you. Perhaps that's what you still are.'

'No, Kieran. Just let me go and see Sasha and find out—'

'What? If she'll let you get engaged to me?' Kieran shook his head. 'Don't bother. I thought you and me had something special. I thought . . .' He shook his head again as though unable to find the words to explain his feelings. 'When two people love one another they put each other first, not their ruddy sister.'

'Kieran, that's not fair.'

'Isn't it? How would you feel if I told you that I wasn't allowed to love you because *my* sister didn't want me to?'

He had a point, Lou knew.

'It's different with twins,' was the only lame answer she could come up with, but all it seemed to do was further ignite Kieran's anger.

'Twins! Don't remind me about that. Caused me enough trouble, the pair of you did back in Liverpool, without you causing me any more. The trouble is that I thought you'd grown up and become a woman, but I was wrong. Well, I'll tell you what, Lou – you go and find out if your twin will let you love me, but don't bother coming to tell me what she said, because I don't want a girl who needs permission to love me; I want a girl – a woman – who knows her own mind and who makes it up for herself. I thought you were that girl, but obviously you aren't.'

'Kieran,' Lou protested, but it was too late, he was striding away and through the pub door.

As badly as she wanted to run after him, Lou knew that she couldn't.

Francine's heart had felt heavier with every mile that the tired train, with its soot-blackened windows, and full carriages packed mainly with young women in uniform, had carried her north. Marcus had rejoined his men. The whole of southern England had become a gigantic armed camp with huge tank, truck and artillery parks and innumerable arms dumps. Enough to equip the forces of over 3,500,000 assembled for the invasion. Was that the reason why there were so few men in uniform on board the train? Because they had already all travelled south and were right now awaiting the order that could carry the Allies to their victory, but which most certainly would carry many of those young men to their deaths?

Fran gave a shiver, uncomfortably conscious of the way she stood out a little from the other travellers in her smart powder-blue costume, with its gay little matching hat trimmed with a small bunch of artificial lilies of the valley, and wishing now that she had chosen to wear something less elegant. The soft pale grey kid of her court shoes and matching handbag seemed to rebuke her for their obvious luxury. She had seen the way the other occupants of the first-class carriage – young women officers in tailored uniforms, which might have been made for them at Austin Reed but which were still made from inferior cloth, as part of the war effort – had looked at her and then studiedly avoided looking at her again. The trouble was that all her clothes were equally smart. Unlike most British women she was not having to rely on clothes bought before the war had begun, thanks to having only returned from working in America just after the start of the war, and the time she had spent in Egypt.

The young women officers made her feel frivolous and useless, adding to her misery. Better to think in general terms about the coming invasion instead of dwelling on her own private despair.

After all, almost every occupied country in Europe was joining in the planned invasion: the

French, the Poles, the Belgians, the Dutch, the Norwegians and the Czechs. The Australians and the New Zealanders were mobilising five air squadrons each, at least according to the papers. But whenever the invasion took place it was the British and the Americans who would go in first, and that meant Marcus. Fear for him clutched at Francine's stomach, at the thought of what he would be facing.

She had telephoned Emily to tell her that she was coming and it had been arranged that Wilhelm would take Jack to the cottage to meet her.

Francine had been rehearsing what she was going to say to him and, ridiculously for someone who had been a singer and used to appearing on stage in front of an audience, she was desperately afraid that she wouldn't be able to say what had to be said without her emotions overwhelming her.

'It's all right, Wilhelm. I can wait for my aunt on my own. Mum needs you. She gets upset when I'm here.'

Wilhelm patted Tommy on the shoulder and nodded, saying warmly, 'You are a good boy, Tommy.'

Tommy. Jack wished that he really was Tommy and that he didn't have to be here. He wished that Emily really was his mum and that he could stay with her.

He wished too that his auntie Fran wouldn't cry whenever she saw him because it made him feel guilty.

* * *

380

Francine could see Jack waiting outside the cottage for her when the taxi dropped her off.

He'd obviously ridden over on his bicycle because he was standing beside it, looking awkward and uncomfortable, and so endearingly lovable that Francine just wanted to hold him and breathe in the now familiar scent of boy and chalk and country air. But she knew from experience that if she did he would go rigid in her hold and turn his face away from her, so instead she simply said, 'It's a lovely day,' as she looked from the blue sky, with its white fluffy clouds, to the new leaves on the trees, and then at the lambs in the field beyond the cottage garden. New life burgeoning everywhere. Spring, with all its promise and its hope was surely the worst time in which to suffer the loss of a loved one, and soon now there would be many, many households amongst the Allied forces where such losses were going to have to be borne.

'Let's go inside, shall we, Jack?' As she went to put her hand on his shoulder, he moved away from her. Tears stung the backs of her eyes. She longed for Marcus and his calm support, but she knew that this was something that she had to do herself. After all, Jack was her child. But he didn't want to be her child. He wanted Emily as his mother.

The cottage had been stocked for her visit with fresh milk and even a couple of eggs, but Jack refused a cup of tea and Francine could tell from the longing way he was looking through the window just where he really wanted to be.

There was no point in putting it off, no point

in prolonging his distress in order that she could delay her own, by stealing another day with him before she finally told him what she had to tell him.

She went over to him and said to him quietly, trying to conceal the desperation she was feeling for his sake as well as her own, 'Please come and sit down, Jack. There's something I want to . . . to tell you.' Not really something she wanted to tell him but something she *had* to tell him, Francine admitted to herself. In London, in the apartment, rehearsing what she would say she had felt far more in control than she did right now. Funny to think that she stood up and sung in front of audiences of hundreds without a qualm and yet here she was, shaking in her elegant shoes at the thought of speaking to one boy. This, though, was different. She might have given herself a set role to play, set lines to learn, but they could provide only a thin covering for her feelings, which didn't protect her at all.

She could see the wary look in Jack's eyes; the way he moved back from her and looked longingly towards the door, wanting to escape from her. Francine ached to hold him close and reassure him. But doing that would not reassure him. It would increase his anxiety because it was Emily from whom he wanted to receive a mother's embrace, not her.

He was sitting down now, or rather perching on the edge of an old-fashioned rush-bottomed chair, his short trousers revealing his thin legs, the knees polished and shiny as though he had scrubbed

them before coming out. Francine could picture
Emily instructing him to do so, determined to let
her see that she provided all the mothering he
needed. The laces of one of his shoes were coming
undone, the shoes themselves well polished.
Francine closed her eyes. As clearly as though it
had been yesterday she could hear her own mother
telling her children that you could judge a person
by the state of their shoes. She could see her mother
too, kneeling down every evening to polish the
shoes she had spread out on an old newspaper.
Her mother would have loved Jack.

'Do you remember the fun we had together when
we stayed at your auntie Jean's, Jack?' she asked
him.

For a minute she thought that he wasn't going
to reply but then with obvious reluctance he
nodded. Emily was obviously bringing him up to
be honest and truthful. Francine felt as though a
knife was being twisted in her heart.

'I'm sorry that you weren't happy with Vi and
Edwin.'

He was tense now, his body stiff and unmoving.

'They were unkind to you, I know.'

'I'm not going back to them.'

His voice was unexpectedly sturdy and strong,
but Francine could see the fear in his eyes.

'Were they ever kind to you, Jack?' she asked
him. 'Can you remember? Perhaps when you were
little?'

What was she hoping for? That he would say
something that would take away her own guilt
and pain?

'Auntie Jean was always nice to me. And Luke and Grace and the twins.'

'Oh, Jack!'

He was retreating from her again, pushing himself back into the chair.

'I was always in trouble at home for doing things wrong.' It was the first piece of information he had given her voluntarily.

'It wasn't you who had done wrong, Jack,' she told him sadly. 'It was me.'

Vi and Edwin had punished Jack for her sins, but Francine knew that she would never get her sister to admit as much.

Jack was frowning now and looking puzzled.

Having come this far she couldn't stop now. It wouldn't be fair to him, no matter how hard she was finding it to tell him the truth.

She took a deep breath and then pulled up another chair so that she could sit directly in front of him. The temptation to take hold of his hands and hold them in her own was hard for her to resist, but she knew that if she touched him he would withdraw from her.

'Jack, there's something I have to tell you,' she began quietly.

He was looking at her at last, his gaze still wary.

'I know this isn't going to be easy for you to understand. It isn't easy for me to tell you, but the truth is that . . .' Her mouth had gone dry, her voice cracking. She had to take another deep breath. 'The truth is that Vi and Edwin aren't really your parents. They . . . they adopted you when you were a baby because . . . because your own mother couldn't look after you.'

Now she had his attention, his eyes rounding as he focused on her.

'I know this must be hard for you to hear—'

'No. I'm glad that they aren't my mum and dad,' Jack told her emphatically. 'I suppose that's why they were always so angry with me, because they didn't really want me.'

'Oh, Jack, they did want you,' Francine protested. 'Vi wanted you very very much. She begged to have you and she promised—'

'She said I was a nuisance and that I got on her nerves and under her feet.'

'Oh, Jack!' She wanted desperately to hold him, so very desperately, but she knew that she mustn't and that he wouldn't welcome her hold.

'I'm sorry you were unhappy.'

There was a small silence whilst Jack looked at her and then away, before looking back at her again. 'If they aren't my mum and dad, then who is?'

Francine took a deep breath. 'Well, I am your mother, Jack.'

'You?'

'Yes, me.'

She could see that he was struggling to assimilate what she had told him, so she waited several minutes before explaining, 'It was because I wasn't married when I had you and because I was very young, only sixteen, that I had to let you go. I wanted to do the best I could for you, Jack.'

Would he understand? Could he understand or was he too young?

385

'When my sister Vi said that she and Edwin wanted to be your parents I agreed that they should be. I wanted you to stay with the family, you see. I thought I was doing the right thing – the best thing for you.'

'So they aren't my mum and dad at all then, they're my aunt and uncle, and you had me but you had to give me to them because you weren't married?'

Francine exhaled. 'Yes. That's right. I'm so sorry that Vi and Edwin were unkind to you. I didn't know. I wish I had.' Francine could feel her self-control slipping away from her. If only Marcus were here with her. She wasn't sure she had the strength for this.

'It wasn't your fault.' Her son's voice was gruff, almost grown up, enabling her to regain control. Almost grown up, but he was also scuffing his foot as the embarrassed boy that he still was, as he asked her, 'So if I haven't got a proper mother does that mean I can choose who I want to be my mum?'

She mustn't allow herself to give in to her own grief or to ache for the fact that he wasn't throwing himself into her arms and declaring that she was the mother he wanted. After all, she had known that that wouldn't happen. That was why she was here. There would be time enough for her to grieve for what she had lost later, when she was on her own.

This was it, the moment when she had to prove her love for him by putting him first. Francine could feel herself wavering, wanting to reach out and beg him to be hers, but she must not do that – for his sake.

It took every ounce of resolution she had for her to say, 'You can, Jack, but I think I know already who you want to choose. It's Emily, isn't it?'

He nodded. 'I like you,' he told her earnestly, his previous silence with her giving way to a rush of words stemming from relief, Francine thought painfully. He continued, 'But you don't seem like a mother . . .'

'And Emily does?'

'Yes.'

It hurt – of course it did – but she had had to hear it, and to confirm what she already knew.

'Can we go and tell Mum?' His face was alight with eagerness and impatience. 'She's been worrying ever so much that you would try to take me away. She doesn't say anything but I've heard her crying at night.'

'You really love her, don't you, Jack?'

'Yes, she's the best mum in the whole world. I'm glad he's gone, though – Con. I didn't like him and he didn't like me.'

Francine forced a smile. He hadn't asked her about his father and perhaps it was just as well.

It was over and done. And now she was waiting for the train to take her back to London. She felt tired and very alone. She could have gone to see Grace but she hadn't felt in the mood for sympathy; her pain went too deep for that. Francine looked at her watch. Another half an hour before her train was due. She settled back on the wooden platform seat, barely looking up five minutes later when someone sat down beside her, until she realised that that someone was Emily. Emily, out of breath and puffing slightly, her face flushed as though she had been hurrying. Emily, in her green and brown floral print dress, her brown cardigan, and her sturdy sensible shoes. Her nose was shiny and her curls untidy beneath her green pork-pie hat, her appearance in stark contrast to Francine's own city elegance, but it was Emily who had the advantage over her, and not the other way round, Francine acknowledged.

'I've been thinking,' Emily announced without any preamble. 'What you've done for Tommy is something I'll never forget, and nor will he. I can't deny that I wish you'd never seen him and that none of this had ever happened but it has, and well, deep down inside I don't feel right about you giving him up and never seeing him again, so I was thinking, how would it be if you were, in public, like, to be his godmother, and you now come down and see him regular, and p'haps when this war is over have him up to London to stay with you? A bright boy like Tommy should be going to London to them museums there, and that, especially if he's going to go to Oxford.'

Emily had been in such a hurry to get out what she wanted to say that she was out of breath, what with having to hurry so fast to the station as well, in case she missed Francine.

To an onlooker they would have nothing in common, Francine realised. They presented such a contrast to one another: she in her expensive costume, with her face discreetly made up and her blonde hair carefully groomed, and Emily with her countrywoman's appearance. But in reality they were not so much sisters under the skin as mothers. Mothers who both loved and longed for the same child. A tear ran down Francine's cheek to land on her lap, followed by another, and then somehow Emily was holding her and comforting her and the two of them were crying together, and unexpectedly Francine knew that, beyond the pain she felt now, there was something born of their love for one boy that could be the foundation for a future in which they would be allowed to share that love. Out of selflessness had come generosity, out of love had come more love. She had prayed that having found him again she would not lose her son a third time, and now Francine recognised that that prayer had been answered.

It was a funny old world, Emily decided as she walked home – despite the urgings of both Wilhelm and Tommy she flatly refused to learn to ride a bike; who would ever have thought that she would actually grow to respect and, yes, like that too pretty, too young girl she had once watched from the shadows steal Con's attention away from her. She had certainly never imagined that it would be that same girl who would be responsible for the greatest gift her life had given her – both the greatest gifts, if she added in the fact that she would never have moved to Whitchurch if it hadn't been for Tommy and thus she would never have met Wilhelm.

It had been a shock when Francine had announced that she was stepping back and letting Tommy make up his own mind what he wanted to do, a shock and a blessed relief, and yet after Francine had gone and she'd had time to think things over, Tommy having headed for the vegetable plot to relay the good news to Wilhelm, Emily had discovered that beneath her joy and relief she could still imagine how and what Francine would be feeling. She would have all those years of loving Tommy and watching him grow, and how those years would rush by for her. Francine, on the other hand, would have the same number of years thinking about the son she had lost – and for her the years could end up dragging in a misery of grief and loss. Emily believed in fair play and justice being done. Francine had played fair by Tommy and by her, and now it was Emily's turn to play fair by Francine.

It hadn't taken a moment for her to put on her hat and her cardigan and set off for the station, and if she had had doubts about what she was doing on the way there, well, now that she was on her way back there was none.

Tommy was happy now to be relieved of his fear of being taken away from her, but in years to come, and once he was a young man, it seemed to Emily that it would only be natural for him to be curious about the woman who had given birth to him, the family she was part of and, of course, the man who had fathered him.

Far better for Francine to be a part of his life openly than for him to feel as an adult that he couldn't seek Francine out without hurting her, Emily felt.

Because when push came to shove what both she and Francine wanted was the same thing, and that was for Tommy to be happy, and to be able to contribute towards that happiness.

TWENTY-SIX

Tiredly Lou pushed her curls back off her face as she stepped down from the train to the platform at Lime Street Station.

It was just over two weeks since she'd received Sasha's letter telling her about Bobby, just over two weeks since she had had that terrible row with Kieran that had ended their engagement before it had begun and sent him storming out of her life.

Her life, but not her heart. It might have taken a long time for her to get there but now finally she knew just how much she did love him, Lou admitted.

Losing him had left an ache inside her that would never stop, an emptiness in her life that could never be filled, but if she had to make her choice again she would make the same one, she told herself fiercely as she joined the other travellers making their way out of the station and into the bright May sunshine.

Three years ago this same month, Liverpool had almost been destroyed when it had been blitzed by the Germans. The city still bore the scars from that dreadful time, outwardly on its streets and buildings, but also in the hearts of those who had lost loved ones.

Lou and Sasha had still been girls at that time, giggling and dancing their way through life, never imagining that they would ever be apart, much less fall out.

So much had changed since then. The majority of uniforms Lou could see on the street around her were being worn by Americans, their presence in the city taken for granted now with so many of them at the huge supply base near Warrington.

The grey hulls of the convoy ships and their naval escort vessels, both in the docks and lying out at anchor across the Liverpool bar, were a familiar sight, though. The convoys had been making their dangerous journey across the Atlantic and back throughout the whole of the war.

The lifting of the rules about how much fabric could be used in clothes at least meant that the young women thronging the city centre were once again wearing pretty dresses, even if most of them were home-made rather than shop bought.

Lou hadn't had the heart to wear anything pretty herself. What was the point when there was no Kieran to see her? Instead, she had travelled in her uniform blouse and skirt, but even wearing that had brought back painful memories of the night they had spent together, when they had first declared their love for one another.

She'd written to tell both Sasha and her mother that she would be coming home on leave. However, even though she believed with fierce conviction that she had done the right thing, she still felt apprehensive about seeing Sasha. Her sister had seemed so emotionally fragile the last time she had seen her that Lou was worried about how Sash would cope with what had happened to Bobby.

It would surely have been the cruellest of cruel things for her to turn up boasting about her engagement to a fit and healthy man who they had once both fallen for, in the face of her twin's commitment to a man who had been so badly wounded.

The familiar walk home from the city centre took Lou up through Edge Hill to the bottom end of Wavertree, and then off into Ash Grove, where her parents lived, with its neat, immaculately kept houses, their small front gardens showing off carefully cultivated displays of spring flowers to one side of the patterned tiled paths that led up to donkey-whitened front steps and burgundy-painted front doors.

The houses had been built in the aftermath of the First World War, to home the more affluent members of the lower middle class, who had seen the benefits enjoyed by those well off enough to move out of the city into Wavertree proper.

Even the fallen blossom from flowering cherry trees was swept up daily by the Grove's housewives, including her own mother, Lou acknowledged as she cut down the well-trodden path to one side of her home so that she could go in through the back door.

All the houses in the avenue had back gardens as neat as those to the front. A rutted lane separated the gardens from the allotments and Lou could remember her mother standing at the gate that led onto that lane, waiting for her and Sasha to come home from school the first week they had been allowed to walk there on their own.

Now when her mother stood at the gate it was to look towards the allotments, to call Lou's father in for his meals.

Today, though, her mother was in the kitchen, making what smelled like leek and potato soup, the back door ajar to allow in some fresh air, Lou's cheery, 'It's me, Mum, I'm home,' causing her mother to turn round from the stove, putting down the spoon with which she had been stirring the contents of the pan, to hurry over to greet her.

'You're earlier than you said. Me and Sasha were going to walk down to the station to meet you.'

'I managed to catch an earlier connection than I'd expected. How is Sash, Mum?'

'Bearing up. I can't say that it wasn't a terrible shock, though. Now, let me have a look at you. You've lost weight.' Jean's smile gave way to a concerned frown as she turned to study her youngest child.

Lou shook her head ruefully, a young woman now, Jean recognised with a small pang of sadness for the speed with which the years had passed, her sadness immediately banished by her pride in her daughter.

Yes, she had lost weight and that was because she hadn't felt like eating since she and Kieran had had their row, but of course she couldn't tell her mother that.

'It's because we've been so busy, Mum, moving planes all over the place.'

Lou managed to present her mother with a reassuring smile. There was no point in giving her poor mum something else to worry about.

'Well, you should still eat.'

The kitchen, so dearly familiar, and so taken for granted during the years she had lived at home, might have had to go without its biannual coat of distemper, thanks to the war and rationing, the colour on the yellow walls faintly patchy by the cooker from steam and heat, but this was still home, and this room in particular so filled with the warmth of her mother's love for them all.

'Is Sash here? I've been thinking about her all the way home.'

Her poor twin. How was she coping? Lou was both longing to see her and half dreading doing so.

'She's still down at the hospital. The nurses have let her give a hand looking after Bobby – not doing nursing things, of course, but keeping him company and that. I must say, I'm proud of the way she's handling things. She's being ever so sensible and making plans for when Bobby gets out of hospital. She's pestering your dad to let them get married so that she can look after him and make sure he does what the doctors tell him to do. Not that Bobby's the type to feel sorry for himself, bless him.'

Lou was conscious of a small surge of relief as she listened to her mother. She'd been so afraid that Bobby's accident would be too much for Sasha to bear, with her being so dependent on him, but from what their mother was saying, Sash was coping really well.

'Sash still wants to marry Bobby then, despite what's happened?' Lou asked.

Jean's frown deepened. 'Well, that's a fine question to ask, Lou. Of course she does. She loves him and you don't stop loving someone just because they've lost their leg. I should have thought you'd have known better than to think otherwise. Sasha is proving what she's made of and we're all very proud of her.'

Jean saw the expression on Lou's face and immediately her maternal anxiety was aroused. Something was wrong; now that she had had the chance to look at Lou properly she could see that it wasn't just weight she'd lost. She'd lost the sparkle from her eyes, and the glow from her cheeks as well. They'd been replaced by dark circles beneath her eyes and hollows under her cheekbones. Her daughter had something on her mind that was troubling her – or was it something in her heart that was the cause of the sadness in Lou's eyes?

'I'll put the kettle on,' Jean announced. 'Your dad's out and won't be back for a while.'

'Down at the allotment, is he?' Lou asked, summoning a smile. It was all very well for their mother to say that Sasha still wanted to marry Bobby and that she loved him; Lou wanted to hear her twin tell her that herself, before she could believe it. The Sasha she had seen in Newcastle would not have been strong enough to cope with what had happened. She had leaned on Bobby for support, and Lou couldn't visualise her twin taking on the role of being the one to do the supporting. She hated the thought of Sasha having not just to struggle with the awfulness of what had happened but also having to pretend to be brave and strong when inside she really felt frightened and alone and trapped – the very feelings Sasha had described so vividly to Lou over Christmas.

'No. He's gone down to the depot to speak to the bosses to see if there's any chance of them taking Bobby on at the Salvage Unit once he gets his discharge from the army. Sasha told your dad how much Bobby looks up to him and how he'd talked to her about trying to get into salvage work once the war is over.'

Lou took off her coat and went to hang it up in the hall, returning to pull out one of the kitchen chairs and sit down on it.

'But Bobby's lost a leg, and the work they do—'

'They do all sorts, Lou. According to your dad Bobby's very good with his hands, and good at electrics too, so it could be that they'll take him on and train him up to work in that department. The doctor says that once they've sorted him out with a false leg, Bobby will be able to move about very well. He won't need to be in a wheelchair or anything.'

The kettle was singing. Jean picked it up and poured a little of the boiling water into the pot, swilling it round to warm it before emptying it out and then putting in the tea leaves and filling the teapot.

Watching the familiar ritual, Lou felt the tight bands of pain round her heart tighten even further. Would she ever stand in her own kitchen, making tea for the man she loved and the children they would have had together? Blinking away tears, she took the mug of tea her mother handed to her.

Something was wrong, Jean just knew it. And girls being what they were, Jean was pretty sure that the cause of Lou's sadness was some young man.

Some young man? A mother's memory was very keen where her children were concerned. Names mentioned, looks given, things picked up on were never forgotten, simply stored away.

Picking up her own mug, and sitting down across the table from Lou, Jean asked as casually as she could, 'Have you seen anything more of that Mallory boy?'

The mug slipped from Lou's grasp, hot tea spilling on to her mother's immaculately clean kitchen floor, and it wasn't just the hot sting of the tea on her arm that filled her eyes with tears, Lou knew.

'So it is him that's got you looking like a wet weekend,' Jean pronounced once she had cleaned up the mess and made Lou sit down with a cold cloth over her slightly scalded arm. 'You're better off without someone like that, Lou. It was his uncle that caused your Aunt Francine so much trouble, leaving her with a baby and her only just sixteen and him married.'

An awful thought struck Jean. 'It isn't that, is

it, Lou? He hasn't had what he wanted and then left you . . . ?'

At another time she might have been more shocked to learn about Kieran's uncle Con and her aunt Francine, but right now her mother's question had Lou swiftly defending her love.

'It's nothing like that, Mum. Kieran isn't like that. He's honest and decent, and brave . . . and he's got ambitions, plans for what he wants to do after the war.'

Jean's heart sank when she heard the emotion in Lou's voice. She was right then: it was the Mallory boy that was the cause of the bleak look in Lou's eyes.

'Well, I'm sorry if he's hurt you, love, but—'

'It isn't Kieran who's hurt me, Mum. He . . . he wants to marry me. We were going to go and choose the ring the day I got the letters from you and Sasha telling me about Bobby. He wanted us to come to Liverpool so that he could ask Dad's permission for us to be engaged.'

Jean was nonplussed. She could understand a girl feeling low because she was keen on a boy who wasn't keen on her, but for a girl to feel low because the lad she was obviously head over heels about had proposed to her? That was something Jean didn't understand.

'So if you love him and he wants to marry, why the long face?' Jean demanded before asking in a more concerned voice, 'He hasn't got a wife, has he, or . . . or got some poor girl into trouble?'

'No. It's nothing like that, Mum. Kieran's too honourable to do anything like that,' Lou repeated.

'Then what is it?'

Lou hadn't meant to say anything to her mother but now that somehow she had guessed that something was wrong, Lou couldn't see any point in refusing to say what it was.

'It's Sash, Mum.'

'Sasha?'

'Yes. You see, when we first met Kieran, when we were doing our dancing and he was working for his uncle, we were both sweet on him, and if anything I reckon that it was Sash he favoured rather than me. He was just a lad then, Mum,' Lou defended her beloved, guessing what her mother was going to say about a young man encouraging both her young teenage daughters. 'He's different now, more grown up. The war does that to you. He says now that he thought of us just like he does his own siblings – a bit of a nuisance and always getting into scrapes for which he got the blame.

'But it was because we fell out over him that Sasha turned back that night she fell into the bomb crater. When I saw her at Christmas she told me how she has these awful nightmares about being trapped and me leaving her there to run after Kieran. You heard her say not long back that she hated the sound of his name. I told her in Newcastle that I'd never let her down, and that I would never have chosen Kieran over her. I promised her, Mum, and we both said how much we'd missed one another and how we'd never fall out again. When me and Kieran first realised how we felt about one another, I was so happy I couldn't think of anything

401

else, but then when I got Sasha's letter saying what had happened to Bobby I couldn't help thinking how she'd feel about me and Kieran, especially if secretly she is still sweet on him. I can't do that to her, Mum. I can't have her thinking that I've let her down and that she doesn't matter to me.'

In her agitation Lou got up, discarding the towel Jean had placed over her arm, pacing the kitchen floor as her emotions spilled out of her.

'I tried to tell Kieran but he just got angry with me and said that I should put us – him and me – first and that I couldn't love him if Sasha is more important to me than he is.'

Jean stood up and then sat down again. Beneath the anxiety she felt for Lou she was filled with pride and love for this, the youngest and the most turbulent, the most troublesome, some might say, of her four children. Who would have thought that boisterous headstrong Lou would feel so deeply about her loyalty to her twin or be prepared to make such a sacrifice for her?

'Well, your young man does have a point,' she felt obliged to say, forced to confess, 'When your auntie Vi accused me of putting your dad before her I'm afraid she was right. When a girl gets married it's only right that she puts her husband first.'

'It was different with you and Auntie Vi, though, Mum. Auntie Vi isn't like Sash. Sash has been through so much and I didn't even know. But I should have known, with us being twins. I feel really bad about that . . .'

'And you want to make it up to her for not

knowing. I do understand, love. I'm a twin myself, remember.'

Mother and daughter exchanged a look of mutual comprehension, and then Lou went and sat down again, leaning across the table to tell her mother fiercely, 'I can't marry Kieran if Sasha secretly loves him too, Mum. And I can't marry him if she hates him because of falling into the bomb shaft, or because he's got both his legs and Bobby hasn't.'

'You're being a good loyal sister, Lou, but do you really think that Sasha doesn't love *you* enough to want you to be happy? If you were in her shoes would you want her sacrificing her happiness for you? Of course you wouldn't.'

'I'm stronger than Sash, Mum,' Lou said simply.

'Well, I don't know what to say except that if I was you I'd wait to make up my mind until I'd seen Sasha and spoken to her. Sasha's stronger than you think, Lou, and this terrible accident to Bobby has proved that. It's as though it's brought out the best in her, and given her strength. And as for her secretly being sweet on your Kieran, well, I wouldn't know about that, but it seems to me that she loves her Bobby very much indeed.'

Your Kieran. How wonderful those words were, but was Kieran still hers or had he given up on her?

'What time does Sasha leave the hospital, Mum, only I thought I might walk down and meet her? I could see Bobby as well, if he's up to having visitors.'

'And if Sister will let you.'

*   *   *

'. . . and the doctor says he's pretty sure that it's twins and that's why I've been feeling so tired all the time. I suppose I should have thought of that for myself, with twins being in the family and me being so big,' Grace smiled ruefully as she relayed what the doctor had told her to Seb, who had nipped home from work especially to see how she was, knowing how miserable feeling so tired had been making her.

Seb was having to work long hours now in the run-up to the invasion, of which no one knew the full details other than the top men involved. He wasn't just listening for enemy messages any more but was picking up highly secret messages from agents dropped behind enemy lines in preparation for the invasion, and that meant that Y Section was on high alert and working round the clock. With Grace just over six months pregnant and beginning to feel the strain of carrying what they now knew could be two babies, Seb was hoping that the invasion would be well underway before the babies were due.

The reason Grace had been to see the doctor today was because Seb had come home earlier in the week to find her crying over the ironing, because she was so exhausted, her pretty face pink and blotchy and her normally delicate ankles badly swollen.

It would be much easier for Grace if she had family living close to her here in Whitchurch, Seb felt, but of course she didn't, and the train journey to Liverpool in wartime conditions to see her mother was not something Seb would want Grace to undertake.

'You need to rest more,' he told her now. 'I'll ask around and see if we can get someone to come in and do the cleaning, and the washing can go to a laundry.'

Grace was horrified. 'No, Seb, I don't want you to do that. People will think I'm not a proper wife to you if I have to have someone in to clean and do the washing just because there's to be a baby.'

'Babies,' Seb reminded her. 'And you are the best and the only wife I could ever want.'

Grace gave him a wan smile. The truth was that she was feeling very poorly and tired indeed, but didn't want to make a fuss. After all, her own mother and her grandmother before her had both had twins, and her mum had had her and Luke to care for as well. Grace couldn't ever remember Jean complaining of tiredness and bursting into tears over a bit of ironing.

'I'm glad it's all been sorted out between Francine and Emily about Jack,' she told Seb instead. 'Mind you, I don't think I could have done what Francine did and give him up.'

'I think that, like Francine, you would have done whatever you thought best for your child. Jack – Tommy – loves Emily and anyone can see how well she looks after him and how much he means to her.'

'I like Emily,' Grace admitted. 'I didn't think I would but I do. She's kind, and although she's younger, in a way she reminds me of Mum. I'm not sure I'll be able to remember to call Jack Tommy, though.'

*   *   *

In the end, mainly because she had been mistaken for Sasha, Lou suspected, she was allowed onto the ward, where she found her twin sitting at Bobby's bedside, the two of them talking, not having seen her. Then Sasha's laughter rang out, a sound Lou had not expected in view of the awfulness of Bobby's injury.

Sasha looked up and saw her, a wide smile lighting up her face as she got up from her chair and hurried over to hug Lou.

'I was going to wait in the foyer for you, but then one of the nurses must have thought I was you and she told me I could come onto the ward.'

'Come and say hello to Bobby. He loves having visitors, especially when they make a fuss of him,' Sasha instructed her.

'I don't want to intrude,' Lou began, but Sasha laughed and shook her head, linking her arm through Lou's as she said, 'How could you be intruding? We were just talking about our wedding, weren't we, Bobby?' She drew Lou towards his bed. 'I've told him that I don't intend to wait until he can walk down the aisle so he'd better make his mind up to that.'

'And I've told her that I will walk down it, and up it again, even if I have to have a couple of mates to hold me up so that I can,' Bobby insisted, smiling warmly at Lou.

They were so relaxed and natural with one another, so apparently happy together and so . . . so accepting of what had happened that just listening to them brought a lump to Lou's throat.

Or was Sasha merely playing a part she felt she had to play for Bobby's sake?

'Do Mum and Dad know about this wedding yet, only I seem to remember Dad saying no wedding until the war is over,' she teased them, trying to match their light-hearted manner.

'Ah, well, because Dad keeps saying that when this invasion finally happens, that will be as good as the end of the war, I've decided that means that once the invasion does start then me and Bobby can get married. I had a word with Bobby's landlady after his accident when I went to tell her what had happened and it turns out that a cousin of hers has a flat she wants to let out 'cos she's moving to Manchester to be with her daughter, and I've put a deposit down on it, and me and Bobby have got first refusal on it.'

Lou was impressed.

'Have you told Mum about any of this yet?'

'No, but I'm going to tell her now that you're home, and we can make some proper plans. It's not going to be a big wedding. Bobby's doing very well, but I don't want him getting set back with a big do. I want only one attendant, Lou, and that's you, and one of Bobby's pals will be our best man.'

'She's only rushing things 'cos she wants to make sure she'll get a widow's pension if I pop me clogs,' Bobby grinned, but Sasha's face went white.

'Don't you dare go tempting fate by saying things like that, Bobby. You know perfectly well that I don't think I'd be able to go on without you. You're my hero. You saved my life. You are my life, Bobby.'

Discreetly Lou turned away to give them a bit of privacy. Either her twin was a far better actress than Lou had ever thought, or she genuinely did love her fiancé.

'Bobby seems to be taking things very well,' Lou told her twin after they had left the hospital.

They were walking arm in arm up Edge Lane on their way home.

'Well, he is now,' Sasha agreed, 'but he wasn't at first. He was all for breaking off our engagement on account of feeling that it wasn't fair on me being tied to someone so badly injured, but I wasn't having any of that, and like I told him: he saved my life and there was no way I was going to turn my back on him.'

'It won't be easy, Sash,' Lou felt bound to say, but to her surprise Sasha contradicted her immediately.

'It will be a lot easier than waking up every day not knowing whether Bobby would still be alive the next day. I was so afraid of him being killed, Lou, and me being left without him. I couldn't bear that. Not having Bobby to keep me safe. He means everything to me, Bobby does. I knew when he took my place in that bomb shaft that he was the one for me, and nothing and no one will ever change that. Lou . . .'

Lou looked at her twin.

'There's something I want to tell you but I want you to promise you will never tell anyone else, or mention ever again after today.'

She was going to tell her that secretly she still loved Kieran. Lou's stomach muscles cramped with misery and despair.

'I promise,' she agreed.

They had stopped walking now and were standing apart and facing one another.

'And I don't want you thinking badly of me either,' Sasha warned her, 'but I've got to get it off my chest, and there's only you I can be honest with about it.'

Lou waited.

'The thing is that when I first heard what had happened to Bobby all I could think was that he would never have to go back working with those bombs again and that he was safe.'

'Well, of course you would think that. Anyone would.'

Sasha shook her head vigorously. 'No, you don't understand, Lou. What I mean is that I was *glad* that he'd lost his leg because that meant that he couldn't go back and couldn't be sent somewhere to fight. I was glad, Lou. And I still am. I'd rather have him safe with me the way he is now than have him with his leg back and in danger.'

The two sisters looked at one another. Lou tried to imagine feeling as Sasha did and couldn't. Kieran had planned his future, their future round his ability to fly – Douglas Bader might have proved that it was possible to fly without legs, but Kieran wanted a job in civilian flying and he would be competing with other men for it. Without a leg Kieran too might be safe, but he would never be satisfied or happy if he didn't achieve what he wanted to achieve. Her peace of mind would mean his despair.

'What are you thinking?'

Lou looked at Sasha and told her honestly, 'I'm thinking that you are very brave, Sash.'

'I'm not brave at all. I'm just so relieved that Bobby is safe. When you fall in love yourself, you'll understand what I mean.'

Lou took a deep breath. 'I understand already.'

It took several seconds for the meaning of her statement to dawn on Sasha but once it had, her twin grabbed hold of her and demanded, 'Tell me. Tell me all about him – how you met, when you met, who he is . . . Tell me, Lou.'

This was it, and it was far, far worse than her first solo flight, worse in fact than anything she had had to do before.

'It's Kieran Mallory.'

There was no need to say any more. After all, Sasha knew who Kieran was and when they had met.

'I knew it. I knew you were still sweet on him, even though you always said you weren't.'

Sasha was laughing and hugging her, her reaction so different from anything Lou had imagined that she was left struggling for words, able to say only, 'You don't mind then, about me and Kieran?'

'Mind? Why should I mind? Oh, you mean because when I was upset after we'd fallen out I sort of blamed him?' Sasha gave a dismissive shrug.

'I was just being silly, like we both were before we grew up, Lou. Of course I don't mind.' Sasha's expression softened. 'I'm pleased for you, Lou, truly I am.'

Her face suddenly lit up as she pulled on Lou's arm and begged her, 'Let's have a double wedding – that way Mum and Dad will have to give in. Say you will, Lou? What's wrong?' she asked when she saw the misery in Lou's eyes.

'We've had a bit of a falling-out and I'm not sure that me and Kieran will be getting engaged now, never mind married.'

Determinedly Sasha coaxed the whole story from her twin and by the time they had finally reached home, they had confessed so much to one another and shared their feelings that Lou felt as close to Sasha as she had done when they were children.

And Sasha was right: all Lou had to do was tell Kieran that she had been wrong, and how much she loved him, and then they could put their differences behind them.

Only it wasn't as easy as that. When Lou returned to Thame Kieran was on ops – flying night missions, which meant that they couldn't meet up. What Lou wanted to say to him she wanted to say in person and in private. By the time he had a day off Lou had been back from Liverpool for over a week, she was on tenterhooks and desperately anxious to see him and to clear the air between them.

They'd arranged to meet at the usual pub, since they could both get lifts there, but when Lou arrived Kieran wasn't there and she'd actually begun to think that he wasn't going to turn up by the time he did arrive.

Just seeing him made her want to fling herself into his arms, but of course she couldn't in a pub full of RAF and ATA pilots.

Even the garden outside the pub was busy, giving no privacy for what she wanted to say to him.

'I'm sorry about us falling out, Kieran,' she told him. 'I should have listened to you.'

Was that a smile she could see beginning to warm his eyes. Impulsively Lou reached across the table and covered his hand with her own.

'I was wrong.'

Kieran's fingers slid between her own and her heart lifted. It was going to be all right. Thank goodness. She couldn't have borne to lose him.

'Sasha laughed when I told her what I'd been worrying about. It's Bobby she loves and . . . Kieran, what is it?' Lou asked anxiously as he pulled away from her, releasing her hand.

'So it's all right for us to be together now, is it, because your sister says so? Well, that might be good enough for you, Lou, but it isn't good enough for me. The girl I want, the girl I marry, won't need her sister's permission to love me, like I've already told you. She'll be woman enough to make her own decisions. I was a fool ever to think that you and me could work. After all, I've seen how it is with you and Sasha.'

'Kieran, it isn't like that. I do love you and I can make my own decisions.' Lou was beside herself, too upset to worry now about their being overheard.

'You say that now, but what about the next time I want us to do something you think Sasha might not like? What then, Lou? Will you go running to her again for permission, leaving me looking like a fool? I'm sorry, Lou, but I'm not prepared to take that risk.'

'Kieran . . .' Lou protested, but she knew there was no point and that he had made up his mind that it was over between them.

So this was what a broken heart felt like, Lou thought miserably as she sat dry-eyed in the open lorry transporting several ATA pilots back to Thame. It hurt too much for tears, too much for there to be room for anything else at all other than pain.

TWENTY-SEVEN

It was here at last, according to the news. The invasion had begun. Francine looked at the empty pillow next to her own. The large bed felt so empty without Marcus here to share it with her.

Two days ago, whilst the country had slept, men, including perhaps Marcus, had been fighting to establish beachheads on the Normandy beaches in the pre-dawn darkness.

Francine looked towards the window, trying to imagine what it must be like on those beaches and then wishing that she hadn't. She was wide awake but she knew that if she tried to sit up in bed she would feel sick again, just as she had done for the past week, and if she did, would it mean what she hoped and prayed: that she was pregnant? A baby. Her and Marcus's baby. A gift, a reward for letting Jack go? One child could never, ever replace another, and for as long as she lived there would be an empty place in her life that Jack should have filled, but to have Marcus's child would be so wonderful.

Marcus. She wished so much that he was here and that she could share her hope with him.

Please God, keep him safe. Please keep them all safe, she prayed.

Bella could feel her heart thudding heavily. Through the kitchen window she could see how blue the sky was. As the kitchen faced north there was no sunshine coming in to strike through the room's chill. Unusually she'd had the morning off from the nursery. She'd been listening to the wireless when the telegram boy had knocked, hoping for more news about the invasion. The Polish squadrons were taking part, and of course Jan would be with them, but it wasn't her husband that Bella was thinking about right now as she sat dry-eyed, staring down at the telegram she had just opened, it was Charlie, her brother. Charlie was dead, killed in action. It was ridiculous, given that it wasn't that long ago that she had last seen him, that she was having difficulty picturing his face. She could hear his voice, smell his scent, remember how irritating he had been when they had both lived at home, but she couldn't see his face and that bothered her.

For some reason he must have named her as his next of kin since the telegram had been addressed to her. Had he done that to protect their mother? It would have been out of character for him to have thought of someone else, and now of course it was too late for her to be able to ask him why he had done it.

How typical of Charlie to do something one wasn't expecting and then not be there to explain why.

It was just as well that her mother was out at a WVS meeting.

Her mother. She'd be devastated, inconsolably grief-stricken. Charlie had been her favourite. Charlie had been her son. *Had been*. How was Bella going to tell her?

Her father would have to be told as well. Charlie was his son too. No, Bella corrected herself carefully, Charlie had been his son. There would be things to be done, arrangements to be made, a church service to be arranged, people to tell. She'd have to ring the nursery and warn Lena that she wouldn't be coming in.

'Stay in bed until the baby comes – but that means for weeks. I can't do that.' Grace glanced wildly from the doctor to Seb, standing at the side of the bed in his RAF uniform, looking so handsome and so protective, his hand holding her own as they both turned to the doctor.

Dr Raines had just retired when the war had started, but he'd come back into practice so that his son, who had taken over from him, could join up. He was bald with a slight stoop, his manner normally reassuring but right now he was looking grave.

For once, the prettiness of her bedroom, with its pink counterpane matching the cabbage roses she and Seb had stencilled onto the distempered walls when they had moved in, were failing to lift Grace's spirits.

'I'm sorry, Grace, but I'm afraid you're going to have to,' the doctor told her firmly.

416

'But why, when all that's wrong with me is that my hands and feet are a bit swollen and I get tired?'

Sunlight shone through the dormer windows and Grace could smell the scent of the climbing rose through the open window.

'I'm sorry, my dear, I really don't want to worry or upset you, but I'm afraid things are rather more serious than that.'

'Serious?' Seb demanded whilst Grace put a protective hand across her swollen body, her heart beginning to pound with anxiety.

She'd been cross with Seb when he'd insisted on calling out the doctor just because he'd come home early and found her lying down and feeling sorry for herself, but now it seemed that Seb had been right to be concerned.

'What is it that's wrong with me, Doctor?' Grace wanted to know.

'It's what we call toxaemia,' he answered her carefully. 'It's a condition that arises sometimes in pregnancy.'

'Toxaemia?' Grace had never heard the term but then she had never worked on a maternity ward. 'Is it . . . is it serious?'

'It can be.' The doctor's smile was no doubt intended to reassure her, Grace knew, but instead she felt thoroughly upset and alarmed.

'How—' she began, but the doctor shook his head.

'The best thing you can do right now for baby and for yourself is to rest. What we need to do is to keep that blood pressure of yours from going any higher.'

Helplessly Grace looked at Seb, needing him to ask the question she could not. He didn't let her down, but then she had known that he wouldn't. He was the most wonderful husband and would be an equally wonderful father. A small sob shuddered in Grace's throat, and Seb's hand tightened on hers.

'And if it does?'

'Well, initially we would have to take Grace into hospital to see if we could get it down.'

'And if you can't?' Grace demanded.

The doctor looked towards the window, avoiding eye contact with either of them.

'Toxaemia is a very serious condition that can kill both the unborn child and its mother. If it can't be controlled with bed rest and the mother's blood pressure kept down, it can result in the mother having fits after giving birth and going into a coma. To avoid that, the normal procedure is to bring the pregnancy to an end, or perform a Caesarean operation if the pregnancy is advanced enough.'

'You mean that you'd kill my baby?' Grace's voice was weak with shocked horror.

'It would be the only way to save your life.'

'Seb . . .' Grace appealed, reaching for her husband's hand.

'It's all right, that isn't going to happen to . . . to us. Dr Raines is only telling us what could happen if you don't rest, isn't that so, Doctor?'

'Yes, indeed. My nurse, Nurse Williams, will come round twice a week to keep an eye on you and take your blood pressure, but I'd be a lot happier if I knew that you had someone with you to make sure that you do stay in bed.'

And, Seb decided, showing the doctor out, he would be a lot happier if he knew that there was someone here with Grace whilst he was at work, in case she took a turn for the worse.

Upstairs in their bedroom Grace told herself that she mustn't cry – or panic. She could feel her heart thudding heavily, her face was burning and her horrid swollen fingers throbbed. Did that mean that the blood pressure was rising?

She could hear Seb coming back upstairs.

'I don't want you to be here on your own, Grace,' he told her, 'not after what the doctor has said. I'm going to telephone your mother and ask her if she'll come and stay.'

'No, Seb, don't do that. Dad would hate Mum being away, and she'd hate it too really. She's got Sasha to think of as well, with what's happened to Bobby, and Luke fighting in Italy. I'll be all right. You heard the doctor; he said that if I rested then—'

'Yes, I heard him,' Seb agreed grimly. 'You need someone with you whilst I'm at work, Grace, someone who won't just make sure that you rest, but someone you can turn to if . . . if you need to.'

Someone who could call the doctor if she took a turn for the worse was what Seb really meant, Grace knew.

'But that means family, Seb, and there's no family here.'

'Yes there is,' Seb astonished her by saying. 'Or at least the nearest thing to it.'

419

'What do you mean?' Grace demanded, but Seb wasn't listening.

'You stay here and don't move until I get back. I won't be long,' he promised her.

Although Emily recognised Seb – his wife, Grace, had invited her and Tommy round to tea several times after Francine had recognised Tommy – it was still a surprise to find him standing outside her front door, but of course she invited him in and took him through to the kitchen, offering him a cup of tea as she did so.

Shaking his head, Seb told her, 'I need your help,' and then quickly explained the situation. 'Grace hasn't got any proper family here in Whitchurch and I thought, well, Tommy is her cousin, and you are his mother, but . . . if I've done the wrong thing—'

'The wrong thing? The wrong thing would have been if you hadn't come to me,' Emily told him forthrightly. 'Of course I'll help. I could come over after Tommy's gone to school, and then Tommy could come to your house, and do his homework there whilst we wait for you to get in. You'll be busy, I expect, with the invasion and everything.'

Emily's practical, calm manner immediately made Seb feel better. She might not be Jean but he suspected that Emily would look after his Grace and their coming babies every bit as caringly as though she were her mother.

'*Emily?* You've asked Emily to come here every day and stay here all day with me? Oh, Seb, how could you? What will she think of me – me, a grown woman, needing to be looked after?'

Seeing that Grace was working herself up, Seb caught hold of her hands and held them in his own, asking her firmly, 'Where would you rather be? Here at home with Emily looking after you or in hospital?'

'I can't go into hospital and leave you here all on your own, and besides, I don't want to take up a bed someone else might need.'

'Good, that's settled then. Emily will be here in the morning.'

'Gavin, it's the memorial service for Charlie tomorrow. I know how busy you are but I'd really like you to come with me.'

They were in the kitchen and Gavin had just come in from work. Both Davie and Janette were in bed, and after weeks of cold silence from Gavin, and an even colder shoulder turned towards her in bed, Lena had decided that enough was enough and that it was time for her to 'say something'. Asking him to go with her to Charlie's memorial service was a good way of beginning things, Lena reckoned, because it gave her a legitimate reason to remind Gavin that they were husband and wife.

Knowing beforehand that he was likely to refuse didn't make her misery any less painful when he demanded brusquely, 'Why?' but Lena wasn't going to let herself be hurt into backing out and pretending that everything was all right. Not any longer. She had a right to know where she and the children stood. If Gavin didn't love her or want her any more then it was up to him to say so.

'Well, to help me do what I can to support Bella, for one thing, and for another, because you're my husband. Bella's been left with all the hard work and arrangements to do, despite the fact that her dad's been round at her mum's goodness knows how many times since they got the news, and stayed overnight one night. Bella says she wouldn't be surprised if, now that Pauline has gone off with someone else, her dad moved back home. Taken Charlie's death really bad, both her mum and her dad have.'

'What about you, Lena? You must have taken it really bad as well, seeing the way you felt about him. And no, I won't go with you to the church. I'll put up with a lot 'cos we're married now, and man and wife, and we've got two kiddies to think of, but I'm not going into church and seeing my wife cry over another chap who means more to her than I do.'

Lena, who had been standing beside the kitchen table, stared at her husband in bewilderment.

'What are you talking about?' she asked. 'Charlie doesn't mean anything to me. You know that.'

'I thought I did,' Gavin agreed grimly. 'But that was before I saw the way he was cuddling you out on the street, like he had the right . . . like you had given him the right, that weekend he came home.'

'Cuddling me?' Lena had to sit down. Her head was spinning and her body had gone all weak.

422

'I saw the pair of you, Lena. I was up the ladder pruning one of the trees and I saw you.'

'What you saw was me telling Charlie to go and get lost,' Lena told her husband firmly. 'I told him straight that I'm a respectable married woman now who knows when she's got a good man in her life, and that there was no way I'd ever be daft enough to be taken in by someone as worthless as him a second time. And as for me shedding tears at his funeral, the only tears I'll be crying will be for poor Bella, who's worried sick about her Jan, and who's being run ragged by her selfish mother, who never lifts a finger to do anything for herself. I'm surprised at you, Gavin, I really am. I can't believe you've been thinking like that for all these months and never said a single word. How could you think something like that after all we've bin to one another, and after I've said how much I love you and how grateful I am to you?' Lena paused for breath.

Gavin might not have said anything about what he'd seen, but he thought plenty about it. Not a day had gone by without him thinking about it and what it must mean.

'I know the way I was before we met,' Lena continued, 'and that my behaviour wasn't what it should have been, going and getting meself into trouble like I did. Heading for a bad end, I was, and no mistake, and it's thanks to Bella and you that I didn't end up on the streets. The last person I'd shed tears over is Charlie, and the fact is that whilst I wouldn't ever wish anyone dead, I'm not sorry that he has gone. For one thing, it means that he isn't going to be around to maybe cause trouble for our Janette when she gets older, and I wouldn't have put that past him. A real nasty streak he had, speaking to me like he did when you saw us.'

There was no mistaking Lena's indignation or the honesty of what she was saying, Gavin recognised, but there were still questions he wanted answered.

'Very well then, if it was all as you say it was, how come when you came home you didn't say anything to me about having seen him? Why keep it a secret?'

Lena could hear the anxiety mixed with male pride and pain in Gavin's voice. Was *this* what all the misery of these last long months had been all about? Mingled with her relief, Lena felt exasperation.

'Why do you think I didn't tell you? Because I knew how you'd take on, and the last thing I wanted was you going round to Bella's mum's and sorting Charlie out man to man. A fine thing that would have been for Bella to have to cope with, after all she's done for us. Not that there wasn't a minute when Charlie was acting like he thought I'd be willing to jump into bed with him, that I didn't wish you'd been there to put him in his place, 'cos I did. I don't know, Gavin, there's me been thinking all these months that you'd stopped loving me and that you were wishing you hadn't married me, and all along you was thinking that I was still daft enough to go hankering after Charlie. I can't pretend that I'm not upset that you'd think that of me.'

'I was jealous,' Gavin admitted, going over to

her. 'Jealous and like a bear with a sore head on account of that jealousy. As for me not loving you any more,' his voice thickened, 'that will never happen, Lena. The fact is that every day I love you more. You and the kiddies mean everything to me.'

'You've hardly bothered with little Davie,' Lena couldn't help reproaching him. 'You'd never think that he was your own and—' She broke off and looked at Gavin, small patches of colour burning along her cheekbones as she demanded, 'You're never thinking that he isn't yours, I hope, because if you are—'

Immediately Gavin shook his head. 'Of course not.'

'Then . . .'

'I just didn't want Janette thinking that Davie was more important to me than her,' Gavin told her sheepishly. 'I remember as plain as day my sister saying how put out she felt when I came along and pushed her nose out of joint because I was a boy. I don't want our Janette growing up feeling like that.'

'Oh, Gavin.'

Having Lena hugging him tightly, her tears dampening his neck after all the months when there'd been silence and distance between them had Gavin wrapping his own arms around her, and showing her very determinedly just how much she meant to him and how much he loved her.

'I'll just take your blood pressure for you, Grace, and then I'll go downstairs and make you a cup of tea.'

It was over a week now since Emily had first started helping out and spending the day with Grace, and now she had persuaded Nurse Williams to show her how to take Grace's blood pressure so that she and Grace could both be easy in their minds between the nurse's visits.

'How is it?' Grace asked anxiously.

'No change,' Emily assured her. 'The doctor will be pleased about that.'

Grace gave her a wan smile. 'I was so pleased when we learned that I might be having twins, with Mum being one, and then her having Sasha and Lou, but now . . .' Fear clouded Grace's eyes as she placed her badly swollen hands on the mound of her stomach. 'I'm not a complete fool, Emily. No one's said anything but I know it would be better, safer, for them if I was only having the one, just in case they have to operate and deliver them by Caesarean section. They'll be small, you see, with there being two, and if my blood pressure goes up and they have to operate earlier than they should have been born, they'll be even smaller, and weaker.'

'It's thinking thoughts like that and then worrying yourself about them that you shouldn't be doing,' Emily reminded her, 'and besides, from the size of you Nurse Williams reckons that you've definitely got a pair of eight pounders apiece in there.'

As always, listening to Emily's reassuring voice made Grace feel much calmer. Whenever she tried to talk to Seb about her fears, she could see how anxious he himself was, even though he didn't say so, and that made her feel even worse. Emily, on the other hand, behaved and spoke as though it was a foregone conclusion that Grace would deliver her babies safely without any complications.

'I've brought me knitting with me today,' Emily told her when she had been downstairs and come back with a fresh cup of tea, the first one out of the pot, just as Grace liked it best, although how on earth she knew that Grace had no idea because she had certainly never told her.

'What are you knitting? Something for Tommy?' Grace asked. When she was feeling really unwell and afraid she would try to imagine her twins Tommy's age, but these last two days, when she had tried to visualise them she hadn't been able to. Her heart gave a panicky thud, her swollen hands pulsing with the pressure of her blood.

She must keep calm, Grace reminded herself.

'In white wool?' Emily laughed, answering Grace's question and showing her the several inches of pretty blackberry stitch border she had already knitted. 'No, I'm doing a couple of matinée jackets for the twins. I remembered I'd got some white three ply I'd bought just in case it ever came in handy, and I reckon I've got enough. I had the pattern in a pull-out from *Woman's Weekly*. Ever so pretty, it is. I can see the babies in them now. What do you think?'

She showed Grace the pull-out with a bouncing baby on its cover, dressed in a snowy white matinée jacket and matching knitted leggings.

Emotionally Grace touched the border Emily had already knitted. She was having a bad day today and

427

felt really poorly, and touching the soft wool brought all the fears she was trying to bury to the surface.

Seeing her distress, Emily put down her knitting and put her arms around her.

'I'm so frightened, Emily,' Grace admitted. 'I keep trying to imagine the babies here and well, but I can't and I keep thinking . . . I don't want to die, Emily, I don't want to leave Seb, and sometimes I wake up in the night and . . .' Grace gulped and then rushed on, 'Sometimes I wish that I wasn't having them . . . that there wasn't going to be any baby and that it was just me and Seb again and that everything was all right. And then I feel so guilty, as though I'm not fit to be a mother, and I start thinking that because of that I'll be punished and the twins will die.'

Emily looked towards the window, trying to imagine how she would feel in Grace's place, how she would feel if Grace was her daughter.

'Well, I'm not surprised you have moments when you feel like that,' she said calmly. 'I'd be exactly the same way myself, and I dare say that if they were honest most women would say the same.'

'You don't think I'm hateful then and . . . and not fit to be a mother?'

'Of course not. The thing is, Grace, that no matter how much other people sympathise and want to help, when it comes to giving birth, it's like death – no one can go through it for you or with you, and I don't think there's a woman on this earth who can say that that isn't frightening. And you've got all the worry of this toxaemia hanging over you as well.'

'Sometimes I lie here imagining the twins, giving them Seb's nose and his lovely eyes, and I can see them so clearly that it's as though I already know them, and then there are other times when I can't picture them at all, and then I get frightened because I think it means that I won't ever get to see them and hold them. I'm so afraid now, Emily. If things go wrong for me, it's too late now for . . . for . . .' she couldn't bring herself to use the word 'abortion' so instead, she said, 'for you-know-what, and it's too soon for them to be delivered. Eight months is the earliest they would want to do a Caesarean, and that's three weeks away.'

Emily continued to hold her. Three weeks might not sound very long, but when, as she had been warned by Nurse Williams, Grace's blood pressure could rise so swiftly that three hours could produce an emergency, three weeks seemed a very long time indeed.

'Your mum's coming to see you this weekend,' Emily reminded her.

'Yes. But I don't want Mum worrying about me, Emily.'

'Then we'll have to put on a good show and make sure that she doesn't.'

Grace gave Emily a grateful look. 'I really don't know what I'd have done without you. I didn't like it when Seb told me what he'd done, asking you to come, but now . . . You truly are the kindest person I know, Emily. Mum will think I'm such a softie, making all this fuss and work.'

'No she won't. She'll be proud of you – any mother would be,' Emily corrected her.

'You are such a comfort, Emily. You remind me of Katie, in a way.'

'Katie?'

'Yes, the girl that Luke was engaged to. She was lovely. We all wanted them to get married, but well, things didn't work out. Mum was ever so disappointed. She really took to Katie. She had that way about her that you have, sort of calm and kind and caring. I know that family is family, and that we all rally round to help one another, but I'm ever so grateful to you, Emily.'

'Well, like you said, family is family.'

Family! Emily's heart swelled with gratitude and pride. After all this time she had so much of what she'd always longed for: a son, and Wilhelm, and now this – a family. She was family, Grace had said so.

TWENTY-EIGHT

Kieran lit a cigarette and squinted through the smoke he had just exhaled toward the skyline. Every day since D-Day his squadron had flown from their base into Normandy, joining the 'cab rank' of other planes there ready to be called upon to do whatever was needed to help the Allied forces push forward.

They had dropped guns and ammunition and radio parts for the French Resistance, leaflets over Paris to say that the invasion was under way, stores for infantry on the ground, medics and medical supplies, and that was in between making regular bombing runs into German-held territory to destroy strategic targets. He had seen comrades die, their planes plunging earthwards in burning pyres of flames and metal; he had seen them dragged from the wreckage of their planes so badly injured that they were unrecognisable; he had witnessed acts of heroism and self-sacrifice that had made him want to weep, and acts of greed and selfishness that had shown him the dark side of human nature, but none of that – nothing, no one – had burned into his thoughts and his heart in the way that Lou had done. She had pierced it as sharply as a piece of shrapnel that couldn't be removed without him bleeding to death, so that he had to live with the pain of it in him or die with its removal. Looking back now he could see that deep down he had known way back, when they had first met, that there was something about her that had got under his skin. He had thought then that it was because she was so aggravating, an aggravating kid who was too naïve to look after herself. A man's pride required, though, that certain rules to a relationship had to be abided by. Lou had broken the first and most important of those rules when she had shown him that her sister was more important to her than he was. A man, a real man, would never put up with something like that, not if he still wanted to call himself a man. Those were the rules.

With the invasion underway the demand for replacement planes was high. That meant that Lou would be busy collecting new Spitfires from the factory at Castle Bromwich and then taking them to the maintenance units. He remembered her telling him how the ATA pilots always flew the same course to and from Castle Bromwich, flying low under the clouds. It was virtually a straight route and it would be easy enough for another pilot to find her. If he so wished. *If?*

It was his rest day and technically he wasn't supposed to fly, but a Lancaster that had just been repaired was standing idle on the runway.

Kieran blew the smoke from his cigarette down his nostrils and then ground out the cigarette beneath the heel of his flying boot, before starting to walk toward the admin block.

Ten minutes later, as Kieran strolled toward the Lancaster, an engineer called out to him, 'Hey, what are you doing?'

'Test flight,' Kieran replied, as he hauled himself up onto the wing. 'Orders. Give the prop a swing, will you?'

The familiar cockpit enclosed him, the Lancaster oddly light on take-off without its crew. Kieran headed east, flying slowly and beneath the cloud.

The run to Castle Bromwich and back to the maintenance units had become so familiar to her now that Lou suspected she could almost have flown it in her sleep, which was why she decided later that she didn't even see the Lancaster until it had drawn level with her, the sight of it coming out of nowhere giving her such a shock that without thinking she let the Spit surge to 250 miles per hour instead of keeping it below the regulation 200.

What was going on? The Lancaster had no business being down at this altitude – bombers flew above the cloud, not beneath them – and then she saw the pilot and her heart somersaulted with as much breathtaking speed as though it was a Spitfire rolling and banking and then looping the loop.

Kieran.

She was less than five miles from the maintenance

unit. Very carefully refusing to look to see if the Lancaster was still there, Lou began to lose speed, dropping down slowly. The maintenance units were concealed often by trees, the tops of which were held down by ropes whilst the unit was being constructed, the ropes removed when the work was completed to spring back to full height, thus concealing the unit. Landing at one of them took care and skill. There was normally only a very small landing strip, sometimes little more than a flat field. Ferry pilots were trained to land one after the other, quickly and efficiently, but that didn't help Lou to feel very happy about having a huge heavy bomber racing down the runway behind her. The minute she was down she taxied off the runway, and then sat rigidly in her seat, trying to find the courage to get out and face Kieran, the man who had rejected her and walked away from her. She must show him that she wasn't the silly little girl she had been in Liverpool. She must be calm and professional, just treating him as she would any other pilot she happened to come across in the course of her own work. She must . . .

Her door was yanked open and Kieran was there confronting her.

'Not planning to stay there all day, are you, only I've got to get the Lancaster back before anyone realises it's missing.'

Beneath them on the ground an aggrieved engineer was demanding, 'What the hell's going on? We were expecting one Spitfire, not one Spitfire and a ruddy Lancaster.'

Lou heard the engineer but she wasn't paying much attention to him and that was because Kieran had reached for her left hand and was flicking open a small leather box, inside which a diamond solitaire ring sparkled in the sunlight.

'Well? Shall I put it on?' he was asking her. 'And I warn you, if you say yes it's never going to come off, Lou, at least not until I put a wedding ring in its place.'

Her mouth had gone dry and her heart was racing like a jet engine.

'I thought you'd given up on me,' was all she could manage to say.

'So did I, but it seems that I was wrong. Mind you, I should have done,' Kieran told her.

'So why haven't you?'

'Do you want me to tell you or show you?'

Lou thought for a moment and then said firmly, 'Both.'

Grace's blood pressure had been up for the last two days, though only very slightly, which was why Emily hadn't said anything to her, not wanting to upset her and make things worse. But yesterday her hands had been dreadfully swollen, more so than they had been, Emily was sure, and Grace had just not been herself. Emily knew how desperate Grace was to stay at home instead of having to go into hospital, and she understood why she felt like that, which was why instead of going to Grace's Emily was now on her way to Nurse Williams' house in the hope that she could catch her before she set off on her bicycle on her rounds for the day.

Her anxiety for Grace made Emily quicken her pace, which was just as well, she acknowledged as she arrived at the cottage, just as Nurse Williams was getting astride her bike.

Quickly Emily explained why she was there.

'Grace's blood pressure isn't up very much, but she isn't herself at all, and knowing how upset she's been I thought it best to have a word with you.'

'Well, if it's not up much . . .' Nurse Williams frowned and pursed her lips. 'I've got a new mother to see at Shaw Farm, and then there's Mrs Haddon's leg that needs dressing. I could come after that, I suppose, but that will be this afternoon.'

'She's been talking about dying, her and the twins,' Emily put in determinedly, 'and I'm not sure I'm doing the blood pressure properly.' That wasn't true, but Emily wasn't at all happy about Grace.

'Mmm, well, all right then. I'll tell you what, I'll cycle over there now and just say that I thought I'd call. I'll check her blood pressure and have a bit of a chat with her.'

'That's ever so good of you, Nurse Williams,' Emily thanked her dutifully, 'especially when you're so busy.'

'I'll probably have left by the time you've walked there. It won't take me long to check her over.'

As she rode away Emily suspected that the nurse thought she was worrying unnecessarily.

Emily had almost reached the lane that led to Seb and Grace's cottage when an ambulance came racing past her, its siren going. When it turned into the lane Emily's heart leaped into her throat.

She wasn't athletic, but she still ran down the lane as fast as she could, arriving at the open door of the cottage just in time to see Grace being carried out into the ambulance. Her eyes were closed and her face looked pallid.

Nurse Williams came bustling out after the ambulance men.

'Just as well I called,' she told Emily, making no mention of Emily's part in that decision. 'Found her next to unconscious, or as good as.'

'What will happen now?' Emily asked anxiously.

'Well, it's up to the doctor, but I reckon they'll try for a Caesar.'

From the ambulance, Emily heard an agonised cry and a sobbed, 'Mum . . .'

'I'm going with her,' she told the nurse, jumping into the ambulance before anyone could stop her and going to crouch at Grace's side, taking hold of her hand.

'Mum,' Grace gasped.

'She'll be here soon, Grace. Don't you worry. Everything's going to be all right, and before you know it you'll be holding your two little ones. Pity I didn't spend a bit more time on them matinée jackets . . .'

The medic sitting taking Grace's pulse gave Emily a nod of approval. 'Keep talking to her,' he told Emily. 'We don't want her going into a panic.'

And so Emily did, all the way to the hospital and all the way onto the ward, until Grace had been sedated and Emily was free to go and telephone Seb and Grace's mother to tell them what had happened.

'The doctor says that they're going to do a Caesarean,' Emily informed Jean, who had left the number of a neighbour's phone with Grace, 'just in case.' 'He thinks it's for the best.'

There was no point in worrying Grace's mother senseless by telling her that the doctor had told her that it was touch and go whether he could deliver the babies alive, and whether after that Grace herself would survive.

Back on the ward, Emily took hold of Grace's hand, and even though Grace was now sedated, Emily still spoke to her as though she was conscious, telling her firmly, 'Everything's going to be all right, Grace. All you have to do is keep calm and think of how soon you're going to be holding those babies. I can see you with them now, and ever so proud you look too, with roses blooming in your cheeks and you looking so pretty that it's no wonder Seb is so proud of you. It won't be long now, so you just hold on. The doctor says that he reckons the babies will be a good weight now so you don't need to worry about that.'

The doctor had said no such thing, but Emily didn't believe in giving a person something to worry about when worrying was going to make them feel worse.

By the time Seb arrived, Grace was just about to be taken down to the operating theatre. There was just time for Seb to slip into the chair at Grace's bedside, which Emily had vacated for him, and for Emily to leave them alone together for a few precious minutes before Grace was wheeled away.

'I still can't believe that we're together and that everything's all right,' Lou admitted to Kieran as they sat side by side in the window seat of the pub, her engagement ring on her finger. 'It was never about me loving Sasha more than I do you, Kieran. It was more that I felt so guilty because of you and me when I thought she loved you as well.'

She'd explained to him now about the bomb shaft and Sasha's fears, and they had both agreed that they should put the whole episode behind them.

'No more fights, no more misunderstandings, and no more delays,' Kieran told her tenderly. 'The first chance I get I'm going to see your dad and ask him to let us get married a.s.a.p.'

'What if he says we've got to wait until the war's over?'

'He won't say that,' Kieran told her, 'because I don't intend to take no for an answer.'

'Sasha's going to want it to be a double wedding with her and Bobby, but if you don't want to, then she'll just have to be disappointed. You come first, Kieran.'

Kieran's smile told Lou that he understood and appreciated what she was saying.

'Oh, I don't mind a double wedding. Just as long as you don't expect me to agree to a double honeymoon. Then I'm definitely going to want you all to myself.'

'Katie! At last. It seems ages since we've seen one another, properly, I mean.'

Katie returned Gerry's happy smile as she walked into the kitchen of their shared billet and found the other girl there.

'We do seem to keep missing one another,' Katie agreed, adding, 'Phew, it's hot outside. I did a bit of a detour coming home this evening and walked through Hyde Park, just to try and get some fresh air.'

'Shall I put the kettle on?' Gerry offered.

Katie nodded her head in grateful, if somewhat surprised, acceptance. It was almost unheard of for Gerry to offer to undertake any of their shared domestic tasks.

'My feet are killing me,' Katie complained, easing them out of her pre-war sandals, and wiggling her happy-to-be-free toes.

'I've got something to tell you.' Gerry had filled the kettle and put it on the cooker lighting the gas jet underneath it, but now as she turned round Katie could see that her face was alight with happiness. It was almost spilling out of her, illuminating and flushing her cheeks a soft pink. 'I wanted you to be the first to know because – well, because really it's because of you and what you said to me that it's happened and that me and Ian are getting engaged.' Gerry shook her head. 'I never thought that I'd end up engaged to a boy who went to school with my brothers and who I've known all my life.'

The kettle was boiling, and tactfully Katie got up and went to it, warming the pot and then emptying it before spooning in some of their precious allowance of tea, whilst Gerry stood watching her, looking so blissfully happy that it was hard for Katie not to feel a small pang of envy.

'If it hadn't been for you saying that I should go home for Christmas, it wouldn't have happened. Ian came round to see my parents 'cos he'd heard about my brothers.' Gerry's happiness was momentarily dimmed. 'He's in the Merchant Navy, and he'd been away when it happened. He always was mad on going to sea. I can remember him talking about it when he used to come round to play with my brothers. Of course, none of us knew then that there'd be the war. Anyway, he asked me out, and I said yes, and then he took me to a dance on New Year's Eve, and then on New Year's Day when he came round to say goodbye before rejoining his ship, we had a good long talk, and I told him . . .'

Gerry broke off from what she was saying to take the mug of tea that Katie was handing to her, only to put it down on the table and continue emotionally, 'I told him everything Katie, like he was one of my brothers or . . . or my best friend, and then afterwards he just looked at me and said that he'd done a bit of running wild himself when he was on the New York convoy run. Then he hugged me, Katie, and I think I knew then. He didn't say anything and neither did I because, well, we'd been such good pals over the Christmas holiday that I didn't want to spoil that.

'When I came back to London I told myself that was that, but then he wrote to me, sent the letter via my parents, and I wrote back, and well, to cut a long story short we've been seeing one another whenever we could – when he was at home and I could get leave, but I've kept quiet about it because . . . well, I wasn't really sure until a few weeks ago how he felt, and then when he did tell me, I wanted to keep it just between the two of us for a while.' Gerry gave Katie a bashful look. 'Especially after the way I'd been carrying on before him and me got together. But then last weekend, Ian told my mum and dad that he wants us to be married. He's brought me ever such a beautiful ring back from New York, Katie, but I'm not wearing it just yet. It would have been my brother Chris's birthday in two weeks' time so we're going to get engaged officially then. Somehow that sort of makes Chris and Danny part of . . . of everything.'

There were tears in Gerry's eyes as she mentioned her dead brothers, and tears in Katie's too when she hugged her and told her how pleased she was for her.

'It's you I've got to thank, you and Peggy, for doing what you did for me. Putting me straight and, well, just being so kind to me. I'll never forget that, Katie.'

They hugged again, and then Gerry detached herself with a small wail, protesting, 'That can't possibly be the time. I'm working this evening.

I'm going to have to fly,' before gulping down her now cold tea and racing for the door.

She was happy for Gerry, Katie acknowledged, washing their mugs and then drying them, but the other girl's happiness had left a small ache in her own heart.

None of them would ever forget the dreadful fear that had accompanied the birth of Grace's twins; for the babies – being born so early at seven months, and one of them so very weak they had feared he had not survived the birth; and for Grace herself, whose dangerously high blood pressure could have led to fits, which could have sent her into a coma and then death.

Emily thought she would remember for ever the anguish and love she had seen on Seb's face when he had arrived at the hospital.

'They said that Harry, the second twin, was blue when they lifted him out, and they thought that they'd lost him, but the nurse realised that his heart was beating so they cleared his lungs and he was as right as rain,' Jean told Emily as they sat together in Emily's kitchen whilst Jean went through the events of that night – events already described to Emily by Nurse Williams, but of course Emily didn't say that to Jean, not wanting to deprive her of the right, as Grace's mother, to relay the story to her.

'It was nearly midnight when my train got in, but thankfully Seb was there to meet me. I've never seen anyone looking like he looked. I thought at first that our Grace had already gone and that we'd lost her, he looked so bad. Fair had my heart in my mouth, it did, but then he said as how she'd had the Caesarean and the twins were safe and well, that it was touch and go for her to see if she was going to pull through from the toxaemia.

'Of course, he said that they wouldn't let me see her, but well, the thought of her . . . of anything happening to her and me not being there – I just couldn't bear that, Emily, I really couldn't.'

'Another cup of tea?' Emily asked

'Well, I don't mind if I do. And like I was saying,' Jean continued whilst Emily poured her a second cup of tea, 'I told the sister in charge of the ward as much, and she said that I could sit with Grace just as long as I didn't disturb her. Grace looked that pale that I really thought . . . but then she opened her eyes and looked at me.' Jean's own eyes filled with tears. '"I'm sorry, Mum," she said. Her, sorry . . . "You've got nothing to be sorry for, Grace," I told her, "except that them two little lads will be wanting their mum." Did I tell you that they're to be Sam and Harry, after Grace and Seb's dads?'

Emily nodded.

'Anyway like I was saying, no sooner had I said that than Grace was sitting up and saying that she wanted to see her babies, and then they were taking her blood pressure and saying that it was all right. Ever such a relief, that was, Emily, I can tell you. That's the thing about motherhood: you don't stop worrying about them just because they're grown

444

up, as you'll discover once your Tommy becomes a young man.'

Her Tommy – Emily glowed with pride.

'I still can't believe that Dad's actually given in and that he's letting us get married as soon as Bobby is out of hospital.' Sasha was plainly delighted and glowing with excitement.

The three of them – Lou, Kieran and Sasha – were all sitting round Bobby's bed, an unheard-of concession from Sister, who had permitted this only because Kieran had promised her that they wouldn't disturb the rest of the ward and because they were there to discuss their shared wedding plans.

The meeting Lou had been worrying about – between her and Kieran and Sasha – had gone far better than she had expected, Lou acknowledged. Kieran had kissed Sasha on the cheek and she had told him that he was lucky to have won Lou, and from there things had gone so well that Lou wondered now why she had ever worried that there might be some awkwardness. Now the four of them were busy making plans, with Kieran and Bobby getting on so well together and teasing both of them that the two men might have grown up on the same street.

Kieran had taken Lou to meet his mother, once her father had given his permission for them to marry, and Lou had immediately liked her mother-in-law-to-be.

It was a pity that their own mother was still

away in Whitchurch looking after Grace and her new babies now they were all out of hospital and at home, and couldn't join in the wedding discussions, but since she was due home at the end of the week Lou and Sasha knew they wouldn't have to wait long to discuss their plans with her.

'I can't wait to see Grace and Seb's twins,' Sasha broke off from wedding talk to say, so easily picking up on her own thoughts that Lou had to smile.

'Don't you go getting any ideas,' Kieran immediately warned Lou, with a teasing look. 'I want you to myself for a while before any babies come along.'

He looked so handsome in his RAF uniform that Lou's heart turned over. She was also in uniform, but she'd removed her jacket, and really the skirt was so smart that when she wore it with the cotton floral-patterned blouse she was wearing today it didn't look 'uniformy'.

'It's the same for me and Sash,' Bobby chipped in, holding Sasha's hand tightly.

She too was wearing a floral blouse, very similar to Lou's, even though they hadn't bought them together.

'Now that Sash's dad has got me a job as an electrician with his lot, I want to do my best to prove that I'm up to the job before we start having babies to worry about.'

'Of course you're up to the job,' Sasha immediately scolded him, 'and don't you go thinking any different.'

A year ago she could never have imagined any

of this happening, Lou acknowledged as Kieran reached for her hand and held it in his own. Or being this happy.

'Well, these two are coming on nicely. Sam's put on two ounces and Harry's put on nearly as much.'

Grace smiled at her mother as Jean fussed over her twin grandsons, lying on their blanket on the grass under one of the apple trees, at the bottom of the garden of the house Grace and Seb were renting.

It was a perfect summer day, the twins protected from the glare of the sunshine by the shade of the tree. With her hair brushed back off her face and done in what they were calling a 'victory roll', Seb thought that Grace looked a picture in her pretty pink cotton dress.

Grace looked at her babies, her heart contracting with maternal love. She'd been so afraid when she'd been taken into hospital, afraid that the twins might die, afraid that she might die herself, afraid of everything, even the fact that she hadn't told anyone how increasingly poorly she'd been feeling, but now thanks, so the doctor had told her, to Emily, all was well and they were all alive and healthy. If Emily hadn't had that impulse to go and see Nurse Williams, and if she hadn't come straight to the cottage, and if Emily had arrived at her normal time later in the morning, then it could all have been too late and she might well have already slipped into a coma, Grace knew.

'I'm ever so glad that you're here, Mum,' Grace told her mother, 'and I'm grateful to Emily too. Without her—'

'I should have been here with you.'

Jean knew she would never have forgiven herself if anything had happened either to her daughter or to the two babies now lying peacefully on their shared blanket, and who already had curled their tiny fingers tightly into their grandmother's loving heart.

'Now don't start that, Mum,' Grace scolded her briskly. 'I told Seb not to ask you to come and stay with us because I knew how Dad would be. I don't know what I'd have done without Emily, though. I must say that I never expected to get on with her so well, and in fact I was cross with Seb when he told me what he'd done, going round there and asking her to help, but now . . . well . . . she's ever so easy to be around, Mum. She reminds me of Katie in a way.'

Jean nodded. She still missed her young billetee and regretted the fact that she was not now going to become her daughter-in-law.

'Oh, look at that!' Grace exclaimed, laughing. 'They're holding hands.'

Jean smiled tenderly as she looked down at the two babies, their tiny fingers entwined.

'I can remember Sasha and Lou doing that,' she told Grace.

'I'm so happy, Mum,' Grace said. 'I was so afraid that something awful would happen and that I wouldn't . . .' She swallowed painfully as Jean hugged her. And then shook her head. 'I'm just so lucky to have Seb, and these two, and you and Dad, and . . . everything.'

Jean patted her daughter's back as Grace's tears fell.

TWENTY-NINE

London was under attack. Just when everyone had been thinking that the war was all but over.

Hitler's deadly V1 flying bombs were raining down on the city night and day. So far, in only five days, forty-two people had been killed, including twenty-four in one blast in a pub, with hundreds more being injured. In one day seventy-three of the deadly bombs had fallen on London. Sent from bases in the Pas de Calais, the flying bombs were fitted with a pulse jet engine programmed to cut out over London. Once the engine had cut out the bomb nose-dived silently to earth in fifteen seconds, with its warhead of nearly a ton of explosives.

One of the girls at work had told Katie that she had heard that the damage from just one bomb could spread over a radius of up to a quarter of a mile.

Anyone in the vicinity of a bomb when it exploded stood the risk of being killed outright, buried alive or being lacerated by the debris thrown up by the explosion.

From triumph over the D-Day landings, and the feeling that now it was only a matter of time before Hitler was defeated, those living and working in London had become fearful of the deadly effect of Hitler's flying bombs.

People were saying that you knew your number was up when you could no longer hear the thudding roar of the bomb's jet engine and instead there was silence. All you could do then was dive to the ground and hope for the best.

Sloane Street was busy, as always, with people in uniform and workers returning home after their day's work. The dust from the destruction caused by the bombs hung over the city like a fine gossamer shroud in the warm June sunshine. You could feel the dust against your skin, taste it in your mouth, and Katie was tempted to head for Hyde Park instead of going straight to her billet, just for the hope of breathing in some fresh air, but she could do that later, she decided. The reason for her desire to go straight to her billet was the hope that there might be a letter from Luke waiting for her. She hadn't heard from him since she had written to him about Eddie. Was that because he simply hadn't had time to write back to her or because he had been put off by the intimacy of detail in her letter and had felt it best not to respond as a hint to her that she had overstepped the mark?

Another option, and one that she was not going to think about, was that Luke might have been injured again – or worse. Automatically Katie started to walk faster as though doing so could keep such thoughts at bay, her head down as she quickened her pace, so that she didn't realise until she was only a few doors away from her billet that someone was pacing to and fro in front of the house.

Someone?

It took several seconds of disbelief and incredulity before she was able to say shakily, 'Luke.' And then run towards him, only to stop just inches short of him when she realised she had been about to throw herself into his arms.

Luke, for his part, had to remind himself that Katie was no longer his, and that overwhelming longing he had just felt to hold her tight was not one he was allowed to have.

'Luke,' Katie repeated, still feeling shaken as she looked at him, her gaze greedily observing the new breadth to his shoulders in the uniform he was wearing so proudly, his tanned face and hands, and most of all the fact that he was whole and uninjured.

'I'm on leave. A troopship dropped us all off at Portsmouth. When I realised that I'd have to change trains here in London I thought I'd take a chance and see if you had time for us to have a cup of tea together and a catch-up.'

That was a lie. The first thing he'd thought once he'd known he was getting leave was that he'd be able to see Katie instead of merely being able to write to her.

'Of course I've got time.' Katie looked towards the closed door. 'I'd invite you in but we aren't supposed . . . I don't really need to go in for anything.

There's a decent little café in Sloane Square we could go to, if you don't mind the walk.'

Luke grinned at her. 'Let's go. You lead the way.'

Katie laughed, relaxing. Luke *had* changed – she could sense it in his relaxed good-humoured manner towards her. There was no sign of the dark angry jealousy she had witnessed in him before.

That impression of the change in Luke was re-inforced for Katie as they walked together down Sloane Street. It was very obvious to her that he was far more at ease with himself, far more mature and relaxed about things, his conversation about his pals in the army showing her a sense of humour and a warmth that reminded her of why she had loved him.

Had loved him?

'We'll have to watch out for doodlebugs,' Katie warned him, forcing herself to be practical rather than emotional.

'Doodlebugs?' Luke raised a querying eyebrow, looking so heart-stoppingly handsome that Katie had to fight hard not to move closer to him, just as though they were still a couple. 'What the devil are they?'

'Flying bombs,' Katie answered. 'They're dreadful, Luke. First you hear them coming in and then there's a silence as they start to fall.' Katie gave a small shudder. 'We had seventy-three of them yesterday alone.'

'A bit like during the Liverpool blitz,' Luke commented.

Katie looked at him and he looked back at her. They had discovered their love for one another during the height of the Liverpool blitz and now, looking at Luke, Katie was reminded of those days and how it had felt to tumble so head over heels in love with him that she had been left giddy with joy, and breathless. She was feeling rather breathless right now too.

'Katie—'

'The café's just round this corner,' she interrupted Luke as they turned into Sloane Square. 'It gets very busy so I hope we'll be able to find a table . . .'

'Katie—'

'It's just over there . . .'

'Katie!'

Now Luke had reached for her hand and was holding it firmly within his own. She could feel the calluses on his skin, put there fighting for his country and for the safety of all those in it.

They'd reached the café and nothing more could be said until they had found a table – outside, and facing Peter Jones department store on the other side of the square, and it wasn't until they had given the waitress their order of a pot of tea for two that they were able to talk properly.

'I got your letter about Eddie.' Luke touched the khaki pocket of his battledress tunic.

'I'm sorry if what I wrote was too . . . too personal. Me feeling guilty about whether or not I did the right thing isn't something I should be burdening you with.'

Immediately Luke shook his head. 'I'm glad you did write to me the way you did, Katie, although—'

He had to break off as the waitress brought their tea and, to Katie, it seemed to take an age for her to remove their cups and saucers, the tea and hot-water pots, the milk and everything else from her tray onto their table, but finally she seemed satisfied that everything was where it should be and they were left alone so that Katie could pour their tea and avoid making direct eye contact with Luke as she pressed him 'Although what?'

'Although I'm sorry that you had to bear so much alone.'

Luke was concerned for her? Katie felt her heart start to beat faster, far too fast, in fact. And there was certainly no reason for her to wish that she was wearing something a bit prettier than her dull navy skirt and pin-tucked cream blouse, something feminine like a dress and a dainty pair of sandals instead of the old ones she had from before the war. Luke looked unfairly handsome in his uniform, his dark hair flopping onto his forehead as well as curling slightly onto his collar. There obviously hadn't been time for him to undergo the regulation services short back and sides. There were new lines fanning out from his eyes, put there by the desert sun? There was so much she wanted to ask him and so much she didn't. Like, had he met someone else?

'It's Eddie's family who have had much to bear,' she told him, forcing herself to concentrate on what he had said. 'I didn't want to marry him, Luke. I liked him very much, he was good fun and I don't think for one minute that he would have really wanted to get married at all – to anyone – quite so soon if it hadn't been for Leonard dying. Eddie wanted to put his family's mind at ease. It's hard for people like us to fully understand how important passing on something like a title and an estate is to people like them. Really and truthfully, Eddie should have proposed to someone named something like Arabella, with a lineage and a pedigree as long as his own, but I think poor Eddie felt that there just wasn't going to be time to find his Arabella.'

'If you want my opinion, Eddie and his family would have done very well for themselves indeed if you had married him, Katie. Any man would be proud to have you as his wife and the mother of his children.'

Katie shook her head. She could feel herself starting to colour up a little. What was the matter with her? Luke didn't mean anything personal by his comment; he was just trying to comfort her. She raised her hand to tuck her hair behind her ear to keep it from being blown into her eyes by the breeze.

'I still keep asking myself if things would have been different if I'd been honest that night when Eddie asked me.'

Luke shook his head. 'My guess from what you've said about him, is that Eddie was the sort who would have acted on impulse no matter what, and that the minute he saw that fight, his instinct would have been to try to break it up. That's the way it is, Katie, if you're the right sort. You don't have anything to blame yourself over. Eddie did the honourable thing, as a serving officer. That would have been what was to the forefront of his mind, not his family or you.' Luke leaned forward, smiling at her as he reached out to tuck another wayward strand of her hair behind her ear. Katie couldn't move, she could barely even breathe. Her skin tingled where Luke's fingertips had grazed it. Her heart was thudding so heavily now she was surprised that Luke couldn't hear it. This wasn't just silly, it was . . . it was dangerous, Katie warned herself as she managed to take a deep breath.

'You have nothing with which to reproach yourself, Katie.' Luke's voice was deep and warm. 'I promise you that breaking up that fight would have had Eddie's full attention. There's a sense of responsibility that comes to the right sort when they're in uniform that it's hard to explain, even to closest family. Your platoon, those you serve with, are your closest family, you have to be able to trust the man guarding your back to do just that, as you do it for him. Eddie gave his life doing what he thought was right, trying to prevent two men from killing one another. I would have liked to have met him. He sounded like a good man.'

Katie had to blink away the threat of tears.

'You would have liked him, Luke. He was so much fun, always joking and teasing, and a terrible flirt, or should I say a very accomplished flirt,' she laughed ruefully.

Luke's words had lifted a weight from her shoulders. She wanted to tell him how grateful she was for his wise words but she didn't want him to feel she was making things more personal than he would want them to be, so instead she said quietly, 'I've really enjoyed your letters. I've felt that I've got to know you so much better now that we're friends.'

'It's kind of you not to remind me what an arrogant, judgemental idiot I was, Katie. I—' He broke off and looked up at the sky as a warning thrumming sound filled the air, growing louder by the second.

'It's a bomb,' Katie told him unnecessarily, standing up and grabbing hold of his hand.

'Where's the nearest shelter?' Luke demanded.

'Peter Jones' basement is our best bet,' Katie answered him, 'right across the square.'

They'd almost reached the store when the silence began. 'Down – lie flat,' Katie told Luke, who needed no second urging, following Katie to the pavement and covering her body with his own. As they waited for what seemed to be an eternity, Katie could feel the steady thud of Luke's heartbeat against her own body. He had protected her like this once before, the night Liverpool had been blitzed, and she had seen those poor people on the bus blown to bits.

The noise as the bomb exploded made Katie wince. Protected by Luke's body, she could still hear the sound of glass breaking, the noise mingling with the shrill, terrified cry of a small child.

'It's all right,' Katie could hear Luke saying reassuringly against her left ear, 'the bomb fell too far away to do much damage here, apart from blow out a few windows.'

As he pulled away from her and then stood up,

458

reaching down to give Katie a helping hand to her feet, Luke gave her such a heart-stopping smile that Katie literally held her breath, overwhelmed by an intense sadness and sense of loss that wasn't helped by Luke's rueful, 'For a moment then we could almost have been back where we started.'

Determined to prove to herself as well as Luke that she wasn't the kind of silly woman who wanted to reignite dead ashes, Katie responded lightly, 'And neither of us would want that, would we.'

It had been a statement rather than a question but Luke was still holding her hand after helping her to her feet, and now he moved closer to her and looked at her.

If she was feeling dizzy it was because she had stood up so quickly, nothing more, Katie told herself, but her heart wasn't listening; it was racing and thudding and behaving as though she was still that girl who in the middle of a blitz had fallen passionately in love with a man she had seen then as a hero rather than a fellow human being.

'Start again, you mean?' Luke was asking her. 'If we did, I like to think that I'd be a damn sight better this time around at showing you how much you mean to me without acting like a possessive chump. War changes so much; it's changed me, taught me, *forced* me to accept that the narrow rules I'd made for myself and others were the rules of someone who didn't really understand the reality of life, but there are some things that don't change. I may have changed, Katie, but the way I feel about you hasn't.'

They looked at one another, both oblivious to the dust from the explosion and the movement of people around them as they picked themselves up and dusted themselves off. They could have been alone together, just the two of them.

'Could we try again, do you think? Slowly this time, not rushing things, just giving our real feelings a chance and giving ourselves the time to feel comfortable with them?'

'I . . . I'd like that,' Katie admitted.

'I'm staying overnight with Francine, but then tomorrow I'm free, if you want to meet up, if that's not too soon, and I'm not interfering with any plans you've already made.'

Katie had to smile. The old Luke would have gone into an immediate suspicious sulk if he'd thought that she might have plans that meant she couldn't see him.

'No plans,' she answered him, 'and, yes, I'd like us to meet up.'

'Is it too soon for me to kiss you, do you think?'

'I don't know,' Katie responded truthfully.

'Shall we find out?'

Some questions, it seemed, could be answered without words, Katie realised as Luke took her in his arms and kissed her very carefully, as though waiting to gauge her response.

This was where she was meant to be, Katie recognised. Here, in Luke's arms, where she had ached to be all the time they'd been apart.

She kissed him back. Not as the hesitant uncertain Katie she had been, kissing the Luke who's emotional intensity and inability to control his

jealousy had overwhelmed her, but as the Katie
she now was, tested by the rigours of war, kissing
the Luke that Katie knew instinctively was now
a man she could love and trust and feel safe in
doing so.

Luke's arms tightened round her, and this time
when he kissed her there was no holding back
for either of them. They would take their time,
they would not rush, and this time they would
make it.

A nightingale might or might not ever have sung
in Berkeley Square, but in Sloane Square Katie's
heart was certainly singing – a quiet anthem of love
and gratitude.

EPILOGUE

'The German war is at an end. Advance Britannia. Long live the cause of Freedom. God save the King.'

Those words, spoken by Mr Churchill from number 10 Downing Street at 3.00 p.m. on 8 May 1945 announced the formal end of the war.

'I still can't believe that the war is really over,' Jean was saying breathlessly to Grace, as she rushed into her kitchen, adding, 'Pass me a couple more of those plates of bloater paste sandwiches, will you, Grace love, and I'll get them out on the table?'

It was a week since VE Day, and the residents of Ash Grove were throwing a street party to celebrate. Outside, bunting in red, white and blue, quickly made from painted paper, was strung from every lamp-post, whilst trestle tables groaned under the weight of food prepared by the Grove's housewives.

'If you ask me, that tinned fruit salad that Jessie Hawthorne from number fourteen's put out is definitely black market,' Jean sniffed, as Grace continued to butter bread with the butter she and Seb had brought from Whitchurch.

'Well, I dare say it will go down a treat with the cream that me and Seb brought with us, no matter where it's come from,' Grace responded to her mother, adding, 'It's a pity it's too early for Dad's strawberries and raspberries.'

'I shouldn't be complaining,' Jean smiled, as she picked up the plates of sandwiches and headed for the open front door, 'not when me and your dad have got all four of you here with us.'

The street was buzzing with activity, with small children running around and hiding from one another under the tables, the men standing together round the beer barrel, which had been set up on a table of its own, whilst the women dashed to and fro with plates of food.

'Here, let me take those for you, Auntie Jean,' Bella offered outside, relieving Jean of the plates. 'Where do you want me to put them?'

'Over there, please, Bella love,' Jean told her, preparing to hurry back to the kitchen for the next lot of sandwiches. 'We'll let everyone get started and stuck in in a few more minutes. Thank goodness it's not raining; it would have ruined everything.'

Jean's smile faded a little as she spoke to her niece. As Jean had said to Bella when she and Jan had arrived, it was understandable that Vi hadn't felt like coming with her or celebrating. After all, it was less than a year since she had lost Charlie.

Thinking of Vi now had Jean putting her hand on Bella's arm and telling her truthfully, 'You could have knocked me down with a feather when you first told me about Vi and Edwin getting back together.'

Bella gave Jean a rueful look. 'I was surprised as well,' she admitted. 'It was losing Charlie that did it. Oh, I can't quite reach,' Bella complained as she struggled to lean far enough over the table to put the plates down because of the swell of the baby she was carrying – conceived at Christmas, much to her own and Jan's joy. Seeing the look they exchanged when Jan took the plates from her to put them down, Jean reflected on how much her niece had changed.

'Here you are, Mum, that's the last plateful,' Grace announced, emerging from the house carrying another plate of sandwiches.

Bella smiled at Grace. Sometimes she felt guilty about feeling so happy, especially when she thought about Charlie, but she and Jan were both so thrilled about the coming baby.

'Do you remember that Tennis Club dance at the start of the war, when I was so horrid to you, Grace?' she asked her cousin.

'Yes,' Grace laughed, 'but I can forgive you because it was thanks to you that I first met Seb.' They both turned to look at Grace's husband, who had his hands full – literally – with his twin sons, who were demanding to be put down so that they could show off their newly learned almost walking skills.

'We were only girls then,' Bella said. 'The war's brought so many changes, including a whole new generation of children, what with your twins, and

464

Francine's little girl, and this one to join them in a few months' time.'

'It's lovely that Francine and Marcus are here,' Jean chipped in, looking across the table to where her sister and her husband were standing, with their baby daughter, Claire, who was now nearly four months old and who had her mother and her auntie Grace's strawberry-blonde curls.

On the other side of the table Francine leaned her head against Marcus's shoulder. This time last year she could never have imagined it would be possible to be this happy. Then all she had been able to think about was getting Jack back. It was funny the way things worked out. She had thought, when she had given her son up to Emily, that she was making a sacrifice for his sake, but instead her sacrifice had become a gift of great joy and love, thanks to Emily, who had showed her the true generosity of a loving heart.

As Tommy's unofficial godmother, Francine had attended his end-of-school-year prize-giving, and had watched as her son had been lauded by his headmaster and house head for his scholastic ability, and his good sportsmanship. She had received with pride the smile Tommy had given her, after he had smiled at Emily, and she had cried a few tears along with Emily when they had fussed over him together after the ceremony, two very, very proud mothers, joined in love.

Now she and Marcus had their own little Claire who could already wind her daddy and her half-brother round her little finger.

It was time for people to start eating, before

the sandwiches started to curl up, Jean and the other women had agreed, but getting that message across to such a large group of people was a man's job, not a woman's. Purposefully Jean inched past the family groups of adults chatting together, avoiding the children scampering around excitedly as she made her way to where Sam was standing, drawing pints of frothing beer from the barrel.

'Sam, we need you to tell everyone that it's time to eat,' Jean told him, tugging on the sleeve of his shirt to get his attention.

From the end of the street it was lovely to see all the young women out of uniform and dressed in their best, the bright colours of their summer frocks making bold splashes of colour in the warm sunshine.

Sam pulled himself up to his full height, his arms brown and weathered where he had rolled up his sleeves, Jean's heart filled with pride and love as she watched him. He was a good man, her Sam. One of the best.

Sam clapped his hands. Gradually those around him fell silent, the silence spreading out like ripples on water, until everyone was turning to look at him.

'Grub's up,' he announced. 'Come on, everyone, tuck in.'

'Grub's up?' Jean repeated indignantly. 'That was a fine thing to say.'

'It did the job, didn't it?' Sam protested, taking a bite out of an egg sandwich.

Jean shook her head. There were some things, some niceties of life, that men – even the best of them – simply did not understand.

466

'Come on, Emily,' Grace urged, holding out a plate of sandwiches to her. 'Don't hold back. You're family now.'

Family. Emily's heart swelled with happiness. She, Wilhelm and Tommy had travelled up to Liverpool on the train with Grace, Seb and the twins. The three of them would be spending the night at her old house, before returning to Whitchurch in the morning.

How very blessed she was, Emily thought humbly, as she watched Wilhelm talking with Jean's husband, Sam. The two men had got on like a house on fire once Sam had realised that Wilhelm was as keen on growing vegetables and the like as he was.

She and Wilhelm had already made enquiries about them marrying, and had been assured that there should be no problem. Next week they were going to look at a farm just outside Nantwich, nothing fancy, just a nice sensible house and enough land for Wilhelm to graze a few sheep and grow his veggies and some crops.

Further down the street, she could see Jean's youngest daughters with their husbands. Both girls had a look of Jean, and ever so pretty they looked too in their polished cotton summer dresses, one red with little black poodles on it, the other blue with white kittens, white belts showing off their slim waists. Had anyone other than her noticed the similarities in looks between Lou's husband, Kieran, and her own Tommy? It was no wonder they had a look of one another: after all, Con, Tommy's father, had also been Kieran's uncle. She looked down at her adopted son, her heart filled with love and gratitude. He was the best gift that life had ever given her.

'How did Kieran get on with his interview with that chap who wants to set up his own private freight company?' Sasha asked Lou as they stood together whilst the men, including their own husbands, gravitated together.

'He's been offered a job – but he won't be taking it up until he's been demobbed, and that won't be for a while because his squadron are still needed to fly supplies over to Germany.'

'I feel so sorry for the German women and children, with nowhere to live, and no food,' Sasha said sadly

'So do I,' Lou agreed, 'but the United Nations Relief and Rehabilitation people are doing their best for them. Just think how it would have been if we hadn't fought Hitler and he had won. We wouldn't just be homeless and starving.'

They looked at one another in mutual understanding. The full horror of the gas chambers and everything that went with them had been revealed to a shocked public after the fall of Berlin.

Today they might all be celebrating victory and the safety of those they loved, but that didn't mean that they weren't all also thinking of everything that had been endured to reach that victory, and of all those who had suffered and who had paid the ultimate price.

*   *   *

Bella tucked her arm through Jan's. They'd been at another VE Day party earlier in the week, given by the Polish community in Liverpool, and Bella had felt so proud of Jan. Now that she was nearly five months pregnant she felt so relieved, after the anxiety of the first three months when she'd worried so much that she might lose her baby, even though their doctor had assured her that there was no cause for alarm. A part of her would always grieve for that little one who had never had the chance to live, thanks to the cruelty of the man who had fathered him – her first husband. That baby would never be forgotten by her, or by Jan.

Jean had told her that she was free to invite Lena and Gavin and their little ones to join the party, but Lena had said that Gavin's family were throwing a party of their own, and Bella had understood that Lena felt that she and Gavin should go there.

As for Bella's mother and father, it had been a surprise to them all when Vi had announced that Edwin had asked her to move out to his house at Neston, so that the two of them could start again, which meant that Bella now had her mother's house to herself, something which delighted her, with Jan on a long leave.

Jean looked around at her family, her heart filled with pride and love.

Somehow they had won through, somehow they were all safe: Grace and Seb with their twins; Lou and Kieran with their plans for the future; Sasha and Bobby, who had made a place for himself with the Salvage Corps and who got around so nimbly on his artificial leg that you'd almost never know it wasn't real; Fran, happy now with Marcus and little Claire; Jack with Emily; Bella with Jan, their expected baby such a relief to Bella, Jean knew, after her fears that there might not be one; and, of course, Luke and Katie.

Jean had been so pleased when Luke had told her that he and Katie were going to give things another try. Katie had come to the twins' wedding, helping out with that same quiet kindness that was so much a part of her, and looking at Luke with her love for him shining in her eyes, just as she was doing now, and Luke looking back at her in just the same way, just as he too was doing now.

'Those two were meant to be together,' Jean murmured to herself.

'Have you made your mind up yet?'

Katie turned her attention away from Grace's gorgeous sons to look at Luke.

'About what?' she began teasingly, before stopping and telling him lovingly, 'You know I have, Luke. In fact I made up my mind, that afternoon in Sloane Square, when I was lying underneath you, wondering where that doodlebug was going to land, that given the chance I wasn't going to let you escape a second time.'

Luke laughed. 'If one of us was worrying about the other escaping then it was me. The minute I read what you'd written about Eddie I knew that I had to find a way of convincing you to give me a second chance before some other chap stepped in ahead of me.'

There was a small pause and then he asked, 'So you will marry me, then?'

'Yes,' Katie confirmed, both of them laughing as somewhere close at hand someone opened one of the bottles of champagne Fran and Marcus had brought with them as part of their contribution to the party.

The war was over. It was time to move on – and forward into the future.

What's next?

Tell us the name of an author you love

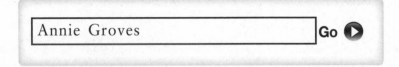

Annie Groves | Go ▶

and we'll find your next great book.

www.bookarmy.com

\multicolumn{8}{c}{**NEATH PORT TALBOT LIBRARY AND INFORMATION SERVICES**}

1	5/11	25		49		73	
2		26		50		74	
3		27		51		75	
4		28		52		76	
5		29		53		77	
6		30		54		78	
7		31		55		79	
8		32		56		80	
9		33		57		81	
10		34		58		82	
11		35		59		83	
12		36		60		84	
13		37		61		85	
14		38		62		86	
15		39		63		87	
16		40		64		88	
17		41		65		89	
18		42		66		90	
19		43		67		91	
20		44		68		92	
21		45		69		COMMUNITY SERVICES	
22		46		70			
23		47		71		NPT/111	
24		48		72			